WAX

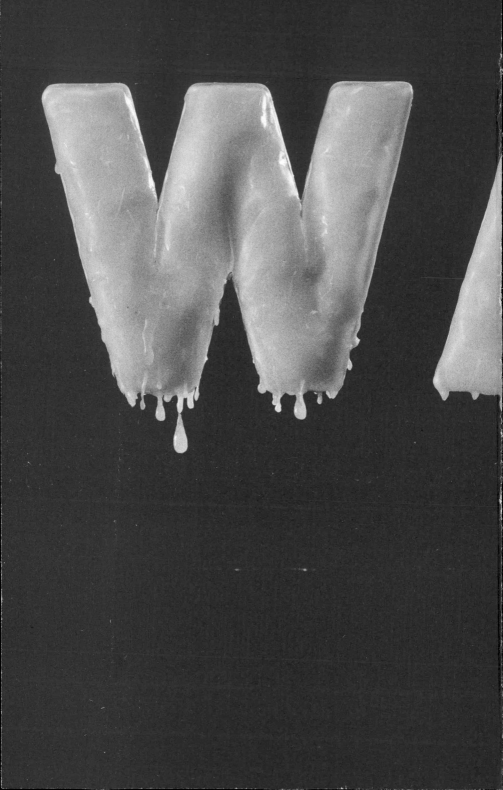

GINA DAMICO

HOUGHTON MIFFLIN HARCOURT

Boston   New York

www.hmhco.com

Text set in Minion Pro

Book design by Lisa Vega

Library of Congress Cataloging-in-Publication Data

Names: Damico, Gina, author.

Title: Wax / Gina Damico.

Description: Boston : Houghton Mifflin Harcourt, 2016. | Summary: Seventeen-year-old Poppy stumbles into a secret workshop at the infamous Grosholtz Candle Factory and soon, a wax boy called Dud is helping her uncover an evil plot that threatens her hometown of Paraffin, Vermont.

Identifiers: LCCN 2015035202 | ISBN 9780544633155 (hardback)

Subjects: | CYAC: Wax figures—Fiction. | Supernatural—Fiction. | Mystery and detective stories. | Humorous stories. | BISAC: JUVENILE FICTION / Humorous Stories. | JUVENILE FICTION / Mysteries & Detective Stories.

Classification: LCC PZ7.D1838 Wax 2016 | DDC [Fic]—dc23 LC record available at https://lccn.loc.gov/2015035202

Manufactured in the United States of America

DOC 10 9 8 7 6 5 4 3 2 1

4500602745

For the CCE.
Sex, murder, comedy . . .
all in a night's work.

Acknowledgments

Here is what you'd find in the Acknowledgments Wing of my wax museum:

A shrine to my agent, Tina Wexler: confidante, hilarious-story trader, doodler of a magnifying glass named Grandpa. Thank you for being a wonderful friend and a wonderful agent, in that order.

An altar to my editor, Julie Tibbott: When I got the idea for this book, my very next thought was, *This is something Julie will totally dig.* Thank you for liking weird things. And *Jesus Christ Superstar.*

A family diorama: These poor souls, predicted to have left me long ago, stuck around through hell, high water, and painful revisions. Only the strong have endured, and to them, I say thank you.

A collection of stately busts of those working tirelessly behind the scenes: Betsy Groban, Julia Richardson, Lisa DiSarro, Hayley Gonnason, Ruth Homberg, Helen Seachrist, Amy Carlisle, and all the other rock stars at Houghton Mifflin Harcourt; Katie O'Connor at Audible; Roxane Eduard at Curtis Brown; Berni Barta at ICM; Maxine Bartow, copyeditor extraordinaire; and Lisa Vega and Steve Gardner for that gorgeous, creeptastic cover.

A series of commemorative candles lit to honor those who champion my books and all books: librarians, teachers, booksellers, bloggers, and word-of-mouthers, plus an especially fragrant one for Dodie Ownes.

And finally, a mirror. That's YOU, dear reader! Thank you for lending me your eyeballs for a while (or ears, if you are listening to the audiobook). No matter which organs you use to consume this story: I hope you enjoy.

Thanks for visiting the Acknowledgments Wing! No refunds.

THE TOWN OF PARAFFIN SMELLED OF ROT.

And apples and oranges. Cranberries and peaches. Ginger and cinnamon, coconut and honeysuckle. Roses, lilies, lavender, and freshly cut grass. Chocolate chip cookies, banana splits, vanilla beans, and snickerdoodles.

It smelled of Citrus Dreams, Tahiti Sunsets, The Night Before Christmas, and New Car Leather. Babbling Brooks, Sun-Kissed Linens, Ocean Breezes, and Stolen Midnights.

Spice and musk and tea and rum. Love and home and peace and America.

The town of Paraffin smelled of everything.

Everywhere.

At the same time.

All the time.

Each scent layered one on top of the other, mixing and mingling, fusing and swelling into an odorous abomination that could knock an unsuspecting sniffer off his feet — a gag-inducing whiff that attacked the nostrils with a ruthless barrage of cinnamon-and-death-scented stink.

Other than that, Paraffin was a lovely place to visit.

Its population numbered 1,014. The streets were tree-lined, the lampposts adorned with Star-Spangled Banners. The town square overlooked a little blue lake, where human-hating geese assembled to peck at bread and discuss their plans for world domination. Across the lake rose Mount Cerumen, a postcard-perfect background for the fireworks that exploded over the waterfront every Wednesday night in the summertime. Main Street featured country shops stocked to brimming with farmhouse tchotchkes, animal-themed coffee sets, and wooden signs with painted homespun sayings like "If You Want Breakfast in Bed, Sleep in the Kitchen" and "When I Get the Urge to Clean, I Lie Down Until It Passes!" plus enough chocolate, cheese, and pure Vermont maple syrup to sustain the populace well into the apocalypse.

But these and any other regional attractions paled in comparison with the ever-present behemoth across the lake. Nestled in the foothills of Mount Cerumen sat Paraffin's bread and butter, the *real* cash cow with which no amount of cow-shaped dairy creamers could compete: the Grosholtz Candle Factory.

The building was a strange amalgamation, a mutant hybrid from two vastly different eras: the front, a modern retail experience comprising clean lines, bright colors, and welcoming customer service; the back, a soaring candelabra of a structure, a castle straight out of Transylvania, with spires looming so high that in the dead of winter they cast eerie, spiky shadows onto Paraffin's sidewalks.

It had been there for as long as anyone could remember. Its provenance was murky; spotty record-keeping at the time had all but doomed its origins to the frustrated conjectures of local historians. To have the archives tell it, the entire enterprise seemed to have popped up overnight. And while the layers of architectural schizophrenia suggested that it had changed hands more than once, the names of the owners of those hands were lost to the icy Vermont winds.

But no one really cared where it came from. Whatever its past, the Grosholtz Candle Factory had grown from its humble beginnings into a wax-poured juggernaut of industry, posting annual sales of half a billion dollars and growing. Convinced that happiness was only a twenty-dollar hunk of wax away, candle enthusiasts came from all over the world to gape at the groaning shelves of merchandise, watch the children's barnyard animal show, peruse the candle museum, make their own candles and wax hand molds, and, of course, take the factory tour.

The tourists — a special brand of sightseers, happy to endure a multiple-hour car ride as long as there were tasteful wicker basket displays at the end of it — *loved* the conglomerated smell. As if on a pilgrimage, they'd walk through the store's swishing automatic doors, close their eyes, and inhale deeply, dragging every note of sage and sandalwood and Santa's Sleigh down to the bottommost pocket of their lungs.

Those who lived in Paraffin year-round thought these people were bonkers. Every morning at sunrise that ubiquitous funk would waft down from the factory, skate across the pond, and wriggle between each and every molecule of clean mountain air. Some townspeople claimed that they could no longer smell it. Those townspeople were lying.

Though probably with good reason. Because with the stench came a small, barely quantifiable feeling of unease that no one in town could put a finger on. With its spectral architecture, the factory had a certain quality — something out of a dark and twisted fairy tale, perhaps. Although additions had been made to bring it up to modern standards, the wooden structures of the original remained, tucked away from the tour buses, snaking up the side of the mountain like the legs of a prowling spider. Over the years, urban legends had bubbled up, stories about malevolent spirits and dark presences. With the smokestacks puffing late into the night, the entire framework seemed to breathe, savoring the scents of its own making.

But other than the weirdness, the smell, and the blatant tourist-trappiness of it all, Paraffiners had nothing but love for the Grosholtz Candle Factory. It created jobs and kept the economy afloat at a time when many other small manufacturing towns in the area had perished. And with candles stuffed into the nooks and crannies of every home, no one was left in the dark when the occasional nor'easter knocked the power out.

Yes, the town of Paraffin was a happy place. The grass was green; the streets were clean. The residents were good, wholesome cheese-loving people. They worked hard, they loved their kids, and they greeted every day with a smile. They said hello to one another in passing, and they watered their neighbors' plants while they were away. They had no reason to distrust their fellow citizens or suspect that they were up to anything heinous, no reason at all.

Until, one day, they did.

1

Pick a fight with a computer

POPPY PALLADINO HAD TRIPPED, FALLEN, AND HUMILIATED
herself on live television in front of thirty million Americans, but
convincing the CVS touchscreen to reverse its stance on her bun-
gled self-checkout transaction — *that* was pure torture.

"Help is on the way!" the computer chirped.

"I don't *need* help," Poppy told it. "I *need* you to take my coupon."

The pharmacist leaned out over her pharmacy battlements.
"You need some help, hon?"

"I'm told it's already on the way."

The pharmacist came to her aid, a woman with limp hair and
glasses that in all likelihood had been swiped from the nearby rotating eyewear display. She must have been a recent transplant; Poppy
had never seen her around town before. The name tag on her blue
polo shirt said JEAN!

"Hi, Jean!" Poppy said. Politeness went a long way in the art of
savings.

"Hi there. What seems to be the problem?"

"Sorry to pull you away from your drugs. It's my coupon." Poppy showed her the crumpled-up coupon smelling of receipt ink and old gum that had been trawling around the bottom of her bag since her mother imparted it two weeks earlier. "It didn't work."

"Well, let's give it another try." She took the coupon from Poppy and smoothed it between her hands, as if Poppy had not done this half a dozen times by now.

Only twenty minutes were left before she had to get back to school for rehearsal, but Poppy remained patient — albeit less than thrilled to have to sit through yet another round of Let the Adult Fix the Thing That the Idiot Teenager Broke. "The machine told me to scan my coupons," she explained, "so I did. Then it beeped. Then it scolded me. Then it stopped talking altogether and decided to have an existential crisis instead."

"Sorry about that. These things can be finicky sometimes." JEAN! put a hand on her chin and looked from the screen to Poppy. "Did you wave it across the scanner in a fluid mo —"

She froze. Her mascara-laden lids began to blink rapidly. "Wait a sec. Are you . . ."

Oh, crapnugget.

"Yes," Poppy said through the tiny hole her mouth had formed. "Yes, I am." Immediately she looked down at the floor and rubbed the scar at the edge of her hairline, her default reaction whenever someone recognized her. It wasn't her favorite reflex; she'd prefer to strike a heroic stance and burst out of the nearest plate-glass window in an epic display of bravado and fearlessness. But some bug in her internal programming wouldn't allow it.

JEAN! put a hand to her mouth, which Poppy could tell was twitching at the edges. "Oh, my."

"Please, just —"

"Poor thing." Despite the woman's best efforts to be polite, her eyes crinkled in that way that suggested there was a laugh coming, a bombastic chortle barreling its way up her throat with no regard for tact or civility or the feelings of an emotionally fractured seventeen-year-old. "How are you holding up, dear?"

Poppy's tight mouth contorted into a tight smile. "I'm fine."

On paper, at least. Poppy's therapist had officially labeled her "No Longer Traumatized," a phrase that her best friend, Jill, had found so hilarious, she had it printed on a T-shirt and gave it to Poppy for her birthday. "Everything's fine," she reiterated.

The pharmacist, fully embracing the fineness of the situation, was fighting the giggles so hard, her neck wattle was quivering. "It wasn't that bad, you know."

Poppy was beginning to think that a dollar off deodorant wasn't worth this level of ballyhoo. "I'm sorry, but the coupon . . ."

"Oh, yes! You know what, hon? Just take it." She pushed the deodorant into Poppy's hand, then grabbed a package of Skittles and a ChapStick and piled those on top as well. "After all you've been through? You deserve it."

Poppy considered her offerings. "You're right. After all I've been through, I do deserve the promise of moist, kissable lips."

JEAN! gave her a loving pat on the hand and ushered Poppy

toward the exit, gallantly waving her arm at the sensors to make the automatic doors swish open.

The doors closed behind Poppy as she left, but not fast enough to muffle the explosion of laughter from within.

* * *

Poppy had not always been America's preferred object of ridicule. Six months prior, no one outside Paraffin had known her name. And within Paraffin, she was simply That Girl. The Blond One. With a Penchant for Maple Ice Cream and Musical Theater.

She'd had no reason to suspect that trying out for *Triple Threat* would be a bad idea. After all, she could sing, act, and dance, thereby satisfying the trio of purported hazards. And she wasn't delusional, either — it was more or less agreed upon by all who saw her perform that she was good. Maybe big-fish-in-a-small-pond good, but certainly not the sort of train wreck those reality show talent competitions love to poke fun at, with goofy sound effects and dramatic close-ups of the judges, their beautiful faces twisted into dual looks of pity and God-given superiority.

She would do right by *The Sound of Music*. She would make her hometown proud. She would never be relegated to the blooper reel.

But what everyone at home and in the audience at Radio City Music Hall had failed to account for on that steamy June evening was one simple, fateful equation: incompetent stagehands + an inconsiderate preceding act = imminent tragedy.

It wasn't her fault.

It wasn't her fault that the El Paso Players were absolute morons and decided to stage the musical number "Be Our Guest" from *Beauty and the Beast* complete with real food that would be tossed and smashed around on a stage that was already slicker than an ice-skating rink — all while citing their commitment to "authenticity," as if singing and dancing cutlery were the epitome of realism. It wasn't her fault that the wreckage got nothing more than a quick mop during the commercial break. It wasn't her fault that she was scheduled to go on after them. And it certainly wasn't her fault that she slipped on an errant bit of pie and pudding (*en flambé*) and crashed to the floor in a pile of screeches and flailing and braids and sensible Austrian costumery.

It . . . *was* her fault that she chose to continue with her performance despite the gigantic gash that had opened up in her forehead. Blood gushed down her face as she crooned "*'The hills are alive . . .'*" with a sweet, maniacal smile, gamely attempting to look as though she hadn't been mauled by an Alpine wolf.

Because the show, as everyone knows, must go on.

In the moment, she thought she'd recovered quite well. She didn't realize that the audience was sitting there horrified, transfixed, and that the judges were yelling for her to stop. She'd plunged gashfirst into the zone, the Theater Zone, and hadn't snapped out of it until she'd sung through the last note — at which point she realized that she was drenched in gore, her teeth had turned red, and everyone in that theater and in homes across America was pissing themselves with laughter.

Then she passed out from blood loss.

When she regained consciousness, she was no longer the plucky young ingénue from small-town Vermont whom Katy Perry had called "adorbs." She was Maria von Tripp. Julie Androops. The undisputed queen of the Internet. Clips of her demise got millions of hits in mere hours. Major newspapers printed her photo. *Saturday Night Live* did a sketch about her.

Of course, not everyone had been mean-spirited. The paramedics had a lot of comforting things to say. She got cards and flowers from well-meaning viewers across the country. Ellen had extended an invitation to her talk show. (Poppy's parents, fearing overexposure and the opportunity for another dance-related catastrophe, declined.)

But overall, the damage had been done. Her confidence: shattered. Her nails: bitten to the quick. She couldn't sleep without the aid of Forty Winks, a Grosholtz candle her parents had imposed upon her, insisting that it was scientifically proven (it wasn't) to induce drowsiness and treat insomnia. And even now, five months later, all it took was a JEAN! to throw a little snicker her way for the wounds of humiliation to be freshly torn anew.

Which was why Poppy was so pleased that her next errand involved the one and only Mr. Kosnitzky, who, she was positive, had never laughed a day in his life.

"Not again," he muttered when the bell over his shop door rang, slumping as he spotted her head bobbing toward him. He'd recognize his most frequent customer anywhere — blond hair secured with a pencil into a messy bun, the ends pointing up and fanned out into a sunburst. "Why aren't you in school?" he demanded.

"Good afternoon, sir! I had free period last, so I was allowed to leave early." Poppy smiled and shook his hand with a practiced combination of firmness and warmth, as if she were running for office.

She was, in a way. And not just because she'd been elected president of Paraffin High's drama club, the Giddy Committee, in a blitzkrieg of a campaign that the *Paraffin High School Gazette* called "well-run," "hard-fought," and "glitter-and-elbow-macaroni-fueled." (Also "unnecessary," as she had run unopposed.) But in a larger sense, Poppy's life post *Triple Threat* was now one big campaign. A drive to win back the hearts and minds of everyone she'd ever met or would meet. A crusade to show all potential college admission boards that she was more than just a joke, more than just That Girl. The One Who Sang and Fell and Bled Everywhere. Ha-Ha, Remember That? Pull Up the Video, Let's Watch It Again.

Two and a half months into the school year, *some* progress had been made in restoring her reputation; people were finally starting to treat her like normal again, and she'd been going above and beyond to remind everyone that she was the same old Poppy she always was. She got stellar grades. She aced her SATs. She clogged her schedule with extracurriculars. Sooner or later, she thought, everyone would be forced to admit that they were wrong about her, simply through her sheer force of being relentlessly, unequivocally respectable.

Case in point: She was still shaking the engraver's hand. "How is Nancy, sir?" she asked with genuine concern. "That pesky yeast infection clear up?"

"Er, yes," he muttered, pulling his hand away. Most people in Paraffin were comfortable with the small-town inevitability of knowing one another's personal details, but Mr. Kosnitzky preferred to keep his wife's yeast where it belonged: at home. "What can I do for you, Poppy?" He spit out her name in a bouncy yet mocking tone, as though resentful that he was being forced to say something cheerful.

Poppy couldn't blame him; she hated her name too. Despised everything about it. Its ditziness, its whimsicality, the sheer Britishness of it. The way it was full of round, unwieldy letters. It undermined her, she felt — or, at the very least, made her feel like a googly-eyed Muppet that had wandered off set.

(Her father claimed that it had all been her mother's doing. *He'd* wanted to name her either Coolbreeze or Jubilation. But Poppy's parents were on another plane of crazy altogether.)

She plunked an oddly shaped award onto the counter.

Mr. Kosnitzky sighed. "Another one?"

"Yes." She slid a piece of paper toward him. "But it's not for me this time."

He read the name off the paper. "Connor Galpert?"

"Correct."

Sighing again, he picked up the trophy and held it to the light. This one had a faux-marble base, like many of the others she'd brought in over the years, but where there usually sat a plastic gold figure of a shuttlecock (badminton team) or a paintbrush (Art Club) or a jazz hand (the Merry Maladies, a group Poppy had spearheaded that went into local hospitals to foist cheer and Broadway songs upon defenseless patients), this particular chunk of gold plastic more closely resembled a large slug.

He waved it at her. "This a turd?"

Poppy stifled a grunt. He was the third one to ask that today. "No, sir."

Mr. Kosnitzky squinted through the lenses of his plastic-rimmed glasses at the paper Poppy had given him, then at the inscription on the copper plate, frowning as he fed it into the engraving machine. "What does SPCY stand for?"

"The Society for the Prevention of Cruelty to Yams."

He raised an eyebrow. "And what does 'yams' stand for?"

"Oh, it doesn't stand for anything, sir. A yam is a type of sweet potato, a starchy tuber that grows in the —"

"I know what a yam is. Why does it need its own society?"

She pulled a pamphlet out of her bag and slid it across the counter with a firm finger. "Mr. Kosnitzky, I don't want to alarm you, but yam farmers in our state receive, on average, fifty percent *less*—"

"You don't say," he said, finishing the inscription and fitting it back onto the base. "And why aren't you in school?"

"I already told you, sir — I had free period last today, so I was allowed to leave early." When he glared at her, she added, "It's in the handbook."

He went back to his work, grumbling. Poppy didn't take his disdain personally; as a rule, Mr. Kosnitzky hated all teenagers. He'd gone so far as to appoint himself Paraffin High's honorary truant officer. Every morning before opening for business, he'd camp out at his storefront window, scan the town square and its prominent gazebo through a pair of ancient binoculars, and call the principal's office the second he spotted anyone unlucky enough to appear adolescent. He was correct roughly sixty percent of the time, and he still felt pretty good about the other forty percent because he still got to yell into the phone.

"So the farmers want this Connor's name engraved onto a giant yam for, what, heroic weeding efforts or something?" he asked.

"Oh, no," said Poppy. "Connor won the yam-eating contest. It was all part of the first annual Paraffin Yamboree, to raise money for the farmers. Didn't you hear about it? I put up flyers all over town. There are two in your front window."

Mr. Kosnitzky frowned and looked over her shoulder. "I don't remember posting those."

"I took the liberty. And it's a good thing I did — we got a great turnout!"

He stared. She beamed. He stared some more. "That'll be five dollars and six cents."

She blinked her giant eyes at him — always a disarming gesture, as they were slightly too large for her head — and placed a neat stack of dollar bills on the counter. "Can I leave some yamphlets too?"

"Heh?"

"Pamphlets," she said, fanning a stack of no less than a hundred. "About the yams."

"No."

He took her money and started punching buttons on his antiquated cash register as the door bell rattled again. "Be with you in a minute," he said to the new customer, who stepped up behind Poppy, boots screeching on the tiled floor.

Poppy could tell from the combined scent of Orbit gum and cheap body spray that it was a teenager. Tall, judging by the way he blocked the light from outside. A watch jangled on his wrist, one of those oversize titanium gimmicks that were bought only by scuba divers or people who wanted to appear as cool as scuba divers. He let out a low chuckle, then advanced another step.

"*The hills are aliiiiiive,*" he quietly sang.

Poppy's ears reddened. She glanced at his stringy reflection in a plaque on the wall.

Blake Bursaw.

Crapnugget.

The self-appointed first family of Paraffin, the Bursaw clan ran every inch of the town — or at least every inch that the candle factory didn't touch. The matriarch, a corpulent floral-print-wearing old woman who resembled a roll of wallpaper and was known colloquially as Miss Bea, served as Paraffin's mayor. Her campaign motto, AN EXTRAORDINARY WOMAN, had blanketed the town for years, everyone still too fearful of her sparkly-eyed wrath to take any of the posters down. Her son, a middle-aged blowhard called Big Bob, sat on the town council and was widely assumed to be next in line for the mayor's office. And *his* son, Blake, treated Paraffin as his own personal dog park, pissing on everything just to mark it as his.

The three of them lived together in an ostentatious mansion

modeled on the White House and worked hard to maintain their position as the Worst. Everyone knew it. Everyone thought it.

But no one said it. Not out loud, at least. And so they got away with everything.

"*With the sound of loooosers,*" Blake kept on singing.

"That doesn't even make sense," Poppy said under her breath. What was he doing in a trophy shop? The kid had never won anything in his life. Except maybe a World's Biggest Douchebag contest.

Poppy nearly laughed at the image of what a giant douchebag trophy would look like, but she reminded herself not to engage. Ever since senior year started, Blake had proved himself to be terribly adept at wreaking havoc upon the tatters of Poppy's once-pristine reputation, orchestrating a reign of mockery that was showing no signs of toppling. The whole school was still talking about the Halloween party debacle two weeks prior, of which Blake had been the chief architect. Poppy had exacted some measure of revenge with a well-timed pantsing in gym class — and the fact that he'd been wearing SpongeBob boxers was a nice bonus — but she'd never be able to top his level of malice.

To Blake, bullying was an art. And Poppy was his muse.

She would not give him the satisfaction of turning around. Yet her palms were getting sweaty, leaving gross condensation marks when she tapped them on the glass counter. "Let's hurry it up, Mr. Koz."

"I'm trying to get rid of the pennies. Just a second." After what seemed like eons, he shut the cash register drawer perhaps a little harder than was necessary and dumped the change into her waiting hands. "Here."

"Thanks!" Without making eye contact with Blake, she whirled around and bolted for the door.

"Wait!" Mr. Kosnitzky called after her. "You forgot your turd!"

Poppy froze in her tracks.

Well. That ought to do it.

Blake promptly burst into a hyenalike fit of giggling. His lanky frame, stretched taut and tough like a piece of jerky, doubled over. *"Turd?"*

Poppy slunk back to the counter and grabbed the trophy out of Mr. Kosnitzky's hand. "Yam." She stuffed it into her bag and headed for the exit once more, glaring so hard at Blake that she missed the handle and slammed into the door, prompting yet another explosion of laughter.

Gritting her teeth, Poppy darted out of the shop, trying — yet not succeeding — to hold her head high.

2

~~Engage in childish name-calling~~

"GIVE *YOU* A TURD, JERKFACE," POPPY MUTTERED, RETURNING to the school's main hallway just as the final bell rang. "Right in your stupid ugly *jerkface*."

"Pardon me?"

She glanced up at Principal Lincoln, a tall, baggy-eyed, gaunt-cheeked, cheerless man whom Poppy liked to think of as Abraham Lincoln's less successful, undead twin. "Oh—nothing, sir," she said, staring up the full length of his ski-slope nose. "Just talking to myself."

"Mmm." He turned his attention back to the masses, no doubt yearning for a bottle from the long-rumored wine rack under his desk, while Poppy struggled against the surging current of students as she made her way to her personal sanctuary: the Gaudy Auditorium.

Once upon a time, a well-intentioned benefactor had mistakenly come under the impression that Paraffin High had any regard at all for the arts, and consequently had donated a heap of

19

money to build a hideous theater. (Had he done his homework, he might have learned that the school routinely sank ninety percent of its extracurricular-activity budget into sports programs and the other ten percent into the only arts group in service of those sports programs: the Paraffin High Marching Band. And that the surplus wax the Grosholtz Candle Factory had donated over the years had never been sculpted into masterpieces, but rather had taken up residence as a rarely used, unsightly gray lump in the art room closet.)

The Gaudy Auditorium immediately fell into disrepair, as it was only ever used for graduation and the occasional Giddy Committee performance; students graduating at the end of four years were surprised to find that their school even *had* an auditorium. So Poppy and her crew had full run of the place, using it whenever they wanted, for whatever purposes their theatrical minds could concoct. It maintained a constant temperature of a million degrees (two million onstage, as the space underneath the floorboards was directly connected to the furnace room), the curtains were disintegrating, the seats smelled of mold, and the slop room they used for storage was so full of past props and costumes that it threatened to plunge the school into a glittery sinkhole at any moment — but it was all the Giddy Committee had, so Poppy was proud to call it home.

She had her hand on the door and was about to push it open when a miraculous voice rose above the hallway clamor.

"Poppy?"

Oh, no.

She was in *no* condition, having run back from Mr. Kosnitzky's store, upset and flushed with embarrassment, to interact with Mr. Crawford right then.

Mr. Crawford, the Adonis of Paraffin High.

Mr. Crawford, the most beautiful high school biology teacher on the planet.

Mr. Crawford, a fully mature adult who did not engage in the cruelness of teenage boys, and therefore the only member of the male species to have attracted Poppy's lustful, unswerving attention, smoldering under it like an ant beneath a magnifying glass.

Mr. Crawford, who had been talking for a full minute while Poppy stared, and who had now paused, waiting for an answer.

Poppy said, "What?"

"I know, it's a big decision." He flashed that irresistible smile. *He is made of MaaaAAAaaaaGIC,* Poppy's fevered brain sang. "But give it some thought. I think you and your family would be wonderful candidates."

"For the, um —"

"Poppy, trust me." He ran a hand through his hair, dispensing an intoxicating aroma of coconut, lavender, and whatever chemical was used to preserve the dissected animals in the biology lab. "My family hosted an international exchange student when I was in high school, and it was such an incredible experience. We're still friends to this day!"

She nodded. "Friends are great."

His lips disappeared into his smile, pinching his mouth as he tried not to laugh. "They sure are," he said, backing up and pointing at her as he left. "The letter should arrive today. Talk to your parents!"

No longer capable of doing anything but waving, Poppy waved at him, dove into the Gaudy Auditorium, and took a deep breath as the door shut behind her.

Silence. Emptiness. Lacquered hardwood floors.

Simply by standing there, breathing the space's distinctive air, she felt a sense of peace diffuse through her body. All the Blake unpleasantness and the Mr. Crawford infatuation drifted away with the current.

Theater calmed her. It sustained her. All was right with the world when viewed through a proscenium arch. And though theater had forsaken her, trampled her, and danced the lambada on the bloody corpse that had once been her budding career, it was nevertheless her one true love, and you don't throw away your one true love over something as silly as profound emotional scarring.

Plus, theater people were *her* people. They understood that the show must go on, even if you are bleeding from the head.

Performing still stung — a shallowness of breath choked her whenever she neared the wings of the stage or caught a whiff of pancake makeup — but her directorial talents had not suffered. When she was in the director's chair, the nerves and shame disappeared. She became focused and confident, a fearless Captain von Trapp rather than a helpless, writhing Maria.

And that's the mode she'd switched to when her theater people barged into the auditorium. They found their intrepid director already in position: third row, fifth seat from the aisle, notebook open, Sharpie poised, bullhorn on, staring expectantly.

"Well?" Poppy said to them. "Get on up there. Broadway isn't going to salute itself."

As the Giddy Committee took their places, Jill sank down next to Poppy and threw her feet up over the seats in front of them. "Broadway does nothing *but* salute itself."

"Don't you have a stage to manage?"

"Is the stage on fire? No? Then I've got everything under control."

Jill Cho was Poppy's favorite person in the world. On their first day back to school after *Triple Threat*, Jill had got there early, opened Poppy's locker (they'd known each other's combinations since seventh grade), and cleaned up all the fake blood that she instinctively knew would be in there courtesy of Blake Bursaw. "Now it smells like a hotel pool," she told Poppy once it had been bleached. "Pretend you're on a fabulous vacation at the Off-Ramp Burlington Ramada."

And that was it. Aside from indulging Poppy in her weekend-long festival of self-loathing and the requisite gorging of every ice cream pint on the market, Jill had gone back to treating her the same as she always had. And Poppy was eternally grateful.

Poppy readied her bullhorn. "I want to run the *Jesus Christ Superstar* number first," she blared, her tinny voice filling the auditorium. "Where's my Almighty Lord and Savior?"

A judgmental noise issued forth from Louisa, a tiny wisp of a person who always wore her dirty-blond hair in dual braids and looked as though the wind might blow her away at any moment. Her first love was ballet, but since Paraffin High didn't have a dance program, she was forced to settle for the only performing art available to her, no matter how lowly and base she deemed musical theater. And deem it she did. Aloud. And often. "Probably off performing miracles," she sneered. "Turning a cask of water into a bong, and such."

Poppy wanted to scold her, as Louisa's constant negative attitude wasn't exactly an asset to a group that was already kind of depressing, but she was probably right on this account. The boy playing Jesus Christ was a freshman who had recently moved to Paraffin, and no one knew much about him, including his real name. He was deposited into rehearsal one day, sentenced to join the Giddy Committee by Principal Lincoln for either smoking pot or setting something on fire or bringing a paintball gun to school (he later claimed it was all three). Poppy couldn't help but feel insulted that her life's passion was being used as a form of punishment, but Principal Lincoln must have had his reasons — maybe he thought she'd set a good example — so she went along with it. But since the boy had never filled out an audition form, she'd never learned his name — and when she cast him as the Prince of Peace, he'd insisted that it would just be easier to call him Jesus. So that's what they did.

"Was he in school today?" Poppy asked Jill.

"Is he ever?" Jill got up. "I'll go find him."

"Check the bathroom," Banks advised on her way in, slinging her backpack onto an empty seat. "The tacos at lunch today were questionable."

Aside from Jill, Banks was the only other nonwhite student at Paraffin High, and people simply didn't know what to do with her. Her father was Hispanic, her mother was black, her height was five foot eleven, and her opinion was that she did not care one bit about public opinion. So she joined the outcast repository that was the Giddy Committee — "because I don't fit in anywhere else, and why the hell not."

A flash of satin entered the auditorium. "Hey, Connor," Poppy said, waving him down, "come here a sec."

The pudgy junior with the beautiful operatic voice whom Poppy had cast as the Phantom of the Opera skittered to a stop on his way to the stage. Though they were not yet in dress rehearsals, he was already wearing his cape. "Yes, my angel of music?" he boomed.

Connor liked to stay in character. It was equal parts charming and annoying.

"I've got something for you." Poppy removed the trophy from her bag and handed it to him.

He cradled it to his breast. "Sweet, sweet yam! *'You alone can make my song take flight!'*"

"Okay, that's enough of that. Get onstage. We're doing your number right after — sweet *Jesus,* where *is* he?"

"Right here," Jill said, pulling him into the auditorium by his ear. "Hanging out by the girls' locker room again."

"Hey!" Christ protested. "Let go of me, woman!"

"You 'woman' me again, and I will end you."

"Why you gotta be like that? I wasn't doing anything wrong!"

Poppy tsked. "That's what the real Jesus said. And then he got arrested and put on trial and things didn't turn out too well for him, did they? Now *let's go.*"

Yet for all of Jesus's whining, the *Superstar* medley went well, the ensemble not even missing a beat when Connor, playing Judas, ripped his pants.

"Betrayed by a defective inseam," Jill remarked. "The irony."

*   *   *

Several hours later Poppy burst through the front door of her home. "Sorry I'm late," she said, dropping her backpack to the living room floor. "The *Annie* number turned into a fight over which orphan was the most pitiful. Hair was pulled, toes were stomped."

Her mother and little brother were seated at their usual places on the couch, tray tables lined up in front of them, as her father bustled in from the kitchen. "Hello, family!" he boomed, plate in hand.

"Hurry *up*," Owen insisted with the life-or-death intensity that only a five-year-old can bring to a conversation. "It's *starting!*"

"Food's on the stove," Poppy's mother told her. "There's extra flax if you need it."

Of course there was extra flax. The Palladino pantry looked like a Whole Foods had exploded — neatly, mind you, into color-coded

Mason jars. The health nuttiness of Poppy's family didn't bother her, as she was the kind of person who ate anything and everything, but there were times she wished things could go back to the way they'd allowed her to eat the week she'd returned from *Triple Threat*: Ice cream. Every damn day. For every damn meal.

Poppy made her way into the kitchen and found a tofu menagerie waiting for her. Tofu shaped like a bird. Tofu shaped like an elephant. Tofu shaped like an octopus. There was also a camera lying askew atop the counter, as well as a handful of notes her mother had abandoned in her haste to get dinner ready on time. She'd no doubt pore over them later that evening, readying her blog post for the next day. Poppy, who had an uncanny knack for discerning what the title of her mom's posts would be just by inspecting the aftermath of the cooking frenzy, surmised that "Tofu Zoo!" was a strong contender that night.

She selected a giraffe, plunked a pile of mashed potatoes next to it, grabbed the freshly blended wheatgrass-kale smoothie from the fridge, and headed into the living room, sinking into her favorite armchair beneath the framed painting her father had commissioned from one of his artist friends. Its overly pretentious title was *A Pulchritude of Peacocks* — but since it featured one flamboyant male getting all the attention from the ladies while another male sulked in the corner, the Palladinos lovingly referred to it as *The Pissed-Off Peacock*.

Owen bounced along to the rhythm as the *Dr. Steve* jingle cued up. A man with questionable medical credentials, Dr. Steve had

somehow conned a producer into giving him a television show —
and as practitioners of questionable lifestyle choices themselves,
Poppy's parents couldn't get enough of him. Neither could Owen.

Neither could Poppy, but only because she'd fashioned a drinking game around his habit of advising people to stop eating food.

"Oh, good, he's gonna talk about the hidden dangers of lem-
ons," her father said. "I read something about that."

Her mother nodded intently. "Me too. The seeds have arsenic in
them? Or something?"

Poppy held her tongue, a well-practiced maneuver by now. Her
parents were sweet, creative, enthusiastic, caring, energetic, wonderful people, and they loved her very much, and she loved them
very much, and they were idiots.

Perhaps that was too strong a word. "Ditzy" was more accurate,
or maybe "flighty." "March to the beat of a different drum," Poppy's
teachers would say after meeting them at parent-teacher confer-
ences. They wanted her to do well in school, of course, but Poppy's
parents were of the opinion that not all wisdom could be found in
books. "The greatest education is experience!" they said — though,
thankfully, never to her teachers' faces.

But what they lacked in book learning, they made up for elsewhere. Both employed as yoga teachers at the Paraffin Resort and
Spa, they were well-liked members of the community. They worked
hard to give their children a good life, and most of the time Poppy
was able to take their silliness as it came. And, she had to admit, they
did have a certain wisdom about them that she couldn't identify — a

sort of unwavering satisfaction with the world and their lives, as if they'd learned some secret that the rest of humanity hadn't figured out yet.

Whatever it was, she envied it.

"These potatoes are amazing, Mom," she said when Dr. Steve had finished inciting his war on citrus and the show went to commercial. "What did you do to them?"

Her mother grinned, her blond hair sticking out like straw just like her daughter's. "Oh, you know. I put the love in."

Her father joined in on the grinning. "And *I* helped peel the love."

Poppy beheaded the giraffe and gummed her tofu. "Mr. Kosnitzky says hi, by the way."

"How's his wife's yeast infection?" asked her mother, who took it upon herself to know every facet of her yoga students' health.

"All cleared up."

"Dr. Steve says yeast leads to salmonella," said Owen, building his mashed potatoes into a mountain. "He did an experiment and made it foam up like a bubble bath and ooze out all over the floor. Is that what happened to Mrs. Kosnitzky?"

"Yes," said Poppy. "The hospital had to be evacuated."

"Not the same thing, buddy," said their father. "Hey, Pops, something came in the mail from your school — something about international something? Is that something?"

A hot flash consumed Poppy at the memory of her encounter with Mr. Crawford, recalling his irresistible coconut-lavender-formaldehyde scent. "It's nothing," she said, keeping her eyes on the screen. "They want us to host an exchange student. You can throw it out."

"Oh, *why?*" said her mother. "That would be so fun!"

"And educational!" Her father pointed his fork at his children. "Family," he lectured, "we should always endeavor to open our home and hearts to those who are different from us."

"Yeah, well," said Poppy, "I don't think it's a good idea." Though she was loath to disappoint Mr. Crawford, hosting an exchange student was bound to be a terrible decision. "One thing I do not need in my life right now is to be belittled in multiple languages."

They couldn't argue with that.

"Any grand plans for the weekend, Poppy?" her mother asked, changing the subject. "Owen has a couple of soccer games tomorrow, so we'll be gone all day."

"No plans." Poppy stabbed her giraffe through the heart. "Probably hanging out with Jill, drag racing on the strip, meeting up with some arms dealers. The usual."

"Mrs. Goodwin told me that the Rotary Club needs volunteers to help build their float for the Paraffin Day parade, so we're going to that, if you want to come," her father said. "Spoiler alert: it's a goose!"

"No, thanks."

"Come on, Popsicle. Are we so tragically unhip that you can't bear to be seen with your parents anymore?" He made a frowny face. "I promise to leave my leisure suit at home!"

"I won't even wear my Crocs!" added her mother.

"We'll let you Instagram the whole thing!"

"And tweet all the Twitters!"

Poppy let out a snicker. If anything, *they* should be ashamed to be seen with *her*. "I don't want anything to do with that parade. The Paraffin High Marching Band was asked to perform in it and the Giddy Committee was not. Paraffin Day is dead to me."

"But it'll be fun!"

"Fun is also dead to me."

Her parents let it drop. Good-naturedly, of course, but a distinct deflation whooshed through the room as their eyes turned back to the television. Though Poppy never talked about it openly, they knew about the bullying, the abuse she suffered at school. It was important, the therapist had told them, not to be overprotective and to let her feel her own way back into the thick of things. But Poppy had noticed that lately they'd been going for the hard sell a lot more often. Family fun time had taken precedence, and it was getting harder and harder to weasel out of it.

"We're still on for the *Dr. Steve* marathon on Sunday night, though," she promised them. "Come hell or high water. Wouldn't miss it."

That brought the smiles back. "Attagirl," said her father.

As if buoyed by the attention, Dr. Steve now spouted his nonsense at top volume. ". . . And once we added it all up, the exhaustive cataloging of healthful benefits was irrefutable!" he shouted. "And do you know what *that* means?"

"Here it comes," Poppy said, her eyes glued to the screen. "Here it comes!"

Dr. Steve pointed at the camera. "Avoid beets," he advised, *"at all costs!"*

"Drink!"

The family chugged their wheatgrass in unison.

*   *   *

Around eleven thirty, the phone rang.

Poppy had gone up to her room to listen to some music and add more strips of fabric to Joseph's Amazing Technicolor Dreamcoat. She wasn't officially in charge of costumes, but the previous week, when Poppy asked the costumer whether she'd found any cowboy hats for the *Oklahoma* number yet, the poor girl had burst into tears and quit the Giddy Committee altogether. So it was now up to Poppy. It wasn't the first time she'd been forced to wear many hats for the good of the production, and it wouldn't be the last.

Which reminded her. She grabbed The List out of her backpack, uncapped her trusty black Sharpie, and wrote:

#19024: Buy cowboy hats

The epic ink-laden List was such a Paraffin High legend that it deserved its own page in the yearbook. (And there was a good chance that could happen, as Poppy was one of its editors.) It all started in sixth grade, when she'd been put in charge of her soccer team's bake sale and had come up with a list of no less than two dozen confectionary wonders, each of which she assigned with due haste to the bewildered parents. She'd kept The List going ever since, using it as a long-running to-do list that seldom saw a task go unfulfilled. When she reached the end of one notebook, she simply moved on to another. Pages upon pages of notes, each one crossed out with a thick black, outrageously satisfying line. She was now on Volume 7.

With my own friggin' money, she added to item #19024, scribbling bitterly. The marching band was currently in Madrid. Performing for a *queen*. And here she was, ripping up Owen's old baby clothes to make a dreamcoat because the Giddy Committee would never see a fraction of that budget.

So unfair.

The *Les Misérables* soundtrack popped up on her playlist next. Poppy sang along as she slashed her beloved X-Acto knife through the fabric, delighting in the devious thrill that came from uttering the line, *"Comforter, philosopher, and lifelong SHIT."* Broadway singing-swearing! The best kind! *"God knows how I've lasted, living with this BASTARD in—"*

The downstairs phone rang.

Poppy lifted her head but kept on humming. It was odd to get a call that late at night on the landline, but not unheard of. She'd just reached for an exceptionally vibrant strip of periwinkle fabric when she heard her mother let out a yelp.

Poppy muted the music and put down her X-Acto knife. Now her parents were talking in hushed, anxious tones.

A familiar weight thunked into Poppy's gut. The air in her room seemed to go stale, all the oxygen sucked out through the gaps in their old, warped wood windows.

Her cell phone. With a jolt, she remembered: she'd silenced it for rehearsal and had forgotten to turn the sound back on. She excavated it from the bottom of her backpack, lit up the screen, and drew a sharp breath.

Eight missed calls from Jill. Twenty-three texts.

Just as she was about to read them, her door swung open. Her father stood in the hall, his face pained.

"Um," he said, twisting his hands, "don't freak out, okay?"

3

Freak ~~out~~

POPPY PERCHED ON THE EDGE OF THE LIVING ROOM COUCH
and stared at the television screen, DVR paused on the Channel Six
eleven o'clock news graphic and the face of lead anchor Veronica
Fahey. Her father handed her the remote, which sat in her clammy
hand like an alien device.

Her stomach twisted. She pressed play.

"And now for something," said Veronica, smiling mildly at the
camera, "on the lighter side of the news. Colt?"

The shot switched to Colt Lamberty, Channel Six's ace reporter,
who had swept onto the local news scene about six months earlier
from someplace much sunnier and with far more attractive people.
He resembled one of those sketches of what scientists think that
people in the future will look like once the world is completely
globalized and all the races have finished banging one another: a
picture of ethnically balanced perfection.

Colt stood in the Paraffin town square, a spotlight-blasted

beacon amid the encroaching darkness. He spoke into the microphone with ease, confidence, and just the right amount of playfulness in his non-regional dialect. "Thanks, Veronica! The Paraffin Day bicentennial celebrations aren't set to begin until Tuesday, but according to footage uploaded by an anonymous viewer to our Channel Six YouNews app, it seems that a few pranksters—and Paraffin's favorite local celebrity—have started up the fun a little early."

The screen switched to some shaky footage that had obviously been recorded on a cell phone. Laughter could be heard in the background—distinctive, hyenalike laughter—as the image bounced and blurred through the darkness. It came to rest on the gazebo, the scene lit with what looked like flashlights.

"The return," said the video's narrator, "of Hogwash."

The remote tumbled from Poppy's hand.

*   *   *

#18984: Write essay for English

#18985: Do calc equations

#18986: Buy fabric and chicken wire for Ham costume

#18987: Make Ham costume (reread Chapter 27 of TKAM to check details)

#18988: Do Practice SAT Exam #5

#18989: Go to the Bursaw Halloween party?

#18990: STRANGLE BLAKE BURSAW WITH MY GODDAMN BARE HANDS

Poppy glanced up from The List — specifically, the section from last month, the one she'd sworn never to reread.

But reread it she had. And spent the previous thirty minutes seething over its cruel foreshadowing.

The instant she'd watched that news clip, she knew Blake was responsible. It smacked of his trademark pranking style: mean and immature, with enough creative flair that you had to give him a few points for originality. That was probably why there hadn't been more outrage over what happened on Halloween — the scheme Blake had concocted was cruel but funny, at least to everyone who was not Poppy. And when it came to viral videos, funny trumped basic human decency every time.

But it still didn't seem all that hilarious to her.

In retrospect, she never should have attended the party in the first place. For heaven's sake, it was at the Bursaws' house! It was walking directly into enemy territory! But it had been a few months since *Triple Threat* had aired, and she had just begun to gain back an iota of confidence. Plus, she hadn't wanted to break her and Jill's grand Halloween tradition of costuming themselves as props from great works of literature. So off they went, Poppy as Scout's pageant ham costume from *To Kill a Mockingbird* and Jill as the conch shell from *Lord of the Flies*. Amid a sea of slutty nurses and slutty devils and slutty angels, there were Poppy and Jill, waddling around like sumo wrestlers in their bulky, chicken-wired, decidedly unsexy monstrosities.

She may as well have been wearing a light-up sandwich board that said TAKE ME DOWN A PEG, PLEASE.

The night had started on a promising note. The mayor herself answered the door, for one thing. Looking hopelessly out of place in orthopedic shoes, a clueless smile, and a darling felted hat with an extra-darling felted flower sticking out of it, Miss Bea gave the girls a warm welcome. Big Bob wasn't far behind; Poppy shook his hand, trying not to recoil as she looked into his leathery face. He was a slimy sort of fellow — he looked a lot like that strong-chinned guy who ran for president a few years back whose name everyone had already forgotten — and not a word came out of his mouth that sounded genuine. He'd recently launched a crackdown on local teen drug use, though his motto, "Drugs are not rad!" did not exactly resonate with the local teens, and his own son, who spent most of his time drinking or snorting or smoking whatever lay within arms' reach, was not exactly the poster boy for moderation. Still, Poppy was comforted by his presence. It lent a nice illusion of responsibility to the proceedings.

But it didn't take long for her to realize that Big Bob was only doing what he always did, which was to turn a blind eye to Blake's unending reign of terror.

Inside the sprawling mansion, the party raged. It was hot. It was crowded. Outside, kids skateboarded in the empty concrete pool. There was alcohol, though Poppy wasn't drinking any and neither was Jill. They were probably the only sober ones who stumbled into that hazy circle of kids who had gathered in the conservatory (*Who has a conservatory?* Poppy remembered thinking. *Are we in the Clue house?*) and started telling ghost stories.

"But I saw her!" one boy was insisting. "I swear!"

The other kids booed him. "Dude, everyone else stopped believing in Bloody Mary when they were ten!" said a girl with a blue streak in her hair, turning her voice smokier as she added, "But the Hollow Ones . . ."

The circle went quiet.

"What about them?" someone asked. "Have you seen them?"

"I haven't, but this older girl I used to work with at the movie theater said that her roommate was coming home from a bar once late at night, and she pulled over to puke in the woods, and there was one in the trees. Just staring back at her."

"So?" said the Bloody Mary boy. "It was probably just some perv in the woods. How could she tell that—"

"Because," said Blue Streak, "when the moon came out from behind a cloud, his skin looked way too smooth, like it was made out of wax. And then"—she leaned farther into the circle—"he opened his mouth. And when she looked inside his mouth, the back of his throat was *glowing*. Like, flickering. Like there was a flame burning down in his gut and reflecting up his windpipe."

Silence again.

But then Jill said, "That's it?" The other kids looked at her with mixed expressions of relief and annoyance. "He didn't breathe fire like a dragon, or, I don't know, do something remotely interesting?"

Blue Streak looked as though she might start breathing fire herself. "I'm just—"

"What is this, open mike night?" Jill carried on. "We've spent our lives hearing and telling and retelling the story of the Hollow Ones, or the Candle Men, or the Paraffin Demons, or whatever the hell you want to call them. It's Hallo*ween*, kids. Step it up and think of something more original!"

Just then Poppy got yanked out of the circle — by a fed-up Jill, she thought. But because of the way the ham costume impeded her movement and peripheral vision, she was unable to confirm the identity of the person who was dragging her by the hambone out of the conservatory, across the living room, out the door, and into the backyard.

It was not Jill.

By the time she realized that it was Blake and that humiliation was imminent, it was too late. Floodlights snapped on. A crowd materialized. She was given a light kick and sent tumbling down a slope. Then off went the hoses, dousing Poppy in water as she hopped and slipped and cavorted across the slippery concrete floor of the empty pool, its steep walls making escape impossible.

The video was titled "Hogwash." It got a million more hits than *Triple Threat*.

(The irony was not lost on anyone that she'd been hijacked while dressed up as a giant ham, as *To Kill a Mockingbird* itself had foretold. Mrs. Shelburne even mentioned it in English class the following week. It became part of the lesson plan.)

Poppy never did find out what happened to the ham costume after that. Which was a shame, really — it had been her best yet. Even better than the *Don Quixote* windmill of sophomore year. Glazed to a blinding sheen, it didn't deserve to be crumpled up and thrown into the garbage, which she assumed is what happened to it after she'd wriggled out and fled the scene.

But oh ho! It had *not* been trashed! It had been saved, decrumpled, and restored to its former glory!

How did Poppy know this? Because the news report blaring into her life that night revealed that for a few brief hours before someone had the good sense to take it down, the costume had been worn by a sculpted statue of Poppy propped up in the gazebo, the video narration stating, "In honor of Paraffin's own Poppy Palladino, who really knows how to bring home the bacon!"

* * *

Back upstairs in her room, Poppy lay on her bed and stared at the bevy of autographed Broadway posters covering her walls. Ordinarily, she found comfort in their familiarity, their art, the cast photos, the loopy signatures. The memories of trips to New York City with her parents, the excitement of waiting at the stage door after the performance for the actors to emerge. The potential for her future, the possibility that one day she could be among them.

But not tonight. Tonight those same autographs looked like asbestos-coated spikes itching to drop down and impale her.

Abruptly sitting up, she reached for her pen. Gripping it so hard she heard the plastic crack, she flipped to the end of The List and wrote on the next blank line.

#19025: KILL BLAKE BURSAW. FOR REAL THIS TIME.

4

~~Devise a strategy~~

WHEN POPPY CALLED HER AROUND MIDNIGHT, JILL DIDN'T waste time with pleasantries. "What's the plan?" she asked, getting down to business.

"I'll pick you up tomorrow at nine," Poppy said. "We'll head over to Smitty's for supplies—"

"Donuts, right? You mean donuts?"

"Of course I mean donuts."

"Okay. Continue."

"Then we begin plans for our counterattack. I think we need to start with . . ." Poppy trailed off, replaying the news segment in her mind.

With what? A simple reciprocal prank wouldn't work this time. It would have to be epic. It would have to match what Blake did, then surpass it. It would have to destroy him. Humiliate him. REVENGE WOULD BE HERS.

You're only perpetuating the bullying cycle, her internal voice of reason piped up. *You're only going to provoke him further, escalating the war until everyone loses.*

All good points. But on the other hand: REVENGE.

"This is all blowback from the pantsing fiasco," Jill was saying. "He thought you were weak. He didn't expect you to fight back. But you did, and voilà, here's the fallout."

"*. . . revenge. . . .*"

"What?"

"Nothing. I mean, you're right. I'm not weak. And this time I'm going to prove it. We're gonna get Blake Bursaw so bad, he's gonna wish *he* was the one Katy Perry had to console in the ambulance!"

"That's a confusing metaphor."

"We shall fight *fire* with *fire!*"

"How about you knock off the figurative language and say what it is your depleted brain is trying to say?"

"We're gonna do the same thing to him," Poppy said slowly, "but do it better."

"Huh?"

"Think about it, Jill — the statue thing's not *that* cruel. For one thing, my cheekbones looked fabulous. Plus, it's just a replica of a thing that had already happened. He didn't break any new ground. He fell back on the pig thing again. Where's the skill in that? He's getting lazy!"

"And you're getting something that rhymes with 'lazy.'"

"We need a sculpture of *him*," Poppy continued, her mind churning. "We need to find out how he got one made of me.

Remember what he did with the wax in art class last year? He made a butt. And not even a good butt! A lumpy, asymmetrical butt!"

"Yet still a butt that seems to have landed a cherished place in your long-term memory."

"My point is that there's no way he could have sculpted it on his own. He must have commissioned it or something. And we all know there's only one place he could have gotten a thing like that."

"I don't know, Poppy. I don't think they do special orders with intent to disgrace."

"Maybe they do! Maybe Blake bribed an employee to do it! I mean, he's Blake friggin' Bursaw. Who's going to say no to him?"

"And who might this mysterious employee be?"

"That's what we have to find out."

"Fine. Tomorrow, nine o'clock."

"See you then. And, Jill?"

"Yeah?"

"Be sure to wear a jacket. Revenge is a dish best served *ice-cold*."

"I'm going to punch you."

* * *

Jill did just that when Poppy picked her up the next morning.

"Ow," said Poppy, rubbing her arm.

"Sorry," Jill said as they drove past the town square. "You forced my hand."

It was a screamingly beautiful Saturday morning, the sun high and blinding against the electric blue November sky. The sure-to-be-brutal Vermont winter hadn't started in earnest yet, but the air was cold and crisp, and Paraffin was cranking up the adorable. Kids rode their bikes, squeezing in a few last days of fun before the snow started to fall. New parents pushed carriages down the sidewalk and cooed at their gurgling spawn. Elderly couples walked hand in hand on the shore of the lake and tossed bread at the geese, who thanked them by pecking at their ankles, the bastards. A large banner strewn across Main Street reminded everyone of the bicentennial celebration on Tuesday, as if anyone could forget. It had been declared a town-wide holiday — schools, banks, and the post office would be closed — and promised entertainment, fireworks, a raffle, and, of course, the big parade.

Poppy opened up her mouth to complain about the marching band, but Jill interrupted her with, "Not a word about the marching band."

"I . . . wasn't. I was going to say that I'm . . . glad my wax twin has vacated the gazebo."

"Wonder what happened to it."

"Oh, the sanitation department destroyed it. They called early this morning to make sure that was all right."

"And you didn't ask to keep it? But your cheekbones!"

Poppy pulled the car into a parking spot across from Smitty's. She got out, stretched, and looked across the lake. The equilaterally triangular Mount Cerumen perked up like the ear of a cat, listening to everything going on in town. Beside it, on a smaller hill, sat two tanks the Grosholtz Candle Factory had once used to store its surplus liquid wax. The tanks had been designed to look like two large pillar candles, and flames were sometimes lit atop their roofs to complete the picture — but other than that, they were no longer operational. Lightning had struck them both years ago, ripping holes in their exteriors and thereby destroying their ability to retain heat, and so the factory had abandoned them in favor of more modern wax storage technologies.

Jill had already crossed the street. "You coming?" she asked. "Or is staring slack-jawed at the lake part of your ingenious plan?"

"Coming! Hang on!" Poppy removed her bag from the back seat and began the laborious process of cramming The List into it.

"Leave The List," Jill said, exasperated. "What possible task could you need to fulfill at a donut shop other than stuffing your face?"

Poppy relented. "Fine," she said, walking to the back of the car. "But I'm putting it in the trunk for safekeeping! Prying eyes and such!"

Smitty's was packed. The gossipy townsfolk had emerged in droves to gab about the prank — the same people who had waved at the cameras when *Triple Threat* came to town to do a puff piece on their hometown hero. Before the bloodletting, of course.

"She's our shining star!" Smitty had said on camera of Poppy, the label of "Local Donut Shop Owner" below his name, his forehead glistening with sweat. Smitty always reminded Poppy of a garden gnome — short, pudgy, cherry nose, bald on top with a ring of hair around the back of his head, and beloved by a minority for reasons incomprehensible to the majority. "Always knew she'd hit the big league," he'd crowed. Then something had occurred to

46

him — something involving the word "marketing" — and his grin grew wider. "Now, how about a maple cruller? Vermont's finest!"

And now here he was again, gleefully shilling confections to his hungry clientele, bragging loudly about his new bagel oven. It was allegedly the largest of its kind in New England, so specialized that only he was allowed to use it or even be in the same room as it. "Can bake seven hundred and twenty-four at once!" he boasted. "Stick *that* in your bagel hole!"

Jill lingered outside the café's entrance, staring with disgust at the nattering hordes. "Maybe we should go somewhere else."

"Nonsense, poopypants," Poppy said, striding toward the café with all the confidence of a victorious general returning home from the war. "We continue unabated." She opened the door for Jill, who stopped short to make way for an exiting couple.

"Oh, sorry," Jill said, skittering out of their way with more speed once she saw who they were.

Anita and Preston Chandler, CEO and president of the Grosholtz Candle Factory, respectively, looked at Jill with expressions of . . . nothing. Her presence barely registered as a blip on their worldview — nothing but a faint gust of wind between them and the next sip of their vanilla lattes.

The Chandlers had swooped into Paraffin years ago, and though the story went that they had inherited the Grosholtz Candle Factory through some nebulous family connections, it sometimes seemed as though they had taken control solely through brute force charm. Anita and Preston were beautiful, beautiful people. Their skin was flawless, their smiles achingly wide. They were a wedding cake topper come to life — plastic, eyes straight ahead, solidly standing on top of the world.

"Gutbag," Anita muttered dismissively at Jill, putting a French-tip manicured finger on the door. "Are you coming?" she asked Preston.

"My tie got coffee on it —"

"You have one hundred and eighty-three ties, Preston. Surely one of them will be a suitable replacement."

He followed her out the door, muttering, "Hundred and eighty-*two* now."

Jill watched them go. "Did she call me a gutbag?" she asked Poppy.

"We continue unabated!"

They continued, unabated, into the café.

Everyone stared, as Poppy knew they would. Everyone stopped eating, as she knew they would. Everyone looked confused, as she knew they would, when she waved and smiled and marched right up to the counter to order half a dozen chocolate glazed donuts. As she *hoped* they would.

She refused to cower. She refused to be embarrassed for the myriad misfortunes that had befallen her. They weren't remotely her fault. Embarrassment was the most useless of emotions in this situation, and Poppy was sick of letting it wash over her without her permission.

She was in charge now.

She would have her donuts.

* * *

"That was bitchin'," Jill said as they left, stuffing several hundred calories' worth of chocolate into her face. "Did you see Mrs. Debenport? I think she choked on her bagel."

"Oh yeah?"

"I couldn't tell for sure. A glob of cream cheese was spat into her coffee, at least."

Mrs. Debenport's ruined coffee did brighten Poppy's spirits, but it was time to focus — and to ignore the many eyes watching her pull out of the parking space. Though Poppy had lost many things during her time on *Triple Threat* — dignity, confidence, a pint of blood — she did win a car, having received the most (pity) votes for Audience Favorite. Clementine was bright orange, somehow simultaneously boxy and bulbous, and made Poppy immediately identifiable wherever she drove — but humiliation perks, humiliating as they were, were still perks.

As she steered Clementine around the lake, the Grosholtz Candle Factory loomed ahead of them like a mullet: jolly commercialized store out front, creepy Gothic dungeon out back. Its spires seemed taller today, their emaciated fingers stretching imploringly toward the sky while its storefront welcomed them with open arms, a sunny hello, and a color-coded map.

"Here's your map!" the greeter bubbled, handing Poppy and Jill one copy each. She wore a red vest and a customized pin that said BARBARA'S FAVORITE GROSHOLTZ CANDLE SCENT IS: NEW-FALLEN SNOW! "If you have questions, ask any of our Waxperts in the red vests. Enjoy your day at the Grosholtz Candle Factory!"

Poppy and Jill nodded their thanks, because for the next thirty seconds, they could not speak. They made it a few feet into the foyer of the store, until they couldn't hold their breath any longer. Jill was the first to blow, followed a few seconds later by Poppy.

The first inhalation was the worst.

"Bluuugh," Poppy moaned, sticking out her tongue.

"Gaargh," Jill gagged, crinkling her nose.

Hazelnut-melon Christmas. Buttercream-pumpkin seaweed. Herbal-sandcastle coffee. Berry-rubber holiday. Autumn-hamburger landfill. Patchouli-patchouli patchouli.

Poppy fanned her hand across her nose and exchanged a foul glance with Jill. "Instead of maps, they should hand out gas masks."

"And suicide pills."

But the agony had just begun. The entrance area alone boasted no less than forty varieties of jams and jellies, a greasy food court, a kiosk offering freshly made fudge, several Scent Stations, and, of course, the main attraction: walls and walls and walls of jars and tins and molds of candles.

"I am going to be sick," Jill announced. "Excuse me while I duck into one of these Scent Stations and unload the contents of my stomach."

"Don't. They'll probably make it into a candle."

"Half-Digested Donut."

"Chocolate-Glazed Upchuck."

The line for the make-your-own-candle area was growing by the minute, winding slowly past a conveniently placed price list — CUSTOM LABELS: $5.00; RAINBOW SWIRLS: $3.00; HIDE A SECRET

NOTE IN A CANDLE: $10.00 — that kids looked upon with delight and parents looked upon with abject hatred. Another vestibule held bottles of Tackety Wax, the Grosholtz Candle Factory's first foray into infomercial-worthy products — a sticky wax that promised a tight seal on anything that needed sealing. And eclipsing them all: a large display with a sign that read INTRODUCING: BiScENTENNIALS! COMING TOMORROW!

"'In honor of our town's bicentennial celebrations,'" Poppy read off the sign, "'the Grosholtz Candle Factory will be releasing two brand-new, small-batch, exclusive special-edition BiScentennial candles *every day.* For the rest of our bicentennial *year!*'"

"My heavens," Jill said as they walked farther into the store. "We'll need another full year to recover from the excitement."

Poppy tried to ignore the costumed musical atrocity that was befalling the food court, but it was not designed to be ignored. A dancing pig dressed in overalls swung his bucket oh so merrily across a raised stage while a trio of cows sang and wiggled their udders. There was also a terrifying anthropomorphic representation of the state of Vermont ambling and cavorting about, his ceaseless, dead stare no doubt sucking the souls from the slack-jawed children who had the misfortune to fall under his tyranny.

"I will miss my eyes," said Jill, "when I gouge them out. But I see no other course of action."

"Waterbury gets Ben and Jerry's," Poppy lamented. "Cabot gets endless cheese. Paraffin gets candles and Vermonty, New England's most beloved nightmare goblin."

It was then that Vermonty entreated the audience to join him in a stirring rendition of Vermont's state song, "These Green Mountains," at which point Poppy and Jill bolted as fast as their loganberry-laden lungs would allow.

They found themselves in a waiting room of sorts, where a large sign announced that the next tour would begin in five minutes. Beside it stood the Waxpert tour guide, a perky-looking girl wearing a red vest and a brightly colored felt hat shaped like — wait for it — a candle. Covering the room was a beautiful glass-domed roof, affording spectators a neck-craning view of the defunct storage tanks, conveniently located just up the adjacent hill. Stained into the glass in elegant, loopy letters was the Grosholtz Candle Factory motto: "One fire, many flames."

A gaggle of tourists, not a one under the age of fifty, dallied about the room, waiting for the next tour to start. Some studied their maps with the intensity of air traffic controllers, not wanting to lose a precious second of candle factory fun time to poor planning. Others were reading the informational placards on the wall or shouting the contents of the informational placards into their significant others' hearing aids. Still others were sitting on benches, complaining about their feet.

But most were captivated by the extensive diorama that wrapped around the perimeter of the room. Behind a wall of glass in a climate-controlled display, no less than two dozen beautifully sculpted life-size wax figures stood frozen in scenes of Vermontian history and noble pastoral labor. Some tilled fields, some churned butter, some gathered eggs. A crowd of villagers traded wares in the town square. One girl who looked to be about Poppy's age sat on a stool next to a cow, squeezing its udders with a look on her face that could only be described as vengeful.

In fact, her cheekbones kind of looked like those of Poppy's gazebo twin.

Poppy tugged on Jill's sleeve and pointed out the deranged milkmaid. "Fancy a tour?"

Jill groaned. "We already did the tour. In fifth grade. Anthony Colucchio stepped on my Hello Kitty sneaker and made me cry. What if history repeats itself, Poppy? Do you really want that on your conscience?"

"I am willing to risk it, yes."

"You're a terrible friend."

"But look at the tour guide's jaunty hat! How bad could it be?"

* * *

The tour was bad. The jaunty hat could not save it.

Somewhere around the point at which the tour guide cooed, "And *this* is the *wicking* room!" Jill slumped her head up against Poppy and whimpered. "I can't take it anymore," she said. "We get it. It's wax. It melts. It smells. End of story."

"The *story* be*gins*," Poppy said in a pitch-perfect imitation of the tour guide's opening sentence, "in 1865, when the *Gro-sholtz*—"

"Stooooop."

Poppy smirked, but her patience had worn as thin as Jill's. The tour was duller than her ten-year-old self remembered, and it had been a waste of time to boot; she hadn't spotted any sort of custom-made-statue opportunities. All she'd learned was that Blake may or may not have gone on this same tour and that the popularity of tea lights was on the rise.

"And here we have a drum of Forty Winks wax — careful, you may begin to feel drowsy after prolonged sniffing!" the tour guide said with a chuckle. "The Grosholtz Candle Factory is at the forefront of the aromatherapy movement, infusing innovative new blends into our candles that will improve people's moods . . . *and* lives. We've partnered exclusively with the Paraffin Resort and Spa on a new line of relaxation melts, and we're even working on a product called Beacon, a powder that can be used by emergency responders as a sort of olfactory flare gun, for victims to 'follow their nose' toward help. Just sprinkle it in any flame, and you've got the opposite of citronella — reeling them in, instead of warding them off!"

"Because that's what we need," Jill joked to Poppy. "*More* candle weirdos."

"And now for a special treat," the tour guide continued once they'd shuffled from the wicking room into a hallway. "Say hello to Anita and Preston Chandler, the CEO and president of the Grosholtz Candle Factory!"

She pulled open a curtain on the wall, revealing a large window. On the other side of the glass was a luxurious office featuring deep brown mahogany walls, a majestic fireplace complete with roaring fire, and red velvet armchairs with tall seat backs. A living Christmas card, Anita and Preston Chandler stood in front of the fireplace, waving, Smitty's Donut Shop vanilla lattes still in hand.

The senior citizens crowded around the window as if it were the monkey enclosure at a zoo, scrambling to take photos of the fancy people in their natural habitat. Poppy and Jill stayed put in the back.

After a full minute of flash photography, the tour guide put an end to the gawking. "Thanks, Anita and Preston! Time for them to get back to work," she said, pulling the curtain closed. "Now, I know what you're all thinking. When is this dang tour guide going to talk about hollows? Hollow candles, for those of you not in the know, are wax shells shaped like candles, but they *do not melt!* Instead, they feature a cavity into which you can insert a smaller candle — a tea light or votive — thereby producing a muted, flickering light that's ideal for —"

"Oh my God, a candle *within* a candle?" Jill said to Poppy, hysteria rising in her voice. "This tour is becoming a Russian nesting doll of insanity!"

Impatient, Poppy pushed to the front of the group, interrupting the guide. "Those sculptures back in the waiting room diorama, where we started the tour. Is there any way to hire someone from the factory to make something like that?"

The tour guide gave her a curious look. "What is that, the question of the week?"

"Huh?"

"Someone else asked that the other day. But I'm sorry to say it's not a service the Grosholtz Candle Factory provides."

Poppy turned to Jill. "That had to have been Blake!"

"Sure," said Jill. "Fine. I don't care anymore."

"Now," the tour guide went on, "if you'll look to your left, you'll see a picture of a bee. Bees make wax too! And so do our ears."

Jill buried her face in Poppy's shoulder. *"Kill me."*

* * *

Poppy did not grant Jill's request. When an hour later the tour guide led them into a room with a small stage, they were both alive and well and totally miserable.

"Bet there's no furnace under *that* stage," Poppy said grumpily. "Bet *their* actors don't get into orphan fights."

The tour guide hopped up onto the stage and wheeled out a table set with two glass bowls of clear liquid. "What does the future hold for the Grosholtz Candle Factory? Let's just say we've got a few more tricks up our sleeve." She beckoned for an older couple to come forward and held the bowls out toward them. "Go ahead, take a sniff."

They did so, then frowned. "I don't smell anything," said the woman.

"Right. Now do me a favor and dip your fingers in. It won't hurt, I promise!" The couple did as she asked. "Now sniff again!"

The woman sniffed at the bowl into which she'd dipped her finger, then gasped. "It's strawberry shortcake!"

"No, it's not," her surly husband countered, sniffing his own bowl. "It's motor oil."

"It's both!" the tour guide crowed. "It's your favorite scent, whatever that may be!"

"Oh, my," said the woman, bringing a hand to her chest. "It's true! I love to bake, and he's a retired mechanic!"

"This miraculous substance is something our Waxperts have been developing for years," the tour guide continued. "They've nicknamed it Potion, and it's one of the newest advances in waxen technology. By mixing a person's individually secreted oils with Potion — a proprietary mix of wax, pheromones, and scentographic sensors — we'll be able to create an innovative, one-of-a-kind fragrance. Personalized scents are going to revolutionize the industry!"

This was followed by a polite round of applause from most, and a drowned-out "I don't think 'scentographic sensors' are a thing," from Poppy.

"In fact, our new line of BiScentennial candles — which releases tomorrow — will be made with this technology, using data from volunteers found right here in Paraffin," the tour guide continued, wheeling the table with the bowls out of the way. "We are not overexaggerating when we tell you that this is a *total candle game changer.*"

"That must be true," Jill muttered to Poppy, "as the Grosholtz Candle Factory is not prone to overexaggeration."

The tour guide clasped her hands together, beaming. "Yes, here at the Grosholtz Candle Factory, it truly is — say it with me — *one fire, many flames.* And with that, there's only one thing left to do!" she finished with a menacing smile. And of course, *of course,* from the wings of the stage moseyed Vermonty, that destroyer of worlds, as the melody of "These Green Mountains" filled the room.

The elderly contingent happily formed an impromptu, tuneless chorus while Poppy and Jill scanned the room for exits. "I'll push them," Jill told Poppy. "Trampling senior citizens is not beneath me."

"It might be the one thing you were put on this earth to do."

The music got louder. Arthritic hands clapped along with the rhythm. Poppy whipped her head around the room and spotted a door toward the back, labeled EMPLOYEES ONLY.

She swallowed, a rush of blood pulsing in her head. Once she was sure no one was watching her, she crept up to the door and put her ear to its surface— but the song had gotten so loud, it was impossible to hear anything.

Jill saw what Poppy was doing and joined her. "Have you decided to sneak into the back and set the Chandlers on fire?" she asked. "Good idea. If only we had access to anything combustible . . ."

"Look," Poppy said, focusing on the door. "What if Blake snuck in here, found and trapped a couple of employees, and held them hostage until they agreed to fashion a statue of me?"

"Well, the simplest explanation *is* usually the right one."

"I'm serious! What if—"

"Our illustrious state needs a dance partner!" the tour guide crowed while Vermonty do-si-doed with himself. "Have we any volunteers? How about you, in the back there?"

The fickle finger of forced audience participation landed squarely on Jill, whose face went whiter than a jar of New-Fallen Snow. "Oh, no," she whispered, clutching at the door. "No no no. *No.*"

Poppy saw her opportunity, and it would cost exactly one decade-old friendship. "Do it," she commanded Jill. "Be a diversion. I'll slip in here, investigate, and find you afterward. Jill. *Please.*"

Jill's jaw went hard. She drew in a long breath, the resigned inhalation of a battle-worn soldier heading into certain death. "If I do this for you," she said stoically, "you will purchase me *ten pounds* of fudge."

"Done."

Jill gave an imperceptible nod and began the long walk to the stage, where Vermonty enveloped her in a suffocating green-felted hug. The last thing Poppy saw as she slipped through the door was Jill being twirled around like a ballerina, and by the look of homicidal rage on her face, Vermonty was not long for this world.

* * *

It was the strangest thing.

Not the fact that Poppy was so easily able to sneak unnoticed into the restricted area.

Not the fact that as soon as she grabbed a red vest off the coat rack within, every employee traveling the hallway nodded at her as if she were one of them, a certified Waxpert.

Not the fact that it was a really *long* hallway. She'd been walking for five minutes and still hadn't reached an end, seeing fewer and fewer employees along the way. Doors lined both sides of it, some labeled, some not. Windows revealed dull, corporate-looking rooms where product development meetings no doubt took place, where employees would shout things like *I think it whiffs of dragon fruit!* or *Let's call this one Banana Bonanza!* or *What does "freedom" smell like?* A couple of laboratories, more offices, a break room. Another window revealed a market research panel currently in session, the kind that almost everyone in town had been invited to participate in over the years. An employee would present candles for volunteers to smell while analysts watched via a one-way mirror. At the end, the sniffers would leave with a free candle, a coupon booklet, and the fervent hope that they would be invited back in the future.

No, the strangest thing was that the farther Poppy walked, the less sterile and generic the hallway was. The linoleum floor turned to hardwood — and then, farther down, *old* wood, the kind that jutted up in odd places with protruding nail heads. Doors got fewer and farther between, then stopped altogether. The clean white walls faded into dusty yellowed wallpaper, then, like the floor, switched to wood. The air became fusty. She had to be at the rear of the factory, somewhere in those arachnid-looking reaches. By the time Poppy arrived at the end of the hallway, finding only a single wooden door, the only thing she could think to say to herself, in the goofiest voice possible, was, "Well, gee. Knock-knock."

"Come in," came a voice on the other side.

Poppy clapped a hand over her mouth. "Oh, crap, no, I was *kidding*," she whispered into her palm.

She glanced around, but there was nothing to glance at. With that single door, the hallway simply . . . ended. She could either go in or begin the long walk back, ending her investigation with as many unanswered questions and unfulfilled revenge fantasies as she had started with.

The silence between Poppy and the concealed answerer gained weight, sagging there between them in the form of a rotting old door. Heat clogged the hallway. Poppy's skin was sweaty, her mouth dry. If she were a candle, she would be Dehydration Celebration.

Clearly, she would not be going in. She was not an employee. She was not authorized to be there. She had hoped to maybe snoop around undetected, but now? It was time to leave.

And yet out shot her hand, reaching toward the knob. Twisting the knob. Pushing the door open.

The room was dark, but not pitch-black. Muted light entered through windows caked with grime. Dust choked the air, so thick, it was as if a fog had rolled in. The wooden boards creaked as Poppy walked, her feet brushing aside something like dry leaves with each step.

And that was when she spotted the bodies.

People hidden in the foggy shadows. Crowding around her, staring at her, advancing on her. She backed up against the door, but it had closed, trapping her inside. Her sneakers slipped on whatever she was stepping on — panicked, she looked down at the floor — it was blanketed with scrapings of skin —

And all the while she felt a scream gathering in the back of her throat, gasping and clawing and begging to be let out — until she couldn't contain it for a second longer.

5

~~Scream~~

"GOOD HEAVENS," SAID THE VOICE THAT HAD BECKONED HER inside. "Now, there's a racket to wake the dead."

Poppy blinked. Some of the cloudy air had drifted out the door when she opened it, giving her a better view of the room. It did indeed contain several people. They were indeed staring at her.

But none of them were real.

They were models. Dummies. Life-size human replicas.

"I'm sorry to have startled you," one of them said.

Poppy gasped, freaking out all over again until she realized that the one who spoke — *that* woman was a real human being. Right?

It was at this point that Poppy wondered what was in those candles she'd been inhaling all day.

The woman started flitting about like a hummingbird. She skittered over to Poppy, not touching her, but rather picking and interlacing her curved fingers together as if she were knitting an invisible sweater. "Look at you! High cheekbones. Strong bone structure. Large eyes. Asymmetrical lips."

62

Never before had Poppy been greeted with an extensive list of her facial features. She found it unsettling. "Um," she said, backing away as the woman stood on her tiptoes to examine her more closely. "I think I may have stumbled into the wrong—"

"Stay still, my doll." The woman spoke with an accent — French, probably. Paraffin wasn't far from the Canadian border, a fact its citizens were reminded of every summer when Québécois tourists migrated south in flocks. "This won't take long."

The glass eyes of the people-shaped figures stared at Poppy while whatever "this" was continued, until she couldn't take the creepiness anymore and broke away with a full-body shudder. "I'm sorry, but—"

"No, no. It is I who am sorry!" The woman gave a little high-pitched chuckle and backed up, holding her hands aloft in a gesture of benevolence. "I sometimes forget about — what do the kids call it? Personal space."

"Um. Okay."

Cocking her head like a bird, the woman observed Poppy with a keen, shrewd stare through a pair of thin-rimmed spectacles that weren't much bigger than her eyes. A beaky nose jutted out above a pair of pursed lips. She projected a sense of advanced age, yet thick dark brown ringlets framed a face that bore no wrinkles. And she was short — Poppy had at least six inches on her.

The woman started to inch closer again.

And sniff at her.

Poppy flinched. Upon realizing her error, the woman made a *tsk* noise at herself, gave Poppy a rueful look, and retreated among the figures. "Apologies, my doll. Not so good with people anymore, I am afraid. This place . . . they do not let me out much."

"That's probably because they're an evil candle corporation dead set on destroying the human race's sense of smell," Poppy blurted, wasting no time in disparaging the woman's place of employment.

But if the woman was taken aback, she didn't show it. Her reaction was the opposite — her mouth opened wide into a smile and her ringlets shook with excitement. "You think so?"

"I — maybe?"

As if she were physically incapable of being still, the woman started fussing with her creations, patting down some hair here, adjusting a scarf there. She was so *odd*. She stared harder than anyone had the right to stare. She spoke peculiarly. Her birdlike mannerisms were becoming more pronounced by the minute. And yet Poppy felt a strange affinity for the woman, as if she were some long-lost grandmother that her parents had always told her was dead for fear of revealing that mental illness ran in the family.

Ah, she was back to the staring again. "What is your name, my doll?"

"Poppy. Look, I'm sorry for barging in. I'm not supposed to be back here, I know —"

"But you came for the tour! And since you are a girl who disregards signs and barges into places where she's not supposed to be, that means that what you've really come for is the *real* tour."

Poppy made a muddled face. Was she scolding her? Or just being blunt?

"Because you are nosy," the woman added.

Blunt, then.

The woman extended her hand. Here, at last, was proof of her oldness — knobby knuckles, skin paper-thin and liver-spotted. Poppy felt like she was shaking hands with a tree branch.

"I am Madame Grosholtz."

"Oh. *Oh.*" Poppy's eyes went wide. "Sorry I called your factory evil."

Madame Grosholtz let out a laugh. It sounded like a tangled wind chime. "It is nothing to me, my doll! Just a name. As long as I do what they tell me to do down there," she said glibly, with a dismissive hand wave toward the floor, "they let me dabble in all the real dabblings up here."

"Actually," said Poppy, "I'm here to find out if you . . ."

But she trailed off, unable to work up a fit of righteous indignation. How could she accuse the woman now? Besides, maybe she wasn't the one who had sculpted the figure in the gazebo; if she had, wouldn't she have recognized Poppy the moment she entered?

"Do you want to see?" Madame Grosholtz asked, nodding and advancing upon her once again. "My dabblings?"

Poppy gathered from her manic, unblinking stare that the only answer she'd be allowed to give was, "Uh, sure."

Delighted, Madame Grosholtz clapped her hands twice and scampered off. A second later the room lit up, and Poppy realized how wrong she'd been about the figures. There weren't just a few.

There were dozens.

Every size, shape, ethnicity. Fat men and skinny men, tall women and short women, happy and sad, from the palest complexion to the darkest shade. The whole of human history on parade: cavemen, bushmen, Vikings, Egyptian Pharaohs, Amazon women, Roman emperors, Mongol invaders, Aztec warriors, European monarchs, founding fathers, rows and rows of figures that Poppy never would have imagined could be rendered at such a level of artistry and skill.

And though the figures were impeccably made, their features weren't perfect; indeed, it was the astoundingly human *im*perfections that stole Poppy's breath away. A woman's eyes were spaced a shade too far apart; a man's ears stuck out at odd angles. Freckles and birthmarks were in ample supply. One had a large nose that bore a curiously strong resemblance to Madame Grosholtz's.

Just when Poppy thought herself incapable of tearing her gaze away from one figure, another would grab it and not let go, gluing her to every minuscule detail. How dynamically their eyes sparkled. How subtly their expressions sat. How natural their poses were, how *lifelike*. Incredibly, unbelievably real.

As if they're embalmed, Poppy thought with a surge of dread.

"It is wax," Madame Grosholtz said reassuringly, as if she'd anticipated the nasty conclusion to which Poppy's mind had started to slip. "Just wax."

So, not corpses, then? Poppy made a snorting noise at the thought, then, embarrassed, looked down at her feet, at the shavings of what she'd thought was skin.

Not skin. Wax.

She looked back up at Madame Grosholtz. "They're amazing," she said, the word maddeningly inadequate for something so . . . well, amazing. "You made all of these yourself?"

Madame Grosholtz fixed a coy, not-so-humble look on her face. "Yes. I made them."

"Are they for the diorama?"

"Oh, heavens, no, not for the store. I made those dismal farmers years ago, as a favor, and after that—no more! That place is reserved for soulless blobs of wax, good only for providing light and scents and a false sense of warmth. The empty kind. Here, we make the full kind. Come."

She beckoned her guest farther into the studio, and Poppy had no time to dissect the woman's eccentric wording because it was at this point that the theater geek in Poppy went all-out berserk.

The costumes! The props! The stagecraft!

Buckets and cans covered every surface. Many contained paint, judging by the multicolored drippings down their sides; others held startling snippets of anatomy—a jar of fingernails, a tin of teeth, a crock of eyeballs. Hair was also in abundance, with a pegboard of various beards and goatee designs, plus a chorus line of Styrofoam heads sporting wigs of every color and style—wigs that Poppy was sure were made from human hair.

It kind of reminded her of the Gaudy Auditorium slop room—if the Gaudy Auditorium slop room had been pumped full of steroids and sequins and eerie, unblinking glass eyes.

Bolts of fabric—from happy checkered pinks to gritty, threadbare grays—puckered out of shelves behind an ancient sewing machine that Poppy had to physically cross her arms to refrain from caressing. A massive workbench stored drills, chisels, and other tools that would not have been out of place at a dentist's office. The bitter scent of lacquer stung the air, but it wasn't altogether unpleasant — it smelled of dedication, talent, and a lifetime of hard work.

Madame Grosholtz circled the work in progress at the center of the room, a large, muscular man wearing armored pants and holding an ax. A Viking.

Poppy's eyes bulged at his rippling biceps, his rock-hard abs. The word *"huminahuminahumina"* came to mind. Yet despite his fierceness, he had a kindness around his eyes, the same kindness she often observed in Mr. Crawford.

"La cire vivante," Madame Grosholtz whispered.

Poppy was too distracted by the cleft in SexyFace's chin to fully hear what Madame Grosholtz was saying. She gazed into the man's eyes, cool, inviting pools of blue that she wanted to dive into and not come up for air and maybe squeeze his butt a little. Only when she started to envision herself crumpling his fur loincloth into a wad did she snap her eyes shut and take a step back. "What?"

"La cire vivante," Madame Grosholtz repeated.

"I'm sorry, I don't speak French."

Madame Grosholtz gave her an amused look but said nothing.

Poppy opened her mouth to defuse the silence, but something made her pause. A shift in the room's atmosphere, a subtle dislocation — as if she'd had one eye closed since the moment she'd entered the studio and had just now opened it.

"Would you like to know what it means?" Madame Grosholtz said in a slanted tone.

Poppy resolved to keep her breath even, but her heart skipped a bit faster. She stared up at the Viking, at that face that looked more real than the one that looked back at her in the mirror every day.

"Yes."

Madame Grosholtz's face was indescribable, her eyes flickering like fire. She leaned in and spoke at a whisper.

"The living wax."

In an instant, everything in Poppy's body, mind, and soul shrieked at her to flee. Something dark and wrong and *heavy* had seeped into the room — a profound sense of *there is something unnatural going on here* that Poppy knew she should run away from — but couldn't.

She blinked once more at the Viking.

And the Viking blinked back.

6

~~Lose grip on reality~~

POPPY GASPED AND STAGGERED BACKWARDS AS IF SHE'D BEEN shot. Her legs went rubbery, all the blood rushing out of her feet and turning them numb. A panicked pounding filled her ears, her heart making it plainly obvious that if she had any desire to keep it beating, she needed to get out of there.

But she ignored the advice of her organs. Madame Grosholtz was watching her with a curious expression, while the Viking had gone back to his fearsome, unblinking gaze.

It could have been a trick of the light.

It could have been a mechanical device.

It could have been her imagination.

It could have, but Poppy knew it wasn't.

Because of all the reactions that might have gone through her head as she processed what had happened, the one that came through the loudest and clearest wasn't *This is impossible* or *Wax can't move* or even *I am losing my goddamn mind.*

It was *Yes.*

Paraffin was unusual — everyone in town knew it but never spoke of it. Never gave voice to that eerie feeling they got when they looked at the factory in the moonlight or smelled the scents that wafted across the lake and bored dark, petrified holes into their psyches. It hid in the shadows, like the legend of the Hollow Ones. Biding its time. Buried so deep that no one would be able to find it without looking, *really* looking, without picking away at the layers like a vulture gnawing clean the bones of a carcass —

Wait, what?

Poppy gave her head a hard shake.

No.

No eeriness. Nothing unnatural. Just a gritty workshop with a loony old bat who spent way too much time inhaling shellac, and now she was dragging Poppy down into her well of insanity too. Had the last two minutes even happened, or had Poppy imagined them? This was exactly the kind of delirium that had fogged her mind on the Radio City Music Hall stage, and she'd be damned if she was going to succumb to it again.

"Are you all right, my doll?" Madame Grosholtz asked, her face inscrutable.

"Yeah." Poppy fought to regain a regular breathing pattern. "I thought I —"

Madame Grosholtz now looked concerned. *So I did imagine it,* thought Poppy. And just like that, all the mysticism of the workshop vaporized with an almost palpable *whoosh.*

"Nothing," Poppy said. "I'm fine."

Things got quiet for a moment. Feeling awkward, Poppy looked

71

down at the paint-spattered floor, at the center of which had been carved the logo of the candle factory.

"You're that girl, aren't you?"

Poppy's head snapped up. "What?"

"The one from the talent show. They gave you that ghastly orange car, no?"

Poppy squeezed her nails into her palms. "Yes. That was me. How did you know?"

"Well. I *do* have a television."

Poppy grimaced. She was starting to feel pretty damn silly under the harsh glares of all those glass eyeballs.

She walked toward a section of more contemporary figures. No fur loincloths or togas here, but rather modern clothing that looked as though it had been purchased at the Essex Outlets. They could have easily donned fanny packs and I LO♥ERMONT T-shirts, walked out into the store, and blended right in with the other tourists.

In the corner, several of them lay jumbled in a pile, discarded: a woman with snarled red hair, a teenage boy wearing neon yellow Velcro sneakers, a portly gentleman with an arm broken off at the elbow. "What happened to these guys?" Poppy asked.

"They're just duds." Regret passed through Madame Grosholtz's face, followed by something a bit darker. "Sometimes I think I'm onto it, getting closer, and then . . ."

The look she gave Poppy was laced with a streak of madness. She gave the chubby man's leg a hard kick—harder than Poppy would have imagined her small frame capable of performing. The leg shattered against the wall, pieces rocketing across the floor.

"It all falls apart," she said, bitter.

The old wooden floor must have warped over the years, because the man's big toe kept rolling until it hit the exact center of the room, atop the carved factory logo. For a moment, the only sound in the room was of the toe slowly rolling back and forth across the sunken depression, back and forth, back and forth . . .

"So," Poppy said before the unease consumed them both, "you do modern-day sculptures too?"

"Yes. Sometimes."

Poppy took out her cell phone and found the news clip of the gazebo, which was still up on Channel Six's website—a website maintained by so-called adults who should have known better than to prolong the bullying of a teenager, celebrity or otherwise. "Did you make this?" she asked, showing her the video.

Madame Grosholtz squinted at the screen. For the first few seconds she looked like any other old person attempting to interact with technology, but as soon as the shot zoomed in on the sculpture, her eyes widened and her jaw tensed. "When was this?"

"Last night. Look, it's not a big deal—trust me, I've been through a lot worse. I just came here looking for someone to help me out with a little bit of payback on the kid who did this to me . . ."

Madame Grosholtz had stopped listening. She was urgently darting around the workshop, picking up odds and ends and looking inside paint cans, muttering, "That'll do it . . . any day now . . ."

73

So much for revenge. Poppy scowled, imagining Blake Bursaw laughing his hyena laugh at her. "What's wrong?"

"Your friend — the one who set this up —"

"Obviously he is not my friend."

"He is dealing with people he should not be dealing with. He must stay away. You must stay away too. And make sure this sculpture is destroyed!"

"It already has been. But I still don't know who made it."

Madame Grosholtz abandoned her preparations, or reorganization, or whatever it was, and rushed up to Poppy. "You must take one," she told her, glancing at the figures around the room. Her eyes, desperate, fell on the boy with the yellow sneakers. She picked it up and dragged it across the room. "I'll lend you one, to protect you. Like a bodyguard. Yes?"

"Oh, that won't be necessary."

"Why not?"

Um, because they're dolls? Poppy wanted to respond. She didn't want to hurt the woman's feelings, but this was getting ridiculous. Plus, the thought of having any one of these creepatrons in her possession — even that dashing SexyFace Viking — was enough to make her skin crawl. "I'll be fine on my own. This is just a childish prank war that got a little out of control — the kid's a dick, but he's not dangerous. Besides, these belong in a museum, not —"

"It's starting . . ." Madame Grosholtz had put the sculpture down and was back to the muttering. "They'll be starting . . ."

"*What* is starting?" Poppy squeezed her head between her

hands, trying to make sense of what was happening. "What's going on?"

"I'll do what I can, but it's up to you now." Madame Grosholtz stood up on her tiptoes to retrieve something on a high shelf. "Open your backpack!"

She said it with such authority that Poppy did so immediately. Madame Grosholtz dropped the item into her bag—a hefty pillar candle, about the size of a can of tennis balls. Though the wax of the candle was black, it was encased in a tube of solid white stone.

Poppy struggled to lift the bag and zip it at the same time. "What am I supposed to do with this?"

"You must—"

Poppy's phone rang. She held up a finger to Madame Grosholtz, who gave her the look of annoyance common to all who have been relegated to second place by a cell phone. "Hello?"

The seething could be felt over the airwaves. "Where *are* you?"

"Oh God, Jill, I'm sorry." Poppy reflexively started walking toward the door, and Madame Grosholtz followed. "I got a little sidetracked—"

"Well, I hope you had fun. Vermonty and I are now man and wife."

"Don't you mean state and wife?"

"*Poppy.*"

"Okay, okay, I'm coming." Poppy turned the doorknob and, careful not to trip on any of the warped planks, headed out into the wooden hallway. "Where are you?"

"In the citronella section, but I don't think it works as well on perverts as it does on insects. Aagh, there he is!"

Jill clicked off, but Poppy pretended she was still on the line. "Oh, really? Brown sugar and freshly cut grass? What a creative combination!" Hoping to forgo an awkward goodbye, she gave Madame Grosholtz an exasperated look and an "I have to go deal with this" face. Madame Grosholtz simply stared. "I'm sorry, I gotta run," Poppy told her, putting her hand over the mouthpiece and shouldering her bag. "Lovely meeting you. Thank you for the candle. And for showing me your—" Horrors. Nightmares. Physical manifestations of psychosis. "—art."

Madame Grosholtz: staring.

Poppy couldn't be sure, as she gabbed loudly into her silent phone and didn't look back, but it felt like Madame Grosholtz watched her all the way down the endless hallway, those piercing eyes burning into the back of her neck.

And then she caught a glance of another eye: that of a security camera in the ceiling, trained directly on her fleeing form.

*　*　*

"Oh, good, you're still alive. Now I can murder you."

Poppy found Jill in the Lost Children Fun Zone with a gift bag in her left hand, a mostly empty box of popcorn in her right, and a scowl on her face that rivaled the grumpiest of Internet cats. "I'm sorry times a *million*," Poppy said.

"You damn well better be," said Jill. "See this popcorn? I had to hurl it into the face of the security guard who had the audacity to say I was 'making a scene.'"

"Were you?"

"Depends on your definition of 'scene.'"

"I see. What's in the bag?"

Jill handed it to her. "I got you a gift to commemorate my feelings about this special day."

Poppy pulled out a wax hand mold. "It's beautiful," she said, turning it to appreciate every angle of Jill's prominent middle finger. "I'm surprised they let you get away with this."

"They didn't. Hence the security guard."

"And yet it's not the most outrageous wax sculpture I've seen today."

"That's nice. Where's my fudge?"

Jill wouldn't hear another word about Poppy's adventures until her ten pounds of promised chocolate were firmly in hand, so it was back to the food court to do battle with the throngs of sugar-zombied children and their exhausted parents.

Ten minutes later they finally got to the front of the line. "Hurry *up*," Jill said, looking around as Poppy counted out her money. "I think I'm on a most-wanted list now. If security finds me —"

"They'll make you into a candle. Right. I got it."

Dodging the legions of senior citizen groups returning to their tour buses, they made the trek back through the immense parking lot to the car. "I don't think Clementine is going to be able to handle all of this," Jill said as she got into the passenger seat, hefting up the plastic bag that strained under the weight of all the fudge therein. "Her back tires are looking a little flat already."

"That might be because I've never filled them?"

"Oh, Poppy. Sweet, dumb Poppy."

Clementine was regularly abused by way of negligence. As Poppy hadn't ever planned on owning a car of her own, she had virtually no idea how to maintain one. "Do I need to get them replaced?" she asked, tossing her backpack onto the back seat.

"You need to get your head replaced. To the gas station with us."

On the way, Poppy relayed to Jill the story of Madame Grosholtz's secret room, including the wax figures — but excluding the hallucinated blink of the Viking. After her dealings with Vermonty, Jill wasn't in the mood to entertain any more ideas of animate objects that should not be animate.

"That sounds inexcusably creepy," Jill said, leaning against Clementine's side as they pumped the tires. "Why didn't you run out of there screaming?"

"I was worried that they'd capture me and use the revolutionary Potion to turn my fear into a scent."

"Nature's Panic."

"The Fright Stuff."

Jill checked her watch. "We still have half a day left. Any more revenge fantasies to fulfill, Count of Monte Cristo?"

"No. I need to regroup and come up with a new plan. And my head kind of hurts anyway." Which was true. Ever since she'd left Madame Grosholtz's workshop, a pressure had been building behind her eyes.

"You still want to hang out tonight?" Jill asked.

"Yeah, but until then I think I'll go home and work on more show stuff."

"The *Annie* mop buckets need to be dented up," Jill said through a mouthful of chocolate. "You could throw those against a wall for an hour or so. That should help with the headache."

"You used to be nice, Jill. Vermonty has changed you."

"Don't you say that about my man! You don't know him like I do!"

"I just don't think you're right for each other."

"He loves me, okay? Why can't you be happy for us?"

Poppy's car made a thumping noise. She frowned and checked the tire pump. "Is it supposed to sound like that?"

"Who knows?" Jill popped the rest of the fudge square into her mouth. "Maybe the candle witch cursed your transmission."

Poppy started to make a joke at Madame Grosholtz's expense but found that it wouldn't come out. As cracked as the woman had seemed, it felt wrong to mock her. Disloyal, somehow.

"Come on," Poppy said, disconnecting the air pump and getting into the car. "Let's get you and your shipment of fudge home."

"I'll text Dad to ready the forklift."

* * *

Poppy's house was empty, and her bedcovers were cool and dark — the ideal place in which to stick her head like an ostrich and sift through the tender thoughts throbbing through her skull. *Maybe I have a brain tumor,* she mused. Maybe everything she saw in that workshop was due to a chemical imbalance, a misfiring of neurons that had tricked her into thinking that lifeless blobs of goo could come to life.

Troubling as these notions were, fatigue swallowed them up. Poppy fell into a murky sleep without the aid of Forty Winks, disappearing into the abyss for who knew how many hours — yet when she woke up, her headache was still there.

She groaned into her pillow. *What if there's really something wrong with me? What are the symptoms of head diseases?* Internet research was required, but the thought of staring at a glowing screen made her eyeballs ache more. She emerged from the sheets, shook her rumpled hair out of her face, and reached for a pen to make a note of it: #19026: Research brain-related calamities — but The List wasn't there.

"Egh," she groaned, remembering that she'd tossed it into the trunk before going to Smitty's. Had she even taken it into the factory? She didn't think so, but it was getting harder to separate the day's realities from fantasies.

She stood up and took a few woozy steps out into the hallway. The sun was setting, the house still empty. Her parents must have taken Owen out for a treat after his soccer game — which translated, in the Palladino household, to a trip to the buffet at the new Whole Foods, which everyone decried when it opened yet flocked to like avocado-starved seagulls. At least they'd probably get it to go, and bring home a box for her.

She stumbled down the stairs, grabbed her keys from the hook, and walked out to the driveway, squinting against the setting sun.

Mrs. Goodwin, the gardening goddess of Springwater Terrace, was ankle-deep in trimmings next door. She waved a dirty spade at Poppy. Poppy made some approximation of a wave back but refrained from saying hello at the risk of getting roped into a discussion about begonias. She was still hoping to squeeze in another hour of sleep before her family came home to find their daughter all tired, weirded out, and dying of a brain worm.

Or lung cancer, she thought, jamming her key into the trunk's lock. *Who knows what sort of toxins were in those wax shavings —*

But her worries evaporated the instant she opened her trunk. *Every* thought in her head evaporated the instant she opened her trunk.

The List was there, all right. Alongside a naked, yelling, wild-eyed boy.

7

~~Freak out again~~

"WHO ARE YOU?" THE BOY YELLED.

In a reflexive panic, Poppy slammed the trunk shut. She put her hands on top, scarcely registering the metallic heat scorching through her palms.

"*What in the ever-loving crap?*" she whispered.

Mrs. Goodwin had stood up at the commotion, peering in Poppy's direction. Poppy gave her a full wave this time, plus a look that said *Everything's fine here, no one has been stuffed into a trunk, garden's looking great!* Mrs. Goodwin gave her an uncertain nod and headed back into her house.

An unquantifiable deluge of strategies zoomed through Poppy's head — *drive somewhere else and then open the trunk; pull the car into the garage and then open the trunk; maybe NEVER open the trunk and let the guy suffocate because who does he think he is, stowing away in my car like that?* — but in the end, her problem-solving instincts overthrew her reasoning ones and forced her hand to pop the trunk open once more.

Out lunged the boy, ready this time. He was naked only from the waist up, Poppy noted with some degree of relief. He started running around the front yard in circles, alternating his cries between "Who are you?" and "Who am I?" and "What is this?"

Surely Mrs. Goodwin could hear him; all the neighbors would be able to hear him, though fortunately, none of them had yet emerged from their houses to investigate.

Damage control. Poppy reached into the trunk to grab the can of pepper spray Jill had gotten for her after "Hogwash." Though the kid was easily a foot taller than she was, Poppy ran at him like a crazed linebacker, slammed into him, and pushed him all the way to the steps of her front door. Spotting the reappearance of Mrs. Goodwin's gardening clogs, Poppy gave him one last shove into the house before closing the door and turning to face him.

"What are you?" he yelled.

"Shhh!" Poppy hissed.

"What is 'shhh'?"

"Quiet!"

"What is 'quiet'?"

Though flustered, Poppy managed to shoot a stream of pepper spray at his face. The boy fell backwards, landing hard on his butt on the main staircase.

That shut him up. "Oof."

The pepper spray, however, seemed to have no effect. Sticking his tongue out, the boy licked a bit of it off his lip. "Hmm," he said thoughtfully, as if savoring its spicy flavor.

This puzzled Poppy. Had the spray gone bad? "Don't move," she said, reaching into her pocket with her other hand. "I'm calling the police."

"What is 'police'?"

"Shut up!" She dug desperately into her pocket, cursing when she realized she'd left her phone upstairs. "Who are you?"

"Who are you?"

"No. *No.* Stop repeating what I'm saying and answer my question. *Who are you?*"

The boy looked as though he was about to repeat her words regardless, but he stopped himself and bit his lip, looking thoroughly confused and scared.

At this, Poppy softened a bit. "Why were you in my trunk?" she asked, switching up her tactics.

"Trunk," he said eagerly, as if they were making headway.

Poppy relaxed her grip on the pepper spray but didn't let go. He seemed harmless, but ever since *Triple Threat,* she'd somewhat cooled on the idea of depending on the harmlessness of strangers. "Where did you come from?"

Brow knitted, hands clasped, jaw slack, he looked around the room in utter bewilderment while Poppy studied him for clues, from the curliest hair on his head to the neon yellow Velcro sneakers on his feet.

Wait. Where had she seen those sneakers before?

Her head snapped back up to his face. Something abnormal had caught her eye — although the house was growing darker by the minute, she thought she'd spotted a flash of light. "Look at me," she demanded. "Open your mouth."

Poppy peered down his throat, past his tongue and dancing uvula, and gasped.

A faint light flickered up against the back wall of his throat, like a fire in a cave.

*   *   *

"I'm confused. Where is the living wax sculpture man now?" Jill asked on the other end of the phone.

"I locked him in my closet. And he's not a man. He's, like, our age."

Jill made an impatient noise. "How can he be 'our age' if he was created out of nothing?"

"Dark!" the boy yelled from within the closet, followed by the sound of a person being poked in the eye by a hanger. "Oof!"

"We don't have time to argue about semantics," Poppy said, pacing around her bedroom and grasping her cell phone so hard, she was sure it would snap in half. "We need to figure out what to do. About him."

"I think we first need to figure out the exact moment you hit your head and started hallucinating."

"*Jill.* I am not hallucinating! Here, I'll send you a picture. Call you right back." She gingerly made her way to the closet. "I'm opening the door," she announced. "Don't spring at me or anything."

He was sitting on the floor, a blouse of Poppy's draped over his head. "Hi."

Poppy winced, unsure how to react to that. It was the first vaguely normal thing he'd said. "Hi. Can you come out here?"

"We don't have time to argue about semantics!"

"Whoa, we're not . . . oh, you're repeating what I said on the phone. Fun. Now get up, please."

The boy scrambled to his feet and bounded to the center of the room like an eager-to-please puppy. "Now what?"

"Hold still." Poppy snapped a photo with her cell phone. While she texted it to Jill, the boy stared up at her ceiling fan, whirling his head around as he followed the path of the blades.

Poppy studied him. He didn't *look* dangerous. Wide, curious eyes. Goofy, dumb smile. A hint of stubble on his jaw, a small paunch around his belly. Unruly strawberry-blond hair that was just long enough to flare out from behind his ears, giving the impression of wings. A baritone voice with a bit of a rasp, made more pleasant by the heaping doses of awe infused into every word he said. Though he was taller than Poppy, with broad shoulders and a thick chest, and though he was technically an unholy abomination, Poppy's fear began to ebb.

"Hi," he said again, waving with his fingers wide like a toddler.

Poppy's phone rang. "Okay," said Jill. "I will give you that there is a large and not entirely unattractive boy in your room. But I am forced to point out that he could be any number of human boys, and not some magical being made out of wax."

"But he *is* a magical being made out of wax," Poppy insisted. "Listen to me. Back there in Madame Grosholtz's workshop — she was telling me about these creations of hers, these — oh, crap, what did she call them —"

"*La cire vivante,*" the boy said.

"Right. Wait, what?" She looked up at him. "So you *do* understand what I'm saying?"

He waved again. "Hi."

Poppy grunted and turned her attention back to Jill. "The point is that there were a bunch of these sculptures, and I know it sounds crazy, but I could have sworn that one of them *blinked*. And at the time, I thought I was losing my mind, but it now seems that I was fully sane and in complete control of my faculties, because one of those sculptures is currently sitting on my bed and going through my bag and — gimme that!" she said, grabbing a tampon out of his hand.

"Yep," Jill was saying. "Fully sane."

"Next thing you know, I get home and open my trunk and there he is. I don't know *how* he — oh!" She smacked herself on the forehead. "The bodyguard thing!"

"The what now?"

"Madame Grosholtz recognized me from *Triple Threat* and offered me one of her sculptures as protection from further bullying! I said no thanks, then you called, and I got the heck outta there. I guess she somehow stuffed one into my trunk anyway while we were getting the fudge . . ."

"Good for her. She realized that you were a danger to yourself and others."

"But I don't get why she'd give me something out of the trash." If Poppy *had* to have a sentient wax being bestowed upon her as a bodyguard, couldn't she have gotten SexyFace? "I remember this kid. He was sitting in a pile of rejects. Duds, she called them."

"Dud?" the boy asked.

"Maybe she got desperate and grabbed whatever was closest," Poppy said. "She *was* getting all worked up and panicky about something—"

"Or maybe she's getting in on the town fad of playing pranks on you," Jill said. "I hear candle witches have a delightful sense of humor."

Poppy scowled. She wasn't getting anywhere with this. Jill was the least likely person to believe in anything supernatural. Jill didn't even believe in yoga.

Then, suddenly, it all became clear. "Wait a minute! I'll just take him back!" Poppy said, astonishment in her voice at the simplicity of the solution. She scrambled for her shoes. "I'll hop in the car and return him to Madame Grosholtz! Come on, dud," she said, patting her knees as if she were calling a dog. "Let's go."

"Don't forget your receipt," said Jill.

* * *

Hopping into the car was easier said than done. First, Poppy had to find the kid a shirt, eventually settling on an oversize promotional Killington Ski Resort tee she'd won on a field trip years before. Then she had to wrangle him into the car, adjust the seat to accommodate his frame, and put on his seat belt. Once he was all strapped in and ready to go, he opened the glove compartment and swept its contents onto the floor.

"Oops," he said, his scrambling sneakers ripping the registration.

Poppy rubbed her temples. "Maybe you don't deserve to ride shotgun."

"Shot . . . gun?"

"Front seat of the car — forget it."

Poppy scanned the street for witnesses. Luckily, Mrs. Goodwin had finished her gardening, but Poppy's parents could arrive home any minute. She gunned it out of the driveway, narrowly missing the mailbox her mother had painted to look like a watermelon.

Fascinated, the boy watched suburbia fly by the window. "Better than trunk," he said with a sage nod.

Poppy glared at him. "Do you have a name?"

"Dud?"

"No — sorry, I only called you that because —"

"Dud! Dud! Dud!"

"Okay, okay. Here — be quiet and listen to the radio."

She hit the button, and one of Madonna's more recent songs screeched out. Dud put his hands over his ears.

"Fair enough." She pointed at the scan button. "Press this until you find something you like."

Tentatively, the boy pushed the button, pausing briefly at each station until he landed on Poppy's parents' religion of choice: National Public Radio. He sat back in his seat and smiled.

"Talking," he said with enthusiasm. "Learning talking."

Poppy gaped at him. "You're learning how to talk just by listening? So you've only learned what I've been saying —"

"Shh," he said, holding up a finger. *"This American Life."*

Poppy rolled her eyes. "Excuse *me,*" she said, though she did shut up. No point in trying to compete with Ira Glass.

They were rumbling along toward the center of town, listening to a heartbreaking story about migrant diaper factory workers, when Poppy turned the corner — and abruptly sat taller in her seat.

The town square had become a sea of flashing red and blue lights. Sirens split the air; smoke darkened the sky. A cavalcade of fire trucks, police cruisers, and ambulances tore down the road, screeching around the edges of the lake.

With a sinking feeling, Poppy looked across the water.

Towering orange flames licked at the spires of the Grosholtz Candle Factory, the whole rear of the building lit up like a blazing candelabra.

8

~~Weave a merry web of lies~~

"This quinoa is delicious," Poppy said, shoving a spoonful into her face. "What am I tasting here — cumin?"

The Whole Foods buffet-to-go boxes had gone untouched. *Dr. Steve* had gone unwatched. One hundred percent of her parents' attention was focused on the boy shoved awkwardly into a folding chair and looking at a fork as though he had never seen a fork before.

"Coriander," her mom answered flatly.

Dud speared a carrot with such force that the fork plowed through the cardboard of the container, dispensing some of its contents onto the carpet. Owen giggled.

"Poppy?" said her father, bending down to pick up the runaway chickpeas. "Could we have a moment to chat with you? Alone?"

"But I'm eating." Poppy arranged her mouth into a shape that was a smile in name only. Behind it was nothing but sheer panic. The second she'd spotted the fire that had consumed the Grosholtz Candle Factory — and was still consuming it, judging by the occasional fire truck screaming by — she'd bolted, for motives that she couldn't herself determine. Maybe she wanted to keep out of danger. Maybe it was a gut feeling.

Or maybe it was the fear that she'd somehow, inexplicably, caused it.

Whatever the reason, she'd sped home at once. Worry clouded her thoughts — was Madame Grosholtz okay? Had she gotten out in time? Poppy hadn't been able to see too well from across the lake, but it looked as though the flames were concentrated toward the back of the factory. And the way the building was shaped, with that one narrow hallway, escape would have been near impossible . . .

When she got home, she wrangled Dud back up to her room and into her closet again, trying to think. But thinking was a higher brain function that Poppy had lost the capacity for. In the space of fifteen minutes she'd devolved to the mental level of a dung beetle — and like the dung beetle, all she could think about was the immense pile of shit she was in.

She was still "thinking" by the time her parents and Owen got home, and that's when her mutated insect brain decided it would be a good idea to remove Dud from the closet, take him downstairs, and introduce him to her family as if he were a cherished guest star on a sitcom. She'd half expected an unseen studio audience to burst into applause.

But all she'd got was a gust of stunned silence, six widened eyeballs, and Owen blurting, "Who's *that?*"

At which point it became obvious that this half-baked plan of hers was crumbling fast, and no amount of coriander could save it.

"Poppy," her father repeated. "A word."

"Can we please watch the news? I want to know what they're saying about the fire at the —"

"Poppy."

"Yeah, okay," she muttered, standing up from the couch. "Um —" She looked at Dud, who was evidently unsettled by the existence of bean sprouts, and then at Owen, whose expression was that of a child who'd been given a life-size action figure for Christmas.

"Watch him," she told her brother. "Make sure he doesn't break anything."

"Sure," said Owen, watching Dud slice a single pea.

Poppy followed her parents into the kitchen and then into the privacy of the pantry, where they closed the door and stared her down. As the space in the pantry was limited, the awkwardness was nice and concentrated.

Her parents were busy shooting each other a lot of uncertain glances, which gave Poppy enough time to decide to charge forth from an offensive position rather than retreating into the canned tomatoes. "That was *very* rude of you," she hissed at them.

"Excuse me?" said her father.

"I thought about what you said. That we should *open* our home, with *open* arms, and *open* our hearts to a scared young foreigner who wants nothing more than to learn all about our strange, vegetable-loving ways."

"We did not say 'open' that many times," her mother said.

Her father agreed with a huff. "And we did not mean that you should pick up a random exchange student as soon as you found one! These things take months to set up! You're supposed to do this with the help of placement coordinators, there are interviews —"

"So I cut out the middleman!" Poppy exclaimed. "Look. Dud needs a home, and I need a better reputation. Do you have any idea how good this will look on a college application? It's right up there with Habitat for Humanity. All the karma, none of the nail gun accidents."

That mollified them a bit. "What about his family?" her mom asked. "Aren't we supposed to be in contact with them?"

"I already talked to his mother," Poppy said, which technically wasn't untrue. "She was fine with it. Practically shoved him into my car!"

"I don't know, Poppy. This whole thing feels . . . what's the word . . ."

"Illegal?" her father supplied.

"Yes. This feels like kidnapping."

"*Mom.* It's *not.* I even cleared it with the school. You can check with them on Monday," Poppy said, making a mental note to add #19026: Bribe a school official to The List.

The lies were working. Her parents were now shooting each other deliberating glances. Her mom asked, "Where is he from?"

"Um. Canada?"

Wrong answer. They deflated. "Canada?" her father whined. "That's not very foreign."

"Sorry, Dad. I was unable to secure a Parisian debutante on such short notice." Her father's nostrils flared. She was losing them.

"Of *course* he's not from Canada," she said. "I meant he arrived *via* Canada. He's originally from—" *Think, Poppy. Somewhere exotic.* "An island." *More specific.* "Tristan da Cunha!"

Their stares got blanker, if that was possible. "I've never heard of Tris—how do you say it?" her mother said, not very subtly glancing at the food in the pantry to see if Poppy had stolen the name from a can of beans.

"Tristan da Cunha. It's a real place!" Poppy said too forcefully. "It was discovered by and named for a Portuguese explorer, then it was annexed by Britain and settled by only a handful of people, and the tiny population living there now are all descended from that first small bunch," she rattled off, grasping to recall the salient points from the report she did in tenth grade. "It's one of the most isolated places on the *planet.*"

Her mother was captivated. "Is that true?"

Poppy batted her giant eyes, trying with all her might to inject as much gravitas as she could into her tale. "It's all true, Mom. Wikipedia it."

"I *will.*"

"That's why he seems a bit off," Poppy continued. "He's lived in such a remote place with the same three hundred or so people his entire life. So if he doesn't know how to, like, use a telephone, or, like, use a fork . . . that is why."

Her father was still staring at her, trying to discern whether he'd raised a lying, evil monster or merely a lying, well-meaning monster. "Tristan da Cunha," he repeated.

"It's near Africa," Poppy threw in.

As soon as she said it, she realized that she should have led with the A-word right off the bat. Relieved smiles drifted onto her parents' faces. At last: *Africa*. A continent full of culture. And exotic, healthy cuisine. And blood diamonds and genocides and all sorts of other atrocities for her parents to get all up in arms against.

"Come on, you guys. Pleeease? Can I keep him?" she begged, adding once more under her breath for good measure, *"Africa?"*

"Well," her father said, "as long as it's okay with the school, he can stay with us. Of *course* he's welcome," he insisted, retroactively inserting goodwill and diplomacy into his tone. "Think of the education we'll get!"

"Have you learned anything from him so far?" her mom asked, now joyous. "Does he have any unique customs?"

As if in answer, the shrill, deafening shriek of a smoke detector blared from the living room.

*   *   *

The television was aflame.

While her father dashed for the fire extinguisher and her brother screamed and her mother inexplicably searched for the remote control, perhaps hoping to find a "cancel fire" button, Poppy scanned the room for Dud.

He was gone. Her box of food was smushed into the carpet, the Nike swoosh rendered in butternut squash.

The fire was small, but the acrid fumes of melted technology were starting to choke the air. As her father battled the flames,

Poppy grabbed handfuls of Owen and her mother and hauled them both out of the house — into equally smoky conditions, thanks to the fire on the other side of town. "What happened?" she shouted at Owen over the *whoosh* of the extinguisher.

Owen looked dazed. "I don't know. We were sitting there — he was eating his peas one by one, and then he sniffed at them, and then he sneezed, and then the television caught on fire."

Poppy had gone her entire life without having seen a fire anywhere other than where fires were supposed to be, and today, within the space of four hours, she'd seen two? It couldn't be a coincidence. "He was just sitting there? Are you sure he didn't . . . I don't know, breathe toward the TV or anything?"

"Poppy," her mother said dismissively, "Africans can't set things on fire by sneezing on them. They don't have magical powers. Don't be racist."

Poppy dearly wanted to devote a hunk of time to dissecting that little gem, but Dud was now missing, and for all she knew, this particular flame-throated fake African *could* in fact sneeze things on fire. "Did you see where he went?" she asked Owen.

He shook his head. "He looked at the fire, then ran out the door."

"Bad news, family." Poppy's father emerged from the house and tossed some melted DVD cases into the front yard. "We lost a couple of throw pillows and *Dr. Steve's Cauliflower Hour.*"

"And the television," Owen added.

"Well, yes. And the television." He wiped a puddle of sweat

from his forehead and glanced up at the sky, where the smoke from the factory still swooped up into a column, blocking out the moon. "Geez, two fires in one night? What are the odds?"

A faint whimpering issued forth from Mrs. Goodwin's bed of roses.

"Oof," it said.

"Why would he run into a pricker bush?" Owen loudly inquired.

Poppy could see him now — a dark form hunched inside the shrub, trying not to move. "I'll get him," she told her family. "You guys go back inside and open some windows."

Dud was curled up in a ball again, his eyes wide and panicked as Poppy approached. She lifted a branch. "Dud?" she whispered. "Are you okay?"

"What happened?" he yelled.

"Shh!" She glanced at Mrs. Goodwin's windows. "We need to work on your volume control."

"What?" he shouted again.

"Shh!"

"What?"

"*No* — okay, when I make that noise, that *shh?* That means you lower your voice. Whisper. Like I'm doing."

Dud lowered his head, as if doing so would also help lower his voice. "Whisper like I'm doing," he rasped in what was technically a whisper, but a loud one.

"Just stop talking until we get back into the house." She grabbed hold of his forearms. "Come on, let's get you out of — oh, that feels *weird*."

98

His skin wasn't . . . cold, exactly. But it didn't feel warm, either. Not even lukewarm.

He was precisely room temperature.

Putting that aside for now, Poppy pulled him up. For all the mass he occupied, he felt awfully light. She was able to lift him out of the bushes with hardly any effort — except for the thorns snagging on his clothes. "Careful!" Poppy said, watching one plunge into his shoulder and tear through his skin. But when it came out, there was no blood. No cut. Not even a scrape.

Dud looked at his arm. "Hmm."

Poppy deemed this to be an understatement. "Did you feel that?"

He didn't answer.

"Hey. Did you feel that?"

"You said to stop talking until we get to the house."

"I did! Good listening skills. But I'm giving you permission to answer this question: Did you feel that?"

"Yes."

"Did it hurt?"

"What is 'hurt'?"

"It's — 'hurt' means 'pain.' Like something that feels bad."

Dud looked down at his vegetable-covered shoes. "I feel bad about the squash."

Poppy gave a little snicker but retracted it when she saw how sincere he was. "No, hurts — like this." She gently pinched the skin on the underside of his arm. "Do you feel that?"

"Yes."

"And it doesn't feel bad?"

"No. But I did feel bad when I felt the fire. It was hot and my face melted."

It was hard to see in the darkness, but now that he mentioned it, his face did look a little melty. *Obviously,* she thought. *He's made of wax. Of course he'll melt in the heat.*

"Is that not normal?" he asked.

Poppy hesitated. He *was* aware that he was made of wax, right? Because that was not a conversation she was up for at the moment. She reached up and smoothed out the skin that had sagged under his eyes. "There," she said. "Good as new."

"And new as good!"

Poppy sighed inwardly. Were all their interactions to turn into *Sesame Street* segments? "Let's go back inside." She steered Dud toward the house. "Oh, and if anyone asks, you're from an island near Africa."

"What's an Africa?"

* * *

Poppy's parents somehow got it into their heads that a quality family dinner could still be salvaged after such a calamity. "So, Dudley!" her mother said, scooping some of her carrots onto a plate for Dud as the family hovered around the oft-neglected dining room table. They were so unfamiliar with the thing, they didn't know how to properly sit at it. "I hear you grew up on an island!"

Dud frowned. "Dud — *ley?*"

"It's just Dud, Mom," Poppy said.

"Just Dud?"

"Yeah," said Poppy, pulling her chirping phone out of her pocket. "It's a traditional . . . island . . . name."

Jill had texted her: *we still on for ice cream now that you returned the mannequin for store credit?*

Poppy replied: *i didn't return him, the factory was on fire*

Jill, ever unflappable, said: *okay*

well

might ice cream help you cope?

"You must have learned all sorts of fascinating nautical skills," Poppy's father was saying to Dud. He'd perched one leg up on a chair and was balancing his plate on his pasty white knee.

for the love of god yes get me out of this house, Poppy answered, putting the phone away. "Dad, he doesn't want to —"

"Sure he does. How many knots can you tie, Dud?" Unsure, Dud held up three fingers, but the Question Train kept chugging. "How many words do you have in your native language for 'sand'?"

"Dad."

Then Owen started in. "Can you climb a coconut tree and get the coconuts down?"

"Oh, Dud, you *must* give me some new coconut recipes," Poppy's mom said. "A few months back I was on a huge kick — did a blog series about it, 'Cuckoo for Coconuts' — but I must have run out of steam after about sixty or so dishes because I stopped, and I can't remember why —"

"Because you constipated us!" Poppy burst out, unable to take another second. "You constipated us all!"

Everyone stared at her.

"We have to go meet Jill," she said, grabbing Dud's arm and dragging him out of the dining room.

"Don't stay out too late!" her mother called after them.

Poppy shoved Dud out the front door, but not before hearing her father say, "She's right, though. You put our bowels through the ringer."

9

~~Drown problems in hot fudge~~

MOST SATURDAY NIGHTS, POPPY AND JILL DID WHAT ANY SELF-respecting high-schoolers without alcohol problems or criminal records did: they went out for ice cream.

Unlike everyone else in the state of Vermont, however, Poppy's and Jill's loyalties lay not with Ben & Jerry's, but with Friendly's. This made them villainous traitors in their fellow residents' eyes, but they didn't care. They had their reasons, and their reasons usually came down to one thing: Friendly's served fried food and Ben & Jerry's did not.

Paraffin's outpost had all the trappings of every other Friendly's location in America — colorful menus, sticky carpets, and screaming children in highchairs amidst a sea of sprinkles and crayons. But Poppy and Jill's haunt of choice had one thing the rest did not: Greg.

Greg was the most enthusiastic Friendly's employee in the nation. Every guest was greeted with the goofiest-sounding "Well, *hi!*" uttered by a human, promptly escorted to a spotless table, and enthusiastically asked in short order about their day, their job, their kids, their grandkids, and their general goals in life. He was there *all the time.* No one could figure out if he had a family — though Jill's current hypothesis was that he did, and that it consisted of a merry band of pampered ferrets.

Every interaction with Greg led to smiles. He made everyone feel special. He was the embodiment of the concept of Friendliness. His panache led some to speculate that before coming to Friendly's employ, he may have worked as a clown who finally snapped, murdered a family of five, and was politely asked to leave the circus . . . but most people were decidedly fans.

"Well, *hi!*" he shouted excitedly at Poppy and Dud before giving the hostess a chance to greet them. "Party of two?"

"Three. And, uh," Poppy said, noticing that Dud was staring at the children's menus, "can we have one of those place mats? And some crayons? He's foreign," she added.

The corners of Greg's smile seemed to extend beyond the margins of his face. "You got it!" he said, gathering menus.

"What is 'foreign'?" Dud asked Poppy as they were escorted to their table.

"A flimsy backstory that probably won't hold up for long," Poppy muttered. Poppy's parents were laid-back, but not naïve enough to accept a total stranger into their house without some evidence of bureaucracy. She'd have to fake some documents, though they were likely to get "filed" in the messy box her mom kept on the dining room table for school stuff that was destined to be ignored.

"Can I get you started with some apps?" Greg asked once they'd been seated, placing menus in front of them with the amount of care required to handle Fabergé eggs. "Waffle fries, chicken quesadillas, mini mozzarella bites—"

"I think we'll wait for my friend," Poppy interrupted before Greg could finish reciting the menu in its entirety, as had happened on more than one occasion.

"No problem!"

Greg skipped off to the kitchen to sprinkle fairy dust into the deep fryer as Jill slunk through the entrance. Spotting Poppy, she stomped through the restaurant in her clunky boots, sank into the booth, and proceeded to stare a hole through Dud.

"Wow," she said after a good full minute. "Lifelike."

"Not life*like*," Poppy insisted. "Life*real*. Life*actual*."

"I'm Dud!" Dud shouted.

"Shh!" Poppy glanced around the restaurant, hoping that the sort of people who chose to spend their swingin' Saturday nights at Friendly's were too besotted with their SuperMelts to look up. "We're still working on volume control."

"I see." Jill performed a thorough eyeballing of Dud, starting with his poreless skin and ending with his incessant smile. "Creepy."

Dud waved at her. "Hi, Creepy!"

"No," Poppy said, shaking her head. "No. Erroneous."

"Hi, Erroneous!"

"I'm Jill," Jill said. "The best friend."

Dud solemnly nodded. "*I* made friends with a rosebush."

"How'd that work out for you?"

"Bad!"

Jill shrugged. "Looks human to me," she told Poppy.

"I know. But when he got all torn up by the thorns, he didn't bleed, and it didn't hurt him. How can you explain that?"

"I can't and I won't."

"And what about the flame in his throat? Look."

Poppy grabbed his head and pulled his jaw open. Dud provided no resistance.

Jill squinted. "All I see is a throat."

Poppy tsked and let go of Dud, who went right back to coloring his place mat. "It's too bright in here," she explained.

"Mmm-hmm. So, what, he's a Hollow One?"

"You say that like, 'oh, so he's left-handed?' It's a *fire* inside his *body*, Jill. It must be how he's able to, like, be alive. Why am I the only one freaking out about this?"

"Because I'm still having a difficult time believing this kid is made of wax. Or that anything fishy is going on down at the candle factory, other than insurance fraud." Then, because Jill couldn't take anything seriously for more than five seconds, she grabbed a menu and forgot all about the prospect of a live wax person sitting across the table from her. "Now," she said, perusing the appetizers. "On to the chicken."

"What is 'chicken'?" asked Dud.

Jill's face took a devious turn. "It means 'scared.'"

"What is 'scared'?" Dud asked, looking scared.

Poppy kicked Jill under the table. "What are you doing?"

"Teaching him English! Dud, English is the language we speak. England is a country, but not the one we live in."

"*Jill.*"

"'Fries' is short for 'french fries,' but we're not in France. 'Fry' is also the way you cook fries. 'Fry' and 'fry' are homonyms."

"What's a homonym?"

"A boy who loves a boy, or a girl who loves a girl."

"Jill, *stop —*"

"What do you think, sir?" Greg had materialized at their table, ready to dive headfirst into some serious app discussion. He pointed at the menu Dud was holding. "How are we feeling about those nachos?"

"Erroneous!"

Poppy was beginning to realize that the longer they stayed, the more opportunity for disaster to strike. "We're just here for dessert," she told Greg.

"You *got* it! Be right back with those ice cream menus!"

Poppy recounted the rest of the evening's exploits to Jill, who listened with either rapt attention or bored indifference. It was always hard to tell with Jill. Dud, meanwhile, removed the paper wrapper from one of his crayons, and by the time Greg returned, he had begun whittling it with a butter knife.

"Here you go!" Greg chirped, sliding ice cream menus into their hands.

Dud's eyes went wide at the colorful array of sprinkles and candies. "Ooh."

Poppy took the menu from him before he could start gnawing on the plastic. "We'll split a banana split," she told Greg.

"Ha *ha!*" he crowed. "Good one! And for you, ma'am?"

Jill set her jaw, stared straight ahead, and said in a calculated, even voice, "Three scoops of Forbidden Chocolate."

"Ohh," Greg groaned. "Oh, no."

Jill steeled herself for the impending wisecrackery. "What."

"I'm so sorry, but . . ."

"But what."

"It's — it's forbidden!"

"Oh drat."

There was a painfully long pause.

". . . Just kidding!" Greg chirped. "Be right back!"

Jill mimed stabbing herself in the eye with a fork. "If you hate that joke so much," Poppy said, "why do you keep ordering it?"

"It's a disease. Establish a Forbidden Chocolate Anonymous, and then we'll talk."

Poppy's phone chirped. "Ooh," she said, tapping the screen. "It's an alert from Channel Six."

Jill frowned. "Don't tell me you signed up for that dumb YouNews thing."

"Um, *yeah,* I did. Gotta keep tabs on any impending disgraces." She navigated through the menu, looking for the link. "Maybe they found out who set the fire. Or should I say maybe they *proved* that *Blake* set the fire."

Jill was reluctant to agree. "I don't know. Blake's a dick and a half — maybe even two dicks — okay, Blake is a triple dick, just astoundingly anatomically impossible, but I don't think he's an arsonist."

"How can you be so sure? With all the crap he's pulled, who knows what Blake Bursaw is capable of? He's practically a criminal, he thinks he can get away with anything, *and* he has a recent connection to the factory, since that's where he got the sculpture of me!"

"Do we know that for sure?"

"No, but — no." Irritated at this sound logic, Poppy tapped her spoon on the table while the video loaded. "Fine," she said, glaring at Jill. "Then who do *you* think did it?"

Jill shrugged. "A jilted, heartsick Vermonty with revenge on the brain."

"Come on. Seriously."

"Seriously? I don't think anyone did it. But by all means, let us watch the news. You will be proven wrong, and I will get to do my I-told-you-so dance."

Poppy grunted. This would not be the first time Jill had performed such a dance. It usually involved way too many fist pumps. "We'll see," she said, tilting the phone so that Jill could watch.

The anchors lit up the screen, their faces arranged into approximate expressions of tragedy. "The news at the top of the hour is the *savage* fire that *raged* through the world-famous Grosholtz Candle Factory. We now go to lead reporter Colt Lamberty, live at the scene. Colt?"

Cut to Colt's exquisite face. "Thanks, Veronica. As you can see behind me, plenty of fire trucks and police cars are still here, but as of about eight thirty this evening, the fire was officially extinguished.

No fatalities have been reported so far, and the owners of the factory, Anita and Preston Chandler, say that the store was evacuated in an orderly — and, more important, *safe* — manner."

They cut to a clip of Anita, who looked far more composed than someone who'd just faced a tragedy should look. "The fire alarm went off," she huffed into the microphone, sounding peeved, "and everyone remained calm. I'd like to thank my staff for keeping their wits about them and for getting our guests out of the building so quickly."

Preston butted his face into the shot. "And not to worry — all the candles are safe."

There was a millisecond of Anita rolling her eyes before the camera cut back to Colt. "No injuries were reported among the shoppers or retail staff, but three men in the back of the building — two factory workers and one accountant — were taken to the hospital with minor injuries, mostly smoke inhalation. This has led investigators to believe that the fire originated in the rear of the factory, where the structure is older and not as well ventilated. The advanced age of the building may have been a factor as well, and while investigators are looking into faulty wiring and a few other possibilities, some evidence does point to the possibility of arson. However, investigators urge our viewers to remember that those findings are preliminary, and to wait for the official report."

"See?" Poppy said to Jill. "*Arson.* Sorry, folks, but tonight's performance of Miss Cho's I-told-you-so dance is canceled. No refunds!"

"Poppy, investigators are *urging* panicky teenage girls to remember that those findings are *preliminary*—"

"Oh, come on. This has got Blake written all over it!"

"Sorry, Pops," Jill said with an infuriating smirk, "but you can't prove a thing."

Poppy clenched her jaw shut. She couldn't prove anything, it was true. But something was up. Something wasn't right.

And if they hadn't found any bodies, and if all the injured were men, then what had happened to Madame Grosholtz? Where was she now?

"I think the bigger question is what the hell is up with this?" Jill asked, pointing at the crayon Dud had mutilated.

But he hadn't mutilated it. He'd *sculpted* it. Into a tiny human figure. With rippling muscles, a powerful stance—

"What is that?" Jill asked.

Poppy was almost too stunned to answer. "Um. That would be a Viking."

"Here we go!" Greg seemed to be going for a personal best this evening, delivering their ice cream in record time. "Enjoy!" he said, dropping a handful of long-handled spoons and the check in his wake.

Dud unceremoniously dropped the Viking and started to devour the banana split. "Mmm," he said, smacking it around his mouth. "Mushy."

"So he's an art prodigy too?" said Jill.

"Apparently? I guess . . . some of Madame Grosholtz's sculpting talent rubbed off?"

"And why is he eating? Since when does wax need sustenance?"

"I don't know, *Jill*, I've never done this before. Your guess is as good as mine."

Jill had already dispatched one of her three scoops by the time Poppy spooned a bite of banana off the split. Dud had paused his gorging to pick the cherry off the top and sniff it.

"It's a cherry," Jill said between bites.

"It's red," Dud said.

"'Red' also means 'communist.'"

"Jill," Poppy said, "so help me God, I will drag you into the kitchen and drown you in a vat of caramel—"

"He's here," a deep voice chanted, *"the Phaaaantom of the Ooop-eraaaa . . ."*

Poppy whipped around in her seat. She'd been so focused on the problems at hand that she hadn't noticed that Connor and the rest of the Giddy Committee had entered the restaurant and been seated in an adjacent booth.

She blinked manically at them. "What are you guys doing here?"

"I organized a cast bonding night!" Connor said proudly.

Louisa gave Poppy a sour look. "That's right. An opportunity for us to blow off some steam without the oppressive, ever-watchful eyes of the production team lording over us."

"That was not the wording in my invitation," Connor assured Poppy.

"Want to join us?" Banks scooted over, crushing Louisa's pencil-thin frame into the wall. "Plenty of room."

"Oh, thanks, but no," Poppy said, trying to be breezy. They hadn't noticed Dud yet, as he was hunched over, snarfing his banana split. "We're pretty much done eating, and you're right — you guys should have some fun without us. It's fine, I'm not insulted."

"I am," said Jill.

"Okay, well, Jill is insulted. Hope you can live with that."

"All right all right all *riiiight!*" Jesus noisily burst through the entrance of the restaurant and clomped between the tables, shooting finger guns at the Giddy Committee as he approached. "Time to get our hot fudge on! What up, Madame Director?" He leaned in to Connor. "I thought she wasn't gonna be here."

"We *aren't* here," Poppy said, pulling herself out of the booth. "We're leaving."

"Hold on! Who's your friend?"

Dud popped his head up like a meerkat. He met every pair of Giddy Committee eyes looking at him and, of course, waved. "Hi."

"He's . . . my cousin," said Poppy, tossing a handful of cash onto the table. "From overseas. And he's jet-lagged, so we're going home now."

She yanked both Dud and Jill out of their seats and across the restaurant, depriving Greg of the chance to flash them his customary goodbye grin. They had just reached Clementine when Poppy's phone chirped again. "Hang on," she said, stopping to check it. "Another news update."

"Look, Poppy!" Dud said, pointing at two squirrels chasing each other up a nearby tree. "Monsters!"

"Shh."

Dud watched the tree monsters, rapt, while Poppy and Jill crowded around her phone. The new video was of Colt, still standing in front of the crime scene. "I'd like to remind our viewers that the investigation is still in a preliminary stage, but we've just received word that police *have* established a person of interest. Security footage from inside the Grosholtz Candle Factory shows an unidentified individual in the restricted area of the building, a person *not* believed to be an employee. The footage is blurry, as the individual was running at the time, but they did appear to be fleeing the area in which the investigators believe the fire started; therefore, analysis of the video has become a top priority. For more updates, stay tuned to Channel Six News."

Poppy's knees had gone weak, the phone shaking in her hand. "*I'm* an individual who was in the restricted area of the building," she said numbly. "Am *I* the person of interest?"

Jill shrugged. "Told you it wasn't Blake."

*   *   *

Yes, Poppy was excruciatingly close to being identified as the prime suspect in an arson investigation. Yes, the *real* crazed arsonist was still on the loose. But all paled in comparison with the problem Poppy faced when she got home with Dud in tow: sleeping arrangements.

Poppy's parents understandably did not approve of a boy shacking up in their teenage daughter's room, but somewhere around the twelve-minute mark of Poppy's lecture about how Tristan da Cunha inhabitants traditionally sleep eight to a room and to make him bunk alone for the night would cause him to start losing touch with his African roots, they gave in.

"But he stays on the floor," her mother said as she smoothed out the sleeping bag. "And leave the door open."

"Yes, Mother."

Her father was clapping a firm hand on Dud's shoulder and delivering a series of veiled threats. "I don't own a shotgun," he was saying, "as I am a peace-loving man, but that's my only daughter, and if anyone hurts her, I won't hesitate to do what needs to be done. Understand, Dud?"

"No."

"*Welp,* we're bushed," Poppy said, busting out with a loud yawn. "'Night, you guys."

"I thought shotgun was the front seat of a car," Dud said as they left.

"It is," she said, rubbing her eyes. "Stay here. I'm going to brush my teeth."

It was a messy affair, as usual. Despite years of practice, Poppy routinely got toothpaste on seemingly every surface other than her teeth — the sink, the mirror, the floor, her pajamas, her hair. But she was so distracted that night, she barely noticed.

I am harboring a fake wax thing, she thought, wondering if perhaps enumerating her many problems would help her solve them quicker. *The police will soon suspect me of arson, if they haven't identified me already. My best friend thinks I'm nuts. And my parents think I'm an expert on Africa.*

She was so lost in thought that when she walked back into her bedroom, she didn't notice Dud until it was too late.

Poppy screamed, every drop of blood in her body rushing right into her face.

10

~~Hide the booty~~

HER PARENTS COULD BE HEARD HURRYING DOWN THE HALL-way, but Poppy cut them off at her bedroom door, closing it behind her. "What's wrong?" her father asked.

"I . . . stubbed my toe," Poppy explained. "I'm fine."

"Are you sure?" her mother asked. "That scream, my goodness — we thought you were being stabbed!"

"What a colorful imagination you have! But honestly, I'm fine. Going to bed for real now. Good night!"

Once they'd walked back to their room, Poppy reentered her own room and faced Dud. It took a monumental amount of self-control to say rather than shout, "Why are you naked?"

Dud put his hands on his exposed hips. "What's a naked?"

"Why," she seethed, staring intently at the floor and definitely *not* at anything else, "aren't you wearing any clothes?"

"Because it's time to wear the sleeping bag?"

Poppy blindly pawed for the sweatpants her father had lent Dud, averting her gaze. *Avert. AVERT.* "The sleeping bag is not something you wear, it's something you put yourself *into*. Where are your pants?"

"But I put my arms *into* my sleeves—"

"Dud? Pants?"

"—and I put my feet *into* my shoes—"

"Found them!" Poppy shoved the pants up against his anatomically correct pelvis, then practically threw herself onto the other side of the room. Her face felt as if it were about to burst into flame. "Get dressed. Now, please."

He gave her a look of concern, dropping the pants in the process. "What's wrong, Poppy?"

"Nothing. Just—"

Don't look at it, don't look at it.

. . .

OH GOD I LOOKED AT IT.

"Clothing is important," she blurted. "I'm wearing clothes. Everyone wears clothes. It's rude to suddenly not be wearing clothes."

"Oh. Okay. Sorry." He put the pants back on and grinned. "Good?"

"Good. I'm going to open a window, it's broiling in here."

"Is it?"

"It's *sweltering*."

She opened her window and sat on the sill. The crisp fall air thwacked her back like a spray of cold water. It felt amazing.

It smelled less than amazing. The ever-present stench of the town mixed with the smoke of the factory fire to create heretofore unsmelled levels of stink. She glanced at Mount Cerumen in the distance, its façade still hazy.

She looked back at Dud, his nudity startling her once more. "Can you put your shirt back on too?"

Dud picked up his shirt but stopped there. "Wait. Can I ask a question? What are these things?" he asked, pointing to his chest.

Poppy calmly licked her lips and focused on keeping her voice even. "Nipples."

"What do they do?"

"For boys? Nothing."

"What do they do for girls?"

"Um, well—when women have babies, milk comes out of them—"

"Milk comes out of the babies?"

"No, milk comes out of the nipples."

"Milk comes out of the *nipples?*"

"Yeah, to feed the babies."

"*Wow.*"

They sat quietly for a moment. Poppy fanned herself. Dud thought some more.

"Poppy?"

"Yes?"

"Where do babies come from?"

"It is officially bedtime." She sprang up from the sill and shut the window. "If you require further information, I think we still have that educational DVD my mom bought for me. I can dig it out of the basement tomorrow—"

"Wait, wait!" Dud bit on his fingernail. "Can I ask one more? It's not about nipples."

"Look, the film will explain—"

"What's this thing?" He started to pull down the waistband of his shorts.

"Whoa whoa *whoa*—" Poppy felt the blood rising once more and put her hands out to object, but she stopped once she saw that all he'd exposed was the edge of his hip. "Wait. What *is* that?"

"I asked you first," he replied, then laughed at his joke as if he'd invented it. "Ha *ha!*"

"It's a ... scar," Poppy said, lightly brushing her fingers over his skin. The mark was made up of a series of short straight lines — deep in the middle and raised on the edges, as if it had been gouged directly into his skin.

"What's a scar?" Dud asked.

"It's a mark that's left over after you get hurt, once the wound has healed. But—"

"But what?"

She thought back to the rosebushes, to the lacerations that hadn't lasted for more than a few seconds. "But I don't see how that's possible with you. Unless it was put there when you were first sculpted. What if she ... what? Why are you looking at me like that?"

Dud was frowning and somehow doing the opposite of blinking—every couple of seconds, his eyes widened. "Sculpted?"

"Yeah. By Madame Grosholtz. At the factory."

He eye-bulged again. "Huh?"

She spoke slowly. "Because you're made of wax."

He stared at her. "I am?"

"Oh, you've got to be kidding me," she muttered under her breath.

So he didn't know. How was she supposed to explain? She had never come up against this problem before, since not a soul on earth had come up against this problem before. There were no educational DVDs on how to break the news to someone that they weren't human. There were no *Dr. Steve* episodes devoted exclusively to the subject.

Poppy opened her mouth and waited for the right words to come. *Well, sometimes when a lonely old woman and a block of wax love each other very much . . .*

"Most people — humans — are made of skin and bones and blood and muscle," she explained. "But you are made of wax instead."

Dud cocked his head.

Off to a terrible start. "When I visited the candle factory today," she tried again, "I met this lady named Madame Grosholtz, and I was invited into her studio, and I saw you there. You were a wax sculpture, like — like the crayon you sculpted at Friendly's, remember? That's what you were. And then *somehow* — in a way that I can't explain — you came to life."

"But you said I was from an island near Africa."

"I know. That was just a little fib I had to tell my parents so they would let you stay with us."

"What's a fib?"

"It's what people use to get through their daily lives without killing one another."

"What is 'killing'?"

This was not going well. "What's your first memory?" she asked, trying a different tactic. "What's the first thing you remember?"

He thought for a second. "It was dark, and then it got bright, and then I jumped out, and you were yelling."

"Okay, well, that actually doesn't sound all that different from a regular birth, but — but *you're* talking about coming out of the trunk of a *car*. That's not how people are born. First they're babies, then they're kids like Owen, then they grow up. Humans don't spring into existence fully formed, like you did."

Dud looked at his hands. "I'm not human?" he said quietly.

Poppy's shoulders slumped. This was turning out to be harder than she thought it would be. "Well, no. Not as such. But if it makes you feel any better, you're a lot more human than some of the soul-sucking monsters I've met in my life."

Dud looked at her with big injured-puppy eyes. "Poppy, I . . ."

Oh, God. Was he going to cry? "What?"

"The monsters I saw." Dud said. "They were furry and had fluffy tails and ran up a tree! Then they went like this." He put his fingertips together and mimed eating a nut.

With that, Poppy relaxed, enjoyed a silent internal chuckle, and made a mental note for next time not to get all worried about the emotional state of a lump of wax. "They're called squirrels."

"Squirrels are funny."

"They sure are. Now show me that scar again."

Dud obliged. Poppy squinted at the lines Madame Grosholtz had carved. It looked as though they were arranged into letters, but— "AMT?" she said. "What does that mean? Amount? Anger management therapy? American musical theater?" She was really hoping for that last one, but she couldn't think of a way it could possibly apply.

She reached for her phone. "Time for a little research."

"What's research?"

"It's when we look up information on the Internet."

"What's the Internet?"

"A waste of time for the most part, but it can occasionally have its uses."

Unfortunately, all the search results were just as unlikely: American Medical Technologists, alternative minimum tax, a stock symbol. Nothing related to candles or wax or scary old ladies.

The more she stared at the screen, the heavier her eyelids grew. "I give up," she said through a yawn. "Time to hit the hay. Maybe when I wake up in the morning, this will all have been a delightful romp of a nightmare."

After showing Dud how to stuff himself into the sleeping bag, Poppy turned off the lamp on her nightstand and got into bed. She gave her eyes a vigorous rub, then lit her Forty Winks candle, tried to relax, and —

"Poppy?"

"Yeah?"

"What is hay and why would you hit it?"

"Go to sleep, Dud."

"What is sleep?"

Poppy snapped the light on.

"You don't sleep?" she said irritably. "Close your eyes and lose consciousness for seven to nine hours?"

"That sounds scary."

It did, now that he mentioned it. Though the idea of him watching her sleep was worse. "Well, it's kind of something most people need to do. Can you give it a try?"

"Okay!"

But once the light was off and the room was still and quiet, the demons of the day began to crawl out of the shadows. The frightening things she'd seen. The stale, dry air of the studio on her skin. She found herself staring at her beloved *Lion King* poster, Simba barely visible beneath all the autographs. This time, in the light of her candle, they looked ominous, like threats scribbled in blood.

"Poppy?"

"What?"

"Can I lose consciousness in the closet?"

Poppy turned the lamp on again. Thankful for the distraction, she got up, opened the closet door, and gestured grandly. "Go for it, kid. Just don't try on my bathing suit or fondle my shoes or anything kinky like that."

"Okay!" Dud jumped up and hopped with his sleeping bag into the closet as if he were in a potato sack race. He settled on the floor, content. "Thank you, Poppy."

"You're welcome. Good night."

"Good night!"

She shut the door.

"Poppy?"

She opened the door.

"What now?"

"It's too dark in here."

Poppy rubbed her eyes and reconsidered every fleeting thought she'd ever had about one day having children. "I can leave the light on, if you want."

"Can I have a candle?"

"No, you cannot. This house almost burned down once today, and I see no reason to finish the job."

"But you have a candle."

"That's different. It's aromatherapy."

"What's aromatherapy?"

"A bunch of hooey, obviously, because otherwise I'd be asleep by now."

"Pleeeease?"

Poppy sighed. "Fine. I think we have some extra ones in the — oh, wait, I've got one," she interrupted herself, remembering the candle Madame Grosholtz had thrust upon her. She pulled it out of her backpack and placed it on the floor next to Dud's head, taking a moment to clear away some of her more flammable items.

"I'll watch it," Dud promised as Poppy lit the wick. "I won't let it burn anything."

His incapacity for sleep coupled with the intensity with which he stared at the flame was enough to convince her. Besides, if her admittedly lame wardrobe burned up and she had to start again from scratch, she wouldn't complain.

She stepped out of the closet. "I'll see you in the morning."

"Okay. 'Night, Poppy."

"Good night."

She pulled the closet doors shut and plunged back into bed.

All was quiet.

Until the rustling started.

She tried to ignore it. She tried to jam a pillow into her ears. But it kept going. It sounded like he was looking through her things. All her things. Every single thing.

Exasperated, she flung off the covers and marched to the closet — and that's when the noises stopped.

Curious, she looked in through the horizontal wooden slats.

Dud was nestled in his sleeping bag and staring at the flame of the candle, a pair of headphones pulled over his ears. He'd found her old radio, the one her grandfather had bought at a thrift shop and given to her for her seventh birthday. She hadn't had the heart to tell Grandpa that no one listened to radios anymore, but she also never had the heart to give it away, so she had stuffed it into her closet and forgotten all about it.

Dud fiddled with the radio. Then snuggled the radio.

Poppy got back into bed. *Harmless enough,* she thought, the tranquil voices of NPR lulling them both to sleep.

* * *

"Poppy."

"Mmm?"

"Wake up."

"No, thank you."

"Pop-*py*."

Pop-*py* groaned and fumbled for her phone, squinting at the bright screen. "Dud, it's three thirty-two in the morning. I know you're new to the concept of sleep and all, but this is what's known as an 'ungodly hour'—"

"But the candle is talking."

She switched on her bedside light.

"Come again?"

Dud, still stuffed into the sleeping bag in the closet, pulled open the wooden door and waved at her. "I mean, not talking like we're talking," he said, holding up the flickering candle. "But when I smell it, I can hear someone talking in my head a little. She says 'my doll' a lot."

Poppy frowned. "Maybe you were semiconscious when she was sculpting you, so you have early memories of her voice. Or maybe you fell asleep and you were dreaming."

"Or maybe the candle has *special powers*," he said with awe.

"Yeah, maybe. But I really need to get some sleep, okay?"

"Okay. You can read it in the morning."

"Read what?"

"The candle."

"What?"

"The writing in the candle."

"The . . . what?"

Dud disentangled himself from his sleeping bag, walked across the room, and handed Poppy the stone candle. She peered inside.

The wax had burned down about half an inch, revealing tiny, painstakingly carved letters that had been etched into the inside of the tube. The melted black wax had filled in the engravings, making them easy to read against the white stone.

"Holy *crap*," she whispered, jolting herself into an upright position. "It's a message!"

Dud sat down on the bed next to her. "I thought you really needed sleep."

"I am willing to make an exception for a hidden message carved into the inside of a candle that can only be revealed by the burning of the wax, which is only the coolest thing I've ever seen." She squinted at the letters. "Madame Grosholtz must have written this — she's the one who gave it to me."

"What's it say?"

She pulled a magnifying glass out of the drawer of her nightstand — "Thanks again, Grandpa" — and began to read the tiny writing aloud:

"IF YOU ARE READING THIS, THAT MEANS I AM DEAD."

Poppy looked at Dud, then read on, turning the candle as the writing spiraled downward.

"I KNOW THAT SOUNDS LIKE A CLICHÉ, BUT IT IS TRUE. AT LEAST, I HOPE IT IS TRUE. I HOPE I AM DEAD. I HAVE WANTED TO DIE FOR MANY YEARS NOW. IF I HAVE ENTRUSTED THIS CANDLE TO YOUR CARE, THAT MEANS I HAVE ENTRUSTED YOU WITH MY STORY. IT IS UP TO YOU WHETHER YOU ACT UPON MY WARNINGS OR NOT.

"I DO NOT CARE WHAT YOU CHOOSE. BECAUSE I AM DEAD."

"It's Madame Grosholtz, all right," said Poppy.

"THEREFORE, CONSIDER THIS THE LAST WILL AND TESTAMENT — AND CONFESSION — OF ANNE-MARIE GROSHOLTZ. OR, IF IT"

That's where the words stopped, the unmelted wax blocking the rest from view.

She blew out the flame. "Maybe we can chisel it out." She reached for her X-Acto knife, tapped it into the wax —

The blade instantly snapped.

"Whoa." Ever the prepared crafter, she had a spare ready to go — but that one broke too. "This is, like, a superwax or something," she said, tapping it with her finger. "Hard as a rock. Madame Grosholtz must have been some kind of mad wax scientist."

A mad wax scientist with a death wish, she thought.

So many questions. Was Madame Grosholtz really dead? If so,

how had she known that her death was imminent? Had she known when she gave Poppy the candle? She must have, if she intended for Poppy to read her will, but that would mean Madame Grosholtz would have had advance notice of the fire. But if that was the case, why hadn't she tried to stop it? The studio, all those beautiful works of art . . .

That poor woman.

So many questions, and so many potential answers — answers trapped inside this candle. "I guess we have to let it burn if we want to read the rest." Poppy relit the wick, placed it on her nightstand, and flung herself back onto her bed with a groan. "How am I going to fall asleep *now?*"

Within seconds, she was snoring.

*　　*　　*

Poppy had not realized how exhausting it would be to infiltrate a mysterious candle factory, stumble upon a talented yet batty genius, adopt a scientifically impossible being, concoct a parentally tolerable lie, incur the suspicion of the police, eat a banana split, and discover a lost will and testament all in one day, but when she opened her bleary eyes the next morning and looked at the time on her phone, she saw that it was already noon.

"Don't judge, Simba," she told her poster, disentangling herself from her sheets. "I had a rough night."

She sat up.

Remembered that she was supposed to have a roommate.

Noticed that the closet door was open.

And Dud was gone.

"Oh, no." She staggered out of bed as the remainder of her brain switched on. "No. Bad."

She pulled on a sweatshirt, grabbed her phone, and hurried downstairs, listing the various ends Dud could have come to. *He melted. He escaped. He jumped out the window and got hit by a car. Someone mistook him for a candle and lit his hair on —*

"Fire in the hole!"

An unlikely display greeted Poppy as she walked into the living room: Dud kneeling on the floor; Owen holding a box of Cheerios and winging them one by one at Dud's face; and Mr. and Mrs. Palladino sitting on the couch, applauding.

"Hi, Poppy!" Dud grinned at her. "We're throwing breakfast."

She turned to her parents. "Why are you allowing this to happen?"

"It's a *traditional* island *tradition*," her father explained in a tone that suggested she was being offensive. "Every morning the villagers wake up and toss food into one another's mouths."

"Dad. They're not seals."

"Well, that's what he told us!"

"Is that what Dud told you, or what Owen told you after you'd already caught him flinging cereal around the living room?"

"Dud, I apologize for our insensitive daughter," her mother said. "You go right back to your culture."

Dud tried to give Poppy a conspiratorial wink, but he had not yet learned how to wink, so he just blinked both of his eyes shut really hard.

"And we're all okay with this. Sure. Why not." Poppy shook her head in disbelief. "What are you guys doing here?" she asked her parents. As yoga teachers, Sundays were usually their busiest work-days.

"Classes were canceled," her mother said. "The studios at the spa smelled too much like smoke from the fire, so they're taking a day to air them out. And lucky us — we get to spend some time with the newest member of our family!"

Poppy rolled her eyes. They landed on the painting of the pissed-off peacock.

Then slid below the peacock's feet, to the artist's signature.

No, not his full signature — his initials.

"Oh my God, that's it," Poppy whispered to herself. "AMT! She signed him, like a work of art! AMT is her name. Her initials. Anne-Marie . . ."

Luckily, no one was paying attention to Poppy as she paced back and forth. Owen had turned on some terrible children's music, and now he and Dud were prancing around the room, singing, *"I can walk from here to there, I can walk most anywhere!"*

"But her name was Madame *Grosholtz,*" Poppy continued, frowning, pacing. "There should be a *G* in there somewhere. Unless they're someone else's initials. But why would she carve someone else's initials into him?"

Maybe Dud was based on someone from Madame Grosholtz's past. A teenage crush. Or — *oh,* Poppy realized with a crushing dread — maybe her son? Her *dead* son?

Poppy hadn't thought about it before. Did Madame Grosholtz

have a son? The candle factory was supposedly a family business, so it must have been handed down to the next generation. Unless the business was her husband's? Was she married?

How much did Poppy even know about Madame Grosholtz?

In retrospect, she realized that it was ridiculous that she hadn't thought of it earlier. She tapped the letters into her phone, her fingers shaking. All she'd had to do was Google the name Grosholtz, and bam: there she was, first on the list of search results.

"Poppy?" Dud said, pausing his shenanigans. "Are you okay? Your face is doing a lot of things."

It was, but Poppy couldn't help it. Because the woman staring back at her from the screen — the woman who was most definitely Madame Grosholtz — was here labeled with a different name, along with a brief description:

Anne-Marie "Marie" Tussaud was a French-born artist of German descent who became known for her wax sculptures and Madame Tussaud's, the wax museum she founded in London.

But it was the next line that really made Poppy's eye twitch:

Died: April 16, 1850.

11

~~Do research~~

POPPY BOOKED IT UPSTAIRS, TAKING THE STEPS TWO AT A time and nearly knocking over the stone candle as she grabbed it from her nightstand and read the words that had appeared overnight:

> THEREFORE, CONSIDER THIS THE LAST WILL AND TESTAMENT — AND CONFESSION — OF ANNE-MARIE GROSHOLTZ. OR, IF IT PLEASE YOU, BY MY OTHER NAME: MADAME TUSSAUD. YOU MAY HAVE HEARD OF ME. I AM MILDLY FAMOUS. I SPENT DECADES SCULPTING FIGURES OUT OF WAX, AND I BECAME WELL-KNOWN FOR IT. I AM PROUD OF THE WORK THAT I DID IN MY LIFE.
>
> I AM NOT PROUD OF WHAT I DID AFTER MY DEATH.

Poppy's stomach gave a lurch.

YOU SEE, CREATING ART — CREATING REAL, GOOD ART —
IS A LONELY PROCESS. MANY HOURS ALONE. IF YOU TALK,
IT IS ONLY TO YOURSELF. AND MAYBE TO YOUR WORK.
AFTER A WHILE, THE WORK BECOMES YOUR FRIEND. AND
AFTER A LITTLE WHILE MORE, THE WORK SEEMS TO COME
A LITTLE BIT ALIVE. SO WHY NOT . . . ALL THE WAY ALIVE?
ENTER: LES CIRES VIVANTES.

"The living wax," Poppy whispered.

IT IS SOMETHING I HAD BEEN EXPERIMENTING WITH FOR
YEARS. I CAME CLOSE A FEW TIMES. TWITCHING MUSCLES.
BLINKING EYES. BEATING HEARTS. BUT THEY NEVER
STAYED ALIVE FOR LONG. I DIDN'T HAVE MUCH TIME LEFT
MYSELF — I COULD FEEL MY BONES GROWING OLD AND
WEARY. ONE DAY MY EYES FELL UPON A SELF-REPLICA
I'D SCULPTED, AND I FOUND MYSELF WISHING I COULD
INHABIT THAT WAX DUPLICATE OF MYSELF. I'D NEVER DIE,
NEVER GET ANY OLDER. I COULD GO ON SCULPTING FOR-
EVER.

I DARE NOT SET DOWN HERE — NOR ANYWHERE ELSE —
HOW I DID IT. THAT KNOWLEDGE IS LOST TO THE AGES,
AND I PLAN TO KEEP IT THAT WAY. SUFFICE IT TO SAY THAT
I GOT RIGHT TO WORK SCULPTING ANOTHER SCULPTURE
OF MYSELF — A HOLLOW ONE THIS TIME. I WAS ABLE TO

DISTILL MY SOUL INTO THE FORM OF A FLAME AND LIGHT THE HOLLOW FROM WITHIN, HOPING TO ANIMATE IT. AND TO MY SURPRISE, DELIGHT — AND MUCH LATER, HORROR — IT WORKED.

FOR SOME TIME, THERE WERE TWO OF US — THE ORIGINAL ME, IN THE FLESH, AND MY WAX DUPLICATE — A CLONE THAT CONTAINED ALL MY MEMORIES AND PERSONALITY, BUT ITS OWN CONSCIOUSNESS. THE REAL TEST CAME, OF COURSE, A FEW YEARS LATER, WHEN MY EARTHLY BODY FAILED ME AT LAST. I TOOK MY LAST BREATH, CLOSED MY EYES — AND OPENED THEM ONCE AGAIN IN MY NEW WAX BODY. OUR TWO FLAME-SOULS MERGED, AND I WAS WHOLE ONCE MORE.

I HAVE EXTENDED MY LIFE THUSLY EVER SINCE. WHEN ONE HOLLOW BECAME DAMAGED OR WORN OUT, I WOULD CREATE A NEW ONE, LIGHT IT WITH MY FLAME-SOUL, AND JUMP INTO MY NEW BODY. OF COURSE, SEVERAL CANDLES THAT WERE LIT WITH THE ORIGINAL WERE AT ALL TIMES BURNING SAFE WITHIN MY HOME — IF ONE WENT OUT, I HAD MANY BACKUP FLAMES WITH WHICH TO RELIGHT.

MADAME TUSSAUD HAD LONG SINCE "DIED," IN THE TRADITIONAL MANNER OF SPEAKING — THERE WAS A FUNERAL, IT WAS IN THE PAPERS — AND SO I TOILED AWAY IN RELATIVE OBSCURITY UNDER MY MAIDEN NAME, SCULPTING

AND WORKING AND REDISCOVERING THE JOY OF THE ART THAT I'D LOST AFTER SO MANY YEARS OF MUSEUMS AND COMMERCIAL SUCCESS. BUT PEOPLE

That was as far as the wax had burned.

Poppy's phone rang.

She jumped.

"Jill!" she shouted into it. "Madame Grosholtz was Madame Tussaud, and she's been alive for over two centuries because she made herself immortal using wax duplicates!"

"Um," said Jill. "Sorry, wrong number."

"*Jill.*"

Poppy slowed herself down to an intelligible speaking speed and explained, to the best of her ability, what she'd learned. "So you're telling me," Jill said patiently, "that the woman you met at the candle factory was not in fact a real, live, walking, talking, sculpting, staring *descendent* of Madame Tussaud, but the actual dead, buried, dearly departed Madame Tussaud herself."

"Yes. That is what I am telling you."

"Like, what — a ghost?"

"No, not a ghost. I'm saying that she was real *then,* and she's real *now.* Or she *was* real now. Well — not now. Now she's not anywhere."

"You sound like you're having a stroke."

"It was *her,* Jill! I swear!"

"That's quite a jump to make, Pops. A jump that, dare I say, is impossible."

"Well—"

"And stupid."

"But—"

"Aaand impossible."

Poppy pulled her phone away from her ear and put it on speaker. "Anne-Marie Grosholtz," she said to Jill, scanning the Wikipedia page on the screen. "Grosholtz was her *maiden* name—she was of German descent but born in France—so it was a *French*-French accent, not French-Canadian like I thought—arrested during the Reign of Terror—made death masks of those killed in the French Revolution—collected *human heads,* Jill—married François, had two sons—completed many sculpture collections—died at the age of eighty-eight—"

"The key word here being 'died.'"

"You want proof? I have proof! There's this *message*—"

"Pops, I had a reason for calling. Did you see the news?"

"No. I just woke up."

"You just woke up? It's after noon."

"*Don't judge.* What's going on?"

"The police announced that they'll be holding a press conference at three o'clock. They say they have new information about the arson investigation."

"*What?*" Poppy looked from the candle in one hand to her phone in the other. Surely human brains were not built for so much information and danger to be crammed in there all at once. "Do you think it's about me? Did they make any progress on the security footage?"

"I don't know."

Poppy fumbled for her jeans, putting the Madame Grosholtz business on hold for the moment in the name of self-preservation. All that goodwill she'd built up since *Triple Threat,* the restoration of her reputation—it would mean nothing if her mug shot were splashed all over the place. "I have to get out of here before the police arrive. I have to figure out how to clear my name."

"Are you crazy? Do you know how much worse it'll get if it looks like you're running away? The best thing you can do is cooperate and answer their questions. The *worst* thing you could do is leave the house—"

"Meet me at Secret Service Way in fifteen minutes!"

✝ ✴ ✴

Against her better judgment, Poppy decided to leave Dud in the questionably capable hands of Owen for the day. Their list of shared interests was growing by the hour: in addition to cereal, they both enjoyed playing with toy cars, jumping on the furniture, playing hide-and-seek, and rolling leftover brownies into shapes that looked hilariously (to them) like dog poo.

"Have fun," she said, leaving her parents as she'd found them: curled up on the couch drinking kale smoothies, captivated by Dud's perplexing island ways. "Just make sure not to let him leave the house. It's Sunday, which is sacred to Tristaners, because the, uh—the island was discovered on a Sunday, and they usually spend the day draping themselves in seaweed to commemorate the occasion. But he should be fine with keeping it sacred . . . at home."

It would have to do. She mouthed, "Behave," to Dud and headed for the door.

"We've got some leftover kale you can drape, Dud," she heard her mother saying as she left. "Would that work?"

* * *

Secret Service Way had nothing to do with the government agency of the same name. "Service Way" because it was a gravelly back road through the woods that bypassed the town and served as a shortcut to both the Grosholtz Candle Factory and the Paraffin Resort and Spa, and "Secret" because only the employees knew about it.

And their children. And their children's best friends.

Poppy bounced Clementine down the dirt road and came to a stop next to Jill, who was sitting in her mom's parked car. Up ahead, looking like a disoriented outhouse, was one of Paraffin Resort and Spa's patented "personal saunas" — a smattering of veritable closets dispersed throughout the woods where one could "be at one with nature" in a "totally private setting" to "sweat out the bad, soak in the good."

Poppy could soak in a little good herself right about now. She rolled down her window.

"For the record," Jill told her, "I am only here to prevent you from incriminating yourself further."

"You think I want to be here? I had to leave Dud with my *parents*. Who knows what kind of a smoking crater my house will be reduced to by the time I get back?"

"And why *are* we here? What is this grand plan of yours?"

"We'll never get close to the crime scene if we go through the front. But if we go around the secret back way . . ." She grinned and stepped on the accelerator, leaving Jill and her reasonable protests in the dust.

Poppy hung a left and steered Clementine onto a smaller, less-used dirt road that wound deeper into the woods, up the small hill next to Mount Cerumen. Jill followed. After a few seconds of uphill driving, the trees began to thin, then clear completely at the top.

The girls got out of their cars. Below them, at the foot of the mountain, sat the Grosholtz Candle Factory, and above them —

"Whoa," said Poppy, craning her neck upward. Her father had taken her here a few times when she was a kid to fly kites, but she'd forgotten how tall the towers were. "The motherships."

The two shiny white cylindrical storage tanks stood before them, lording over the surrounding pines like teeth that had been knocked out of a giant's mouth. Each at least a hundred feet tall, with metal staircases curved up their walls, they were labeled GRO-SHOLTZ CANDLE FACTORY #1 and GROSHOLTZ CANDLE FACTORY #2.

"I still haven't heard a valid argument for this plan of yours," Jill said, joining her. "Why on earth would you want to get *closer* to the crime scene?"

"I don't know yet," said Poppy. "But there's gotta be something there that'll prove I had nothing to do with this. And that Blake has everything to do with this. And with Madame Grosholtz being made of wax and all, maybe — Jill? Jill!"

"What?"

"Why aren't you listening to me?"

"I'm—" Jill was frowning and sniffing the air. "Do you smell that?"

"Huh?"

"Smell. The air." She closed her eyes and took a long, luxurious breath.

Poppy did the same—and stiffened. "What the heck?"

The air smelled of . . . nothing. No berries. No sandalwood. No coconut-pine-cinnamon-lime. That omnipresent, amalgamated odor that oozed its way into every crevice of Paraffin had dissolved into oblivion and was replaced by a flat, distilled scent.

"What *is* that?" Poppy asked.

"I don't know," Jill said, giving tank #1 a kick. "But I think it's coming from this."

Poppy frowned. "I thought these things broke when they got struck by lightning." She walked up to #1's wall and tentatively put a hand on its surface. The thick metal was warm to the touch, but not so hot that she had to draw her hand back. It felt like an enormous coffee urn.

Poppy tapped her chin as she surveyed the tank's exterior. One spot featured a large gaping hole—created by the lightning strike, judging by its seared, jagged edges—but it was patched with nothing more than a thick translucent plastic tarp and what appeared to be a tight seal of Tackety Wax. Nearby, a large red button was set into the wall, and as it had been pushed in, Poppy guessed that it controlled the heat.

"I thought these were out of commission forever," Poppy said, testing the tarp. It barely yielded beneath her touch, but it was clear from the way it bulged that there was some sort of liquid inside. "Why fix them when they've got such better, more advanced wax storage tanks?"

"I dunno," said Jill. "I found a tank full of wax, and you have a waxy mystery to solve. Do I have to do all the work?"

Just then they heard a car crunching along the gravel of Secret Service Way.

Then it slowed.

Then turned.

And began climbing the road to the tanks.

Poppy inhaled. Was it the police? Or maybe the crazed arsonist, back to finish the job? "What do we do?" she asked Jill. "Hide?"

"They'll still see our cars!"

"So?"

"So your car is the most recognizable car in Vermont!"

"Not to a deranged mountain hermit arsonist who doesn't own a TV!"

While they argued, the car crested the top of the hill, rendering their conversation moot. And the driver turned out to be much worse than a deranged mountain hermit.

Blake got out of his car — Poppy didn't know what kind it was, only that it probably cost more than her house — and looked at the two girls standing before him. Confusion muddled his face. "What are you doing here?" he asked.

At the sound of his voice, Poppy recoiled. She'd worked hard to get rid of this habit, but it never failed to crop up in his presence, as if he were crumpling her soul like a used-up Post-it. But this time, with her innocence on the line, she managed to scrape up an ounce or two of bravery and stand her ground. "What are *you* doing here?" she shot back.

"Asked you first, Your Porkness. Surprised those stumpy little hooves of yours were able to get up this hill." Cue the hyena laugh.

But . . . it didn't seem as though his heart was in it. And his eyes weren't narrowed and penetrating and mean the way they usually were. He seemed distracted, his gaze darting around the trees as if he thought he was being watched. As if he was going through the motions of insulting Poppy because that's what he was supposed to do, but in reality he had more important things on his mind.

Out of all the arson-related questions she could have asked next, even Poppy was surprised to hear herself blurt, "Who did you hire to make that sculpture of me?"

Blake glanced anxiously at the tanks. "I didn't."

He left it at that. And that's when Poppy *knew* something was wrong. Blake Bursaw never, ever missed an opportunity to boast about his reprehensible accomplishments. He hadn't shut up about "Hogwash" for one second since Halloween. But now he wasn't rubbing his wickedness in her face. He wasn't bragging or swaggering — it was as if the prank had become an afterthought, only a day later.

"Oh, come on, Blake, I know it was you," Poppy said. "I saw the video — that was your voice. You obviously —"

"I didn't hire anyone to sculpt it," he said, "because it was already sculpted."

"What?"

But by this point Blake was full-on ignoring her. He walked right past the girls, toward the trees beyond the tanks — on a mission, it seemed. "Blake, wait!" Poppy sputtered. "Did you set the fire?"

He didn't answer. He kept walking until he reached the edge of the clearing, then disappeared into the trees.

"Forget about him," Jill said, pulling on Poppy's sleeve. "Let's get out of here before someone sees us —"

Before she could properly think it through, Poppy took off running, flying through the trees in an effort to keep Blake in her sights. Dodging branches and taking care not to trip over any tree roots, she soon spotted him up ahead, moving quickly but assuredly down the hill until he burst out of the trees. Moments later, so did Poppy.

She stood there, staring, as the dimensions in her brain reprogrammed themselves. She was looking at the Grosholtz Candle Factory, but from behind — an angle she'd never seen it from before. The retail store was in the distance; slightly closer was the warehouse area, a mess of delivery trucks and loading docks. Closest of all was the rear of the factory — including the charred ruins of Madame Grosholtz's studio. Bands of bright yellow police tape roped off the perimeter, but they didn't seem to deter Blake, who was confidently striding toward them.

That flutter of yellow snapped Poppy out of her confusion. *Why would he return to the scene of the crime?*

And where is everyone?

The rubble was deserted. There wasn't a single police officer, detective, or fire marshal on site.

Blake didn't seem at all surprised by this. He ducked under the caution tape without hesitation.

Poppy shouted his name. He froze in an awkward crouching position.

She hurried down the rest of the hill, blowing past a Paraffin Resort personal sauna in the process — then retreating and turning left at the structure instead, as she'd blundered into a patch of thistles. She tried not to think about Madame Grosholtz when she finally stepped onto the warped wooden floor of the studio, but reminders of her were everywhere — piles of scorched fabric, the smell of burned lacquer in the air, the sheer cragginess of it all. And wax — so much wax, the molten residue of all those beautiful sculptures, colors swirled together, smooth and puddled and hardened on the floor in one big sheet, like a marbled ice-skating rink.

Poppy's breath caught. There, poking up out of the solidified wax —

Madame Grosholtz's glasses.

A few feet away: Her heavy black dress. A wad of hair. And a pair of dainty black boots that couldn't have belonged to anyone else.

It was one thing to pull facts from Wikipedia or read what had been written in the stone candle's engraved message. It was quite another to stand atop the proof, to literally walk across the melted remains of a centuries-old wax sculptress.

Poppy did what she could to pull herself together. "Where

146

are the police?" she demanded of Blake. Her distress at Madame Grosholtz's disappearance had nowhere else to go, so it bubbled over and splashed directly onto him. "And what are you doing here?"

"I could ask you the same thing."

"*You* started this, I know you did!" Poppy had no idea where all this nerve was coming from, but she kept rolling with it. "And in the course of trying to prove that, I came into possession of something . . . weird . . . and it came from this factory, and — and —" *And the owner of this studio, who was supposed to be very much dead, was very much alive until yesterday,* she wanted to say. But she couldn't trust Blake with something as big as that. "And I've got a lot of questions, but then *someone* burned down the only way I can get answers. And pretty soon the police are going to think *I* was the one who did it! But I didn't!"

Blake looked at her — not as a snake looks at a mouse, but as one decent person might look at another decent person. "I didn't either."

"Then, seriously, why are you here?"

Reluctant, Blake sucked his lips into his teeth. He looked back up the hill, then out toward the town. "Late Friday night, the Chandlers called my house to talk to my dad and my grandma. My dad said it got heated. Then yesterday, Dad and Gram left early in the morning — which is weird, because they usually sleep in on the weekends. They wouldn't tell me where they were going, but I heard them say something about candles or scents or something as they left."

He scratched his head, looking pained. "They came back a little

147

while later, but something was *off*. I don't know how to describe it. Like . . . different. Like they weren't themselves. Dad —" He paused. "This is going to sound crazy, but Dad's face? It looked, like, wrong. Like he'd gotten plastic surgery. Probably not noticeable to anyone but me, but I could tell something was different. And Gram wasn't wearing her glasses," he continued before Poppy could answer. "I've never once seen Gram without her glasses. Whoever heard of an eighty-year-old woman's eyesight getting better overnight?"

"She *is* an extraordinary woman," Poppy deadpanned.

As a mark of how preoccupied he was, he didn't stop to retort. "I just can't — I don't know. Something is off," he repeated.

Poppy was about to keep giving him the badass treatment, but the wounded way he was talking made her soften her tone. "What had the Chandlers called about the night before?"

"They were threatening to press charges against me for theft."

"What did you steal?"

"That sculpture of you."

Poppy started. "Wait wait wait. You stole the sculpture from the Chandlers? Why did the Chandlers have a sculpture of me?"

He turned his head away from her, but it sounded like he muttered, "Not just you."

"What?"

Blake let out a huff. "Why should I keep talking to you about any of this, Palladino? So you can run off to the police and turn me in?"

"*I'm* the one they're looking for! I was caught on camera in the factory, in an area I was not supposed to be in, not long before the fire was set!" Blake scoffed, but Poppy wasn't letting up. "Can you at least tell me where you got it?"

"I broke into their property. Actually, I didn't *break* into anything, it was already open. So, really, it was just there for the taking."

"The Chandlers had a sculpture of me that was just there for the taking."

"Yes."

Poppy was baffled. "*Why?*"

"I don't —" Blake's face remained pensive for another second or two, but then he made a dismissive noise and narrowed his eyes. "You should go," he said, reverting to his sneering self.

"Excuse me?"

"I'm gonna dig around and see what I can find. So you should get out of here."

"I am absolutely not going anywhere."

"You'll slow me down!" He took a step toward her. "I want to find out what's going on with my family!"

She took a step toward him. "And I don't want to get arrested!"

Suddenly the floor gave way beneath them. They fell a couple of feet, flailing, crashing into each other, and finally landing painfully on a set of concrete stairs.

"Owww," Poppy groaned, rubbing her bruised back. She picked up a piece of the shattered wooden floor, a portion of the Grosholtz Candle Factory logo carved into its surface. She looked up to find a rectangular opening. "A trapdoor," she said, realizing the spot they'd stepped on was the sunken area she'd noticed the day before, the divot in which that big toe had swirled around.

Blake agreed with a grunt. "Must have caved under the weight of the wax. And us. Well, *you*."

Poppy ignored the barb, taking a few steps down the darkened stairway. *Maybe Madame Grosholtz is inside!* she thought, hoping that the old woman had used the crawlspace as an emergency shelter. But when the stairs ended in a dark, narrow hallway, she realized it wasn't a crawlspace.

It was a tunnel. And it led directly into the mountain.

Poppy hesitated, but only for a second. Jill had probably lost interest and gone home by now. And this spurt of bravery certainly wasn't going to last forever.

Slowly, she turned to Blake and held his gaze. "I'm game if you're game."

Blake heaved a grunty sigh — but didn't say no.

Poppy felt around as she walked through the tunnel, using her cell phone as a flashlight. The walls were made of black stone that was smooth and frigid to the touch — as if it were made of solid ice.

"Where are we?" Blake whispered after they'd walked for a minute.

"I don't know."

"Do you want me to go in front?"

Poppy did want him to go in front — she would have preferred any bullets or butcher knives or flaming arrows to go into the guy who'd made her life a living hell — but her utter aversion to acting like a damsel in distress won out. "No, I'm *fine*," she said, turning around to look at him so that he could see how fine she was.

"Then you might want to watch out for that—"

"Ow!"

"Door." His smirk was nearly audible. "You seem to have a lot of trouble with doors."

Poppy shook off the embarrassment and raised her cell phone flashlight. In place of a doorknob was a metal ring shaped like a figure eight, through which Poppy looped her finger. It felt cold in her hand, and heavier than seemed possible for its size — as if it had been forged out of some metal that didn't play nice with the laws of physics. When she gave it a yank, it yanked back, slipping from her hand and dropping back onto the wood with a crash.

Poppy cringed. "Well, now we've knocked." She backed up, careful not to bump into Blake. "Guess we just have to wait."

"For what?" Blake said with a laugh as the door swung ajar beneath his touch. "It's open."

And he slipped inside, as if this place, like everything else in Paraffin, belonged to him.

12

~~Trespass~~

POPPY HAD EXPECTED WHATEVER WAS ON THE OTHER SIDE OF the door to be as cold and dank and dark as the tunnel they'd gone through to get there, but when she stepped over the threshold, what struck her was:

Warmth.

Comfort.

Tranquillity.

And *light*.

Hundreds of thin white tapered candles in every direction she looked. In sconces on the walls, in candelabras hanging from the ceiling, in elaborate wrought-iron stands groping up from the floor. Countless little licks of flame, bathing the room in a flickering, buttery glow.

"What is this place?" Blake asked, craning his head up.

"I don't know," Poppy whispered. Whispering felt appropriate. "It looks like a cathedral."

It certainly echoed like one. Even with the luminosity of the candles, the empty space yawned out in front of them, a disquieting hollowness that sent shivers up and down Poppy's arms. Though the architecture of the cavern was undoubtedly Gothic — pointed arches, dramatic ornamentation, and ribbed, vaulted ceilings — there was something alien about it too. The space felt unnaturally tall, taller than it should have been, given its depth inside the mountain. No windows. The ridges in the walls seemed almost organic in nature — sinewy, like tendons. Wax coated every surface, ranging from smooth pools to bulging globs. Hardened stalagmites stuck up out of the ground, and precarious stalactites hung from the lofty roof above, poised like the teeth of some great beast. It was as if the entire structure had been trickled into existence, drip by drip.

Shadows jerked everywhere, the little flames throwing monstrous shapes onto the walls. Poppy's and Blake's figures looked distorted as they walked, their shoes squelching into the soft wax on the floor. "Look," Blake said, pointing. "Footprints."

It was hard to tell how many sets there were. Poppy could identify a high heel and maybe a work boot, but she couldn't get more specific than that — especially since they crisscrossed all over the wax, approaching five different doors. Two of them, labeled IN and OUT, were set into the right-hand wall, and two more, labeled UP and ACROSS, were on the left.

Poppy turned around and looked at the door through which they'd entered: BETWEEN. "Where do you think the rest go?" she asked Blake.

"Don't know." He tried each one in succession, but they were locked. Poppy knocked on ACROSS, but the solidness of it was a tangible thing—it tossed her fist back with cold indifference. A giant faucet stuck out of the door labeled IN, its surface made of clean, shiny metal, as if it had been recently retrofitted into the door. Nearly two feet in diameter, it emptied into a pool—almost like a baptismal font, but with a globby hill of wax accumulated around its drain.

Also in keeping with the cathedral theme, a rectangular slab of heavy stone sat on a raised platform at the head of the space—an altar of sorts. Dark, dried drops oozed over its edges, layered on top of older, inkier stains.

"Is that blood?" Poppy asked Blake.

"How should I know?"

Poppy pulled The List out of her bag, carefully placed it on the altar, and began to sketch out a general map of the cathedral, labeling each door so that she could obsess over them later. "You might not *know,* but you should at least *care.*"

Blake was neither knowing nor caring nor listening to a word Poppy was saying. Behind the altar, the chamber ended in a rounded wall—further cementing the feeling of a church—and it was this wall that now commanded Blake's attention. He walked toward it, frowning.

Poppy looked up from her sketch and followed his gaze. "Are those photographs?"

"Tintypes," Blake said without thinking—then his eyes widened as he realized how uncool it was for him to know something like that. "I mean, I think. I saw something on TV about them."

"Oh, ex*cuse* me," said Poppy, deciding to milk this moment for all it was worth. "*Do* tell me more about the history of photography, Professor."

He scowled at her. "They're old, okay? That's all I know. Like, eighteen hundreds."

They *were* old. The portrait on the left was of a young but severe-looking woman with a heart-shaped face and piercing, ambitious eyes. The portrait on the right was of a man with a thin black mustache and an expression that conveyed either puzzlement or indigestion. They both wore nineteenth-century attire, and each portrait was placed inside a gilded frame.

Blake took a sharp breath. "Holy . . ."

"What?" Poppy abandoned her diagram and stepped down from the altar to join him at the wall.

He looked from the portraits to her, incredulous. "Are you not seeing it?"

Poppy stared at the photos. Then stared some more. Then, like one of those hidden 3-D images, it snapped into place.

"Whoa," she said, backing away. "They look just like the Chandlers!"

"Yeah." His voice had gotten tighter, his breaths shallow. "They do."

"Must be their great-grandparents or something." She took some quick snapshots of the portraits with her phone. No matter what angle she stood at, their eyes seemed to follow. "But wait — does that mean Anita and Preston are brother and sister? I always thought they were married —"

With a lunge, Blake tried to pry the frames off the wall, but they held fast. Poppy cringed as his grunts echoed through the cavern. "Calm down, Blake."

"No, I won't calm down! These bastards did something to my family!" He walked up to each door and tried to kick them down as his rage intensified, railing and shouting, punching the walls —

Click.

The door marked UP parted down the middle, revealing an elevator.

Blake, panting, stared at it. Then walked right in.

"Blake! Are you crazy?" Yet Poppy followed him — not so much because she wanted to, but the idea of being left alone in that spooky place was not a pleasant one. She hurried to scoot inside just as the door closed behind her.

They rode up in silence, Poppy trying to keep her breath under control, trying not to stare at the dark stains on the floor.

When the door opened, Poppy almost laughed out loud. In her wildest dreams she had never imagined that she'd end up in this position: standing next to Blake Bursaw, peering out at the tall-backed chairs in the office of the owners of the Grosholtz Candle Factory.

After pausing to make sure the office was empty, Poppy and Blake stepped out into the room as the door closed — or rather, as the false wall of the fireplace silently slipped back into place behind them, concealing the elevator within.

"Not even a real fire," muttered Blake, waving his hand through the flame. "It's like a hologram or something."

The office looked the same as it had when Poppy had gotten a glimpse through the window during the tour — mahogany walls, lots of bookcases, a few doors that led to parts unknown, the roaring fire that she now knew was fake. As she ran a hand over the velvet chairs, she wondered — had Big Bob and Miss Bea sat in those same spots before the factory opened for the day? Who knows what could have happened, with no one around?

Blake was probably thinking the same thing. He was silent for another few seconds, then shook his head and looked at his unnecessarily large watch. "You know what? Screw this. I'm not gonna waste my time poking around in some —"

"Wait," Poppy said. "Do you hear that?"

Blake listened. "Sounds like . . . people . . ."

"Duck!"

As the tour guide whisked open the curtain, Poppy and Blake dove under the window, pressing their backs against the wall and pulling in their feet.

"We need to get out of here," said Poppy.

"You think?"

As the flashes of cameras went off directly over their heads, Poppy's phone chirped. *got bored waiting for your nervous breakdown to run its course,* Jill had texted. *call me later.*

"If I get out of this alive," Poppy muttered, "sure, I'll give you a ring."

As soon as the curtain closed, Blake scrambled to his feet.

"Quick," he said, hurrying toward a door that seemed as if it might lead out into the hallway. "If we time it right, we can blend in with the tour."

Blake opened the door and — bingo. He grabbed Poppy by the wrist and dragged her into the hallway. "Bathroom," he said, plowing to the front of the group and past the tour guide. "Emergency."

"Gee, thanks," said Poppy as they jogged down the hall. "I've been wanting to add 'diarrhea' to the list of ways you've humiliated me."

They didn't stop until they were at the main entrance, where Blake gladly let go of her wrist and Poppy just as gladly put a safe distance between them. They took a moment to assess the Sunday-afternoon hordes, a large portion of which were gathered around the now fully stocked BiScentennial display. Dual piles of lavender and green candles sat beneath the sign, which had been changed to read THEY'RE FINALLY HERE!

The whole spectacle earned a derisive snort from Blake.

"It's part of this new special-edition thing," Poppy said dryly. "They're releasing two new candles per day in honor of the bicentennial. Word on the street is that they're a real game changer."

Rolling his eyes, Blake grabbed one of the lavender candles and inhaled.

Then inhaled again.

His chest rose and fell, his eyes widening.

"What's wrong?" Poppy asked.

"Smells just like my grandmother," he murmured.

Poppy took a sniff herself and almost gasped. She couldn't say whether it smelled of Miss Bea — she'd met the woman on only a couple of occasions — but memories of her own grandmothers instantly washed over her. Warm meals, crocheted blankets, a hint of butterscotch —

Poppy looked at the label. "It's called To Grandmother's House We Go."

Blake backed away from the display, wary. "What'd you say was so special about these things?"

"They're made with this new substance called Potion. It can capture the essence of a person and turn it into a candle scent. Or something." She hurried to sniff the green candles on the other side of the display. "This one is kinda ... metallic. Familiar, but I can't —"

Blake grabbed the jar out of her hand and huffed it. "Money," he said with authority. "It smells like money."

Poppy bit her lip. *If Big Bob were a candle, he'd be ...* "Are you sure?"

"Positive."

"Well, *you* would know."

When Blake read the label, the color went out of his face. "The Smell of Success."

He started pacing, looking as though he wanted to tear the whole world apart. Barbara, Queen of the Color-Coded Maps, approached. "Is everything all right?" she asked.

Smoke was all but coming out of Blake's ears. Poppy told Barbara they were fine, then pulled Blake into the clearance section. He shook her off, nearly knocking over a collection of essential oils.

"What are you saying?" he demanded. "That they kidnapped my dad and grandma and — what, turned them into *scents?* Into *candles?*"

"I have no idea," Poppy said as carefully as she could, regarding him as she would a wild animal. "We need more information. We need —"

Blake's phone beeped. "Text from Dad," he said, running his hand through his hair and taking a deep breath. "He wants me to meet him and Grandma at the press conference. I gotta go." He pushed past her.

"Hey, wait! That's it?"

He turned around, annoyed. "You want a hug?"

"I just — I feel like we're kind of *in* this now. Together."

"*I'm* not," he said with a smirk. "Good luck with those arson charges."

"Hey!" Poppy grabbed him by the shirt and thrust her face into his. Again, no clue where this courage was coming from, but she sure was enjoying it. "Trust me, Bursaw, I don't want to be in this any more than you do. But we both know there's something going on here. So if I come across any new information, or if you learn anything from your dad or grandma, wouldn't it be beneficial to both of us to, I don't know, keep each other in the loop?"

Blake looked a little nauseated at the idea of teamwork, but he gave her a gruff nod. "Yeah, okay. Find me tomorrow at school, and we'll talk."

"We should exchange phone numbers too."

He stared at her. "You want my phone number?"

"In case we find out anything new. Not to, like, plan a sexy rendezvous. I still think you're a triple dick."

"A what?"

"Just give me your phone."

Once they'd swapped numbers, Blake turned around without another word and ran out the exit.

The candle store was noisy, humming and pulsing with the press of the weekend crowd. Poppy swept her eyes across the throngs, allowing them to carry her back to the diorama display. She looked up through the stained-glass window dome at the storage tanks looming above, then at the poor waxen farmers in the pastoral scene. They gazed straight ahead, unamused, powerless to stop people from taking selfies with them.

"Excuse me," she said, flagging down a passing Waxpert. "Did they rearrange the figures? I was just here yesterday, and I think they were in different spots."

The Waxpert followed Poppy's gaze. "Oh, yeah! Guess you're right!" She shrugged and gave Poppy a dopey grin. "Probably the Chandlers' doing — sometimes they like to redecorate after hours."

Poppy raised an eyebrow as the Waxpert ran off. "Interesting."

*　*　*

Over the years, Poppy had been forced to wade through plenty of unusual things when she entered her house: yoga mats, boxes of granola, hand-woven blankets that came with the insistence that "if they're good enough for Peruvian alpacas, they're good enough for the Palladino family." But this was the first time she'd stepped around shards of broken glass jars.

They were in boxes, at least. Spotting the telltale Grosholtz Candle Factory logo on a couple of the fragments, Poppy followed the trail into the kitchen.

Standing around the table: her family.

Seated at the head of the table: Dud.

On the table: the townspeople of Paraffin.

In a miniature echo of the diorama she'd just come from, a community of figurines now littered Poppy's kitchen. Rendered in the vibrant colors of Grosholtz wax were a dozen six-inch figures, each sculpted and posed in a way that was undeniably, definitively *those people*. There was Greg, the Friendly's waiter, merrily hoisting a tray of chicken finger platters. There was Mrs. Goodwin, gardening shears in hand. There was a judgmental Dr. Steve. And of course, the Palladino clan themselves, in their natural habitat: Mom, Dad, and Owen, smiling and eating out of Whole Foods containers.

"Poppy!" her mother exclaimed as Poppy picked up the Jill figurine and studied its dead-on smirk. "You failed to mention what a talented sculptor Dud is! I've never seen anything like it!"

Her father gestured wildly at Dud, whose tongue stuck out in concentration as he scraped the blade of her X-Acto knife across Colt Lamberty's hair. "It started with one, but then he kept going and going, asking for more!"

Poppy's mother ruffled Dud's hair. "Like a little Oliver Twist."

Poppy would have loved to point out that nothing about Dud was little, and that Oliver Twist's situation was a smidge different from theirs, but she lost focus the more she looked at the figures. How had he been able to glean that much detail about people he'd met or seen for mere seconds? Other than her family and Jill, they were complete strangers to him — yet he'd sculpted them as though he'd known them for years, known what they had for breakfast that morning and how crispy they liked their bacon.

Her gaze swept over the tops of their little heads until it met Dud's, who gave her a shy smile. "I made them for you."

While Poppy's parents busted out with a syrupy "Awww," Poppy leaked a thin, silent stream of air in place of whatever she'd hoped her brain would come up with. Had this wax thing formulated a genuine human emotion? Was he — oh, God — developing something of a crush on her? And was this all seriously happening *in front of her parents and her little brother?*

"Let me grab you another candle," said Poppy's father. "I think there's an extra Ocean Breeze in the closet."

"And I'll go get the camera," her mother said as they hustled out of the kitchen. "Ooh! We can send the photos to Dud's parents!"

"Ooh!" Owen piped up. "I know who else you should make, Dud! Mr. *Crawford.*"

Poppy rounded on her brother. "What?"

"Poppy looooves Mr. Crawford. She wants him to be her husband."

"Where did you hear that?"

"You said it to Jill on the phone! You also said that his lips were like two juicy strawberry Starbursts!"

"Owen, I swear to God—"

"I'm gonna get his yearbook picture!" He ran out of the kitchen.

After pausing to collect herself, Poppy took a seat at the table. "I can't believe you made all these," she said to Dud. "Where did you learn to sculpt like that?"

"I dunno. It's easy."

"Maybe for you, but this doesn't come naturally to most people. Not that you're most people. Or could even be considered 'people.'"

"I'm people! *I can walk from here to there, I can walk most anywhere!*"

"Right. Of course." She rubbed her eyes. "Um, listen, Dud, I'm flattered that you did this for me, but—"

"This stuff smells good," Dud said, cramming a wad of wax up his nose as he took a big whiff.

Poppy stared at him.

Dud stared back at her.

Then he shot the wax bullet out of his nose and across the table, knocking over little wax Mrs. Goodwin.

The moment, clearly, had passed.

"Okay, Dud," her mother crowed as everyone returned to the kitchen. "Gather up those little masterpieces and give us a big smile. Owen, Poppy, you get in there too. Not *that* close, Poppy."

"I *wasn't*—"

"Smile!"

The photo captured Owen grinning, Dud waving, and Poppy looking at her phone, which had beeped. "Poppy, put the phone away," said her mother. "Now I have to take another one—"

"Sorry." Poppy pulled up the Channel Six YouNews app and fled the kitchen for her room before they could object. "The press conference just started."

And then ended, only thirty seconds later.

"Thank you all for coming out," Big Bob said into the bouquet of microphones. Miss Bea stood behind him, the flower in her hat looking limp. "The Grosholtz Candle Factory is Paraffin's greatest treasure, and its citizens are understandably concerned about the cause of the fire that ravaged its walls last night. Today we have some answers: in light of new information given to us by Anita and Preston Chandler, we are officially closing the investigation. It seems that demolition work had been scheduled for the older sections of the factory that were no longer in use, and some hectic rescheduling, combined with poor communication, resulted in an electrical mishap that led to the fire. Precautions have been taken to ensure that this will not happen again, and the Chandlers wish to thank their beloved community for its concern and support. Thank you."

Poppy stared at the screen. Then dialed Jill.

"Not buying it!" Poppy shouted when Jill picked up. "The older section of the factory was most definitely in use—that's where Madame Grosholtz was!"

Jill sounded exquisitely bored. "Why would they lie about that?"

"Because they're trying to cover something up! Trust me—something is up with the Chandlers and the Bursaws. I think they're in cahoots!"

"Cahoots, Poppy? They're in cahoots?"

"Yes. Even Blake is suspicious. *Blake Bursaw*. Isn't that a hint that something weird is going on?"

"It's a hint that the authorities know better than you," said Jill. "To be honest, the weirdest thing about this situation is that in the midst of it, you struck up a friendship with your mortalest enemy."

"God, Jill, it's not a friendship—"

"It's bizarre. And bad. And will come back to bite you in the ass, mark my words. I can't believe that after all that dickwad has put you through, you're taking his side."

"I'm not!"

"Do you even need my help anymore? Why bother calling me?"

Poppy pulled the phone away from her face and let out a frustrated sigh. She hated when Jill got like this. It was all part of those stage manager tendencies of hers—a place for everything and everything in its place—that didn't always work out so well in reality. And definitely not in this bizarre wrinkle of unreality into which Poppy had fallen.

"Hello?" Jill was saying. "Where'd you go?"

"Listen, I'll—see you tomorrow. Maybe this'll make more sense then."

"Okay. Later."

"Later."

Poppy ended the call and stared at the phone, feeling gross.

Arguing with Jill was never any fun. It happened often enough, given that they were both strong-headed control freaks who always thought they were right. It was what had drawn them together. But this time it seemed a little bit worse. Like something fundamental was breaking down between them.

A quiet knock came at the door. "Poppy?" Dud stuck his head in. "Are you okay? What did the press conference say?"

She looked up at him. "I think I'm off the hook."

"What hook?" Dud asked, coming into the room.

"For the fire. They don't think it was arson anymore. Unless . . . unless that's what they want me to think. Maybe they're spreading false information in the hopes that I'll let my guard down."

"Hmm." Dud nodded, as if he had the first clue what she was talking about. "What does the candle say?"

"The candle?" She smacked her head. "Oh my God, the *candle!* I forgot all about it!" She lunged for the heavy white stone, but urgent footsteps were thumping down the hall. "What's going on in here?" her father asked, barging in.

Poppy hid the candle behind her back with an impatient grunt. "What do you want?"

Both of her parents crowded into the doorway, visibly relieved at the lack of bedroom shenanigans. "You two ready for the big *Dr. Steve* marathon?" her father asked. "Starts in an hour!"

"We no longer own a television," Poppy said.

"It's streaming online!" he said, elated.

"It starts at five? Isn't that a little early?"

"Not if you want to cram in eight hours! Word on the street

is that he's got some real damning evidence against elbow maca-roni—"

"Fine. Can you leave, please?"

Her parents exchanged glances.

"Dud," said her mother, "why don't you go find Owen? It's time for his afternoon snack."

"Okay!"

As Dud raced out of the room, Poppy's father sidled in. "What's that behind your back?"

"Nothing." She held it up, blasé, as if it were nothing. "Just a candle."

He squinted at the tiny lettering, which Poppy was thankful he could not read without his glasses. "Ah," he said after a moment, smiling. "I get it."

"Get what?"

He turned to his wife. "I heard about this. Supposedly you can put a secret message into one of those make-your-own-candles from the factory. I bet it's a love letter."

Poppy's mother cooed while Poppy wondered if it was possible to break all ties with her family and start a new life in the creepy candle dungeon. "It's not a love letter, you guys."

"Then what is it?" her mother asked teasingly.

Poppy considered her options. She couldn't tell them it was a message from a somewhat-dead-somewhat-alive art legend. She couldn't tell them that Dud wasn't capable of understanding the concept of nipples, much less love. She couldn't tell them *anything*.

Poppy fixed a defeated scowl on her face. "It's a love letter."

"I knew it!" Her father grabbed the stone candle and held it over his head, out of her reach. "Oof, heavy! Can I reeead it?"

"No!" Poppy jumped up and tried to grab it from him, noticing as he held it aloft that the factory logo was stamped on the bottom along with the factory's motto: *One fire, many flames.* "Give it to me!"

He laughed again and relented, carefully handing her the candle. "But seriously, Popsicle, keep it friendly between you two. Dud's a nice kid. I don't want to have to end his life."

"*Noted.*"

She shoved them both out into the hallway. "Remember Dr. Steve!" her father reminded her. "Come hell or high water, you said!"

She closed the door on them, then whirled around and leaned her back against it. "I would take both hell *and* high water over the problems I've got right now."

There was a polite knock.

"Your dad said I should come give you a firm handshake and nothing more," Dud told her when she opened the door. "I don't know what that means."

"Just get in here."

Dud sat down on the bed next to Poppy as she grabbed her magnifying glass and read Madame Grosholtz's newly revealed writing.

BUT PEOPLE IN THE SMALL VILLAGE WHERE I'D FLED BEGAN TO TALK, OF COURSE. ABOUT THE RECLUSIVE OLD LADY

WHO MADE SUCH LIFELIKE WAX SCULPTURES. WORD GOT AROUND. AND BEFORE LONG, IT FELL INTO THE EARS OF THE WRONG PEOPLE. THE WORST PEOPLE: ACTORS.

"I take offense to that," said Poppy.

IF YOU TAKE OFFENSE TO THIS, I APOLOGIZE. BUT IT WAS ACTORS WHO SPELLED MY RUIN, AND SO I AM NO LONGER CHARITABLE TOWARD THESPIAN FOLK. THE PAIR OF TRAVELING THEATRICALS WHO CAME TO SEE ME WERE INTERESTED IN USING SOME OF MY SCULPTURES IN THEIR PERFORMANCES, LIKE PUPPETS. YET THEY CHANGED THEIR TUNE ONCE THEY SAW WHAT I COULD DO.

I ALWAYS KEPT MY MOST PRIVATE WORK HIDDEN AWAY, BUT I WAS NOT AS GOOD A LIAR AS MY VISITORS WERE, AND THEY SOON FIGURED OUT WHAT I WAS UP TO, WHAT I HAD BEEN DOING TO KEEP MYSELF ALIVE. AFTER THAT, THEY FORGOT ALL ABOUT THEIR FOOLISH PUPPETS. WHAT THEY SAW INSTEAD WAS POTENTIAL. SOMEONE WHO COULD SCULPT REPLICAS OF THEM SO THAT THEY COULD NEVER DIE. OR AGE.

WHY DID I GO ALONG WITH IT? IN TRUTH, I WAS LONELY. AFTER YEARS OF SOLITUDE — MORE THAN ANY HUMAN SHOULD HAVE ENDURED — HERE WERE FRIENDS AGAIN. I'D SCULPT HOLLOW AFTER HOLLOW, AND THE CHANDLERS

**WOULD DO ALL SORTS OF THINGS WITH THEIR DISPOS-
ABLE BODIES — THROW THEMSELVES OFF BRIDGES, SWIM
OUT INTO THE MIDDLE OF THE OCEAN, CLIMB TREACHER-
OUS MOUNTAINS. AND IF THEY FELL AND GOT IMPALED
ON A ROCK — WHAT OF IT? I WOULD SIMPLY REINCAR-
NATE THEM FROM THEIR FLAME-SOULS, LIGHTING THEIR
FRESHLY SCULPTED HOLLOWS BACK IN MY STUDIO. WE
WERE IMMORTAL. WE WERE UNSTOPPABLE.**

OF COURSE

Even if the wax had burned down farther than that, Poppy
wouldn't have been able to read it — her hands were shaking too
hard. She placed the candle on her nightstand and put her head into
her hands. "The Chandlers," she whispered. "The Hollow Ones . . ."

"Poppy?" Dud placed a worried hand on her back. "Are you
okay?"

"No. Nope. The Chandlers —" She swallowed. "The Chandlers
are made of wax. The Chandlers are well over a hundred years old."

"Is that bad?"

"It's —"

Poppy sputtered. It wasn't *inherently* bad. Madame Grosholtz
did the same thing, and she seemed decent enough. Most people, if
given the opportunity to become immortal, would take it, as long as
it didn't hurt anyone in the process.

But the Chandlers seemed so . . . sinister. They were up to
something in that candle dungeon of theirs. Sure, maybe it was a

shrine to all the years that they'd cheated death — but if they'd been existing as nothing but wax Hollows for decades, then what was up with those bloodstains? If it wasn't their blood, whose was it?

"Is it bad?" Poppy repeated. "I don't know. But it's not good."

Her first instinct was to call Jill — but when she picked up her cell phone, her finger paused over the screen. Jill had already made her feelings on this subject known.

Crinkling her nose in disgust, she scrolled through her contacts until she found BLAKE BURSAW.

It rang six times before he picked up. "Hogwash? Didn't think you could dial with those hooves of yours."

"I just made a series of groundbreaking discoveries, Bursaw. Do you want to hear them, or do you want to keep acting like a douche?"

"Can't I do both?"

"I'm hanging up."

"Okay, okay — sorry. Go ahead."

Poppy took a deep breath. "The Chandlers —"

"Gram?" A moment of muffled speech — it sounded like he was talking to Miss Bea. "Sorry. My grandma's being . . . can I call you back in a second? I'm gonna go somewhere private."

Poppy decided that it would be prudent to sort the ground-breaking discoveries in order of importance by the time he called back. They started to run together in her head, and new insights kept popping up — *no wonder the fire was a hologram; it was just to keep up appearances, since a real fire would be the last thing wax beings would want in their proximity* — so she reached into her bag to tear some paper out of The List.

Which wasn't there.

Poppy made a noise not unlike that of a dying whale.

"What's wrong?" Dud asked.

"The List," she croaked, frantically digging into each section of her bag. A queasy feeling of helplessness bobbed around her midsection. "It's not here."

She tore the sheets off her bed, but it wasn't there, either. She must have left it somewhere. School? No. It was in her trunk yesterday. Was it still in the trunk? Or was it . . .

"Oh, no." Her stomach lurched. "Oh, *shit*."

Her phone rang. She answered it with, "I left my notebook in the cavern!"

"So?" said Blake.

Whether the arson investigation had been called off or not, it would be very bad for someone to find her notebook directly beneath the crime scene, giant block letters screaming IF FOUND, RETURN TO POPPY PALLADINO, along with her phone number and address. "So . . . what if they find it?"

"Is this what you called about, Hogwash? Your stupid notebook?"

"Of course not —"

"Then get to the point."

"Fine." Poppy took a deep breath. "Have you ever heard of Madame Tussaud?"

Blake let out a disgusted sigh. "You know what? We're done here. I'm just gonna ask my dad what's going on. He appreciates direct questions. He'll tell me."

Poppy flashed back to the horrible things Madame Grosholtz had said in her message. "No! Blake, listen to me: do not confront them. I think they're mixed up in something really bad — actually, I think we all are —"

"Thanks for your concern, but I think I can handle it. I'll call you afterward, if it'll make you feel any better."

"No, you don't understand! The Chandlers are not who they say they are!"

He hung up.

And though Poppy stared at her phone all through dinner and all through the *Dr. Steve* marathon, and stayed up half the night waiting, he never did call back.

13

~~Try to Monday~~

THE NEXT MORNING, POPPY WAS IN HER CAR AND OFF TO school before her parents came down for breakfast.

"And the worst part," she shouted into the phone at Jill as she drove, "is that the candle won't stay lit! There's more message in there — I *know* there is — but when the *Dr. Steve* marathon finished and I went to check it, the flame was out and it hadn't burned at all! Then I lit it before going to sleep, but when I woke up later during the night — same thing!"

"I'm more concerned," Jill said over the phone, "with your delusion that the Chandlers are evil wax mannequins."

"It's not a delusion — *hey!*" Poppy blared her horn at a car that had cut her off. Or perhaps the car that she'd cut off. "Jill, I've lost the capacity to multitask. I'll explain everything when I see you." She ended the call and focused on the road, hands at ten and two.

"Where are we going?" Dud asked. His yellow sneakers were tapping against the floor of the car, his eyes bouncing around, taking in the sights of the town as they drove past.

"School!" Poppy burst out, irritated. "Can you believe that amid arson and subterranean mountain lairs and the emergence into my life of not one but four sentient beings made of wax, I still have to go to school and take a *gym quiz?*"

"What's a gym quiz?"

"Good question, Dud! A gym quiz is a thing that should not be. Because the height of a basketball hoop is a piece of knowledge that will NEVER ASSIST ME IN MY DAILY LIFE."

"You seem tense."

"As if gym isn't demoralizing enough on its own. Now we need to bring paperwork into this? And the result of this farce will have a bearing on my GPA?"

"What's a GPA?"

"Oh, only the number that will determine my future. Add to that the fun little challenge of getting to school early and explaining to the administration who *you* are and why you need to be enrolled in classes and oh, by the way, if my parents ask, just tell them he's from the incredibly specific 'island near Africa.'"

"I thought it wasn't really that close to Africa."

"It's not!"

Dud put a hand on her shoulder. "Do you need to talk through your feelings?"

Poppy glanced sideways at him. *Did he pick that up from eight hours of Dr. Steve?* "Yes, I do. Let me talk through my feelings. I *feel* like I'm trying to put a jigsaw puzzle together, but half of the pieces are from Teddy Bear Picnic, and the other half are from Kittens Frolicking in Baskets of Yarn, with a few random pieces of Majestic

Bald Eagle Flying Over American Flag thrown in for good measure, and all of them are singed black and mutated from fire damage and smell like Ocean Breezes and broken dreams!"

Dud shook his head. "Too many feelings."

One of them being disappointment; Poppy had hoped that the stone candle's overnight revelations would contain more pertinent information about the Chandlers, but they weren't juicy enough:

OF COURSE, THINGS ALWAYS TURN SOUR. THE CHANDLERS HAD LONG AGO ABANDONED THEIR REAL, NON-WAX BODIES — ONCE THEY SAW WHAT I COULD DO, THEY DID NOT THINK TWICE ABOUT DISROBING THEIR MORTAL TRAPPINGS. ONLY LATER DID THE HARSH REALITY OF WHAT THEY'D DONE SET IN — THE REALIZATION THAT THEY WOULD HAVE TO KEEP REPLACING THEIR WAX BODIES, OVER AND OVER. AND THAT WITHOUT ME THERE TO SCULPT THEM, THEY WERE DOOMED. SO THEY KEPT ME CAPTIVE FOR A WHILE — THEM LIVING THE LIFE, ME TOILING AWAY AS THEIR PRISONER. AND EVENTUALLY THEY GOT GREEDY. THEY WANTED MORE. THEY WANTED TO

"They wanted to what?" she'd shouted at it. "Tell me!"

But the candle did not accommodate her request. And though she dearly wanted to bring it to school and give it a nice cushy spot in her locker and check it obsessively between classes, she just couldn't risk removing it from the safety of her house.

"I heard her again, when I smelled the candle this morning," Dud said quietly.

"Who?" Poppy asked. "Madame Grosholtz?"

He nodded. "In my head."

"What does she say to you?"

"Oh, she doesn't talk to me. She talks to . . . herself, maybe? It's sort of like when you get excited about something and you walk back and forth around your room and talk fast and move your hands around a lot."

"Um," Poppy said, tucking a piece of hair behind her ear, "just so you know, thinking out loud is something a lot of creative people do. It doesn't make them, like, nuts or anything. In fact, it makes them —"

"Can I get more candles?" He pointed at the factory as they rounded the bend of the lake. "To sculpt more things?"

"No."

"Why not?"

Poppy was about to launch into an exhaustive explanation of exactly why not — when she got an idea.

"Because," she said, "I'm going to do you one better."

*　*　*

"Ready?" Poppy asked, straining to carry the dented *Annie* orphans' buckets through the narrow door.

Dud bounced excitedly on the balls of his feet, causing the multitude of props and costumes stacked up in the slop room to sway perilously. "For what?"

She dropped the buckets at his feet. Inside were grayish, disgusting blobs of what appeared to be industrial byproduct. "Here you go."

Dud's eyes almost fell out of his head. "What is it?"

"It's wax!"

His nose scrunched up as he poked at it. "Doesn't look like wax."

"That's because it hasn't been dyed and scented and raped of its original beauty by a soulless corporation." She left out the part about the soulless corporation selflessly donating it to a school that lacked an arts budget. It would have ruined the spirit of her indignation. "Go ahead, try it."

Dud broke off a chunk of the wax and immediately formed it into a squirrel.

"Wow," said Poppy, ever amazed by his speed. "Guess you've already got the hang of it."

Dud let out a whoop and straightaway began chipping more wax out of the bucket, his supplier all but forgotten.

Poppy glanced around the slop room. As it was an offshoot of the Gaudy Auditorium, odds were that no one would come within a hundred feet of it during the school day. Still . . . "Dud, promise me something. Dud. Look at me."

He paused mid-bucket to look up at her. "Hmm?"

"You can stay here all day long and sculpt, as long as you don't leave this room, okay? That way no one will bother you, and you won't bother anyone else. I know they're not ideal conditions, but there's a sink, and some tools, paint, and costumes — and wigs, if you dig around in some of the boxes. And if you need more wax, just hang tight — I'll come back and check on you in a couple of hours. Got all that? Can you promise me you won't leave?"

"What's a promise?"

"It's when you have to do what you say you'll do. Or I'll be sad. And mad."

"Okay," he said, his eyes on the wax. "Promise."

Poppy watched him, unsure. She didn't feel a hundred percent about this, but it had to be better than trying to enroll him. Prospective students tended to be required to prove citizenship, and to have a Social Security number. And a pulse. "Well . . . okay. I'll be back at lunch."

Dud was already busying himself with dumping the gray blobs out of the buckets. "Sounds good!"

Poppy bit her lip as she left the slop room, closing the door behind her. "Does it?"

*   *   *

Paraffin High buzzed feverishly with the events that had transpired at the factory over the weekend. The fire — and who, if anyone, had set it — was all anyone could talk about.

Every class Poppy attended that day used it as a starting point around which to build a lesson. In math, they determined that it had to be arson, using calculations for wind speed and direction. In English, they explored what the act of setting a fire says about the human condition. Mr. Shale, the history teacher who should have retired decades ago, got a little carried away with his Cold

War metaphor and declared that the fire was all the doing of the Soviets.

"In art we were told to sketch how the fire made us *feel*," Jill told Poppy when they met up at her locker for lunch. "I asked if I could drink a gallon of paint instead, but was told that performance art didn't count."

"To be fair, performance art never counts for anything."

Poppy glanced around the hall. She'd kept an eye out for Blake all morning, but she hadn't seen him. Hadn't heard him. Hadn't discovered anything viscous planted in her locker. If she didn't hate his guts so much, she might even have been worried—

"Poppy?"

She whipped around to find Mr. Crawford smiling at her, that adorable dimple sinking so deeply into his chin that a family of bears could crawl in and hibernate there for the winter.

"Bear," Poppy said.

"What?"

"I mean—hi, Mr. Crawford. What's up?"

He scratched his head, looking harried. "I was wondering if you could help me out with something."

"Yes. Anything."

If he noticed her abject desperation, he classily didn't let on. "You know how the Paraffin High Marching Band is supposed to be performing at the bicentennial parade tomorrow?"

Poppy suppressed a scowl. "I am acutely aware of that."

"Well, Principal Lincoln just got a call from the band teacher, and, um—you're not going to believe this." He let out a pained laugh. "They're stuck in Madrid! Another Icelandic volcano erupted and they grounded all flights in and out of Europe."

"Are you kidding me?"

"So now we're scrambling. The mayor's office still wants a performance from the youth of the town, and . . ." He ran a hand through his well-conditioned hair. "Do you think the Giddy Committee could perform in the parade? Just a musical number or two — and it doesn't have to be polished, just something to —"

"*Yes.* Oh my God, yes!" she shouted, prompting some of the students streaming down the hall past them to raise their eyebrows. "Absolutely. We'd be happy to. *I'd* be happy to. Whatever you want. Whatever you need."

His eyes lit up. Sparkled. *Twinkled.* "Really? Oh, man, thank you, Poppy. Think you can rally the troops for a rehearsal today?"

She nodded so hard, her neck cracked. "We were rehearsing anyway for our Broadway revue that's coming up in a couple of weeks, so I can just refocus our rehearsal today for the parade tomorrow, because I'm the director, so I can. We can." She fixed a goofy grin on her face and pumped her fist into the air. "Yes, we can!"

Now he was looking a little weirded out. "Okay. Great. Call time is at eight forty-five a.m. tomorrow in the parking lot behind the Price Chopper. I'll be around, but let me know if you have any questions before then." He gave her a little wave and allowed himself to be swept up by the hallway rush. "See you in biology!"

"Wait!" Poppy called after him anyway. "Do you want to, like, give me your phone number, or —"

"Nah, email's good. Thanks again!"

Poppy slunk back to Jill, who was judging harshly. "I want you to know what you look like right now," said Jill, "which is one of those skeletons you see in a haunted house, with your mouth wide open and giant gaping holes where your eyes should be and the sort of vacant silent scream reserved only for the damned."

Poppy gathered up her textbooks and what was left of her dignity. "Let us dine."

When they got to the cafeteria, Poppy, envying the ordinary day her fellow students were having, unpacked the grapes and neatly compartmentalized cubes of tofu her mother had prepared.

"So back to the Chandlers," Jill said, joylessly chewing her turkey sandwich. "You're saying that they're Hollow Ones?"

"Yes." Poppy took out her phone and showed Jill some pictures she'd taken that morning of the candle message: *They did not think twice about disrobing their mortal trappings.*

"But what about Dud? Did he disrobe his mortal trappings too?"

"You know, I've been thinking about that." Poppy selected three grapes to demonstrate. "Madame Grosholtz, Anita, and Preston all came from their original, nineteenth-century selves. They've been reincarnating wax versions of themselves for decades." She then removed a single tofu cube and put it by itself. "But Dud is different. It's almost like Madame Grosholtz made him from scratch. Like his personality is new, not carried over from anyone else. Like she made him out of thin air. I don't know how, of course, but I'm pretty sure he's different from the other three. The tofu stands alone."

"The tofu . . . stands alone."

"Yes. Exactly."

Jill seemed to have no idea how to respond to that. "What's with the phone?" she asked instead. "Don't you usually scribble your manic digressions in The List?"

"I have temporarily misplaced The List," Poppy said irritably. "But — trust me, it's all right there in the candle."

"I see. And where might this candle be?"

"I left it at home. I can't run the risk of it getting lost, or broken — or stolen."

"Good Lord, Poppy. Paranoid much?"

"It's not paranoia if they're really after your secret-candle-message-hidden-by-a-dead-woman, *Jill*."

Jill rubbed her temples. "Permission to change the subject?"

"Permission granted."

"What's new with Wax Boy? Or — sorry, the Tofu Who Stands Alone."

"Oh, he sculpted the town out of candles."

"Um, what?"

Poppy filled Jill in on what had happened after they'd parted on Sunday. "It's like part of Madame Grosholtz is ingrained in him or something. Programmed."

"How did the sculpture of me look?" Jill asked.

"Pretty dead-on."

"Can I have it?"

"What? No —"

"I'll give you ten bucks for it. Hey, look at that — you might have a pretty lucrative business opportunity here. Open up a little shop, sell the townspeople tiny versions of themselves. Or of other people, that they can then squash. Like voodoo dolls. Voodoo squash dolls. Doubles as a great band name, too."

"Are you making fun of me?"

"I am."

"This is serious, Jill!" Poppy whisper-shouted. "The Chandlers are up to something! Just because I don't know what it is yet doesn't mean it's not happening!" She angrily pushed her lunchbox away.

"Done with your food?"

"Yes. Your rudeness and skepticism have made me lose my appetite."

"Poppy." Jill flashed her a knowing smirk. "Come on."

Poppy grumbled and downed the rest of her tofu in one bite. "Seriously, who are these bizarre people on TV shows who lose their appetite when they get stressed? I could eat an entire lasagna right here, right now, no utensils, just my face, splat." She put her head on the table to demonstrate.

Jill patiently chewed her sandwich and looked out the window. "So where's Dud now?"

Poppy spoke into the laminate. "He wanted to keep sculpting, so I grabbed some of the surplus wax from the art supply and set him up in the slop room."

"Are you sure that's where he is?"

"Yeah."

"Are you sure he's not outside the window, flattening the landscaping with a giant wax version of Mr. Crawford?"

Poppy slowly raised her head.

14

Flee the cafeteria

"DUD! WHAT ARE YOU DOING?"

"Hi, Poppy!" Dud waved Mr. Crawford's wax arm at her.

She dragged him off the front lawn of the school while Dud dragged the wax Mr. Crawford, forming a motley chain of fools that was ultimately wrangled into the groundskeeper's maintenance shed. "I *told* you to stay in the slop room," Poppy said as evenly as she could, not wanting to spook him but finding it hard not to among all the hanging pitchforks and shovels. "You *promised* you'd stay."

A look of genuine remorse washed over his face. "I'm sorry, Poppy. But I thought maybe you'd want to show it to Mr. Crawford because you like him so much!"

"That's sweet of you, but —"

"Maybe if he likes it, he'll *marry* you."

"No. That is not how that works. Teachers don't marry students. And even if they did, he has a wife and two children, and if I haven't

186

figured out a way to get them out of the picture by now, it's probably never going to happen —"

"Poppy Jubilation Palladino." Jill's muffled voice came from outside the shed. She heaved the door open and wedged herself between Poppy and Dud. "You're still weighing your prospects with Crawford? I thought we definitely ruled against that last year. We made a chart and everything."

"He forgot to wear his wedding band last Tuesday," Poppy shot back defensively. "He said he dropped it into the garbage disposal, but wouldn't a man who *really* loved his wife plunge his hand in there to retrieve it?"

Jill turned to Dud. "Your guardian has mentally left the building, so I guess it falls to me to tell you that you have to scram. Your kind isn't allowed here."

Poppy rolled her eyes. "You don't have to be racist about it."

"Against . . . a race of sentient wax beings?"

"Racism is still racism. She didn't mean it, Dud."

Dud grinned cluelessly. "What's a race?"

"A contest to see who's fastest," Jill said.

"What's a contest?"

"A quiz for people in jail."

"Jill, I swear to God . . ."

But Poppy trailed off as she stared at Wax Crawford. It was uncanny. The contours in his face, the easy smile. The paint matched his skin tone. And although he was dressed in a pair of *Oklahoma* overalls and the wig wasn't quite right and his eyeballs weren't made of the more realistic-looking glass ones Madame Grosholtz had had access to, the rest was immaculate.

Poppy sighed. "Can you find your way back to the slop room," she asked Dud, "or do you need me to take you?"

"I can walk from here to there —"

"Smashing. Go. Just don't let anyone see you."

He snuck out of the shed and tiptoed around the back of the school, making sure to stay out of the line of sight of any windows. Only when he was safely through the door to the auditorium did Poppy exhale.

"What do we do with this guy?" Jill asked, linking her arm through Wax Crawford's.

"Beats me. I guess I'll stick him in my trunk and figure out what to do with him later."

"Thereby fulfilling your ultimate fantasy."

"Shut up. Yes. But shut up." Poppy stuck her head out once more to make sure no one was watching. "Stay here and guard him while I pull Clementine around."

"Permission to make out with him while you're gone?"

"Permission denied."

*   *   *

Poppy wrangled Wax Crawford into the car without much ado, without the painful awareness of how open and exposed she was, how high the potential for embarrassment. In a former life — like, three days ago — she might have been terrified of getting mocked by Blake Bursaw, but now she was so focused on the task at hand that she didn't care.

Besides, Blake wasn't anywhere to be found. She still hadn't seen him.

And for the first time ever, she realized she wanted to.

She paused at the school entrance and looked back at the parking lot. Blake's car was not in it.

Maybe he's sick, she thought as she walked back to class. *Maybe he's . . .*

But she couldn't think of any other reason why Blake wouldn't be there. He'd told her he'd see her at school. He'd said he would call her back. Neither of those things had happened.

Something clenched in Poppy's chest. And then something else clenched harder at the thought that Blake Bursaw's well-being was something clenchable.

This distraction followed her all the way into biology, a class where she was typically distracted enough by the Greek god at the front of the room. Today, though, her thoughts drifted not to the noble pursuit of mentally undressing her teacher, but to the mysteries surrounding the candle factory.

Madame Grosholtz/Tussaud was made of wax, she jotted down in her notebook. *And so are the Chandlers. But what does any of this have to do with Big Bob and Miss Bea?*

She paused, her pen hovering above her notebook. She was supposed to be taking notes on how viruses replicate, but so far all she'd done was sketch out some blobby circles, turn those blobby circles into the dreamy blue eyes of Mr. Crawford, scribble it all out, and go back to thinking about the message in the candle.

Madame Grosholtz said that souls can be put into the forms of flames.

One fire, many flames.

One fire, many flames.

"Poppy?"

She looked up. Mr. Crawford was staring down at her, worried. "Are you having an asthma attack?"

"What?"

"You're breathing heavily. Are you all right?"

Poppy forced herself to exhale and regain a normalish composure. She looked around the empty classroom. Class had ended, and she hadn't noticed or heard the bell. "I'm fine. Just . . . got so wrapped up in the magic of horrific diseases. And — and —" There had to be a better way out of this. "And guess what? My parents said yes to hosting an exchange student!"

"Really? That's wonderful!" His grin lit up the room. "Of course, there are still a multitude of steps between saying yes and finally receiving a student." *Oh?* Poppy thought as he hurried to his desk and pulled out a thick folder. *You mean they don't come pre-stuffed into your trunk?* "Here's the informational packet," he said, handing her the folder. "The exchange agreement is in there, along with some FAQs, expected responsibilities of the host family, all that fun stuff. Once that's taken care of, we can begin the process of getting you matched with a student."

She took it from him. "Great."

He cocked his head. "You sure you're okay, Poppy? You look kind of pale. Listen, if this bicentennial parade thing is stressing you out too much —"

"No, no! I'm happy to do it. Thrilled. *Ecstatic.*"

"You seem a little . . . on edge."

"Nope! Just trying to figure out which songs we should sing in the parade. I've narrowed it down to either 'Circle of Life' or 'Hakuna Matata,' but I'm not sure how fast Serengeti Jetty can ship out their animal costumes on such short notice."

"Er —"

"Now, I *did* find a nice gazelle online, but I'd rather save the money for another set of giraffe stilts." If anything was worth blowing her own personal Giddy Committee budget on, it was this. "I've been meaning to ask you — how many wildebeests do you want? Five?"

Mr. Crawford frowned.

Poppy made a note. "I'll get ten to be safe."

He rubbed his chin with a wedding-banded hand that Poppy tried to ignore. "Poppy —"

"Oh, and don't worry, *our* zebras won't be made out of pajamas from Sears." She snickered. "Nice try, Burlington High. Amateurs."

"Actually, I don't think we're going to need anything that extravagant."

Poppy blinked at him. "Oh?"

"I mean, I have no doubt that you could pull off a veritable

191

Broadway production if you wanted to—and I'm sure that's what we'll see at the revue in a couple of weeks." He smiled. Poppy caught a whiff of his patented flowery-sciencey smell. "But for the parade tomorrow," he continued, "I think the people of Paraffin are going to want something light and happy and simple. Something familiar. Something the old folks can sing along to."

Poppy gripped the edges of her desk.

Her voice quivered as she asked, "Like what?"

* * *

The Giddy Committee looked into the third row, fifth seat from the aisle, at their fearless leader, who sat not with her pen poised and her bullhorn raised, but rather slumped in her seat, staring straight ahead.

"What's wrong with her?" Connor boomed, swishing his cape.

Jill hurriedly stepped in to block Poppy's catatonic form. "Everything is fine," she told the group. "There's been a slight change of plans. We've been asked to perform at the bicentennial parade tomorrow—" A delighted cheer went up among the committee, but Jill cut it short. "Which *means* that today's rehearsal will be spent practicing for that. We'll resume the revue rehearsals again on Wednesday."

"What are we performing for the parade?" asked Banks.

Jill glanced back at Poppy, who had turned an unsightly shade of green. "Well," Jill said, addressing the club once more, "we'll be doing a medley from, uh, *The Sound of Music*."

Poppy let out a whimper.

"Get up on the stage and wait in the wings," Jill instructed them, "where you will receive further instructions once our fearless leader decides to *sack up.*"

"Why?" Poppy moaned as Jill sank down into the spring-loaded seat next to her. "Why me?"

"You need to snap out of it," Jill said, snapping her fingers in front of Poppy's face. "I realize that literally nothing is worse than this. Not living wax figures, not interacting with Blake Bursaw, not eight straight hours of *Dr. Steve.* But you said you would do it, so you have to do it. You don't want to let Mr. Crawford down, do you?"

"How could he do this to me, Jill? I used to be one hundred percent positive that he and I were soul mates. Now I'm starting to think it's more like ninety-five percent."

Jill curled her hands into fists. "It's a crowd favorite," she said patiently. "Despite your understandable misgivings, everyone else loves it. It's family-friendly. People know the words. We live not fifty miles away from the von Trapp family lodge. It's practically our official state musical."

"Oh, big surprise, you taking Vermonty's side."

"*Poppy.*"

Poppy let out a loud, exasperated grunt and sat up in her seat. "Fine. Tell them to take their places for the *Oklahoma* number. We'll use the same choreography and just switch the songs around or some bullshit."

"That's the spirit."

Irritated, Poppy sank down again while Jill got up to relay the instructions to the actors. They glanced over at her, pity radiating from their eyes like a laser show.

Doubly irritated, Poppy habitually reached into her bag, then remembered that The List was still missing.

Triply irritated, she grabbed her biology notebook instead, trying to suppress the full-body cringe that came with the idea of mixing class notes with show notes. Still, she uncapped her pen and poised it on the page, ready to give this Austrian abomination her full attention, if only to please Mr. Crawford.

She started barking orders at the stage. "Louder, Banks! I can see you, Connor!"

Connor's flushed, sweating head poked up out of the trapdoor in the center of the stage. "I can't help it! It is literally a furnace down here!"

"Now, now, Connor — is that what a von Trapp would say?"

But before long, her directives began to deteriorate in both politeness and lucidity. "Be more Austrian, Jesus! Louisa, spread out your fingers! Put a little more jazz in that jazz hand!"

Louisa put her jazzless hand on her jazzless hip. "I don't see how a family in peril at the brink of World War Two warrants jazz of any sort."

"Well, I don't see what any of this has to do with Paraffin's bicentennial, either, but life doesn't really make a crapload of sense, does it?"

"Okay, that's it." Jill marched down the aisle, clutched a handful of Poppy's sweater, and yanked her up out of the seat. "I'm cutting you off. Go cool down. Take a walk. Get your toxic attitude out of here so we can get something accomplished."

"*I'm* the one with the toxic attitude? Says *Jill?*"

"Yes, you are. Now go."

"This is a mutiny," Poppy called back to the Giddy Committee as Jill escorted her out of the theater. "You're all mutineers, just like Captain von Trapp! Admiral von Schreiber would be *pissed!*"

*   *   *

"Admiral von Schreiber *would* be pissed," Poppy grumbled to herself as she pushed open the door to the restroom. She turned on the tap, closed her eyes, splashed water on her face, and let loose her thoughts.

First they wandered to the various ways she would like to torture Mr. Rodgers and Mr. Hammerstein.

Then they wandered to Dud. She'd gotten so upset after biology that she'd forgotten to check on him on the way to rehearsal.

Then they wandered to Blake. Where *was* he?

Had Big Bob and Miss Bea done something to him? It seemed unfeasible, but if the Chandlers had done something to *them* . . . because the Chandlers were made of wax and had special waxy magic powers . . .

Poppy snorted at herself. The never-ending voice in her head sounded ridiculous, and this was coming from a girl whose internal monologue regularly included lyrics from *Mamma Mia!* She turned off the water, dried her face with a paper towel, and headed for the slop room.

"Dud?" she said, knocking as she opened the door. "It's just me . . ."

A finger beckoned her forward. It had a nail, a cuticle, and even the trace of a fingerprint. It was attached to a perfectly sculpted hand, which was attached to a perfectly sculpted arm.

Poppy took a few more steps in. "Oh my God. *Dud.*"

That's what she was looking at. A perfect replica of Dud.

It was impeccable. Not an odd angle, not a wrong proportion, not a hair out of place. He'd found the right wig, the right clothes, the right everything. It actually took Poppy a moment, as they stood there together, to figure out which was the real Dud.

Well, the slightly more real Dud.

"What do you think?" he asked with a small, nervous smile.

She shook her head in disbelief. "Stunning. Your work is flawless. It's . . ."

Better than Madame Grosholtz's.

"Nah." Dud waved her off, but looked pleased. "It's easy."

"I'm serious, Dud. This is good on a level that I didn't know existed. You could sell these for thousands of dollars!"

He was unimpressed. "It's just for fun."

"Except that . . ." The joy dissolved. "I don't want anyone to see this. I mean — I *do* want people to see this. It should be in a fancy art gallery in Brooklyn or something. But here . . ." She bit her lip and tried not to imagine what was lurking up at the factory. "I want to make sure it stays safe."

And so for the second time that day, Poppy found herself loading a wax body into her car.

As she slid Wax Dud II into the back seat (as Wax Crawford already occupied the trunk), it occurred to Poppy that she was more or less reenacting what Madame Grosholtz had done right after they'd parted ways. What was running through that woman's head in those last moments? What had she tried to warn Poppy about? Just the Chandlers, or something more?

Poppy covered the sculpture with the big green blanket she kept in the car for impromptu picnics, then slammed the door and sighed.

"What's wrong?" asked Dud.

"I can't believe I'm saying this, but I have to put all of this Madame Grosholtz business on pause. Jill's right. Tomorrow's a big day. A big, stupid von Trapp day, and all I'm *supposed* to be thinking about is doorbells and sleigh bells and schnitzel with noodles. I don't have room in my brain for any of . . . this."

It would have to wait. It was immense, and strange, and unsettling, and pressing, and it would have to wait. The show must go on.

"What's a schnitzel?" Dud asked.

"You know what, Dud? I have no friggin' idea."

But as they turned to head back to Gaudy Auditorium, passing Blake Bursaw's usual parking space, his absence bit at her harder than ever. The end of the day had arrived and she still hadn't seen him. She still hadn't heard from him despite the dozen or so voice mails she'd left. And though the kid regularly ditched school for days at a time just because he could, this felt different. Ominous.

She stared at the empty parking space.

"Aren't you going back to rehearsal?" said Dud.

"Yeah, but first . . ." Poppy lingered for another moment, then pulled her keys out of her pocket. "We need to run an errand."

* * *

"Why aren't you in school?"

"School is over, Mr. Kosnitzky. The final bell rang an hour ago."

Mr. Kosnitzky humphed and glowered at Poppy's perky hair. "Then why are you here?" He glanced suspiciously at her empty hands. "You don't have a trophy."

"No. I have a question: Have you seen Blake Bursaw at all today?"

He rubbed his chin. "Bursaw?"

"Yeah. He wasn't in school, and I figured that if anyone saw him out and about, it would definitely have been you, sir."

"Yes, it would have," he said with a proud nod.

"So you saw him?"

"No."

"Oh." Poppy's shoulders dropped. "Well, do me a favor and keep an eye out. A keener eye than usual, okay? Because Principal Lincoln is really starting to crack down on kids who skip, and he needs all the help he can get."

"I'll do what I can. Now buy something or leave."

Poppy left. "Well, that was a dead end," she muttered. Looking up and down the sidewalk, she felt nervous. Worried. Anxious. Fearful of the state of things and unsure that anything would ever be all right again. So even though she needed to get back to Dud, who was waiting for her in the town square gazebo, she decided to take a quick trip to the place she always went when nothing in the world made sense: Paper Clipz.

"Mmmm," she uttered as she drifted blissfully down the aisles, taking in the decadent scents of office supplies, of paper and ink and binders and index cards and sweet, sweet organization. Proximity to color-coded things always made her feel better. She was about to hug the Sharpie display when she remembered the tragic fate of The List.

Darkness clouded the aisle as she pictured its cruel demise. She certainly wasn't going back into that cavern to retrieve it. But on its own, it would never survive those open flames, the dank moisture, the page-spoiling rot—

"No!" she shouted.

The employee at the counter looked up. "Can I help you with something?"

"No, I—I was having a traumatic stationery-related flashback."

The employee put a sympathetic hand over her heart. "I *completely* understand."

Poppy spent the next ten minutes test-driving the newest makes and models of notebooks. She liked the coil strength of the Noteworthy 3000, but the leather-bound Write It Down! was not without its charms.

Finally she settled on the Pen Dragon 2.0, which boasted extra-weighted paper—the better to clutch worriedly. She paid for her purchase and headed back to the gazebo, where Dud was picking through the grass.

"Poppy, I have a question," he announced.

"Shoot."

"If I find something that belongs to someone else, but that person isn't around, am I allowed to take it?"

"Usually no, but that depends on what it is. And where you find it."

"What if it's a watch that I found over there?"

He pointed at the ground, at a spot a few feet away from the gazebo. Something in the grass glinted in the setting sun. Something silver.

An unnecessarily large titanium scuba diver watch, its face splattered with blood.

*　　*　　*

"I thought you said you're not usually allowed to take things."

"This is one of the times when I am allowed. That's what 'usually' means, that exceptions can be made."

She grasped the watch in one hand and steered with the other, weaving Clementine in and out of traffic. Hopefully, Jill had things under control back at rehearsal. Poppy was too deep into this to stop now.

True, she still couldn't prove any foul play. Blake *was* the sort of person who might lose a thousand-dollar watch and not think anything of it. And the blood? Could have come from a goose. Or a pigeon. Or a goose . . . attacking a pigeon?

"Where are we going now?" Dud asked.

"Somewhere I vowed I'd never return." Poppy glanced at her rearview mirror; she thought it unlikely that she was being followed, but she couldn't be too careful.

"What's a vow?"

"A solemn promise."

"Why are you breaking a promise?"

"Because I guess deep down I'm a good person and I care about what happens to my fellow man, even though my fellow man does nothing but crap all over me time after time after time."

"Oh," said Dud. "Okay."

A wave of revulsion crested as the Bursaws' mansion came into view, its resemblance to the White House more striking in broad daylight. Poppy half expected a team of government snipers to take her out as she turned onto the long circular driveway.

"Stay here," she instructed Dud after parking the car haphazardly — the only way to do so in a circular driveway. "Do not follow me. I'll be out in a few minutes, okay? Here, I'll leave the radio on."

Dud smiled as the melodious sound of NPR filled the car. "Mmm," he said, nodding. *All Things Considered.*

She shut the door as quietly as possible and made her way up the steps to the front door, listening for the hounds that were surely about to maul her. But everything was still. She willed herself not to think about the pool in the backyard, the infamous setting of "Hogwash," but she couldn't help it.

She refocused her hatred on the doorbell, which she pushed harder than necessary. A lilting chime of bells sounded within.

Poppy waited.

The door opened.

She didn't know what she'd been expecting. Maybe a confused butler. Maybe Blake, ready with a cream pie to hurl at her. But not Big Bob Bursaw himself, along with Miss Bea, both with gigantic smiles plastered across their faces, as if they'd been expecting her all along.

"Hello!" said Big Bob.

"Hello!" said Miss Bea.

"Um," said Poppy. "Hi."

"What can we do for you?" they asked in unison.

Poppy didn't know how she managed to keep it together in the face of such weirdness. "I'm looking for Blake. He — we're doing a project together, and he was supposed to be in school today, but I didn't see him, so I wanted to check in and make sure everything was all right."

"Oh, Blake's fine," said Big Bob.

"Just fine!" Miss Bea added.

"He's in his room."

"Studying for a quiz!"

"I'm sure he'll be back to school tomorrow."

"To take the quiz!"

Poppy blinked at them. "O . . . kay." She reached down to scratch her ankle, trying to peek past them into the hall, but they stood as a united front.

"Are you all right?" Miss Bea asked. "You look a bit . . . off-kilter, dear."

Big Bob leaned in. "Drugs are not rad, you know."

"I've heard," Poppy said with a nervous chuckle. "Um, I don't mean to be a pest, but can you check? To see if Blake is here? He borrowed my notes," she lied, "and I need them back." She smiled. "To study for the quiz."

The Bursaws' smiles got wider while their eyes got meaner.

"Of course," Big Bob said hollowly. "Just a moment." He turned around and walked up the immense staircase behind him. Poppy tried to peek around Miss Bea, but alone she still made a formidable wall. All Poppy could make out, through the windows of a French door to the floodlit backyard, was the bright blue tarp covering the pool for the coming winter.

"It's nice to meet a friend of Blake's," Miss Bea said in the tone of someone who was unaccustomed to conversing with teenagers.

Poppy nodded politely. *Friend. Sure.*

Big Bob's voice drifted down from upstairs, but it sounded like he was now talking to someone on the phone. She caught snippets here and there — "all set" — "Anita, wait" — "how should we —"

"What's your name, dear?" asked Miss Bea.

And there, at that moment, Poppy knew for sure something was wrong. That name of hers had been drummed so hard into the citizens of Paraffin that they knew it better than their own.

"Poppy Palladino."

"Oh, my," Miss Bea said with relish. "That's a catchy one."

"Apologies," Big Bob boomed, appearing at the top of the staircase. "Guess he's not here after all."

"Oh." Poppy tried to look innocent. "Well, aren't you worried about him? Like I said, he wasn't in school—"

"We heard you the first time, dear," said Miss Bea, abruptly dropping all pretenses of friendliness as Big Bob walked down the stairs. "And like *we* said, we don't care."

"You don't care? That he might be hurt, or missing, or—"

"No," Miss Bea said flatly. "We don't."

"But maybe *you* should," Big Bob added.

Poppy cocked her head. "Excuse me?"

"Well, I was looking for your notes," he said, twisting his voice into the same fake-innocent tone Poppy had used not two seconds before, "and I came across this little number." He held up a notebook.

The List.

Poppy's jaw thunked open in shock. "That's *mine*. How did you—"

"It doesn't matter," Big Bob said, flipping through the pages. "What matters is this."

He held up the notebook, his finger pointing at a familiar item.

#19025: KILL BLAKE BURSAW. FOR REAL THIS TIME.

Ice slivered through Poppy's veins. "That was just—I didn't mean it, obviously. I didn't *do* anything."

"Perhaps not," said Big Bob. "But if this should fall into the wrong hands — those of the police, say — they wouldn't hesitate to identify you as a person of interest. Again."

Poppy took a couple of steps back from the door, reeling. "What's happening here? Are you *blackmailing* me?"

"That's right, you little gutbag," Miss Bea said cheerfully. "You stop asking questions about Blake, and we'll keep this little evidence of attempted murder between us."

"Attempted *what?*"

Big Bob took a step toward her. "Do we have a deal?"

Poppy silently gaped at them. What else could she do? She couldn't call the police. Heck, she couldn't call *anyone*. Who would believe her? The only one who would was Blake, and he was most definitely missing.

"Do we have a deal?" Big Bob extended his hand.

Poppy cowered under his grinning form.

"Um, okay," she whimpered. "Deal."

When she shook his hand, it took everything in her power not to gasp out loud.

It was as room temperature as Dud's.

15

Practice reading comprehension

"POPPY?" HER MOTHER SAID WITH SURPRISE WHEN POPPY and Dud barreled through the front door. "What are you doing home? I thought you had rehearsal—"

"I do. Can't talk. Forgot something," Poppy huffed as she ran upstairs.

Thankfully, the flame had stayed lit this time—in the hours Poppy and Dud were away at school, more of the message had been revealed. "I don't even know what to hope for," she told Dud as she picked up the stone candle and magnifying glass.

> AND EVENTUALLY THE CHANDLERS GOT GREEDY. THEY WANTED MORE. THEY WANTED TO FEEL WHAT IT WAS LIKE TO BE OTHER PEOPLE. THEY WERE ACTORS, AFTER ALL. THEY WANTED TO "EXPAND THEIR CRAFT," AS THEY PUT IT. AND THAT WAS THE POINT OF NO RETURN. THAT'S WHEN EVERYTHING GOT MESSY AND COULD NOT BE PUT BACK THE WAY IT WAS.

Poppy gulped. Normally she loved being right. But now that she was reading such dire words in black and white, carved into stone, the thought of performing the I-told-you-so dance didn't seem so appealing.

THEY MADE ME SCULPT HOLLOWS THAT WERE DUPLICATES OF OTHER PEOPLE — SOME WERE WELL-KNOWN, OTHERS WERE NOT — ALL WHILE SECRETLY STUDYING THEIR MAN-NERISMS, THE WAY THEY TALKED. THEN THEY'D KIDNAP THEIR TARGETS, INHABIT THE WAX DOUBLES, SWOOP INTO THEIR LIVES, AND TAKE THEIR PLACE. I DO NOT KNOW WHAT HAPPENED TO THEIR VICTIMS. ALL I KNOW IS THAT ONCE THE CHANDLERS HAD THEIR FUN PLAY-ACTING AS NEW PEOPLE, THEY SHED THEIR HOLLOWS, AND THE REAL FOLKS WERE NEVER HEARD FROM AGAIN. SOON THE CHANDLERS FIGURED OUT THAT THEY DID NOT HAVE TO BE BOUND BY ONE CLONE EACH — WITH THEIR ORIGINAL FLAMES, THEY COULD LIGHT AS MANY HOLLOWS AS THEY PLEASED.

"One fire, many flames," said Poppy.

IT WASN'T LONG BEFORE I CAME TO REALIZE THE FULL HORROR OF WHAT I HAD DONE. ONE DAY I MAN-AGED TO ESCAPE AND COME TO THE STATES, BUT THE CHANDLERS TRACKED ME DOWN, IMPRISONED ME ONCE AGAIN, AND STARTED A CANDLE FACTORY IN THE

MEANTIME — BECAUSE WHY NOT MAKE A PROFIT WHILE THEY WERE AT IT? AND NOW THEY HAVE GONE AND DONE SOMETHING TRULY REGRETTABLE. I DO NOT KNOW

Poppy's mouth had gone dry. Her hands desperately squeezed the white stone, the clamminess of her palms making it difficult for her to keep her grip.

Blake had said that his dad and his grandmother didn't seem like themselves. Because the Bursaws *were* no longer themselves. They were nothing but wax puppets with the Chandlers' antiquated souls inside, pulling the strings.

* * *

"Poppy," said Dud, gripping the car door handle with one hand and the stone candle with the other, "are we supposed to be going this fast?"

"Don't worry. Speed limits are more like suggestions."

"And stopping at crosswalks is —"

"Optional."

"Are you sure?"

"Am I not the only one in this car who's taken driver's ed?"

"Who's driver's ed?"

Poppy punched the radio knob and let NPR take over. "No more talking."

She couldn't keep up a conversation anyway. The puzzle pieces were finally clicking into place. Why did the Bursaws call off the fire investigation? Because the Bursaws were really the Chandlers, so they used their newfound authority to get rid of the investigators, lest anyone keep poking around the factory and discover what they were really up to.

Questions were still coming fast and furious — *If the Bursaws I just met are wax Hollows, then what happened to the real ones? And where is Blake?*

Or rather, *What have they done to Blake?*

But Dud wasn't letting up. "What does this button do?"

"Locks the doors."

"What does this button do?"

"Opens the window. But don't —"

Dud opened the window. A gust of wind punched through the car, lifting the blanket off Wax Dud II in the back seat and blowing out the flame of the message candle.

"Dammit, Dud! We need that candle lit!" she shouted, reaching back to cover the sculpture again.

He gave her a repentant look. "I'm sorry."

She'd had misgivings about removing the candle from the safety of her home, but things were escalating, and she needed to read Madame Grosholtz's words as soon as they were exposed. But perhaps assigning Dud to candle watch had been a mistake. "Look around the floor. Maybe you can find some matches —"

"Achoo!"

"Yeah, I'm aware that this car is an allergy factory. I'll get it cleaned as soon as we get this pesky wax-demon problem taken care of. But for now, please look for the matches —"

"No need."

Poppy looked at him. Then at his lap.

"Did you just . . . sneeze that candle lit?"

He grinned. "I did."

Like he'd sneezed the television on fire. And why not? He had a flame in his body, after all.

The boy was a human lighter.

"Well," Poppy said, "that's convenient."

Dud cupped his hand around the candle, now taking his keeper-of-the-flame role seriously. "Where are we going now?"

"Back to the factory. You don't have to come in; I just want to check something. In fact —" Out of habit at this point, she dialed Blake's number again, rehearsing what she was going to say when his voice mail picked up. But this time —

"Hello?"

"Blake!" She pulled over into an illegal parking space. "You picked up!"

"Yeah. It's my phone."

"Where have you been? I've called a million times, left a million messages, you weren't in school —"

"I was sick. Didn't my dad tell you?"

"Well — yeah, but —"

"But what?"

Poppy paused. He sounded different. Gone was the intensity from his voice, the reckless fury that had surfaced when it seemed that his family was in danger.

"I don't know," she said. "I wanted to make sure you were okay."

"I'm fine, Poppy. Talk to you later."

Poppy stared at the phone as the call ended. "Not Hogwash?" she said. "Not Your Porkness? Nothing about my hooves?"

Blake had never once called her by her real name. Maybe he really was sick.

Or maybe he'd caught something much worse.

Poppy swung out of the parking spot, bouncing Clementine up onto the curb as she pulled a U-turn. A chorus of honking erupted. "They're sticking their fingers up," said Dud, putting his hand through the window to do the same and pleasantly waving it at the enraged motorists. "Hi!"

*　*　*

The Grosholtz Candle Factory wasn't as crowded on a Monday afternoon as it had been over the weekend, but Poppy still had to bob and weave past a group of retirees clustered around the main entrance in order to get to the BiScentennial display.

As promised, two new candles: Cup o' Joe and Forever Young.

Poppy picked up the brown Cup o' Joe, sniffed, and was bombarded with the distinctive roasted notes of coffee. "Excuse me," she said, flagging down the nearest Waxpert. "When were these candles made?"

"Oh, the Chandlers manufacture them overnight," the Waxpert said, "then prepare the display before we open every morning. They've spearheaded this BiScentennial campaign all by themselves!"

"I see," Poppy said shakily as the Waxpert left. "Thanks."

Unnerved, she stepped around to the other side and sampled

the other candle — but abruptly clapped her hand over her nose at the mix of Orbit gum, cheap body spray, and all the alcohol and pot and sweaty smells of a raging Saturday-night party.

Blake. Without a doubt.

*　*　*

"STOP EVERYTHING!"

Poppy stampeded down the aisle of Gaudy Auditorium like a spooked buffalo, waving her arms and bringing the "Do-Re-Mi" number onstage to a screeching halt.

"What now?" cried Jill. "We were getting something done for a change —"

"Awesome! Then you won't mind if we pause for a moment to do something else."

"I do mind. A great deal."

"Too bad. I'm mutinying your mutiny."

Powerless to stop her, the members of the Giddy Committee reluctantly obeyed as Poppy spent the next ten minutes placing them in various spots around the stage. "Jesus, move a few steps downstage. No, *down*stage. Walk *toward* me. How do you guys not know your stage directions by now?"

Jill tapped her on the shoulder. "Where's your, um, cousin?"

"Waiting in the car." *Guarding that candle with his life, I hope.*

"Hope you parked in the shade —"

"Shh! I'm trying to concentrate!"

The world premiere of *Poppy Explains the Horrible Wax Situation Using Her Actors as Stand-Ins* was only minutes away, and

212

preliminary reviews had already panned it, calling it "confusing," "impossible," and "I feel as though I have been miscast."

This last comment was from Connor, of course, who was not happy with his role as Madame Grosholtz. "I can do so much more," he insisted, swishing his cape. "I know stage combat."

"Connor, I *literally* just need you to stand there while I narrate and explain to you guys what's going on. These aren't actual roles. This isn't an actual show. You get that, right?"

"But how come Jesus gets to be Big Bob Bursaw?"

"Born talent, bitches!" Jesus shouted.

"Okay, you know what?" Poppy said. "Forget it! Everyone off the stage. Just find a seat and listen to me."

The members of the Giddy Committee sat in the audience in a clump, the old seats making heinous creaking noises, while Poppy sat on the edge of the stage and beheld her captive audience.

"Once upon a time," she said in her best Narrator voice — because a fake performance was still a performance — "there lived a woman named Madame Tussaud."

* * *

When Poppy finished her monologue, the members of the Giddy Committee shifted nervously in their seats, not knowing whether to believe her or challenge her or run screaming to the next available extracurricular activity.

"Prove it," Louisa said.

Poppy locked onto Louisa's cynical, beady eyes. "I can't prove it," she admitted. "It's all been conjecture up to this point, but honestly, there's no other explanation! Tell them, Jill!"

"There's no other explanation," Jill said. "Except for, you know, the thousands of other explanations."

"Seriously," said Louisa. "Never thought I'd have to say this to someone over the age of ten, but the Hollow Ones legend isn't real, Poppy. People can't be made out of wax. Candles can't be made out of people. What drugs are you *on?*"

"Drugs are not rad," said Connor.

"Wait, who's got the drugs?" Jesus asked, perking up.

"I am *not* on drugs, you guys!" Poppy shouted. "How else do you explain Dud?"

"Who's Dud?"

Poppy bit her lip. With all the insanity she'd heaped upon them, she didn't want to add Dud to the pile.

"Let me put it this way," she said. "Think of the Chandlers as matches. Just like you'd use one matchstick to light the individual candles on a birthday cake, the Chandlers lit copies of themselves inside the individual wax sculptures of Miss Bea and Big Bob. Now Miss Bea and Big Bob are imposters, walking around as if they're the real thing, when in fact they are clones of the souls of Anita and Preston Chandler! Respectively!"

She was met with blank stares.

"You *guys.* I am telling you that the Chandlers kidnapped two prominent members of our community. Maybe they are being held hostage. Maybe they are dead. Maybe they have been turned into candles. Is none of this a cause for concern?"

She was met with silence.

"Well, how about this: if Blake —"

"Oh, here we go," Jill interjected. "Best buddy Blake again."

Poppy eyed her — but maybe it was best to leave Blake out of this for now. "If," she reworded, "the Chandlers were able to get to the Bursaws — arguably two of the most untouchable people in Paraffin — then aren't you worried that any one of us could be next?"

Jill shook her head and stood up. "We need to get back to rehearsing for the parade, Pops."

"But it could happen again! We need to stop them! If they've already gotten to Blake —"

"Blake again, huh?" Jill snorted. "You know what? How about you take five and join us once you've . . . regained your composure."

For the sake of the Giddy Committee, Poppy obeyed. But as she watched them get back to their places onstage, she couldn't help but obsess harder.

She looked back down at her notebook, at the doodles she'd scribbled in biology.

One fire, many flames.

She stopped.

Frowning, she looked closer at the cells she had drawn in class.

"Viruses!" she shouted.

Jill, delivering a halfhearted pep talk to the Giddy Committee, put a hand over her brow to squint at Poppy in the audience. "I know you're a little rusty on this one, Pops, but infectious diseases don't figure into *The Sound of Music* as much as you'd think."

Poppy summoned every ounce of righteousness and redemption

she'd been storing up since *Triple Threat.* "The Chandlers are like a virus. They're replicating bad cells — copies of their souls — and passing them off as normal, healthy cells so that the body — Paraffin — won't catch on to what they're doing, won't notice that anything is wrong! Meanwhile, they're slowly taking control of our town, and if no one tries to stop them, it'll happen again. And again! And if we don't stop them soon from spreading, it'll be too late!"

She stood there before them, frenzied and panting and full of every hope she'd scrounged from the bottom up.

"Am I right, or am I right?"

*　*　*

"I *am* right," Poppy grumbled as she trudged through the school parking lot. Jill had asked her, once and for all, to leave the auditorium. And then Jill had locked the door.

Screw Jill, she thought. *And screw the Giddy Committee. I don't need them. I've got a human lighter. Go Team Wax.*

A positive attitude was key.

Her spirits lifted higher when her car came into view, Dud excitedly beckoning from within. "There are more words!" he said, handing her the magnifying glass as she sank into the driver's seat. "Important words, I think!"

Poppy read aloud:

"AND NOW THEY HAVE GONE AND DONE SOMETHING TRULY REGRETTABLE. I DO NOT KNOW WHAT IT IS — ALL I KNOW IS THAT THEY HAVE BEEN GIVING ME PHOTOS OF

TOWNSPEOPLE, I ASSUME, AND FORCING ME TO SCULPT THEIR LIKENESSES. MY GUESS IS THAT THEIR DELU-SIONS OF GRANDEUR HAVE REACHED NEW HEIGHTS, THAT THEY WISH TO INFILTRATE MORE PEOPLE IN THE TOWN AND TO SOMEHOW BUILD UP THEIR FACTORY PROFITS IN THE PROCESS. WHICH IS WHY I AM DOING SOMETHING I SHOULD HAVE DONE MANY, MANY YEARS AGO — BURN DOWN MY STUDIO AND END MY UNNATURALLY LONG LIFE, THEREBY TAKING AWAY THE CHANDLERS' ABILITY TO CONTINUE THEIR REIGN OF TERROR. SOME DAMAGE IS DONE — I CANNOT TAKE BACK THE HOLLOWS I HAVE ALREADY SCULPTED — BUT PERHAPS IF THIS CANDLE FINDS ITS WAY INTO THE RIGHT HANDS, THEY CAN STILL BE STOPPED."

"Are we the right hands?" Dud asked.

Poppy had gone pale.

"I guess we'll have to be." She swallowed and lifted a limp fist into the air. "Go Team Wax."

16

~~Stay on the road~~

ON THE DRIVE HOME, THE THOUGHTS SWIRLED AND TORNA-doed, jumped and bucked, but they always landed on the same conclusion: *Keep it together, Palladino.*

That, more than anything, had to remain her strategy. No matter how much she knew, no matter what she suspected, she could not let on a thing. Not to the authorities, not to the Chandlers, not even to her parents.

After giving Dud a quick lesson on what he should say if her parents asked how school had gone, she parked Clementine in the driveway, took the key out of the ignition, and placed her head on the steering wheel.

"Now what?" asked Dud.

"Now we unload you from the back seat."

As quietly as possible, they removed Wax Dud II from the car. Poppy decided to store it in the gardening shed in the backyard; winter was on its way, so there wasn't much of a chance that her parents would be looking in there anytime soon.

Wax Crawford, on the other hand, was to stay in the trunk. Possibly forever.

Poppy clicked the shed's padlock shut and warily eyed the kitchen window. "Now we attempt dinner."

* * *

A change was taking place in the Palladino household. The stained wooden tray tables had been relegated to the basement. Trivets had been unearthed for the first time in years. And Poppy was flabbergasted to find her family seated at the dining room table when she and Dud walked in, her father at the head, carving a blob of fake meat. "Hello, family!" he crowed. "It's Tofurky time!"

"Good God, what is happening in here?" Poppy asked.

"We decided," her mother said, passing Owen a bowl of carrots, "that it's time for us to start acting a little more civilized. Dr. Steve says that children who eat together with their families at the table accrue fifty percent more healthful benefits than those who don't."

Poppy let her backpack slide to the floor while Dud took a seat next to Owen. "And you're sure this has nothing to do with being embarrassed about our shabby lives in front of our new guest?"

"It has nothing to do with embarrassment," her father said, a point Poppy had to concede. She'd seen photos of her parents from the 1980s and concluded that humiliation was not something with which they had ever concerned themselves. "Besides," he went on, "I'll bet Dud eats together with his family on a boat or at the fire pit, or standing over the innards of a wildebeest. Isn't that right, Dud?"

Dud looked up from his salad, an alfalfa sprout hanging from his lip. "What's a boat?"

"We *do* eat together," Poppy jumped in. "With the added bonus of television. What about Dr. Steve?"

"Well, if you'll recall, Poppy, our television exploded. And I'm sure Dr. Steve can survive without us."

"Dad. We are his *only friends.*"

"Dud!" Mrs. Palladino interjected. "How was school today?"

Clearly rattled by the question despite the training Poppy had given him, Dud opted to deflect. "This food is delicious!"

Poppy's mother gave him a confused yet pleased smile. "Thank you, Dud! It's because I put the love in."

Poppy came to his aid. "Here are the exchange-student forms, by the way," she said, grabbing the packet from her bag and holding it up so that everyone could get a good look at her ruse. "Where do you want them?"

"Oh," her mother said, distaste for paperwork already flitting across her face. "In that box over there."

Poppy gladly dropped the folder into the box, knowing full well that it wouldn't be touched for at least a fortnight. Meanwhile, the question train had roared back to life once more. "I'm curious too, Dud," said Poppy's father. "How was your first day at school?"

He couldn't avoid it any longer. Dud methodically put down his fork, placed his hands in his lap, and looked at his plate. "School was fine," he said in a monotone. "I read a poem in English, sang a song in music, and drew a banana in math."

"Parabola," Poppy hissed.

"Para . . . banabola."

Dammit. He'd gotten it right when they rehearsed in the car. Poppy tensed up, but her parents didn't seem to notice his mistake. "That sounds nice," her mother said. Maybe she didn't know what a parabola was either. "And there were no problems getting you signed up for classes?"

"Nope, they squeezed him in," Poppy said.

"And what's your favorite class so far, Dud?"

He snuck a wry look at Poppy. "Art."

"No wonder." Her father gestured at the small army of wax figures he'd arranged on the kitchen counter, like an off-season nativity. "You're a born artiste!"

Dud beamed.

Poppy choked down her carrots.

Owen decorated his face with Tofurky.

After dinner, Dud announced that he was going upstairs to "MAKE HOMEWORK," which sounded so fishy that even Owen raised an eyebrow, but the adults in the household didn't suspect a thing. "It's amazing how well he's already assimilating," Poppy's mom confided to her as they washed the dishes. "It must be such culture shock for the poor thing. Do the other kids at school like him?"

"I have not heard any complaints."

"Of course not. What a fuzzy little sweetheart! I only hope no one takes advantage of him because he's different. With all the garbage *you've* had go to through —"

"Mom."

"I'm just saying, honey. Lots of bullies at that school. I'd keep an eye on him if I were you."

"He'll be fine."

"You're probably right. I'm sure the ladies are flocking already."

"Mmm."

Poppy's mom threw down her dishrag and leaned in to inspect her daughter's face. "You just turned beet red."

"No, I didn't."

"Yes, you did."

"It's the hot water, Mom."

"You like him."

"I do *not*."

"You realize that this is a tricky pickle, right? You're living in the same house together. That could be a problem."

"It will not be a problem, because I do not like him."

"Like who?" her father said, breezing into the kitchen.

"Poppy likes Dud," her mother said.

"Mom! *I do not!*"

"Ooh," her father said, wincing. "That's a tricky pickle."

Poppy dropped the dish she was washing into the sink, sending a spray of water onto the floor. "You guys need to stop. It's not a problem. It's not a pickle. Because *I. Don't. Like. Him.*"

Her parents exchanged knowing glances. "We said the same thing to our parents when we met."

"That's because you guys were freaks and losers and hopelessly devoted to each other's acid-washed jeans. I, on the other hand, am disencumbered by the mind-fogging drug of lust. I am focused on getting into college. I am focused on not causing myself any more trouble or 'tricky pickles' than I already have this year. Why on earth would I add another potential calamity to the list?"

They nodded. They gave her sympathetic looks. Then her father leaned into her mother and said in a stage whisper, "The lady doth protest too much."

"*Dad!*"

"Love isn't a calamity, sweetie," her mother said. "It's a wonderful thing. But maybe put it on hold while you're living in the same house. Once he goes back home, you two can stay in touch through the Internet, and then you can go visit him in Africa. Or maybe he'll come here for college and you can hook up then!"

"She means get back in touch," her father said. "Not *hook up, hook up.*"

"Right," said her mother. "Although hey, once you're living in a dorm, it's not like we can stop you. Remember Walsh Hall? My goodness, the noises we heard. The noises we *made.*"

Poppy recoiled. "You have to stop talking."

"We're human beings too, Pops!"

"For the love of God. *Cease and desist.*"

Owen wandered in and looked at the puddle of dishwater on the floor. "What's going on?" he asked his parents.

"Poppy likes Dud," they said in unison.

Owen frowned. He looked at his parents. Then he looked at Poppy.

"I thought you were saving yourself for Mr. Crawford."

"Oh my God OH MY GOD."

* * *

As she stomped out of the kitchen and up the stairs, Poppy was sure that every drop of blood in her body had been redirected to her face. She made a beeline for the bathroom, turned on the faucet, and proceeded to splash cold water on her cheeks until she'd returned to a conventional color.

"Poppy?"

"Gah!"

She flung herself backwards into the towel rack as Dud poked his head through the door. "Sorry to scare you," he said. "I wanted to ask what a Tofurky is."

"It's . . ." The best definition Poppy's addled brain could come up with was *a fake bird made out of beans*, but that didn't really clarify anything. "It's complicated," she said, rubbing her temples.

"Are you okay?" he asked, deeply concerned. "You look sad. Is it because those people took your notebook?"

"Yes. Among a lot of other things."

"Do I make you sad?"

"Not exactly. No."

"If I don't make you sad, do I make you happy?"

But Poppy had fallen too deep into her labyrinth of thoughts, rehashing all the things that had been yelled across the kitchen. She knew that as a girl of a certain age and a certain cocktail of hormones, any of her encounters with the opposite sex would be construed by her parents as experiments in wooing — and the more she denied it, the less they'd believe her.

But she really *didn't* like Dud. Not in that way, at least. She liked him as a friend, as a confidant, as an adopted exchange-student brother.

As her only partner on Team Wax.

Dud gently raised his finger to the edge of her hairline. "What's this?"

Poppy looked at their reflections in the bathroom mirror. "Oh. That's a scar."

"You have a scar too? Did someone carve their initials in you too?" he asked, poking apart her hair to see better.

"No," she said, pushing him away with a laugh. "It's not that kind of scar."

"Oh." He thought for a moment. "The other night you said a scar is 'a mark that's left over after you get hurt, once the wound has healed.' How did you get hurt?"

Poppy propped her elbows on the bathroom counter and played with the toothpaste tube. "It's a long story. One that involves my dreams being crushed. And it pales in comparison with the buffet of disasters we now find in front of us, so trust me, it's not a big deal."

"Dream crushing sounds like a big deal."

Her thumbs sank deeper into the smooth plastic of the tube.

"Do you need to talk through your feelings?" he persisted.

Poppy sighed.

"It happened during a talent contest," she relented. "I sang. I danced. I was on TV."

He gasped. "Like Dr. Steve?"

"Yes. Without the medical quackery, but yes. I was on TV, and I fell and hit my head, and I bled all over the damn place, and it was humiliating, and it pretty much demolished my chances of ever making it to Broadway."

"Why?"

"Because! That image of me covered in blood and singing like a psychopath is all people are ever going to see." She did not want to get into this. She did not want to keep talking. "They won't look any deeper than that. They won't see me for my talent — if I had any to begin with. If I get cast in anything, it won't be because I earned it. It'll be because I'm a novelty, a gimmick they can splash onto billboards. Come see the freak! Hogwash, live and in the flesh! Twenty million hits on YouTube can't be wrong!" She angrily flung the toothpaste onto the counter. "That's not what I want. I don't want to build a career on a foundation of pity. I don't want to be a joke."

Dud put his hands on her shoulders. "There, there," he said, just like Dr. Steve. "It'll be okay."

"Honestly, Dud? I don't think it will. I think I blew it." She swallowed, but the growing lump in her throat didn't go away. "And you know what the worst part is? Let's say I really did screw my chances of pursuing a career in theater. Fine. I mean, it would suck — it would hard-core, flat-out *suck* — but I would accept it and move on. But move on to what? What else could I do? It's the only thing I've ever been good at, the only thing I've ever loved." She heaved a limp shrug. "I'd be lost."

Dud's eyes were worried. "*That's* not a healthful benefit."

Surely there were better ways of expressing all this—perhaps to a licensed therapist and not a freshly minted mannequin—but the dam had burst. "See, this is the thing that I haven't been able to tell anyone. Not my shrink, not my parents, not even Jill. That the worst damage wasn't to my skull or to my reputation or to my ego. Those are all things that can heal with time. The thing that terrifies me more than anything is—well, *now* the thing that terrifies me more than anything is that a ruthless army of wax pod people will infiltrate my town and destroy everything without anyone stopping them or realizing what they're up to—but up *until* now, my biggest fear was living a life that didn't matter."

Dud widened his eyes. "You matter to *me*. You let me sculpt things and listen to the radio and eat ice cream and chase squirrel monsters. I never did any of those things before I met you."

She rolled her eyes. "You didn't *exist* before you met me."

"Exactly! You are the *best*."

Poppy shrugged her shoulders out of his grip, but she couldn't help smiling.

"What's going on in here?" she heard her father say from outside the closed door.

"Orgy, Dad. Please leave us alone."

"Ha, ha," her father said, opening the door.

Poppy held her toothbrush aloft. "Just brushing my teeth."

"Well, you don't need Dud for that, do you?"

Poppy ran a hand through her hair and tried to banish all thoughts of murder from her head. "I suppose I do not. Actually, I'm going to take a shower, so both of you can leave."

Her father gave a satisfied nod and disappeared down the hallway. Dud started to follow him, but Poppy called him back. "Dud?"

"Yes?"

"To answer your question: You do make me happy."

He grinned. "Oh, good!"

"And Tofurky is a fake bird made out of beans."

"*Whaaat?*"

17

~~Celebrate a local holiday~~

"SO THEY FINALLY KICKED HIM OUT?" ASKED JILL.

"Not out of the house. Just my bedroom. He has to sleep in Owen's room now, even though *we didn't do anything*."

Poppy's mom elbowed her away from the kitchen sink. "Poppy, get off the phone. Can't we eat breakfast together as a family without the encroachments of modern technology? No offense, Jill!" she shouted toward the phone.

"None taken," Jill's tinny voice echoed back.

"Forget it," Poppy told Jill. "I'll see you at the parade."

Ordinarily, Jill's morning phone calls were like shots of espresso—Poppy always got dual bursts of energy and happiness when she saw her number pop up on the screen. But today grudges prevailed instead. She was still mad at Jill for kicking her out of rehearsal—twice!—plus Jill's incessant apathy and skepticism were starting to wear on her. But she forced herself to put that aside for the moment. If the town was in real danger, she couldn't risk dooming its citizens because of some petty best-friend drama.

And though Poppy was in a terrible mood for a variety of reasons, the main one was that the message candle had stopped delivering its message. With Madame Grosholtz's ominous last words — *but perhaps if this candle finds its way into the right hands, they can still be stopped* — the tiny scratched letters had ended. After that, it was nothing but pure unetched stone.

Poppy put away her phone and glared at her mother. "It's not enough to force us into dinner together, now you're hijacking breakfast, too?"

Her mother shrugged innocently. "Dud seems to like it."

Dud, seated at the kitchen table, held up a plate full of scrambled eggs and gave Poppy a smile that was also full of scrambled eggs. She sat down beside him and put some food on her plate, yawning repeatedly.

Dud watched her, confused. "Are you stretching your teeth?"

"No, I'm yawning. It happens when people are tired."

"You're tired?"

"Ha! Understatement of the year."

Yesterday's discoveries had kept Poppy up into the wee hours of the morning. She couldn't stop turning the facts over, looking at them from different angles. Dud's relocation to Owen's room had turned out to be a blessing — at least with him gone, she could think without being pelted with more unending questions.

"Are you worried about the parade?" he asked.

"The parade is the least of my troubles." She lowered her voice. "We have a crisis going on in this town — we don't have time for a celebration! Things are moving too fast for us to stop them. And I don't know *how* to stop them. Not to mention that our current mayor is an imposter, and the *real* mayor has been kidnapped, and she and Big Bob and Blake are all missing, probably hurt, and possibly dead!"

"What does 'dead' mean?" Dud asked.

Poppy yawned again. "I'm gonna take a rain check on that one."

"Happy Paraffin Day, family!" Her father swept into the kitchen. "Pops, are you at the front of the parade or more toward the back? I want to have the camera ready."

"Can you not?" Poppy dejectedly picked at her eggs. "It's *The Sound of Music,* and it's reliving my nightmare, and it's going to be a train wreck. I don't even want to be doing this in the first place."

"Fraulein Maria didn't want to be a governess in the first place either, and look how well things turned out for her!"

"Running for her life through the Alps in the dead of winter with seven slow-moving children in tow?"

Her mother lightly smacked her with the morning paper. "It's in service to your town, sweetheart. Think of all the people you'll be entertaining!"

"It'll be good for morale," said Dud.

Poppy glared at him. Where was he picking up this stuff? "Do you even know what 'morale' means?"

"It'll be good for morale."

Poppy chugged the rest of her orange juice and stood up, grabbing a few more slices of Fakin' Bacon for the road. "We gotta go," she said, motioning for Dud to join her. "See you guys afterward. Enjoy the festivities."

Her father held up his glass of orange juice, as if delivering a toast. "Break a leg!"

Dud gasped. "That's not nice!"

Everyone laughed except Poppy, who would have gladly welcomed a compound fracture at this point if it meant getting her out of the von Trappery. "It's an expression, Dud," her mother explained. "It means 'good luck.'"

Poppy pulled Dud out of his chair. "We don't have time for English lessons. We're already going to be late."

"Then you better shake a leg," said her father. "Which is *also* an expression."

"Goodbyyye!" Poppy shouted, slamming the door behind her.

* * *

Poppy needed coffee. Badly.

She parked Clementine near the town square, instructed Dud to stay put, and jogged toward Smitty's; crowds were starting to show up, so Poppy quickly scooted through the door while everyone else was trying to decide whether donuts were the right food for parade spectating.

As she entered, the smell bowled her over, knocking an epiphany into place.

Cup o' Joe.

"What can I getcha?" Smitty half shouted at Poppy, causing her to jump at least a foot back from the counter.

"Um . . . coffee?"

He grunted and started to pour her a cup as she raked her eyes over every inch of his face. "What are you doing?" he asked, looking uncomfortable.

"I — I have a question," she improvised, redirecting her focus toward the various baskets of bagels behind the counter. "About a bagel."

"Oh, not this again. I know what you're gonna ask. 'What's on the everything bagel?' Dumbest question I ever heard! The answer's right there in the name! It's got your garlic. It's got your sesame seeds. It's got your onion. It's got —"

"Actually, my question was about the baking technique," said Poppy. "How do you prepare them?"

"Oh. Boil 'em first, then pop 'em in the oven."

"What kind of oven?"

His eye twitched. "The one in the back. It's pretty big."

"How many bagels can it bake at once?"

"A lot."

"I know, but how many *exactly?*"

His nostrils were flaring. "Kid, I don't got time for this! You want a bagel or not?"

Poppy shook her head, handed him a few bills, grabbed her coffee, and fled — but not before hearing him mutter to himself as he counted the money: "Rotten gutbag."

"Smitty is an imposter," Poppy hissed at Dud once she got back into the car. "The real Smitty would never pass up an opportunity to talk up his precious bagel oven. The real Smitty would have known its *exact* capacity — would have shouted it from the rafters! This one's got to be a Hollow!"

"That's bad."

"It's very bad." She nervously blew on her coffee. "So that means they've got all three Bursaws, plus Smitty — hang on a sec." She handed Dud her cup and pulled out her notebook. "The first day of BiScentennial candles was Big Bob and Miss Bea. The second was Blake and Smitty. Which means that today there should be two new candles, but . . ." She looked at her phone. "Crap, we don't have time to get to the factory and see what they are." She slumped in her seat. "Not that it matters. If the Chandlers process everything overnight, their victims are probably beyond saving. Whoever it is, they could already be dead."

"And what is 'dead' again?"

She turned on the radio. "Here, listen to NPR."

He turned it off. "Tell me!"

She sighed. Better he learn it from her than from Dr. Steve. "Well, if you'll recall our lesson on the miracle of life, humans are born, then they grow up, then they hopefully live long, meaningful lives, and then they die. They . . . stop living."

Dud frowned. "I don't understand."

"It is a hard thing to understand. And no one likes to think about it. Or talk about it. So can we not?"

"That means that one day," Dud persisted, "you won't be here anymore? Because you're human?"

Poppy fidgeted in her seat. "Yeah."

"But I will be, because I'm wax?"

"Right." She took the coffee cup back from him and took a sip. "That's what this whole thing is about — the Chandlers moving their souls from body to body. They don't want to die. They want to live forever."

Dud fell silent. He looked out the window. "Oh."

Poppy glanced warily at the teeming crowds as she pulled out of her parking spot. The last time she had seen this many Paraffiners in the same place at the same time was on the satellite feed during her final *Triple Threat* performance. The show had repeatedly cut to that shot of them gathered in the town square, cheering for her and holding up signs. Then, after the fall, to a shot of them no longer cheering. Lowering their signs.

"You know what?" Poppy said. "I changed my mind. I don't think you should come to the parade."

Dud looked at her. "Why?"

"Because . . . there are too many people. And they'll point at me, probably, or stare. And you —"

You are the only one in this town who sees me as a real person and not as a national laughingstock. You might change your tune once you see the way they gawk. You might join in.

"You might be seen as suspicious," she said. "It's a small town — new people stick out, and if anyone starts to ask questions, you might not know how to answer them, and that could lead to trouble."

"And we don't want trouble."

"That's right." She bit her lip and looked away from the crowd of people, feeling their eyes drawn like magnets to her shiny orange car. "How would you feel about a game of hide-and-seek?"

"Okay!"

She turned the wheel. "Emphasis on 'hide.'"

* * *

"So what are you saying? That all the Bursaws bit the dust?" Jill started in again once she and Poppy were reunited.

"Your nonchalance in the face of such tragedy is disturbing, Jill."

"Well, call me insensitive, but it's hard for me to get weepy over things that haven't really happened."

"They *have* happened!"

"Poppy, the Bursaws are alive and well and sitting in the grandstand. I saw them not twenty minutes ago."

"Even Blake?"

"Even Blake."

Poppy frowned. "But those are the wax Bursaws. The real Bursaws are elsewhere — and yes, possibly dead. I mean, there is a *chance* they're still alive — the Chandlers could be holding them hostage. That's the hope, but I'm starting to have my doubts."

Jill looked at her watch. The parade was to start in ten minutes, and the Price Chopper parking lot serving as the staging area was filling up fast. A few other community groups mingled about — the Boys & Girls Club, the American Legion, a loose confederation of elderly dancers who called themselves the Boogie Woogies. A fire engine here, a Lincoln Town Car there, the Coalition for Antique Tractor Collectors. The Rotary Club and the Paraffin Town Library had both produced well-intentioned efforts in the float category, but the Grosholtz Candle Factory promised to be the most popular of the bunch — primarily because it would be giving out free candle samples, with Vermonty performing a dance when it reached the grandstand.

Of course, Poppy was more concerned with the occupants of the grandstand, the waxy pretenders to the throne. Would anyone pick up on the fact that Big Bob and Miss Bea were not who they appeared to be? Probably not, if Wax Blake was doing his best to keep people from getting too close.

Yet Poppy could only make educated guesses about the current status of the Bursaws, trapped as she was in the sticky mess of parade preparations, sneering at the unacceptable amount of merriment around her. She was *so* not where she wanted to be at the moment: far from the center of town, hair braided, and wearing itchy lederhosen, ready to assault Main Street with a grenade of musical theater.

She shot a quick glance at the Price Chopper dumpster. Dud's eyes poked out of it.

She shook her head. He disappeared back inside.

The other members of the Giddy Committee, wearing the vaguely Alpine costumes Jill had cobbled together from their meager supplies, were nervously preparing around her, warming up their vocal chords and practicing their skip-two-threes.

"Madame Director," Connor said with a deep bow, "I took it

upon myself to bring a prop that I felt would add to the performance. What say you?"

Poppy studied the stuffed animal he presented. "Let me guess. Doe, a deer?"

"A *female* deer."

"Fine. Whatever."

Poppy couldn't have cared less. Sure, their performance would reflect on her, the school, and the Giddy Committee — and if she'd been in a better frame of mind, she might have seen it as an opportunity for redemption in the eyes of the townspeople — but for once in her life, she had more important things to deal with than theater.

Especially when she spotted the crew of the Grosholtz Candle Factory float making their final preparations.

Jill turned to her. "So I think we should open with 'The Lonely Goatherd' — Poppy! Come back here!"

Poppy returned a moment later, her face flushed and candles in hand. "They gave me free samples of today's BiScentennials!" She read the two labels aloud. "Italian Leather and Sour Grapes. Who could those be?"

"I don't know," said Jill. "What are your thoughts on the opening number?"

Poppy tapped her chin. "And whoever they are, the question remains: How are the BiScentennial candles being manufactured?"

"Probably with wax," Jill said.

"Well, yes, obviously with wax," Poppy said testily. "But remember, on the tour, how the tour guide said they'd be using that Potion stuff to extract people's essences? She said they'd be using 'data' from Paraffiners, but what does that *mean?*"

"No clue."

"Here's what I'm thinking—"

"Oh, now there's thinking involved? Because up until now it has seemed as though you've thrown rational thought out the window."

"Would you shut up and listen to me for once?" Poppy snapped. "I'm trying to make sense of a completely nonsensical situation by turning to my best friend for help, but all my best friend wants to do is be a skeptical bitch about it!"

Jill's mouth dropped open. They called each other bitches all the time, but always with love, never in earnest. She took a breath and started to reply—

"Good morning, ladies!" Mr. Crawford said, jogging up to Poppy's side. "Is your crew ready for the performance of a lifetime?"

Both Poppy and Jill froze. The fight was imminent, bubbling up behind their teeth, but neither wanted to start it in front of Mr. Crawford. "Yeah," Poppy eventually managed. "I think so . . ."

"Poppy hates *The Sound of Music,*" Jill blurted. Now all three of them looked shocked, even Jill, but her expression quickly turned to one of malice. "*Hates* it. She always has, from before she was on *Triple Threat.* She only performed it because the producers made her. It's her least favorite musical of *all time.*"

Mr. Crawford frowned. "Is that true?"

"No," Poppy said numbly. "No, it isn't."

"Yes, it is," Jill said. "At the end, she roots for the Nazis."

Poppy gasped. "I do not *root* for the *Nazis*."

"She shouts, 'The helpless children are right over that hill! Hurry up! Don't let them get to Switzerland!'"

"That's not true," she told Mr. Crawford, who was now looking at her as though she'd committed a war crime. "She's lying."

"Oh, but I'm not," Jill said with relish. "I believe Miss Palladino's exact words were, 'I hope little Gretl falls off the mountain. So long! Farewell! *Auf Wiedersehen,* goodDIE!'"

If Mr. Crawford had a response to that, Poppy didn't hear it. She turned and ran to the farthest corner of the parking lot, keeping her back to the crowds and staring straight into the trees. Her shoulders heaved as she tried not to cry, two little words scampering like demonic squirrels through her mind.

Jill too?

But her tears quickly turned into hot streams of anger. How *dare* she? Jill had been right there on the front lines for the worst moments of Poppy's life, and now she was using it as ammo. *In front of Mr. Crawford.* How cruel was that?

A light breeze blew through the trees as she stared steely-eyed into the woods, running through the comebacks she wished she'd thought of in the moment — when an odd aroma wafted into her nose.

Instantaneously her mind went blank.

Then, slowly, one thought occurred to her — then grew stronger and stronger until it drowned out everything else, screaming through her brain at a deafening volume.

She allowed herself a brief glance at the throngs assembled for the parade. The Giddy Committee would probably be fine without her. The Soulless Ice Demon Heretofore Known as Jill would have things under control. And Mr. Crawford was never going to speak to her or look at her or kindly rebuke her misplaced flirtations again, so really, what did she have to lose?

With a deep breath, Poppy plunged into the woods.

*   *   *

The forest was disorienting — plus the lederhosen weren't doing her any favors in the speed department. It wasn't until Poppy caught sight of the big white tanks that she realized she'd been heading toward the candle factory. The flame on top of Tank #1 was lit, calling her forth like a beacon.

Of course, she thought as she walked up the metal staircase of #1 without hesitation, *of course that's where I need to go . . . the Grosholtz Candle Factory is a wonderful place . . .*

When she took the final steps onto the roof, a big, silly grin smacked onto her face as she looked at the flame. *"So beautiful,"* she said, her tone oddly high-pitched.

"Poppy?"

She whirled around, her shoes scraping on the rough surface of the roof. "Dud? What are you doing here?"

He let go of the staircase's railing and took a few slow steps toward her. "I saw you go into the woods, and you looked mad and sad and then kind of scary, so I got out of the dumpster to follow you, to make sure you were okay. And now you climbed up onto this roof, so I don't think you are okay."

"Go away, Dud," she said in a harsh voice that did not sound anything like her. "I'm busy." She turned her back on him and continued on toward the flame at the center of the tank's roof, sniffing manically.

"But, Poppy, wait —"

"I said go away!"

She heard an abrupt rush of footsteps behind her. Before she realized what he was doing, Dud clamped his hand over her face. Poppy screamed into his hand, but her scream was too muffled for anyone to hear . . .

. . . *Oh my God, he was bad all along* . . .

. . . *He's gonna kill me* . . . *I'm gonna die right here on this roof* . . . *and I never got to find out what the flame had to tell me* . . .

. . . *Wait, is that really my dying thought?*

Poppy stopped struggling. The fog that had clouded her mind at first sniff began to clear.

She blinked hard.

What am I doing on the roof of this tank?

As she straightened up, now calm, Dud relaxed his grip — except for his fingers, still tightly squeezing her nostrils shut.

"Let go of by dose," she burbled.

Wide-eyed, Dud shook his head. "No way. Whatever you smelled made you go crazy!"

"I realize that. Let go — I'll hold by own dose, I probise."

Terms settled, Dud let go. Poppy pinched her nostrils and looked up at the tall flame, gulping air into her mouth to clear out any residual toxins. The base of it looked like that of a giant lantern, the fuel in its well flecked with a golden, sparkly powder. "Do *you* sbell that?" she asked Dud, not daring to get too close.

"No."

"Well, whatever that sbell is — it, like, hijacked by brain. I kept thinking I had to get up here at all costs!"

Not that the roof was much to look at. It was old and rusted, with a hinged, closed hatch in the center. She peered at the roof of the other tank; it was largely the same, except for a big, unpatched hole — the result of the lightning strike, judging by the burn marks.

Poppy glanced back at the golden flecks in the fuel well of the flame. "I thidk this is that additive they talked about at the tour — the powder you add to a flabe to lure people in!"

Footsteps sounded on the metal steps.

Before they could hide — or figure out if it was possible to hide atop a flat roof — a figure in gardening clogs appeared, taking heavy, zombielike steps toward the flame.

"Bissus Goodwid?" Poppy asked her addled next-door neighbor. "What are you doing here? I thought you were on the Rotary Club float!"

"Float," Mrs. Goodwin repeated in a monotone. She stopped just short of the flame, taking deep breaths and staring at it with a blank expression.

"I think the sbell lured her id too," Poppy whispered to Dud. "Bissus Goodwid, the scent is hypdotizing you! Breathe through your bouth!"

More footsteps on the stairs.

Poppy hurried to the stairs and took a quick peek down, then retreated. "It's Prestod Chaddler!" she whispered to Dud. "We have to get out of here!"

He looked around nervously. "There's nowhere to hide and seek."

Poppy gave Mrs. Goodwin a hard shake. "What do we do?"

"Do," Mrs. Goodwin replied, still captivated by the flame.

Panic began to set in. Preston was almost at the top —

Dud grabbed Poppy and flung her onto his back. "Hold on," he instructed, sprinting to the edge of the roof. And then, to Poppy's utter terror, he sat down, turned around, and lowered them both over the side, holding on to the lip of the roof by his fingertips.

Poppy frantically clung to his shoulders but remained quiet — and managed to pull herself up enough to see what was going on.

Preston was on the roof now. He had his back to her, but she could hear what he was saying. "Where's the other one?" he asked Mrs. Goodwin. "Where's the girl?"

"Girl."

Preston let out a frustrated sigh. "Forget it." He used a large key to unlock the hatch, and then, without any hint of ceremony or consequence, shoved Mrs. Goodwin into the hole. A second later, a splash sounded below.

"I'm gonna get an earful on this one," he muttered to himself, irked, as he locked the hatch and disappeared back down the steps.

Once they were sure he was gone, Dud climbed back up, safely depositing Poppy on the roof. She ran to the hatch. "Bissus

Goodwid!" she shouted, madly pounding on the hatch. If the fall alone didn't kill her, being trapped in a giant drum of liquid would. The woman had to be in her eighties—she'd drown in no time. "Bissus Goodwid!"

No answer.

She pulled on the hatch's handle, but it wasn't budging. Poppy pounded down the stairs of the tank and tried to peel back the repair patch, but the plastic was too thick and the Tackety Wax too strong.

"I can't," Poppy said, panting, tears springing to her eyes as Dud came down the stairs. "I can't save her. What do we do?"

"I don't know." He knitted his fingers together. "This is dangerous."

Poppy wiped her face and steeled her resolve. "Add it's about to get a lot bore so."

*   *   *

Poppy led Dud through the path down the hill, remembering to hang a left at the Paraffin Spa personal sauna. After a while she gave the air a small test whiff. "I think it's gone," she said, taking a deeper breath.

She climbed up into the ruins of Madame Grosholtz's studio and approached the trapdoor. "We're going down there," she told Dud. "And we don't know what or who we're going to find, so from here on out, zip it."

"Zip what?"

"Zip your mouth."

"How do I do that?"

"Just be quiet."

"Oh. Okay."

Poppy took a deep breath, hitched up her lederhosen, and stepped down onto the —

"Poppy?"

"What?"

"Should I be actually zipping my mouth somehow, or is that an expression?"

"*Shh!* It's an expression. It means no more talking."

"Okay."

She stepped through the jagged wood into the hole, found her balance on the first step, and —

"Poppy?"

She looked up at Dud, eyes blazing. "*What?*"

"Break a leg."

"Oh. Thanks."

"Or is it shake a leg?"

"*Please* stop talking."

The staircase was narrower and darker than she remembered. Poppy had to slowly slide her toes down and make sure she had her footing before taking each step. With every second that passed, she was sure that Dud, blindly flailing behind her, was about to crash and send them both tumbling — ironically breaking a leg in the process — but he turned out to be surprisingly graceful.

"Where are we going?" Dud whispered as they made their way through the icy tunnel.

"A cave." She took out her cell phone and used the screen to light the way. "Well, it's more of a cathedral. Well, it's more of . . . it's a long story, is what it is."

Deeper into the mountain they crept, slipping more than once on the glossy stones. Poppy aimed her phone straight ahead, the meager illumination from the screen bathing the tunnel in a sick, ghostly light.

When the door to the cavern came into view, Poppy motioned at Dud to be quiet — but upon creeping on tiptoe to the edge of the door, she found that the cavern was as empty as she and Blake had found it two days prior. More footprints littered the floor, however, and on the altar —

"That is *definitely* blood," Poppy said, inspecting the dark streaks. "Fresher than last time, I think —"

She cut off her words as a rumble from the elevator door sounded. "Oh, crap," she said, grabbing Dud. "We have to hide!"

"Again?"

"Again!" She dragged him into a shadowy corner of the cavern, pressing her backside into the wax until she was relatively sure they were hidden in the darkness.

Anita and Preston emerged from the elevator. Preston made a beeline for the door marked OUT and disappeared through it while Anita turned the large metal spigot attached to the door marked IN. A gooey liquid seeped out of the faucet and into the pool, followed by something much heavier and more unwieldy and human-body shaped, which fell to the bottom with a sickening *sploosh*.

Poppy would recognize that ski slope of a nose anywhere, along with the pungent, fermented scent of old wine.

Sour Grapes.

"Oh my God," she whispered. "It's Principal Lincoln."

She watched, horror-stricken, as Anita calmly lifted the principal's body into a limp, upright position, then let go—but he didn't fall. The thick substance coating his skin was hardening fast, keeping him in a standing position. With an expressionless face, she continued to pose him, putting one arm on his hip and the other over his eyes, as if he were looking into the distance.

Potion, Poppy thought, her mind racing. *That's the "data" they're collecting from Paraffiners. But instead of dipping their fingers, they're drowning their whole bodies! Mrs. Goodwin took Principal Lincoln's place in the tank, and tomorrow she'll end up just like him!*

Meanwhile, Preston emerged with a sculpted wax replica of Mrs. Goodwin, placing it next to the altar. Anita paused in her preparations to say something to Preston—Poppy couldn't hear what it was, but she heard Preston's reply.

"There's only the one today."

Anita blinked at him. "What do you mean?"

"We didn't get the girl."

"*What?*"

"I thought she went up to the roof, but when I got up there, I didn't see her. I don't know what happened."

Angrily, Anita walked away from the stiffened form of Principal

Lincoln and, gripping the Hollow of Mrs. Goodwin by the back of the neck, leaned in to kiss it.

What the heck is she doing? Poppy thought — but realized the answer just as quick. Because as their lips parted, the sculpture came to life, Anita's flame-soul safely transferred into the Hollow body.

The newly awakened Wax Mrs. Goodwin joined in on the Preston bashing, using the same tone as Anita. "This is ridiculous."

"And on release week too," Anita added.

"What's the big deal?" Preston asked. "So we only release one candle tomorrow."

"It's not *Uni*Scentennial, Preston. It's *Bi*Scentennial."

". . . Oh! Is that why we called it that?"

"For shit's sake. Yes. Am I the only one with brains in this operation?"

She stalked to the door labeled ACROSS, pulled it open, and nodded at her recent creation. Wax Mrs. Goodwin nodded back, then disappeared through the door with a sympathetic eye roll.

"I have brains," Preston muttered as Anita returned to him. "*I'm* the one who formulated Potion. Doesn't that count for something?"

"It might have, if it hadn't taken you a goddamned century to finish. All those useless test subjects over the years, roaming the woods, falling off cliffs, too dimwitted and unpredictable to pass as human."

"Some worked in the factory," Preston pointed out. "Hollow slave labor has saved us a *lot* of money."

"Apparently not enough to get Potion made any faster! And *still* it ended up being a rush job, getting the gutbag replicas sculpted, getting everything into place in time to release for this goddamn bicentennial."

They made their way to Principal Lincoln's stiff body and, together, lifted it. "We didn't *have* to do it now. I know," he said, withering under her glare. "I know it's the PR opportunity of a lifetime, but . . . we could have waited."

"For another hundred years?" Her eyes flashed, fire behind them. "No. This is our chance. I am sick of hinging my immortality on fits and starts, one backup Hollow at a time. Once we've got an entire town's worth of insurance policies under our control, then we can reassess our marketing plan." She scowled. "What I wouldn't give for at *least* two more years of development to work out the kinks —"

"But I streamlined the process, just like you asked! I made the fumes fatal! They're dead within minutes!"

"Only the older ones," Anita said testily. "That Bursaw kid lived well into the next morning. Which is why I specifically requested the girl today, so that we could have more data on how age affects potency. You moron."

"Oh," Preston said, cowed. "I — oh."

Anita sneered at her partner in disgust as they maneuvered Principal Lincoln into the elevator, pushed the button, and disappeared behind the doors.

Poppy waited a full five minutes before moving. Not that she could have done much in that time — her head was reeling from what she'd witnessed.

Principal Lincoln was dead.

He'd been used to make that day's BiScentennial candle.

Tomorrow's BiScentennial candle would be made with Mrs. Goodwin, who had been pushed into a tank of poisonous Potion.

A wax replacement of her had been animated with Anita Chandler's flame, then sent out into the world.

Poppy had only narrowly escaped the same fate herself.

And Blake was definitely dead.

Every muscle in her body clenched. Only three short days ago she hadn't cared one iota about Blake Bursaw's well-being. On the contrary — she'd hated his guts. She'd wished him dead more times than she could count. This was what she'd always wanted: for him to suffer, to leave her alone once and for all, to be banished from the face of the earth.

So why did she feel like her insides were turning to bile?

"Poppy?"

She whirled around to face Dud . . . but Dud was not there.

Her heart rate began to spike. "Dud? Where are you?"

"Up here!"

She followed his echoing reply to the door marked OUT, the one Preston had gone into and apparently forgotten to close. Inside was another tunnel, this one sloping upward into darkness. "Dud?"

"Yup!"

"Should I join you?"

"Double yup!"

Owing to the sharp incline, it felt like climbing up a playground slide; Poppy had to grip the walls as best she could to keep from slipping. When she reached the top, she stepped out into a wide-open space — one that was a lot brighter and more sterile than the one they had come from.

Poppy had performed at Radio City Music Hall. She knew how big the theater was, knew how expansive and cavernous the space seemed from her tiny spot onstage. And though she knew for a fact that the size of this storage tank was merely a fraction of that legendary landmark . . .

It *felt* just as big.

The space of Tank #2 yawned open — up and up and out and around, balconies upon ledges that rose to the reaches of the ceiling, with a catwalk stretching across the top. The lightning-made hole in the roof allowed for a column of light to stream down from above. But what occupied those spaces weren't applauding patrons of the arts, nor disgrace-hungry reality show spectators.

Words failed her. She tried to shape her mouth into a speaking position, but it wasn't working. It remained slack, numb, as she struggled to come to grips with what sat on the never-ending mezzanines spiraling around the interior of the steel coliseum.

Every single citizen of Paraffin, rendered in wax.

Sculpted to perfection.

And ready to invade.

18

Retreat

"I THINK," POPPY WHISPERED, BACKING UP AND PULLING DUD with her as she gaped at the scores of figures, "we should leave. Quietly. And calmly."

They didn't quite pull it off, flailing down the slope of the slippery tunnel like a pair of clumsy penguins, Poppy's head whirling uncontrollably. *Not just you,* Blake had said of the Poppy sculpture he'd stolen. He must have seen everything—and hadn't even needed to unlawfully break into Tank #2, with that gaping hole in the roof. No wonder he'd been so spooked, so worried about his family, so hesitant to say anything. It sounded crazy because it *was* crazy.

But the Chandlers had silenced him anyway.

"This way!" Dud said once they were back in the cathedral, pointing at BETWEEN — the tunnel to Madame Grosholtz's studio.

"Hang on." Poppy stared at the ACROSS door, which Wax Mrs. Goodwin had left open to reveal yet another tunnel. "This door was locked last time I was here. Let's find out where it goes." She plunged through the opening, pulled Dud in, and closed the door behind them just to be safe.

The tunnel was identical to the others — except for its scent. "What's that smell?" Dud asked, using Poppy's phone as a flashlight.

The acrid odor made Poppy's nausea worse. *Why* was she feeling this way? Why was she taking Blake's demise so hard?

Because by wishing him dead, I killed him.

She knew that wasn't true. She knew it was irrational thinking.

Because he's the same age as me, and it's upsetting when kids die.

Warmer.

Because I tried to save him, but not hard enough.

Bingo.

"I think it's the lake," Poppy said, snapping her focus back to the smell. There was no time for guilt — not now, anyway. "We must be walking directly beneath it."

Which meant, according to the mental map she drew as they walked, that they were crossing from the factory toward the center of town, and that the tunnel should end right about . . .

"Whoa," Poppy whispered as they climbed a small staircase back up into the world.

"Where are we?" Dud asked.

Poppy looked around the small storage space, a crack of light in the wall illuminating a stack of rakes and several bags of potting soil. But the most telltale sign of their location was the pounding of feet on the ceiling above them, along with a deafening blast of music.

"I think we're under the gazebo," Poppy said.

She approached the crack in the wall and gave it a gentle push. It noiselessly swung open, depositing them in the town square. It seemed that the parade had ended; everyone was now gathered on Main Street, chatting and eating food from street vendors and dancing to the jammin' tunes of the Sugar Maple Leaf Rag Band, the most unfortunately named jazz combo in New England.

And luckily, everyone was having too much fun to notice the two bedraggled, lake-scented kids stumbling out of the bottom of the gazebo. She pushed the door shut, its edges blending seamlessly with the ornamental design on the base, making it virtually invisible from the outside.

"Oh . . . my . . . God," Poppy said with great weight in her voice, in stark contrast to the Boogie Woogies boogie-woogieing around her. "That's it. That's it!" Her hands were spinning wildly, a nice visual representation of what was happening inside her brain. "The Chandlers must light the Hollows down there in the cathedral, then send their newly sentient clones through this tunnel and up and out and—" Her gaze wandered to the masses of people. "And into a massive crowd of everyone in town . . . where they can blend in instantly . . ." Her excitement slowly transformed into dread. "So the rest of them could be . . . anyone at all."

Dud tried to look concerned, but his attention wandered to the mounted police unit. "I want to pet the monsters!" he cried, bolting for the horses.

Poppy, too dazed to stop him, simply watched him go and

assessed the damage that she'd failed to control. *We are screwed,* she chanted in her head. *We are so, so screwed.*

"*There* you are," an unkind voice said behind her.

Poppy turned around. There was Jill, hand on hip and scowl on face.

"Jill!" Everything that had gone down between them earlier that morning dissipated the instant Poppy saw her best friend, pulling her into a fierce hug before Jill could object. "I am so glad to see you."

Jill looked as though she had a few more choice words for Poppy but couldn't decide whether she should unleash them, given Poppy's instant bestowal of forgiveness. "Are you okay? Are — have you been *crying?*"

"Hellooo, everyone!" a woman's voice trilled.

The music had stopped. Wax Miss Bea, with Wax Big Bob standing behind her, was now at the microphone, smiling plastically as she thanked everyone for being part of such a wonderful day, for making Paraffin the wonderful town that it is . . .

"For being helpless lambs to the slaughter," Poppy whispered under her breath. "For falling blind to the crimes and atrocities being committed under their noses —"

"Pops, we're in public," Jill said. "Try and dial back the insanity a smidge."

Poppy exhaled. "Jill, I know you've had a hard time believing me up until now, but trust me: there is some really weird, *really* messed-up stuff going on in this town. And I really have proof this time."

The crowd burst into a raucous round of applause at whatever lies the Bursaws had spewed forth. "And now," Wax Miss Bea added, "for the final event of the day — the raffle drawing! Colt, would you like to do the honors?"

Colt Lamberty, radiant smile in place and microphone in hand, bounded up the gazebo steps in a pair of blindingly polished, expensive-looking shoes. He beamed out over the crowd. "Good afternoon, Paraffin!"

Paraffin responded with hoots and whistles.

"What a beautiful crowd. Gary, get on up here and get a shot of this beautiful crowd."

Colt's long-suffering cameraman obeyed his cruel master and joined Colt onstage, sweeping the lens of the camera over the townspeople. "Stunning," Colt said. "Just stunning. Now! Who's ready for the big raffle drawing?"

More hoots. More hollers.

"Councilman Bursaw, the entries please!"

Wax Big Bob wheeled out the raffle drum, a large gold cylinder into which the citizens of Paraffin had stuffed their hopes and dreams. The crowd oohed.

"I can't take this," said Poppy, the sickness rising again. "Look at them — happy, careless, no idea that their demise is imminent and that their elected officials have been transformed into diabolical wax pod people! We have to tell them! We have to!"

With that, Jill yanked her out of the crowd, all the way down to the edge of the lake.

"What are you doing?" Poppy said, pulling out of Jill's grip. "They have a right to know! How can you —"

"Well, well, well!" The Giddy Committee appeared, now changed out of their Bavarian frocks and back into their civilian clothes — except for Connor, who was still wearing his cape. "Look, everyone," he said, glaring at Poppy. "It's Benedict Arnold von Trapp."

Jesus snorted. "Weak, bro."

"I think that I, Connor Galpert, speak for all of us when I say that when our fearless leader abandons us, we have the right to know why."

Poppy looked at Jill, who shrugged. "They have a point."

Poppy swallowed. "Um —" She swept her gaze around the circle, meeting five pairs of betrayed, inquisitive eyes.

"Let me guess," said Banks. "It has something to do with that pile of insanity you heaped upon us yesterday."

"Yeah, but —"

Louisa grasped Poppy's fluffy collar in her hands and pulled her close. "We brought the *hills* to *life* with the *sound* of *music* for you," she spat with venom. "You owe us an explanation!"

And of course, Dud chose that moment to barrel into her circle of friends and yell, "Poppy, my finger fell off!"

He held out his hand. Where once his thumb resided was a cleanly shorn stub, a flat beige surface — that was noticeably not spurting blood.

Poppy gaped. "It *fell off?*"

"Yes! Well, no. I was petting one of the police monsters, and he ate it."

"You mean a horse? A horse ate your finger?"

"Yep!"

Those same five pairs of eyes switched from being miffed to being baffled, horrified, and about to cause a panic.

"Okay," Poppy said carefully, not wanting to spark the powder keg of hysteria. "Nobody freak out. Let's all sit down and talk about this."

The Giddy Committee sat down on the grass in a circle, staring at Dud. Dud sat next to Poppy, staring at the spot where his thumb used to be.

"To start, this is Dud," Poppy told the group. Dud waved. "He is made of wax. As you can see."

"And he's — what, on our team?" said Louisa. "I thought the wax people were the bad guys!"

"I assure you, Dud is harmless."

"So are beluga whales. That doesn't mean you should adopt one and welcome it into your home."

"*Dud* is not the problem here," Poppy told them. "The problem is that all that stuff I told you yesterday is *true*. The wax imposters, the lighting of the Hollows — it all checks out." She described what she'd seen in the storage tank. "They've stockpiled Hollows of *everyone*. Every single citizen in Paraffin!"

Louisa rolled her eyes. "One wonders where they find the time."

"They've got plenty of time. They don't sleep! Why do you think the factory runs so many market research tests? Almost everyone in town has gone to one of those sessions, answered exhaustive questionnaires about themselves, had their speech patterns and mannerisms filmed, all in the name of market research — when in fact, the

Chandlers have been studying how to act once they inhabit them. They took plenty of photos of us for Madame Grosholtz to sculpt from. Now they're kidnapping townspeople, two at a time. Every day, two new Chandler clones released out into the town. Every day, two new evil wax-pod-people doppelgangers out there, disguised as our fellow citizens. We have to stop them!"

"You keep using the word 'we,'" Louisa said. "Why is that?"

"Because *we* are the only ones who know about this. And we can't tip anyone else off, because everyone else is a suspect. Smitty is one of them! And so is Principal Lincoln! I saw them stiffening the real Principal Lincoln's body, and who knows what they did with it—" She tried to make herself stop yelling and speak more calmly. "We are essentially responsible for saving Paraffin. Why is that so hard to understand?"

Louisa gave Banks a disbelieving look. "Is she listening to herself?"

"Look," Poppy said, "if you don't want to help, fine. Dud and I can tackle it on our own. I just thought—" And here she adopted a mock-innocent face. "I thought that, you know, who better to help identify imposters acting like other people than actors themselves?" She let out a plaintive breath. "But if you guys don't think you can do it, then . . . forget it."

The Giddy Committee was insulted.

"*I* could do it," Connor said. "*I'm* a real actor."

Louisa scoffed. "She never said you weren't. She's just trying to manipulate us."

Poppy held her gaze. "Is it working?"

Louisa relented with a sigh.

"Wait a second," Banks said. "Does this mean they can, like, read each other's minds? If they're all offshoots from Anita and Preston, are Anita and Preston controlling all of them, all at once?"

"That's . . . a good question." Poppy thought for a moment. "No, I don't think so. When I was at the Bursaws'"— she winced at the name— "I'm pretty sure Big Bob had to call Anita to tell her that I was there. They're more like clones. That's how Madame Grosholtz described it in her message, anyway. They're duplicates of Anita and Preston, but they don't share the same consciousness, so there's no automatic communication between them. I'm guessing Preston is in Big Bob and Anita is in Miss Bea, but I suppose it could also be the other way around—"

"Yeah," said Banks dryly, "we wouldn't want to impose gender stereotypes onto the monstrous wax people."

"What's the big deal?" asked Jesus. "If they're only taking the place of assholes anyway, aren't we better off?"

"No, Jesus, we're not," said Poppy, "because (a) immortal beings hell-bent on supreme power are not in fact preferable to the Bursaws, hard as that may be to believe, (b) they're killing the people they're replacing, and (c) you can do simple math, right?"

From the look he gave her, Jesus could not do simple math.

"There are only one thousand and fourteen citizens in Paraffin," she said. "At the rate of two per day, they'll have replaced us completely within a year and a half. And I'm betting that they'll increase that rate as soon as they make enough Hollows to overpower us. I mean, since Saturday they've already made seven clones

261

of themselves — most of whom hold strong positions of power or influence in the community, who will be able to keep up the charade and convince people that nothing out of the ordinary is going on. And before long, it'll hit a tipping point. In no time at all, they'll get you, me, your families. *Everyone.*"

That seemed to do it. The members of the Giddy Committee went silent, going over the math in their heads.

Then Jesus abruptly got to his feet.

"Where are you going?" Poppy asked.

"I just got an idea."

"Can you run it by me first?"

"Nope! Gotta go!"

"Jesus, wait —"

But he ran off before anyone could stop him.

Connor scowled. "Truly, Madame Director, I implore you, a hooligan such as Jesus is not fit for the part of the son of God —"

"Connor. Bigger fish to fry here."

"Poppy, what's your plan to deal with this?" asked Jill. "Do you *have* a plan?"

"Of course I do. We're going to look at people. Hard. If you think they're acting suspicious, follow them. Study them. From now on, *everyone in town* is a suspect."

"That narrows it down," Louisa muttered.

"Louisa, I am *this* close to knocking your block off." Pause. Deep breath. "But you're right. Let's be smart about this."

Poppy took out her notebook. Everyone groaned.

"We need to be organized!" she insisted. "And the best place to start is by listing what we know. Or *who* we know for sure are Hollows." She drew a crude calendar. "Now, Sunday was the first day the BiScentennial candles went on sale. That was Big Bob and Miss Bea. The next day, yesterday, was Blake and Smitty. Today was Principal Lincoln and . . . I don't know who yet. The scent is Italian Leather."

"Palladino is an Italian name," said Louisa.

"Louisa, I am this close. *This close.*" She wrote down a big question mark. "Tomorrow will be my neighbor, Mrs. Goodwin, and — well, it was supposed to be me. And the next day it'll be two more people, unless we figure out a way to stop all this by the end of the day. Which seems kind of impossible."

But Poppy felt a little better. Having a plan made her feel less helpless, and things were falling into place. She just had to figure out what that place was. "Here's what's going to happen: I'm going to go home, lock myself in my room, and not come out until I've figured out what to do about all this. Behold: The Plan." She removed her new notebook and held it up as if it were the Holy Bible. "In the meantime, you guys try and figure out who Italian Leather could be. Ask around. Find out who's acting slightly less than normal. Then call me if you learn anything important, if you think of anything new, or if you see or hear anything odd."

"And if we encounter a Hollow?" asked Banks. "What do we do, bash their heads in?"

"No. I mean, I don't know yet. We'll have to destroy them

somehow, but that's getting ahead of ourselves. Until then, just focus on ID'ing them. Keep your eyes peeled as you have never kept them peeled before!"

The Giddy Committee agreed to the plan, then gathered their stuff and left the park. "How do you peel an eye?" Dud asked Poppy and Jill as they walked up the small hill toward the town square.

"With an eye peeler," Jill said.

"What's an eye peeler?"

"It peels eyes."

They walked for a moment in an awkward silence.

"So, are we okay?" Poppy asked Jill somewhat desperately. "Because I really need us to be okay."

"We are. I'm sorry about what I said to Crawford."

"And I'm sorry I've been such a lunatic."

"Yeah, but—" Jill looked repentant. It looked strange on her. "If you're right about all this stuff, then *I've* been a triple dick for not believing you. And if, heaven forbid, you were in danger or got hurt because I ignored you . . ."

Poppy couldn't help but smile. "It's okay, Jill. Out of respect for you, I won't even do the I-told-you-so dance."

"You are too kind." Jill nodded at something behind Poppy. "Incoming."

"*There* you are!" Poppy's mother emerged from the crowd. "You kids sounded great! It was so crowded, though, it was hard to see you—especially you, Poppy—"

"What have you got there?" Poppy interjected as her father and Owen came into view.

"We won the raffle!" said her father. "A limited-edition copy of Paraffin-opoly. Isn't that exciting?"

"I suppose 'exciting' could conceivably be a word used to describe that, sure."

"And the Grosholtz Candle Factory was selling surplus wax at their booth," her mother added. "So we bought a whole bunch for you to sculpt, Dud! It's waiting in the car!"

"Cool!" Dud spread out his hands excitedly. Poppy grabbed the one that did not have a thumb and, not knowing how else to explain that away, held it in a loosely romantic manner.

"Aww," her parents sighed simultaneously.

* * *

When the Palladino family got home around one o'clock — and after Poppy made Dud surreptitiously resculpt his thumb from the surplus wax — she immediately brushed off her family's pleas for merriment. "I know it's family fun day, but seriously, I'm exhausted," she announced, itching to get started on The Plan.

"But it's a holiday," her mom said, and held up a plate. "I made pie."

"Pear-affin pie," her dad added. "Get it?"

"I do. And — yes, that is very cute. It'll play great on the blog," she told her mom, forcing a smile. "But —"

"We've got the whole day, Pops!" her father crowed. "We could see a movie, we could take a drive, we can go for a bike ride and maybe take off the training wheels this time?" he said, nudging Owen. "The possibilities are endless! Vermont is our oyster!"

265

"I know Vermont is our oyster. But I stayed up late last night planning for the parade today, and honestly, all I want to do is crash."

"Well, all right," her dad said, not bothering to hide the disappointment in his voice. "Dud? How about you? Want to go on a bike ride?"

Dud stared at him. "What is a bike?"

*   *   *

Poppy smushed her head into her mattress, savoring the quiet. The instant Dud had revealed that he'd never been on a bike, her parents swooped in with nonstop talk about heading over to Cycle Town and buying him his first ten-speed and oh won't it be *fun* for him and Owen to learn together and we'll be back later, Poppy, have a good rest!

She glanced at Madame Grosholtz's message candle, still burning. The wax had burned about two-thirds of the way down, but the words had definitely ended; there was at least two inches of blank space.

Madame Grosholtz had said all there was to say.

Poppy shivered. Now that she was all alone, she realized that solitude maybe wasn't the best thing for her right at the moment. The mere concept of Blake Being Dead had grown into a big black cloud choking every inch of her room. It was such an utterly impossible thing. Grownups were the ones who died, who got somber funerals and flower arrangements and the empty consolations that they'd lived full lives. Not someone who was as young and energetic as she was. Blake had used that energy in malicious ways, true, but she'd seen a different side of him over the past couple of days, one that cared about his family and was willing to do anything to save them.

He didn't deserve death. None of the townspeople did. The image of all those dead-eyed Hollows kept swirling through her head, pounding, moaning, *it's hopeless, it's hopeless, it's hopeless* . . .

No. Pessimism had never gotten her anywhere, and it wasn't going to help her now. Blake was dead, and nothing could bring him back — but at least she could make sure it wouldn't happen to anyone else.

She uncapped her pen, cracked open The Plan, and started writing.

19

~~Obsess~~

FROM THE MOMENT SHE GOT HOME UNTIL HER FAMILY returned, Poppy's pen never stopped moving. It scribbled and scratched, zigged and zagged, crossed things out, added things in, created flow charts, maps, graphs, timelines — and by the time she heard footsteps on the stairs, she'd filled nearly half the pages of her Pen Dragon 2.0.

Dud burst into her room. "I learned how to ride a bike!"

"That's nice," she said, not looking up from her notes. "But I've got some murders to avenge."

Either Dud didn't know the meaning of the word "murder" or such grisly enterprises did not interest him, because his reply was, "Okay! I'm gonna go eat some pie. Do you want any?"

"No. And Dud —" She finally looked up, her eyes bloodshot and frantic. "Tell my parents I'm not to be disturbed. I'm working on something top-secret, and I need total concentration."

"Okay!"

But once dinnertime came and went, her father paid a visit.

"We've got a killer game of Paraffin-opoly going," he said. "You sure you don't want to join us?"

"I'm sure."

"What are you up to, Pops? You shouldn't be working so hard on a holiday—"

"I'm writing my college essay!" she shouted, the first thing that came to mind. "So if you want me to get into college, I suggest you leave me alone!"

Cowed, he closed the door. "Okay, hon. Sorry. Let us know if you need any help."

Poppy felt terrible. But she did not have the luxury of feeling feelings at the moment, so she channeled all that guilt down her arm, through her hand, and into her pen.

* * *

Around nine o'clock another knock came at her door.

"I'm. Busy."

Her mom opened the door anyway, sticking her grinning face through the crack. "I know, honey, but . . ." She let out a giddy puff of air and threw up her hands. "You *have* to come see this."

"What?" Poppy stashed her notebook under the sheets of her bed and reluctantly stood up. "Did Dad crown himself king of Paraffin or something?"

"Oh, no. Even better. Dud's been doing some more sculpting with the wax I bought today."

Poppy's feet felt like cinder blocks as she plodded down the staircase. Today had been upsetting and horrific enough. Was there anything on earth that could possibly top it, that could be worthy enough to be a grand finale?

Oh, Poppy thought as she walked into the living room. *Yep. This.*

"I made *you,*" Dud said, biting his lip to contain his grin. "Well, just your head so far. But I want to make the rest. What do you think?"

Poppy thought that it was very odd, staring into her own eyes in her own disembodied wax head. "Unnerving" didn't begin to describe it. "Ghastly" perhaps, or "heebie-jeebie factory."

"It's . . . very accurate," she said.

And it was. He'd captured every detail. Her unnaturally large eyes, her tiny nose, her scattered freckles. Even the expression was dead-on: a mix of optimistic ambition, ambitious desperation, and desperate optimism.

Dud had put the love in.

"Do you like it?" he asked shyly.

"Yes." Poppy looked away from her mirrored glass eyes, back into his. A mix of pride and affection swelled within her. "It's amazing, just like the others. You are so good at this."

"As good as Madame Grosholtz, you think?"

"Definitely."

He let out a quiet, happy gasp of delight. "Good. *Great.* Then my plan might work!"

Poppy's smile cracked. "What plan?"

"And Madame who?" her mother asked.

A jolt of energy seemed to spring up from the soles of Dud's feet. He grabbed Poppy's wrist and dragged her into the kitchen. "Be right back!" he shouted at the rest of the family as he shut himself and Poppy up in the pantry.

Poppy was miffed, mostly because she knew she'd never be able to come up with an explanation of why she was in the pantry with Dud that wouldn't evoke the words "seven," "minutes," or "heaven." "What's going on, Dud?"

"I've been thinking. About what you said about dying. And then about what Madame Grosholtz said. And I thought — okay, maybe *these* Hollow people are bad, but it doesn't have to be that way!"

Poppy raised an eyebrow.

"So I thought," Dud continued, "that maybe we could figure out how to put your flame into a Hollow, and then you can live forever, like me!"

Poppy suddenly felt a strong need to lie down. She settled for leaning a hand against the wall. "Oh, Dud. I don't think that's a good idea."

Dud kept smiling; it was clear that he'd so deeply convinced himself that she was going to be excited that he hadn't processed her negative reaction yet. "What?"

"I don't want to be seventeen forever," she said, her voice rising as she heard the words spoken aloud, realizing the exact magnitude of their horribleness. "This has been the worst year of my life! With the only comfort being that it will be *over* in a few months!"

Dud scratched his head. "But —"

No. He was making this too hard. He was complicating things

where things should not be complicated. There had been no X for a person like Dud in the formula that was her senior year, and adding one now would mess up the equation. And a not-human person, at that — it had to involve exponents. It was too complex.

"I don't want to live forever," she continued, manic, panicking. Even with all the death smacking her in the face over the past few days, this was not something she wanted. "Even if we did know how Madame Grosholtz did it, which we don't."

"But if I got my sculpting talent from her, maybe I could also figure out —"

"Dud, no. Not like that. I mean, in theory, sure, immortality sounds nice, but if that's the kind of person I'd turn into — like the Chandlers, usurping innocent people's lives just to add more years to mine — then no, thank you. Besides, what's the point? I might live forever, but my family wouldn't, my friends wouldn't. I'd be all alone!"

Dud dug his sneaker into the floor. "You'd have me."

She didn't know what to say to that, so she ignored it. "But I *want* to grow up," she insisted. Blake had been robbed of that chance, and she had no intention of squandering her own. "I want to go to college, have a career, have kids, live a full life —"

"So do I!"

Dud looked surprised at his own outburst, then recoiled a little, knitting his fingers together just as Madame Grosholtz had done.

He gave Poppy a heartbreaking glance. "I want all that too. I want to be human. But I can't be. So I thought — if I can't be human, then you could be wax. But I guess if you don't want to be like me, then . . ."

Poppy wanted to comfort him, wanted to say something that would make everything all better. But nothing came to her. So they both remained still and let silence fill in the rest.

*   *   *

Poppy lay awake in bed, though she was exhausted. The horrors of the day — and night — had swelled beneath her consciousness like a rough sea, bouncing her tiny boat about, never letting it settle into calm. Every time she closed her eyes, she saw Dud's, pleading, and hers snapped back open again.

So she tossed.

She turned.

Her stomach rumbled.

And then, just as she was starting to nod off, her phone rang.

"It's him! It's him! It's him!" Connor shouted at the other end before she could say hello.

"Who's 'him'? What's going on?"

"One of the Hollows! On Channel Six!"

Poppy jumped out of bed to run downstairs, then remembered that their television set had gone to that great trash pile in the sky. Grunting, she plugged her earbuds into her phone and opened the Channel Six YouNews app instead.

Naturally, the top story was the bicentennial parade. She tapped on a live feed of Colt himself, standing in front of a spotlight at the center of the darkened town square. In the background, cleanup crews were still sweeping piles of confetti. "Hundreds of Paraffiners gathered here today for a once-in-a-lifetime celebration," he said, stiffly gesturing to the space behind him. "Truly, Paraffin Day was a day to remember."

Poppy brought the screen closer to her face. Putting aside for a moment his striking good looks and dazzling teeth, she immediately perceived that Colt looked *off.* To be fair, he had always seemed a little otherworldly, but now his eyes appeared glassed over and his nose seemed crooked—hardly noticeable at all if you weren't looking for it. She hadn't noticed it at the parade.

"Thank goodness for high definition," she said, staring at the screen.

"And look," said Connor. "Look at his shoes!"

The camera had panned to the confetti-blanketed ground, catching Colt's feet in the action. "So?" Poppy said. "What about his shoes?"

"*Leather.* Fancy leather!"

Poppy gasped. "Oh. My. *God*—"

"Who are you talking to?"

She looked up. Her father's head poked through her bedroom door.

Poppy ripped out her earbuds without saying goodbye to Connor. "Just watching the news," she tried to tell her dad in a breezy voice. She showed him the phone. "There's . . . footage of the parade. I wanted to see if we were on it."

"Oh, right!" Her father took a seat on her bed and gave her

head a hug as he looked at the screen. "You know, I missed you, Pops. There were so many people there, of course, it was hard to see. I caught part of the Giddy Committee — and definitely heard them — but I couldn't find you."

Poppy was beginning to see the flaw in her plan. She'd just invited her father to watch video evidence of her absence. "You know what?" she said, putting her phone away. "I changed my mind. I don't want to watch it."

He frowned. "Why not?"

"Oh, you know . . ." She got that haunted look in her eye, the one that always accompanied *Triple Threat* flashbacks. "I don't think I'm ready to see myself on TV again."

"Ah. Of course. Well, I'm sure you were great, sweetie."

"She was!" Dud said from Owen's room. "She did a backflip!"

Evidently Dud had learned the subtle art of passive aggression.

Her father gaped at her. "I didn't know you could do a backflip."

Poppy held his gaze. "I can. Apparently."

"You'll have to show me!"

"Um —"

"But for now, bed."

"Yes!" She hurriedly got under the covers. "Bed. Bed is what I will go to." She raised her voice. *"Dud and I will both go to bed."*

Her father gave her a wink. "But not together, right?"

"Dad."

20

~~Abandon personal hygiene~~

"GOOD HEAVENS," HER FATHER SAID FROM THE BREAKFAST table, "you look like a malnourished zombie."

Poppy gave him a cranky look. "As opposed to a well-nourished zombie?"

"I imagine there are different levels of healthfulness, even in the zombie world. What do you think?" he asked his wife, who was adding something nauseating to a tub of yogurt.

"You know, I'm not up to date on my knowledge of undead nutrition," she said, spooning a glob into her mouth. "Where's Dud, Owen?"

Oh, Dud? Poppy thought. *He wanted to make an immortal version of me, and I broke his heart for his troubles. I even made him destroy it — that's right, I forced him to systematically smush up that beautiful, flawlessly crafted head of mine. Because there are body snatchers in them there hills, and I don't want any of them to steal my identity. It would have been a nice gift from a good friend, but you know, life sucks and everything turns to dust and I feel like a piece of absolute garbage.*

Owen shrugged at his mother. "He said he doesn't feel good."

"Oh, dear. Would he like some hot oatmeal?"

"No," Poppy interrupted. "In accordance with his island tradition, we are to stay far, far away from him while he battles the 'gods of pestilence.' Or he'll, like, implode."

"Don't be silly, Poppy. He won't implode."

"You want to go tell him his gods are silly?"

She did not. "I'll just leave a bowl outside the room."

Poppy's father jumped up. "And I'll slip some immune boosters under the door!"

Good luck, thought Poppy.

She'd already knocked on Owen's door. She'd pled. She'd apologized.

She'd gotten no reply but silence.

* * *

Upset, and facing a dead end when it came to Dud, Poppy refocused her thoughts on the Hollows. Her hands, slick with sweat, slid around the steering wheel as she drove to school. She didn't want to waste time with school at all — saving the town from invaders seemed like a pretty good reason to skip — but the Giddy Committee was a big part of The Plan, and to get to the Giddy Committee, she had to attend rehearsal. And to attend rehearsal, she had to attend school.

But not all of it.

Poppy hurried up to Jill's locker and whispered, "Skip homeroom with me."

"My, my," Jill said with a grin. "You sure know how to drop a girl's drawers."

"Stay long enough to be counted for attendance, then meet me at Clementine."

Her homeroom teacher took roll call more slowly than usual, it seemed. Poppy was nervous; she'd never skipped school before. She sat ramrod straight in her chair, her nerves stretched taut and ready to snap like a rubber band.

As soon as attendance was over, Poppy asked to use the bathroom and booked it through the main hallway.

"No running," a deep voice rumbled behind her.

Poppy stopped, then slowly turned around. Wax Principal Lincoln emerged from his office, cutting an imposing profile as he stared her down.

"Sorry," Poppy said breathlessly.

He gave her a stern nod, then turned and went back into his office.

Poppy speed-walked the rest of the way, shuddering and whispering "Creepycreepycreepy," all the way to her car.

*　　*　　*

"But you already know who the BiScentennial is going to be today," Jill said as they turned up Secret Service Way. "Mrs. Goodwin, I thought."

"Right. But in order to stay one step ahead of things, we need to figure out who the BiScentennials are going to be *tomorrow*. Those are the ones who would have been lured into the Potion this morning."

"Why didn't you just do a stakeout at the tanks?"

"Because I don't know if they stick to the same time, and I'm sure not camping out in the danger zone all day."

"But you *were* willing to let said luring happen without trying to warn or stop innocent people from getting shoved into a tank?"

"Of course not! But I also have parents. Parents who would definitely notice if their daughter up and left to go do an overnight stakeout."

"But —"

"No, no more. Silence."

Any objections Jill could raise, Poppy had already wrestled with. She simply could not be everywhere. She could not thwart every one of the Chandlers' plans. This thing had gotten too big too fast, and at this point there was bound to be some collateral damage. All she could do was use the tools at her disposal to prevent it from getting worse.

As Clementine crested the hill and the tanks came into view, Poppy rolled down the car windows. "Okay. Smell."

Poppy took a deep breath. Two scents began dueling for her attention, switching off with each gust of wind.

One was sweet.

The other reeked of some pungent, toxic substance.

"What is that?" Poppy asked, wincing. "Ammonia? Vinegar?"

Jill frowned. "Chemicals."

"Who do we know that would smell of—" Poppy gasped. "JEAN!"

"Who in the heck is Jean?"

"She's the new pharmacist at CVS—and I've never seen her before, so I'm pretty sure she just recently moved here! Which totally makes sense. Less of a chance that neighbors will know her well enough to notice a change in her appearance or personality."

"Hmm. Good point."

"But the other one . . ." Poppy took another whiff. "It's sweet, definitely—but I can't—"

Jill started to snicker. "You don't know what it is?"

"No, what?" Poppy asked. "Candy? Cream soda?"

"Nope." Jill gave her an inside-joke smile. "It's Forbidden Chocolate."

Poppy stared back at her. "Oh, get the hell out. Are you sure?"

"You insult me, dear Poppy. Of course I'm sure. I'd stake my life on it."

Goose bumps trickled up Poppy's neck. "If Greg were a candle, he'd be Forbidden Chocolate! Of course!"

"He's such an upright, dare I say *friendly,* guy," Jill replied, equally excited. "Who wouldn't trust that face of his?"

Poppy let out a squeal. "Jill, you magnificent genius!"

Someone popped up from under the blanket in the back seat. "What about me?"

There was much screaming.

"Dud!" Poppy yelled. "What are you doing in here? Why are you hiding? Are you trying to give us massive heart attacks?"

Dud had not yet mastered the skill of answering Poppy's multiple questions at once. "Um —"

"I'll translate," said Jill, turning in her seat. "What's going on, Waxy? I thought you were sick."

"No, I'm okay." He looked at Poppy's reflection in the rearview mirror. "I just didn't want to be alone in the house."

"Do you want to go back to school?" Poppy asked. "To sculpt some more?"

He looked down at his hands. "No."

Poppy's heart broke in yet another place. She'd killed his passion for the only thing he loved. Great. "What do you want to do, then?"

"Can I . . ."

"What?"

He looked at Poppy again. "Can I go sit by the lake?"

"The lake? Why the lake?"

"Well — I really want to go to the melty place —"

"Madame Grosholtz's studio?"

"Yeah, but that seems too dangerous. So I can just look at it from across the lake. I can sit on a bench."

"You want to sit on a bench and look at the lake," Poppy said unsurely. "You know that's something that mostly only old men do, right?"

"That's fine," Dud said.

Poppy looked at Jill, then shrugged. "Seems harmless enough."

Jill furrowed her brow but said nothing.

* * *

When they got to the lake, Dud's bad mood instantly dissipated. "Goose monsters!" he yelped.

"Don't talk to strangers," Poppy said as he got out of the car. "And if you feel like you're in danger, hide. Remember hide-and-seek?"

"Okay!" he said, barreling down toward the shore.

Poppy bit her lip. "He's actually not all that good at hide-and-seek —"

"Listen to me, Poppy," Jill interrupted, fixing an intense stare on Dud's receding form. "You need to *pay attention* to him."

"What do you mean?"

"You know I like Dud. I do. But —" Jill's mouth twisted. "Look, I've been thinking about this a lot, and — I don't trust him. I *can't.*"

"Oh, Jill. He's harmless."

"Is he? If all the other Hollows are being controlled by the Chandlers, how do we know that Dud isn't too?"

"Because he isn't."

"How do you know that?"

"Because I do."

Jill raised an eyebrow. "Do you? Without a doubt?"

Poppy shifted uncomfortably. "No, not without a doubt, but it's *Dud.* He's —" His smile could be seen from a hundred feet away. "He's one of the good guys."

But Jill was right; Poppy couldn't know that for sure. Even if Dud himself were pure and good, one of the other Hollows could have easily booby-trapped him. She *thought* that Madame Grosholtz was the one who planted him in her trunk, but she couldn't prove that. A grenade of evil could be lying in wait somewhere deep inside him, ready to explode as soon as one of them thought it could best be used to their advantage.

He was potentially dangerous.

He was a liability.

"He should be dealt with," said Jill.

Poppy reeled back as if she'd been slapped.

"*No.*" She wrung her increasingly clammy hands. "We're not going to do that. He may be a liability, but he could just as easily be an asset."

"You're letting your feelings cloud your judgment."

Of course she was. Of course it was ridiculous that she should have any emotional connection to a person-shaped ball of wax. Of course she could be putting the town in further danger by trusting him.

But *he* trusted *her.* Didn't that count for something? How could she betray him like that?

"We're not going after Dud," Poppy said, struggling to keep her voice from breaking. "Don't bring it up again."

Jill leaned back in her seat. "Fine."

Dud chose that moment to run back to the car. "Poppy! I saw a snake monster!" he said, his face exploding with wonder.

"Cool, Dud." Poppy gave him a tight smile but couldn't keep it for long — not after she'd spotted Jill out of the corner of her eye, mouthing, *"Snake."*

* * *

The ride back to school was decidedly frosty.

Paraffin High's rotating class schedule had deposited Mr. Crawford's class into the second period of the day, so Poppy made sure to get there in time — but she was so distracted that she didn't get to enjoy her usual ten full minutes of excitement and preparatory primping. She blustered into the biology lab, took her seat, and began nervously tapping her pen against the leg of the desk.

"Mitochondria," Mr. Crawford began after the bell had rung. "Your friends and mine. Let's muck around for a bit in their squirrelly ways, shall we?"

God, he's gorgeous, Poppy allowed herself to think for a brief moment, before remembering, *Oh, right, the town is doomed.* A surge of nausea pounded through her stomach, the odor of the lab definitely not helping.

Mr. Crawford grabbed a marker from his desk and turned around to write something on the board. But Poppy wasn't paying attention.

She was sniffing the air, detecting the chemical smell of the preservative used to keep the dissected animals.

She was listening to the inflections of Mr. Crawford's voice, the way they sounded slightly unnatural, almost rehearsed.

And she was staring at the back of his head.

". . . and of course, all those folds increase surface area. Any questions? Yes, Poppy?"

"What's wrong with your ear?"

His hand flew up to his right earlobe, which had sagged down about half an inch longer than the one on the left. He quickly massaged it between his fingers, and by the time he let go, it was back to normal. "Guess I missed a bit of hair gel," he said, letting out a small self-effacing laugh. "Thank you, Poppy, for pointing it out. In front of everyone."

She should have been embarrassed. She should have wanted to die. And she would have, if he'd been the real Mr. Crawford.

But judging by the infinitesimal sneer he shot at her right before turning back to the board, he was not.

21

~~Self-preserve~~

POPPY HAD NO IDEA HOW SHE MADE IT THROUGH THE REST of that class. She may have somehow put herself into a catatonic play-dead state the way some animals do when they feel threatened.

It shouldn't have come down to a melted earlobe. She should have figured it out sooner — of course the chemical smell was his, not JEAN!'s. She knew Mr. Crawford's scent better than her own!

My beloved, she thought, biting her lip to keep it from quivering. *Could he still be alive in the Potion tank? Or is he dead? And — oh, God, what about his family?* — for the first time considering his wife and children with a sense of something other than abject jealousy.

She'd been there at the tank that very morning! She should have tried to save him! But no, she'd already tried to get to Mrs. Goodwin and had gotten nowhere. That tank was secured too well for her to break through in a pinch.

Better to do things right than rushed. It killed her to have to think that way, so callous and calculating, but the greater good of the town had to come first. The Plan would go into effect tomorrow, no matter what.

Her comatose classroom strategy lasted straight on through calculus, music, history, and gym, which was the easiest of all — she just showed up looking as grim and unenthusiastic as she always did, lingering around the sidelines as basketball happened in front of her. It wasn't until she left the locker room that her nerves ramped up again, when she ran into Jesus.

And the day immediately and without hesitation got worse.

"Hey, Poppy, guess what?" he said. "I melted the principal."

"What?"

He fluffed himself up, looking proud. "I. Melted. The —"

"Oh my God, *shhh*. Come on."

Poppy grabbed his wrist and dragged him into the alcove under the staircase, where kids sometimes went to make out. "Slobber Junction, Palladino?" he said, waggling his eyebrows at her. "I'm flattered."

"No. Never. Please reiterate what you said, and then explain it to me in the greatest of detail."

"I melted the principal!"

"Elaborate."

"It went down like this." He spread his hands out to set the scene. "When I got to school 'bout a half hour ago, that orc of a lunch lady caught me smoking outside. Sent me to the principal's office. So I went, and you know, this ain't my first barbecue — I know how to sweet-talk my way out of detention. So I swagger into the office, bump fists with Miss Fitzgerald — have you met her? The new secretary? *Damn,* the booty on that woman —"

"Jesus! Focus!"

"Hey, I wasn't rude about it! Jesus is a gentleman! So I *respectfully* bump fists with Miss Fitzgerald, wish her the best of mornings, and stride on into Lincoln's office. He doesn't see me come in at first, he's turned around, looking through a file cabinet. I said, '*Sic semper tyrannis,* Lincoln.' That's what I always say. We got a whole thing going on. You know, like John Wilkes —"

"I got it. Continue."

"But this time he jumped, all surprised and shit, and scraped his hand on the corner of the cabinet — which is made of sharp metal, so there shoulda been a cut there. But it didn't bleed! And then he rubbed it real fast and, like, made it go away! I guess he thought I wouldn't notice, but when he took his other hand away, there wasn't even a scratch mark there anymore."

Poppy felt sick. "Go on."

"So I said, '*Busted,* Lincoln!' And of course he went all innocent and shit, 'What are you talking about?' but it was too late."

Poppy's palms were getting sweaty. "Too late for what?"

"I already *told* you! I set him on fire and melted his waxy ass to the ground!"

This claim, now repeated to her for the fourth time, still did not compute. "How . . . did . . . you do that?"

He rolled his eyes, as if there should be no difficulty in

comprehending the words he was saying. "I took out my flame-thrower," he said slowly, explaining, "and burned him up. What don't you get about it?"

"Everything!" she yelled. "What flamethrower?"

"Well, after you told us all that shit yesterday about the wax monsters invading our town, I went home and, you know, got to work. We gotta defend ourselves." He lifted the back of his shirt, removed something from his waistband, and displayed it to Poppy with a flourish.

"A paintball gun?"

"*With* a Zippo attached," he said proudly. "And filled with lighter fluid."

Poppy felt the floor tilt beneath her. "Oh, no. Oh, no no no."

"So he melted." Jesus shrugged as if, now that he'd told his epic tale, it was no big deal. "Bam. Cross him off the list."

It was clear to Poppy that the most pressing issue here was that she'd created a situation in which a boy thought it was okay to fashion an improvised flamethrower and start immolating the school administration, but — "Wait. He really melted?"

"Hell yeah! That office floor was one big puddle o' principal! Ruined the rug, though, which is a shame because it was a nice rug. I rolled it up and threw it out the window, then went outside and dragged it into the woods. Collateral damage."

"Did anyone see you? Or hear you?"

"Nah, and you know what? Lincoln didn't scream. When he saw what I was about to do, he just kind of stood there and glared

289

at me. I don't think he wanted any attention called to it neither, you know? 'Cause then people would see that he was made outta wax, and that's *real* bad for Team Hollow."

"Okay. Okay." Poppy put her clammy hands over her eyes and tried to think. "This is a regrettable development, Jesus. You can't just go around killing them. That's not part of The Plan. We need to *identify* them first, and then figure out —"

"Figure out what? If the situation is as bad as you say it is, we gotta start eliminating 'em, one at a time!"

"No. Nope. That is not how it works. Someone's going to notice that the principal vanished from his office!"

"Nah, I took care of that, too. I wrote up a phony note from the pad on his desk, said he was heading out for an emergency root canal, and showed it to Miss Fitzgerald. Chatted her up for a good minute or so, blocked her view of the door — so she'll think he slipped out while we were talking."

"But his car is in the parking lot. Sooner or later people are going to realize that he's missing!"

Jesus just shrugged. "Not my problem. I did what I had to do."

This was every kind of disaster rolled up into one. "Okay, give me the flamethrower," Poppy said, never having thought she'd have to say *that* sentence out loud. "I will keep it for now."

"You're not gonna break it, are you?"

"No. I'm going to put it into my locker for safekeeping. I think we should keep the ritualistic incinerations limited to one per day."

Jesus pouted. "If you say so."

"Just — go about your day. Avoid authority figures. And

obviously don't tell anyone about this." As soon as she said it, she realized that to someone like Jesus, that may not be obvious. "You got that? You can't tell *anyone*."

"Okay, okay."

"*Or* take them outside to show them the rug."

"Aw, come on now."

*   *   *

Poppy wanted desperately to move on with her day, but she had to double-check Jesus's work. "Hi, Miss Fitzgerald!" Poppy chirped to the secretary, hoping to sneakily get a status update. "Is Principal Lincoln in?"

"No, in fact," Miss Fitzgerald said. "Emergency root canal! He was acting so strangely when he came in this morning — not like himself at all. Must have been in so much pain, the poor man." She clucked her tongue. "Do you want to leave a message? He's been getting calls all morning, but I haven't been able to track him down."

Well, that's because he's melted into a carpet out back. "No, that's okay. Thanks anyway!"

By the time Poppy finished, she'd missed English class completely; when the bell rang for lunch, she went straight back to her locker, where Jill was waiting for her.

"What's up?" Jill said.

Poppy almost deflated with relief upon seeing someone sane and helpful. "Oh, Jill. I don't know where to start."

"You look sick, Pops. What's wrong? You are the whitest thing in this hallway, and that is saying a lot."

291

Forgiving Jill's earlier Dud-related accusations in light of this new Jesus-related melting, Poppy gave her a quick rundown of the situation. "And the real Mr. Crawford is trapped in the tank, probably dead! He's younger than the rest, so maybe he's holding on, but—"

"Wait a sec. Are you *sure* Principal Lincoln was melted?"

"Yes. Why?"

Feeling a remarkable sense of déjà vu, Poppy whirled around. Principal Lincoln was striding through the hallway as though nothing had happened, frowning at students, throwing out the occasional warning of "No horseplay." He didn't look at her as he passed, even though she froze, dropped her books, and stared at him, open-mouthed, while other students were forced to go around the mess she'd made.

Only when Jesus rammed into her from behind did she snap out of it. "Poppy, did you see that? He's *back*. He came back!"

She lifted her books from the floor and hugged them to her chest, dread settling through her bones. "They must have multiple copies."

It made sense. Surely the Chandlers had the capacity to duplicate Madame Grosholtz's originals; why *not* make an exhaustive supply of backups? Poppy hadn't gotten a good look when she'd seen Tank #2, but it was big enough to store them all. She could picture its balconies now: identical copies lined up one behind the other, like rows of a shark's teeth.

Jesus's eyes were all fire and brimstone. "So—what, now we can't melt 'em?"

Poppy detected a teachable moment here. "Well, we'd agreed that we weren't going to melt them *anyway,* correct?"

But Jesus's head was somewhere else. "Yeah, yeah. Unless . . ."

"No, Jesus. No 'unless'!"

But before she could stop him, he took off down the hall and disappeared into the crowd. Poppy and Jill wordlessly watched him go.

"Round up the Giddy Committee," Poppy said numbly. "Emergency lunch period rehearsal. *Now.*"

*　　*　　*

Poppy sat in her usual spot in Gaudy Auditorium, marveling that the rest of the student body was carelessly chowing down in the cafeteria as if it were any other day. As if the fate of the town did not rest on a scrappy gang of musical fanatics and a psychotic plastic-flamethrower manufacturer.

The Giddy Committee slowly trickled in, buzzing with rumors. "What's going on, Poppy?" Banks asked.

"Well, Mr. Crawford is a Hollow, for starters."

"Mr. Crawford is a *Hollow?*"

"I know," Poppy said ruefully. "He's way too hot for something as horrible as this to happen to him, but here we are."

It was then that Jesus bounded into the auditorium and started to make his way down the aisle.

Poppy knew that unnervingly gleeful look on his face. She grabbed Jill and hurried to meet him before anyone else could hear whatever troublesome things he had to say. "What now?"

Jesus winked at her. "I melted him again."

"*Jesus!*"

"No, no, it's okay! Look."

They watched him pull yet another weapon out of his bag.

"Where did you get that?" Poppy asked. "How many different guns do you bring to school on a daily basis?"

"I gotta be prepared! And with all the shit that's going on, I don't hear you complaining!"

"I have been doing nothing *but* complaining!"

"Check it out: the faster we melt their sorry asses, the sooner the copies will get used up! They can't keep up with us forever!"

"Yes! They can! That is the point, Jesus—they're immortal, they don't sleep, they have all the time in the world to replenish their copies!" Poppy gave Jill a hopeless look. "Jill, can you field this one? I can't talk to him anymore."

Jill looked from Jesus to his gun, then back at Jesus again.

"Think you can make one of those for each of us?" she asked.

* * *

"I can't believe you're taking his side," said Poppy. "We're all gonna get expelled."

"Can't get expelled if there's no principal," Jill said.

"Actually, I think that sort of decision falls to a disciplinary board—"

"Poppy, don't you think you're missing the bigger picture here? If we don't start extinguishing these things soon, the board will be made up of the very things we're supposed to extinguish!"

"But they're just going to keep resupplying! They're just going to keep pouring out of that storage tank and into the cathedral and through the tunnel and out of the gazebo and back into our lives again!"

"But Jesus is right — if we do it fast enough, maybe they won't be able to keep up."

Poppy scowled. "Assuming that's even possible. So what are you suggesting — that we arm the Giddy Committee with flamethrowers and say, 'Have at 'em, chappies!'?"

"I guess if you wanted to sound like an old-timey vaudeville performer, you could say that."

"Um, Poppy?" Connor asked. "Lunch period is almost over."

Poppy glanced up at the stage, where she'd placed everyone in accordance with the current incarnation of The Plan. (Except for Jesus. Jesus had been excused so that he could go make more flamethrowers.) Poppy had forgotten about them once she started arguing with Jill. "Sorry, guys. I've had to do a little scrambling in light of today's developments. You can come down."

There was a mad dash off the stage. As there'd been no school the day before, the furnace had been turned up extra high to reheat the building, and the floor of the stage had risen to surface-of-the-sun temperatures. "I have a bone to pick with you, Poppy," Connor announced dramatically, then worriedly followed up with, "A metaphorical bone."

"Look, there's nothing I can do about the furnace. I've asked the janitor a million times —"

"It's not that." Connor put his hands on his hips and reflexively reached behind his back to swish the cape that he was not wearing. He scowled at its absence. "I have to say that while I appreciate the work we have to do in order to not let the townspeople slowly be replaced by evil waxen facsimiles, I fear that our performance is going to suffer if we don't keep rehearsing."

Poppy was starting to feel as though she were running a day-care center. "Connor," she said, sighing, "this is kind of important."

"Yes, but the *craft!* The craft is suffering! And I'm just going to put this out there — but you know what *I'd* want to do if *I* were an evil waxen facsimile and had just completed the exhausting task of infiltrating a town? I'd like to sit back, relax, and immerse myself in the transcendent experience of live musical theater, that's what!"

"You're suggesting we put on a show for the monsters trying to take over our town."

"If they win, they'll certainly deserve it."

Louisa made an impatient noise and shoved in front of Connor. "Enough stalling, Poppy. Do you have a plan or not?"

"And where's Jesus?" Banks asked.

"Jesus is on a special assignment," said Poppy.

"In fact," Jill added, "we all owe Jesus a great deal of gratitude, as he is the one who has figured out how to make a dent in their numbers."

"How?" Banks asked.

Poppy looked at Jill. Jill nodded. Poppy sighed.

"Gather round, kids," said Poppy, "and let me tell you a little story about improvised incendiary devices."

After the bell rang and their flamethrower rap session ended and they all agreed to meet after school to finalize the details, Poppy went back to her locker to retrieve her American government textbook. But seeing the White House on the cover, she was reminded of the Bursaws, and then of the ostensible hopelessness of the situation, and then of the fact that she had not eaten a bite of food all day and was about to pass out.

She hurried across the hall and accosted Jill, who was still at her own locker. "Three things," said Poppy. "I need to get out of here, I need to go pick up Dud, and I need to eat something fried."

Jill crossed her arms. "Poppy Palladino, are you suggesting we ditch school *again?*"

"I'm as surprised as you are."

* * *

Dud scraped his crayon across the Friendly's place mat maze so hard, pieces of wax crumbled off and tumbled around the table.

"I don't know how I feel about this," said Dud.

"You should feel good," Jill said. "You're almost at the pot o' gold!"

He put down the crayon. "No, I mean about the flamethrowers."

"Well, seeing as how we're now producing weapons of mass destruction to be used exclusively against your people, you probably should feel kind of bad."

"Jill," Poppy warned.

Dud asked Poppy, "You're not gonna use them on *me*, are you?"

She waved off his question and continued to stare at the menu, wanting to eat the photo of the waffle fries. "Of course not."

"Aaaand what can I get you guys?" Greg surged to the side of their table, invisible tail wagging. Poppy stiffened but reminded herself to act normal. This midday Friendly's trip wasn't just for kicks; they were also on a mission to prove Greg's Hollowness and incorporate his demise into The Plan. And since they'd already tipped their hand to Principal Lincoln and possibly Smitty, it was important not to let Greg know that they were onto him.

It was also important to eat a lot of food. Poppy had to keep up her energy.

As for Greg's energy, Poppy had to hand it to this Chandler clone, whichever one of them it was. Very convincing. "Ever try the Fishamajig?" Greg asked. "It tastes as fun as its name!"

Poppy was not sure how something could taste fun, but in keeping with her life goal of eating every item on the Friendly's menu, she was willing to find out. "Sure," she said. "I'll give it a whirl."

"A jig!"

"Yes! That too."

"And for the rest of you?"

Jill gave him a salute. "I'm all set."

"And I'll have . . ." Dud scanned the menu. "The buffalo."

"The buffalo wings?"

"Ha!" Dud cracked up. "Buffaloes don't have wings."

Poppy whispered to Greg, "Just bring a pile of chicken."

Greg said, "Right-io!" then danced off.

"Look, I'm not exactly *pro*-flamethrowing," Poppy said, once again in disbelief at the words coming out of her mouth, "but I'm starting to think we don't have much choice. It's not like we can go around stabbing them or chopping their heads off or anything."

"This is making me uncomfortable," said Dud.

"Sorry." Poppy took a long sip from her water. "Let's talk about your day. Did you play with the geese?"

"For a little while, but then Madame Grosholtz started talking in my head again, so I sat down on a bench and listened."

"Oh, really?"

He nodded. "I like to hear her talk. It makes me feel nice."

"That's kind of what memories are," Poppy said. "A way to remember what someone was like so that you can feel nice about them instead of sad."

"But I never met her."

"Well, she's the only family you have. So it's okay that you miss her, even if you didn't know her."

"What does she say to you, Dud?" Jill asked with an edge to her voice.

He shrugged. "Mostly stuff about making sculptures."

"Anything else?"

Dud's smile disappeared under Jill's hard stare. "Um, no."

An awkward silence descended.

And the quieter it got, the more Poppy remembered what Jill had said earlier about him.

And the more she remembered, the more she glared at Jill.

Jill, in turn, kept glaring at Dud.

Dud started color-coding the sugar packets.

The rest of their meal was appropriately thorny. Poppy was mad at Jill, Jill was mad at Poppy, and Dud wasn't mad at anyone but could tell that something was amiss.

"Did we save room for dessert?" Greg asked.

Jill and Dud both declined, clearly wanting to leave, but Poppy said, "Yes," perhaps a little too vehemently. "I'll have a scoop of Forbidden Chocolate."

"Ohh," Greg groaned. "Oh, no."

Poppy looked at him, surprised. "What?"

"I'm so sorry, but . . . it's forbidden!"

"It is?"

Dumbfounded, Poppy watched him prance off. "He knew the Forbidden Chocolate joke?"

"Guess the Chandlers learned to do their homework after Smitty failed your bagel oven test," said Jill.

Poppy frowned. She still wanted to be sure. The Plan didn't have allowances for setting innocent people on fire.

She grabbed her phone and got up from the booth without a clear strategy in place — until she got to the kitchen and inspiration struck. "Hey, Greg," she shouted from the door.

Every employee in the kitchen stopped to look at her, even the line cook, mid–burger flip. "Yes?" Greg said, from the plating station. "Did you need something else?"

Poppy felt a hand on her back. Jill and Dud had sprung up from the booth and were trying to restrain her.

"What are you doing?" Jill asked, pulling on her shirt.

Poppy ignored Jill, keeping her eyes on Greg as she rammed her elbow into the light switch. As there were no windows in the kitchen, the room went dark. Noises of confusion arose from the staff, but Poppy kept her focus squarely on Greg's mouth, expecting to see a lot of flickering going on in that throat of his.

And yet: nothing. No fire in his belly. No light in his mouth.

Greg isn't a Hollow?

But in the corner of her eye, two small, flickering point of lights remained.

One in Dud's mouth.

And one in Jill's.

22

~~Shit self~~

POPPY TURNED THE LIGHTS BACK ON AND BLINKED A FEW times, pretending that the sudden brightness was bothering her — when in fact she was trying to recover her faculties, restore her breathing, and not *FREAK THE HELL OUT.*

Jill is a Hollow. The candle smelled like Forbidden Chocolate because JILL LOVES FORBIDDEN CHOCOLATE.

Poppy had to get out of there. She had to get Dud out of there.

And to do that, she had to act normal.

"I am so sorry about her," Jill told the kitchen staff as Poppy picked up her phone from the floor, having dropped it in shock. "She's preparing for a role as a crazy cat lady and took it a little too much to heart." Jill scrambled for some bills in her pocket. "Here, Greg, this should cover our check. We're leaving."

She dragged Poppy through the restaurant and out the front door. Dud followed, bewildered. Poppy kept a neutral face, but every second was agony, her mind chanting, *Don't tip her off, don't*

302

tip her off, occasionally switching it up with a scream to *RUN. AWAY.*

"What is wrong with you?" Jill said once they were in the parking lot.

"I thought I could—"

"What? See if you could get bounced by a secret Friendly's security squad? You're acting like the kind of person who should be wearing a tinfoil hat and eating her own hair."

"I thought I was a crazy cat lady."

"You are all of those things rolled into one and tied up with a ribbon of damaged brain cells."

That's when Poppy spotted it: her chance for escape.

"*Shut up,* Jill!" she exploded. "God, I am *so* sick of you questioning everything I do! I'm trying to save our asses here!"

Jill glared at her. "I know, but I don't think that—"

"No! Enough! This is not how friends act! Friends are supportive and sympathetic in times of crisis! Not snarky and dismissive and awful!" She turned around and stomped off toward Clementine. "Come on, Dud."

Once they both got into Clementine, she started the car with a roar and pulled out of her spot, but Jill blocked her way. "Poppy, stop."

Poppy rolled down her window. "I'm going to Paper Clipz to print out copies of The Plan for everyone. *I'm* still holding rehearsal, because *I* still want to save this town. Come or don't. I really don't care anymore."

"I'll be there. I promise."

Of course she would be, to listen in on the specifics of The Plan so she could relay them back to the Chandlers. "Well, you'll have to find your own ride. Have a wonderful afternoon, jerk."

With that, Poppy screeched out of the parking lot. It wasn't until she'd driven far enough down Main Street and pulled into a parking spot that she started to shake violently, uncontrollably, with a frantic scream working its way through her body.

"Poppy?" Dud looked terrified. "What's wrong?"

"Jill. She's a Hollow. I don't know when they got her — maybe this morning, before school? But they got her. Which means she knows everything that's been going on today — oh my God." She clapped her hand over her mouth. "I told her everything! And *she's* going to tell *them* everything!" She slammed her hands on the steering wheel. "I'm such a moron!"

Dud, not knowing what to do, rubbed her shoulder. "No, you're not."

"I am! And — oh, *Jill*." A sob bubbled up. "The real Jill. *My* Jill. She's trapped in that tank, drowning in poison, and there's nothing I can do about it! She's probably already dead!"

"Maybe not," Dud said. "They said the younger ones . . ."

He trailed off as Poppy cried. She couldn't breathe. She couldn't see through the tears in her eyes. She grabbed the steering wheel with shaking hands and tried to think clearly.

We have to go to the tank. We have to try to get in. But even as she tested out the idea, she knew it would be fruitless. The tank couldn't be breached — at least not until the whole Plan was carried out, start to finish.

Jill would either be dead, or not. They wouldn't know until tomorrow morning.

"We have to stick to The Plan," she rasped. "It's the only way."

Dud nodded, his eyes huge. "It'll be okay. It's okay, Poppy."

"It's not! Now I have to adjust The Plan to deal with her, too, but I also can't tell her what The Plan *is!* How are we going to defeat these things if she's one of them? We can't keep up the charade forever — sooner or later she'll figure out that we're onto her, and then we'll be targets — or maybe we already are! They'll take us out next, and when we're gone, there'll be no one else to stop them and the town will be doomed! For real!"

Paraffin was a powder keg that was frighteningly close to detonating.

But there was nothing for it. She had to press on.

*   *   *

After doing her best to collect herself, Poppy started the car to head to Paper Clipz — but turned it off again when she looked across the street at Smitty's.

Which was closed.

In the middle of the afternoon.

She reached into her bag for her phone — then swore as the cracked screen failed to respond to her touch. Reaching for the Giddy Committee contact sheet instead, she assessed the street for telephone options.

"Hello, Mr. Kosnitzky," she said, breezing into his shop.

"Why aren't you in school?" he demanded.

"Good afternoon to you too, sir." She smiled brightly. "As I've explained to you many times before, I often have free period at the end of the day, which means it is permissible for me to leave school grounds before the final bell."

He scowled at her. "Hmph."

"I was wondering if I could use your phone, just for a minute? It's an emergency."

"Hmph." But he pushed the antiquated telephone across the counter.

Jesus picked up on the first ring. "Yo?"

"Yo, Jesus. It's Poppy."

"Oh, hey! 'Sup?"

She turned farther away from Mr. Kosnitzky and lowered her voice. "Smitty's is closed. In the middle of the day. Would you know anything about that?"

"Yeah, definitely. I melted him."

"What?" Her heart was still clattering around in her chest like a fly trapped in a window. "What?"

"On my way home from school, I paid him a little visit."

"And you did not simply take note of his Hollowness and leave the donut shop in an orderly fashion?"

"*Hell* no."

Poppy looked to the ceiling. "Let me try to fill in the holes here," she said testily. "You left school. You knew Smitty was a Hollow. So you, what, stopped by his café and did a little stakeout and — oh,

I bet you waited in the back for him to bring the trash out to the dumpster and then—"

"Meltdown!"

"Great. That's just great." She smushed the skin of her forehead into a lump. "Did you at least dispose of the wax?"

"Of course I did. Jesus is a professional."

"Well, that's good if it buys us some time, but that's also bad, because people will *definitely* notice that Smitty is missing. I don't think that donut shop has been closed a day since it opened."

"Sorry, Madame Director. Do you want to blab about this on the phone all day, or do you want me to get to work making more flamethrowers?"

Poppy fumed for a moment.

"I want you to make more flamethrowers," she whispered, then hung up, fending off Mr. Kosnitzky's scrutiny with an innocent smile. "All done! Thanks, Mr. K."

"Don't slam the door on the way out!"

"I have a question," Dud said when Poppy got back into the car. "Why did you tell Jill to come to rehearsal if she's one of the bad guys?"

"Because we can't tip her off. We need to pretend that we think she's the real Jill, so that she doesn't get suspicious and tell her bad-guy buddies."

Dud frowned. "But you also can't tell the Giddy Committee about The Plan with her there, because she'll tell the Hollows and they'll know what to expect."

"Right. So we need to throw her off the trail."

"How do we do that?"

Poppy narrowed her eyes and summoned the full weight of her theatrical prowess.

"We make props."

* * *

Poppy and Dud drove from Paper Clipz to Paraffin High just as school was letting out for the day. "Repeat your job back to me," Poppy said to Dud.

"I wait in the car until you come out."

"Right. And if you start to feel melty?"

"I start the car and turn on the air conditioning, but I don't drive anywhere, because I do not know how to drive and I do not have a driver's license."

"Good. Be back in a bit."

Poppy headed for the front door, easily blending in with the crowd of kids hanging around the entrance of the school. But someone called her name as she entered.

"Poppy Palladino? Is that you?"

Poppy whirled around and smiled at Miss Fitzgerald, the secretary, who was holding a coffee cup and a stack of papers. "Yes! Hi, Miss Fitzgerald."

"Hi, Poppy! Did you leave the campus at any point today?" She frowned and started to leaf through the papers. "Your homeroom teacher listed you as present, but a little while ago a call from Mr. Kosnitzky came in, saying that he saw you in town —"

"Oh?" Rotten Kosnitzky. "That's weird, because I was definitely here. Maybe he saw my mom and thought it was me? We look a lot alike."

"Oh, okay!" Miss Fitzgerald smiled. "Geez, it's like we're running a truancy hotline today! We got a call from Smitty, too —"

"Wait, what? When?"

"About ten minutes ago — said he saw a kid snooping around his dumpster earlier this afternoon."

"Smitty was there? At his coffee shop? Ten minutes ago?"

"Of course he was," Miss Fitzgerald said, laughing. "Smitty's always there."

Poppy nearly screamed. She spun and sprinted down the hall as far as she could go, until she rounded a corner and leaned against the wall to catch her breath.

Her throat tightened as the horrible thoughts cascaded. *Smitty came back already while we were at Paper Clipz. And Jill's not Jill. And if this plan doesn't work, soon I won't be me. Mom won't be Mom, and Dad won't be Dad. It's happening TOO FAST.*

Just then, a man in a suit rounded the corner and gave her a big smile.

"Hello, Poppy," said Principal Lincoln.

* * *

"No way," Jesus's voice screeched through the phone. "No *fucking* way."

Poppy had immediately removed herself from Wax Principal Lincoln's presence and raced into Gaudy Auditorium, where the

Giddy Committee was starting to convene and where Jesus was on speaker on Banks's phone, seething.

"Jesus," Poppy said, "you need to accept it: your blowtorch-the-world plan just isn't working."

"Let me at him again! It'll work this time, I swear —"

"Dude, if you bring back that flamethrower, I will not hesitate to use it on you. Understand? Just get over here *now*."

The wobbliness in her voice made the Giddy Committee wince. "Are you okay, Poppy?" Banks asked.

No, I am not, nothing is okay, my best friend might be dead, and Dud is probably going to melt in the car, she wanted to say — but she couldn't, because at that moment Jill entered the auditorium.

Wax Jill entered the auditorium.

She lingered at the door. "Hey."

"Hey," said Poppy.

A million things were happening on Jill's face, and she opened her mouth to speak several times before settling on "Can I talk to you for a sec? Alone?"

Poppy nodded and got up from her seat. "Be right back," she told the rest. "Talk among yourselves."

As she met Jill at the rear of the auditorium, Poppy took a deep breath. Time for more Acting.

She told Jill about what had happened after they'd parted — the Smitty melting, the subsequent return of Smitty, the return of Principal Lincoln — all of it as honestly and authentically as she could, even though Wax Jill probably already knew everything. Because if she thought for one second that Poppy was holding anything back, anything at all, she'd realize that Poppy was onto her.

When Poppy finished, Jill looked worried — though Poppy knew it was probably more of an expression of frustration that this puny gutbag's plans were so difficult to quash. "Wow," she said. "That's crazy."

Poppy then remembered that she was still supposed to be mad at her for pettier reasons. "Oh?" Poppy said snidely. "You finally believe me this time?"

"Huh? Oh. Yeah." Jill scowled, as if she, too, were annoyed about having to keep up this little charade. "I'm sorry about this afternoon. You're right — I should have your back."

"It's okay. And I'm sorry for all the stuff I said."

They hugged. Poppy imagined their bodies sizzling upon contact, like cold water hitting a hot pan, their secrets smoldering between them and rising up in a smoky cloud of deception and propaganda and *LIES*.

But it was just a plain old hug. With a lot of internal retching.

When they returned to the group — which Jesus had rejoined, looking pouty — Louisa looked at Poppy expectantly. "So what are we supposed to do now?"

Poppy pulled out a stack of still-warm, freshly printed sheets of paper and took a long, luxurious whiff. "Now," she said, "we plot and scheme."

She handed out the detailed instructions to each member of the Giddy Committee, starting with Louisa and ending with Jill. At the top, in gigantic letters, it said THE PLAN, followed by a detailed itinerary and map.

"Tomorrow," she began, "two more people will be captured, and therefore two more Hollows will be released. Melting obviously does nothing to stop them, so *instead* of destroying them, we're going to stop them from being circulated into the general populace. It's not a permanent solution, but hopefully it'll buy us some time."

The Giddy Committee members were staring hard at the papers, their faces contorted by confusion and panic. "What—" Connor started.

"We don't know the exact time the Hollows will be released," Poppy interrupted. "So we'll gather in the space under the gazebo early in the morning — at seven a.m. We wait there until they emerge from the tunnel. When they do, we tackle them and tie them up."

A few beats went by.

"Tie them up?" Banks said, incredulous. "That's so weak! Why not melt them?"

"Because," Poppy said, injecting loads of impatience into her voice, "if we've learned anything from Jesus's adventures today, it's that the Chandlers find out very quickly that their Hollows have been destroyed, and they are equally quick to replace them. This way, at least they'll be stuck, immobilized, bound, and gagged, and the Chandlers won't know about it. We leave them there under the gazebo, and then . . ."

They waited for her to finish, but she didn't. "And then what?" asked Banks.

"Hopefully by then, I'll have figured that out. But this is the best

I can come up with for now. Jill's right — slowing them down is better than doing nothing at all."

Jill nodded.

Poppy sighed and heaved a helpless shrug. "So that's it. We'll meet tomorrow morning at the gazebo at seven."

"What if they don't emerge until much later?" said Louisa. "You want us to skip school?"

"Yes, I do. I need every one of you to promise me that you'll show up. Is everyone onboard with this?" They exchanged wary glances with one another, but nodded. "Good. Plotting-and-scheming meeting adjourned."

The Giddy Committee shuffled out of their seats and up the aisle, uncharacteristically silent and downtrodden, their eyes darting around nervously. Jesus headed toward the main entrance to wait for his mom to pick him up, and Louisa and Banks began their walks home. Poppy and Jill headed into the parking lot, waving to Connor as he got into his car.

Jill got into her mother's car and started it up. "See you tomorrow, then."

"Yeah. See you tomorrow."

Waving, Poppy backed away from Jill's car and walked across the parking lot to Clementine. "Did I do okay?" Dud asked when she got in.

"Shh. Wait," Poppy said, watching.

Jill backed up out of her parking space, drove through the lot, turned onto the main road —

And drove out of sight.

Poppy exploded out of Clementine, shouting, "Go go go!" Dud followed, and Connor, waiting in his own car, did the same. Banks and Louisa could be seen running back toward the school. They all converged in the main hallway, each of them clutching their copies of THE PLAN — but unlike Jill's and Poppy's copies, at the top of theirs was printed, in gigantic letters:

JILL IS A HOLLOW.

THIS IS <u>NOT</u> THE PLAN.

BUT YOU MUST PRETEND THAT IT IS. GO ALONG WITH EVERYTHING I'M SAYING TO YOU — REACT AS YOU NORMALLY WOULD, ASK QUESTIONS AS YOU NORMALLY WOULD, LEAVE THE BUILDING AS YOU NORMALLY WOULD ONCE THE MEETING IS ADJOURNED.

BUT ONCE JILL IS OUT OF SIGHT, <u>RETURN TO SCHOOL AS FAST AS YOU CAN.</u>

"Back to the auditorium," Poppy said breathlessly, pulling her bulging notebook out of her bag once they all arrived. "For the *real* Plan."

23

~~Bundle up~~

6:59 A.M.

Poppy looked at Blake's colossal scuba diver watch. It was the only timepiece she had left, now that her cell phone was broken. With a pang, she figured he would have been okay with her borrowing it if it helped save a life or two.

Because time, in this instance, was definitely of the essence. It wasn't going to be easy, setting off a chain of events without any of the Hollows catching on *or* warning the others *or* calling the police. It wasn't going to be easy to pick off the Hollows without the Chandlers catching wind that something was awry.

It had to go perfectly.

She looked over the inventory of items they'd gathered the night before — ~~oregano, Tackety Wax, microphone~~ — and frowned when she sniffed her hands, which still smelled like lighter fluid from the fire she'd started an hour earlier. Dud was watching the fast-moving clouds; it was a chilly day, but of course that didn't bother him. Poppy, on the other hand, was wrapped up tight in a sweater, scarf, jacket, mittens, and a hat. It was a lot windier up there, and her nose was so cold, she could have chipped it off with an ice pick.

At least the view was nice.

For what felt like the millionth time, she read over The Plan. Each to-do item was to be crossed off as it was completed. Each Hollow was to be marked as witnessed (noted with a pair of eyes 👁👁) by at least one other Hollow. Each member of the Giddy Committee was to play a part, scheduled down to the minute.

"It's going to work," Dud said out of nowhere.

Poppy rubbed her mittened hands together. "I hope so."

"It will," he said with a nod, leaving no room for argument. "You'll make it work. I'll help if you need it, but you won't. You're Poppy." He grabbed the sides of her head and stared intently into her eyes. "You are the most healthful benefit I know."

She smiled, feeling a little warmer. "Thank you," she said quietly. "And you're not such a dud after all. More like a . . . a rousing success."

"That is a terrible name. Let's stick with Dud."

She let out a small laugh. "Happy to."

She uncapped her black Sharpie and looked at her watch.

It *had* to go perfectly.

~~7:00 a.m.: Commence The Plan~~

* * *

Smitty's churned and bubbled with its usual crowd of early-morning regulars. A table of Paraffin High students pounded down crullers while quizzing one another on Spanish vocabulary. The coop of old hens pecked and chattered and sniped from across their booths, trading old gossip and spinning new yarns. Anita and Preston Chandler sat at the counter, sipping lattes and talking to each other in hushed tones.

It was into the blue vinyl stool next to them that Jesus slipped.

"What can I getcha?" Smitty asked him, looking askance at the ridiculous hoodie and sunglasses that hid the boy's face.

"Coffee."

Smitty gave him a gruff nod and shuffled over to the pot. He looked wary, tense; every so often his gaze flickered to the Chandlers.

When he returned with the coffee, Jesus reached out to grab it. "Thanks, bro —"

But the cup slipped between his fingers. Coffee flooded the counter, soaking the Chandlers' morning newspaper — and Smitty's apron.

"Dammit!" Smitty shouted, holding out his arms to keep them from getting wet. His apron failed to live up to its aspirations; coffee had already run off onto his pants.

The Chandlers had recoiled from the spill as well, but they looked more upset with Smitty than with Jesus. They shot the increasingly enraged baker a warning glance. A *don't rock the boat* glance.

~~7:02 a.m.: Anita and Preston 👁 👁 Smitty~~

Smitty scowled at them, then at Jesus, but managed to curtail his temper. "Just be more careful next time, kid." The apron was swiftly removed and rolled into a ball. Smitty stalked down the length of the counter and informed the waitress that he would be right back — and she should mop up the counter.

She gave him a sour look as he retreated into the back room; then she grabbed a dishtowel and began to sop up the coffee.

Jesus, meanwhile, removed his sunglasses, turned to the Chandlers, and said, "My deepest apologies, sir and madam. It was never my intention to soak your newspaper in coffee, but you see —" He broke off, affixed a look of pain to his face, and wrung his hands, massaging each finger. "Ever since I lit that candle, I've been feeling a numbness in my extremities —"

"Candle?" Anita shot a laser-sharp stare at him. "What candle?"

"Oh, it was a gift from my mother, from the Grosholtz Candle Factory. Forty Winks, I think it was called? I know it was supposed to help me sleep, but the fumes made me dizzy. I even puked! And ever since, I've felt really weird, like, neurological-damage weird . . ."

Horror-stricken, the Chandlers folded themselves into a huddle and traded panic.

"— already a bestseller —"

"— sabotage, maybe —"

"— there'll be an investigation —"

"— and lawsuits!"

7:05 a.m.: Anita and Preston Chandler leave Smitty's

*   *   *

"I think next time I'll do zebra stripes," the cashier at Cash Register Number One said to the cashier at Cash Register Number Two. The

318

store had just opened, so business was slow — but it would be picking up with the first wave of the senior citizen tour buses arriving any minute. "Or maybe cheetah spots. What do you think?" She fanned out her fingers, wiggling her nails at him.

The other cashier yawned. "How about giraffe prints?" he suggested.

"Ew, no. Giraffes aren't sexy."

"And zebras are?"

The phone rang. Deciding that whoever was on the other line had to be more interesting than his partner in cashierdom, Cashier Number Two lunged for the phone. "Thank you for calling the Grosholtz Candle Factory," he said, "where every candle is heaven-scent —"

"Shut up and get me Barbara!"

Cashier Number Two was momentarily paralyzed by the sound of Anita Chandler's voice. A common side effect. "Uh . . ."

"Now!"

He slapped his hand over the mouthpiece and scooted out onto the floor, slamming into two teenage girls as he rounded the corner to the main entrance. "Sorry! Sorry, ladies." He reached into the closest display and handed the girls the first thing he could grab. "Here, have a birdhouse."

He rushed on to the esteemed map distributor and held the phone out to her as if it were a squirming eel. "Barbara, Anita's on the line. She sounds *pissed.*"

Barbara accepted the phone. "Anita? What? Slow down, I can't understand you. *What?* Okay. Okay, I'm on it."

She put her game face on and leered at the outlandish display of Forty Winks candles. "Get a box," she told Cashier Number Two. "We're pulling the Winks."

"What? Why?"

"Just do it!"

He nodded and began to sprint off, but not before once again running into those two teenage girls, who had been standing so close, they must have overheard the entire conversation.

One of them smiled sweetly.

"Is something wrong with the candles?"

~~7:10 a.m.: Escalate a scandal~~

* * *

The Smitty's waitress mopped up the last of the spilled coffee from the counter and rinsed the soaked dishrag in the sink. "You want another cup, hon?" she asked through a yawn, turning back to Jesus.

But the seat was vacant.

No one had seen Jesus slip into the kitchen. He was so skinny, he hadn't needed to open the door any farther than the crack Smitty had left in his wake. And, as Smitty was a man of such well-publicized self-sufficiency, Jesus knew there wouldn't be anyone else back there.

Smitty stood in front of the bagel oven, drying his clothes. Mindful of the heat, he was obviously trying not to get too close, but small drops of wax had already fallen onto the concrete floor where he'd started to melt.

So really, Jesus was just finishing the job.

~~7:15 a.m.: Melt Smitty in New England's largest bagel oven~~

*   *   *

"Excuse me!" Banks shouted from the front steps of the Grosholtz Candle Factory. "Mr. and Mrs. Chandler, can we have a word with you?"

The distraught candle factory executives stormed across the parking lot, a task made difficult by the plentiful tour buses unloading their passengers. Every time the Chandlers made a substantial leap forward, a wayward cane or a slow-moving scooter moved in to block them, which made it all the easier for Banks and Louisa to jump into the fray.

Banks shoved a microphone into Preston's face. "Mr. Chandler," she said while Louisa filmed with her phone, "is it true that the Grosholtz Candle Factory is selling contaminated, harmful candles to the public?"

"No!" he shot back, dislodging himself from the geriatric labyrinth and yanking Anita along with him. They kept on marching toward the main entrance. "There is no evidence to suggest that any of our candles —"

"No comment!" Anita shouted over him, elbowing him in the side. *"No comment."*

Banks followed right alongside them, jogging and holding out the microphone while Louisa ran backwards ahead of them like a paparazzo, keeping her phone's camera recording. "I heard a kid died," Banks said, bopping Preston Chandler in the nose with the microphone. "What words of comfort, if any, do you have for his grieving family?"

"*Died?* I didn't hear that —"

"*No comment!*" Anita interjected.

"What about the Forty Winks that have already been shipped across the country?" Louisa asked. "Are they contaminated as well?"

"Will there be a recall?" Banks asked.

"What early symptoms should candle lovers be on the lookout for?"

"How quickly do the seizures set in?"

"Is the blindness permanent?"

"How many limbs can your candle lovers expect to lose?"

As they reached the main entrance, Anita spun around, her chest heaving, her face twisted with rage. "*NO. COMMENT.*"

Banks put a hand on her hip. "The people have a right to know."

Preston stepped in and put his hand over Louisa's phone. "Tell you what, girls. Just turn off that camera, step into our office, and we can all sit down for a nice, unrecorded chat."

Banks gave him a winning smile. "That sounds great, Mr. Chandler."

Preston nodded at Louisa, who was fiddling with her phone. "Sound good to you, kid? You stopped recording, right?"

"Right." Louisa tapped the screen a couple more times, then slid it into her pocket. "All done."

~~7:20 a.m.: Upload interview to Channel Six YouNews~~

*   *   *

Colt Lamberty sat in the Channel Six conference room, practicing his eyebrow raising in the window's reflection. "Colt?" said the station manager, heading up the meeting. "Could you stop that for a minute?"

"These exercises are essential to my gravitas," Colt explained impatiently, not stopping. "Up . . . down. Up . . . down," he whispered to himself. "Miraculous . . . tragic. Intrigued . . . suspicious. Late-breaking . . . hard-hitting. Saucy . . . sexy."

"Please pay attention, Colt."

Colt let out an unnecessarily loud sigh and reached for his phone instead. No emails. No tweets. No tips. It was shaping up to be a slow news day indeed —

Until his YouNews notification pinged.

~~7:25 a.m.: Colt 👀 Anita and Preston~~

*   *   *

"Now, girls." Anita delicately swirled the contents of her latte and leaned forward to expose her cleavage in case either or both of them were into that. "I'm sure we can come to an understanding."

Louisa and Banks felt small in the large velvety armchairs by the fireplace, and they felt even smaller once the Chandlers stood over them and started lecturing, too furious to notice the one major change that Poppy had made to their office. But the girls kept their cool and listened politely. "That depends," said Louisa. "Are the rumors true?"

Preston let out a condescending laugh. "Of course not —"

"*No comment.*" Anita shot him a fiery look and whispered, "You are such an *idiot.*"

All smiles again as she faced the girls. "Now, about that recording. I'm going to need you to erase that."

Louisa crossed her arms. "Why? It's on my phone. I own it."

"Yeah, and it's going on my acting reel," said Banks. "I'm gonna make it big in Hollywood."

"Of course you are," Anita said sarcastically. "But you'll have to do it without that interview." She took two fast, terrifying steps toward Louisa. "Give me your phone!" she demanded in that tone of voice adults think they can use to get children to instantly obey.

Louisa kept her arms crossed and narrowed her eyes like an insolent brat. "Make me."

Losing control, Anita lunged forward, grabbed Louisa's wrists, and pulled her up out of the chair.

"Anita, stop!" Preston shouted, putting a hand on her shoulder. "The tour!"

She froze. All four of them slowly looked toward the display window, where a dozen elderly tourists stood, each of their mouths open in shock at seeing the CEO of a multimillion-dollar company manhandling a teenage girl.

Several took photos.

Anita dropped Louisa back into her chair and flashed a winning smile at the group. "Hello!" she said, waving like a beauty queen. "Welcome to our factory!"

Sensing a bit of urgency, the tour guide ushered the group away from the window and closed the curtain, encouraging them on toward the wicking room.

"Should I go get their cameras?" Preston asked Anita.

"No," she said, thinking. "We'll have to spin this a different way now. We were . . . I don't know, we were rehearsing a play or something. Engaging with the local theater youth, or some nonsense. Yes, that's it!" She lit up. The roaring fire behind her — reeking of lighter fluid, much larger than its hologram version — made her glow, as if she'd been sent from hell. "It was all performance art! We can say the interview was scripted, and turn the contamination rumors into something marketing came up with. Contaminated . . . with fun! Infected . . . with love!"

Preston got into the spirit. "Poisoned . . . with safety!"

Anita was beaming now. "Girls, what do you think?" she asked, extending her hand. "Do we have a deal?"

Louisa looked at Banks. Banks looked at Louisa.

They stood up and extended their hands.

~~7:30 a.m.: Push Anita and Preston Chandler into their office fireplace~~

*   *   *

Colt Lamberty's expensive sports car bumped and jostled over the craggy surface of Channel Six's back-roads shortcut into town. He was about to hang a left when a large boy appeared from nowhere, landing with a disturbing crunch on his windshield.

Colt sighed impatiently.

He got out of the car and assessed the damage. The hood had not been dented, nor the windshield cracked. The boy looked dead, but the paint job seemed to be intact.

"Help!" Connor sprang back to life, gasping and grasping at Colt's lapel. "Sir, you gotta help me!"

Colt recoiled. "Oh. You're alive." As if handling a large insect, he peeled Connor's fingers off his jacket. "Here," he said, pulling a crisp hundred-dollar bill from his wallet and tossing it at Connor. "A little something for your troubles."

Connor watched it flutter to the ground. "I don't need help! My friend does!"

"I do not care about your friend."

"But, sir — he's in *danger!*"

Colt raised a splendidly groomed eyebrow.

"Danger?"

7:35 a.m.: Intercept Colt Lamberty

*   *   *

Mr. Kosnitzky finished washing his storefront window, put the Windex away, and looked at the clock: 7:36.

Just enough time left over to do a little spying.

He sat down in his chair and stared, eagle-eyed, at the town center. No teenagers in the gazebo. No teenagers at the lake. One teenager over by the post office, but he supposed that she could just be mailing something, not up to anything nefarious.

But he could not be certain.

Just then a flash of shiny crimson Euro-ness screeched around the corner. That dolt Colt Lamberty was at the wheel, as usual, chasing some ridiculous lead. A cat trapped in a tree, probably, or the Virgin Mary in someone's pancakes.

But wait — someone rode in the passenger's seat.

Someone wearing a cape.

Someone young.

A *teenager.*

7:40 a.m.: Mr. Kosnitzky reports Connor to Principal Lincoln

* * *

"Where'd you say this place was, kid?"

"On" (gasp) "the" (gasp) "other" (gasp) "side" (gasp) "of —"

"Would you stop crying?" Colt dug around the cup holder, pulled out a napkin from Smitty's, and thrust it at Connor's blubbering face. "And don't you dare get any snot on the seats. They're Italian leather."

"Oh, okay. Sorry, mister."

Connor then burst into a fresh batch of tears.

Colt's lip curled. The sound of children crying was almost as painful as the sound of their laughter. "So tell me again — where is your friend now?"

"Trapped in a well!" Another sob. "We found this shack in the woods, and we thought it was an outhouse, so we went to investigate, and when we opened the door, there was just a big hole in it, and he fell in!"

"And how did you end up so far away from your friend?"

"*I got lost!*" Connor cried. "I've been wandering through the

327

woods all night! I couldn't find my way out! I had to eat a bug to survive!"

"Okay, do me a favor. Stop talking until we get there."

They continued toward the mountain, when Connor let out a squeal. "There!" he said, pointing at the turnoff for Secret Service Way.

Colt set his jaw. How many godforsaken back roads was he going to have to ruin his car on today? "How far?"

"Just a few more — there!"

They came to a stop. Connor flung himself out of the car and huffed up a small hill, thrashing through the high grass. "This way!" he called to Colt.

Picking his way through the mud and ruining his expensive Italian leather shoes in the process, Colt followed Connor with no small amount of fuming. "This better be worth it, kid."

When he finally reached Connor, the boy was standing next to a large wooden structure. "In there," Connor said fearfully.

Colt rolled his eyes. "This isn't a well, kid."

"Yes it is!"

"No, it's not." He grabbed the handle of the door. "These aren't even the deep woods. This is on the spa's property —"

"Oh?" said Connor, moving up behind him. "Really?"

~~7:45 a.m.: Melt Colt Lamberty in a Paraffin Resort personal sauna~~

*   *   *

Principal Lincoln strode down the hallway, his shoes clacking against the floor. He didn't know much about the kid Kosnitzky had called about, but he thought he'd seen a cape-wearing boy often hanging around the auditorium. And if the boy was with Colt, then he obviously had a flair for the dramatic.

7:47 a.m.: Principal Lincoln 👁 👁 Colt

But Principal Lincoln had checked Connor's files, and he'd never been absent from school — not once. Something was up. Something originating, Principal Lincoln had a feeling, with the Giddy Committee.

He knocked on Mr. Crawford's classroom door. "Those kids who sang in the parade," he said. "Is one of them named Connor?"

"How should I know?" Mr. Crawford said. "I've only been this guy for a day."

Principal Lincoln gritted his teeth. "Come with me. I have a feeling about this."

He led Mr. Crawford to the Gaudy Auditorium and paused, waiting for his eyes to adjust to the darkness of the theater — when a bright spotlight snapped on. It was pointed at the stage, upon which sat a giant pile of weed.

Jesus.

Upon the weed sat a person smoking a joint and laughing.

JESUS.

"Hello, Lincoln," Jesus said as the two men made their way down the aisle, their eyes popping out of their heads. "Crawford. Want some?"

Once the shock wore off, Principal Lincoln rubbed his hands together. "You," he said, pulling out his phone, "are going to *burn* for this. Pun intended."

Jesus shrugged, his eyes bleary. "Whatever. I just wanted to, you know, call a truce between us. Let bygones be bygones."

"Shut up, you little pissant."

"No need for language, Lincoln! I'm extending some goodwill here. I tried to kill you a couple times, and you wouldn't die. You win. No hard feelings, bro. Come on up here and join me."

Principal Lincoln ignored him, jabbing at his phone.

"Whatsa matter?" Jesus continued. "You don't like to party?"

Mr. Crawford, who had hung back to watch the unfolding scene, now grasped Principal Lincoln on the shoulder. "Anita, wait —"

But Principal Lincoln shook him off. "Yes, hello?" he said into the phone, grinning evilly. "I'd like to report a felony."

~~7:50 a.m.: Principal Lincoln calls the police~~

*   *   *

Big Bob was sitting in his office, staring at the bust the town had given him.

It was a decent likeness. Tussaud could have sculpted a better one. But the talentless gutbags had tried their best.

First he put it on his desk, but that wasn't high enough. He moved it to the top of his file cabinets, but those didn't convey the air of import that the bust implied. It needed to be somewhere dignified, a place of honor and repute —

His phone rang.

"Hello?"

"Sorry to bother you, Councilman Bursaw, but this is Officer

Reynolds down at the station. I've got Principal Lincoln on the line, ranting and raving about some kid down at the school sitting on a *mountain* of pot."

7:52 a.m.: ~~Big Bob~~ 👁 👁 ~~Principal Lincoln~~

Big Bob grinned and leaned back in his chair. "You don't say."

"It gets better. The principal says the kid is so high that he gave up the location of his stash."

"What? That's fantastic! Call the media. They can film the seizure live —"

"Yes, but — well —"

"What?"

"He says it's in your swimming pool."

"My *pool?*"

"Yes, sir. Apparently he and your son are friends, and that's where they've been keeping it. Like I said, he's stoned out of his mind."

Big Bob grunted.

"What I'm saying, sir, is that we are the only people who know its location, and that I'm giving you a heads-up. Honestly, we're a little short-staffed today — Chief Peltor hasn't shown up for work, and no one knows where she is — so if there *happened* to be a delay, and the stash *happened* to be relocated to a less incriminating place before the media caught wind of it —"

Big Bob nodded. "I understand."

"Or we can call it off altogether — lot of trouble for such a small-time drug bust —"

"No, of course not!" Big Bob shouted, jumping out of his seat. "Drugs are not rad!"

"So . . . you'll move it?"

"Of course I will. Hell of a photo op!" Big Bob cleared his throat. "I'll call you when it's all clear. Shouldn't take too long. And, Officer — thank you for the warning."

"No problem, sir. Good luck."

"Over and out!"

News of the bust spread quickly. As Big Bob strolled down the hallway, the town hall employees erupted in cheers, slapping him on the back and giving him high-fives and shouting, "Drugs are not rad!" The smile remained on his face all the way to the mayor's office, where it was replaced with a contemptuous scowl.

"So?" said Miss Bea after he'd filled her in on the situation. "Why bother sticking your neck out like that? Who cares about any of this?"

"Hey, *you* were the one who said we needed to keep up appearances as much as we could. Big Bob Bursaw cares about this stupid drug thing, so *I* have to care about this stupid drug thing!"

Miss Bea let out a frustrated sigh. "Fine. But I don't see why you need my help. Or the kid's."

He tossed her a set of car keys.

"Because many hands make light work."

~~7:55 a.m.: Big Bob and Miss Bea head home~~

* * *

332

"Don't try to run," Principal Lincoln told Jesus, climbing the stairs to the stage. "The police are on their way."

Jesus laughed. "Like I'd get far! I'm high as shit!"

Principal Lincoln took a few more steps toward Jesus, then looked back at Mr. Crawford. "Preston. Get up here and help me."

"I really don't think—"

"*Preston.*"

Mr. Crawford walked up the steps, cowering slightly behind Principal Lincoln—until Principal Lincoln stopped abruptly. "What's going on here?" he asked, studying Jesus.

"Hmm?"

"Why don't you care that you're being arrested?"

Jesus gave a lazy shrug. "I guess I just ain't all that worried. I got a lot of dirt on you two. Lots of information that could be traded, say, to the Bursaws. To make a deal and whatnot."

Principal Lincoln let out a loud, booming laugh. It echoed through the empty auditorium. "You've got dirt?"

"Yeah, all that wax shit. You're imposters. That's why I tried to melt you, bro."

Principal Lincoln shook his head, chuckling as he stood over Jesus. "You're such an idiot." He knelt down to eye level, pulling Mr. Crawford with him. "I've got some unfortunate news for you, *bro,*" he said, relishing every second. He leaned in, as if to tell a secret, whispering, "*The Bursaws are wax too.*"

Jesus held his gaze. "Is that right."

Principal Lincoln kept on smiling, but his nose began to twitch.

"What's that smell?" he asked, picking up a bag of the weed. "Is that oregano?"

"Nah." Jesus grinned and stood up, opening the trapdoor in the stage. "It's flame-broiled principal."

~~8:00 a.m.: Melt Principal Lincoln and Mr. Crawford in the Gaudy Auditorium furnace~~

* * *

"This is *such* a waste of time," Miss Bea grumbled, the big blue tarp crumpling noisily as they removed it from the swimming pool.

"Seriously," Blake added. "I was having a lovely morning snooping through these people's tax files until you got home. I know we need to keep up appearances, but to get *this* involved—"

"Would you give it a rest?" said Big Bob. "For ten minutes of work, we keep the police out of our backyard, we get to seize the drugs and become local heroes, and the gutbags follow us more blindly than they already do. Where is the downside in this?"

He descended the steps into the shallow end and skidded down the slope into the deep end, where several taped-up packages sat in neat little piles. Blake sidled up behind him, followed by Miss Bea. "That doesn't smell like pot," she said.

"That's . . . because it's not," said Blake, sniffing at a package. "What the—"

"Ahem," said someone behind them.

All three Bursaws turned around and looked up. At the edge

of the pool stood a very tall girl and a very short girl inexplicably brandishing a pair of enormous paintball guns.

"Happy belated Paraffin Day!" Banks and Louisa sang.

~~8:05 a.m.: Flamethrow the hell out of Big Bob and Miss Bea and Blake~~

* * *

The wheels of Colt's sports car left the ground. Connor was driving faster than he ever had in his life, his cape flapping out the window, singing, *"The Phaaaaantom of the Opera is heeeeeere. . . . to meeeelt your faaaaace."*

He screeched to a stop in front of Jill's house and reached for his flamethrower, grinning.

~~8:10 a.m.: Serenade Jill until she comes outside~~

* * *

Poppy tapped her Sharpie on her knee. It was almost time.

Impatient, she got up and walked across the roof of Tank #2. It had been an ideal place for her and Dud to hide out for the duration of The Plan — it was out of the way, so none of the Hollows would spot them or grow suspicious, and at the same time it was so close to the bad-guy headquarters that none of the Hollows would suspect them of hiding there.

She looked across the way at Tank #1. *Please be alive, Jill,* she thought. *Please be alive.* She noted with relief that the flame had still not been lit — which meant that no new victims had been lured in. The ten Hollows the Giddy Committee had destroyed over the course of the morning were the only ones out there.

As for inanimate Hollows, hundreds of them still sat below her feet. Poppy looked through the lightning-made hole at the inventory inside, shuddering. The look on Mrs. Goodwin's face as Poppy had barged into her bedroom that morning with a flamethrower was not one she would soon be forgetting. Though her kindly neighbor insisted on her innocence, Poppy forced herself to press on, knowing the woman was lying. The wax puddle that remained was all the proof she needed, but emotionally speaking, it was still harrowing.

Logistically speaking, it was way too easy.

"You'd think the Chandlers would have gotten a little more intelligent over all their years on earth," Poppy whispered to Dud. "You'd think they'd maybe set the alarm system if they didn't want to get burned up in their sleep. You've only been alive for a week, and I feel like you're smarter than both of them, with all their years combined."

"I have a good teacher," said Dud.

"Why, thank you."

"Oh. I meant Dr. Steve, but — you're good too."

Poppy glanced at Connor's next task in The Plan, flinching at its words: 8:15 a.m.: Melt Jill. Then she looked at Blake's watch again, wishing for the millionth time that her phone still worked. If something went wrong, there was no way for anyone on the Giddy Committee to contact her.

And immediately upon having this thought, she knew that something *had* gone wrong. She'd developed a sixth sense about these moments — every time failure was imminent, the hairs on the back of her neck twitched.

"Uh-oh," said Dud, all but confirming it.

Poppy whipped around. How the intruder had climbed the metal stairs without either of them hearing, she didn't know.

But there she was: Wax Jill, grinning like a monster.

24

~~Lose all hope~~

ANY SENSE OF RELIEF OR SUCCESS THAT HAD BUILT UP OVER
the course of The Plan vaporized in an instant.

She needs to be in the tank! Poppy's mind was screaming. *Or
The Plan won't work!*

"What are you doing here, Jill?" she asked instead, trying to
keep her voice even.

"Oh, drop the act," Jill said, advancing on her. "One of the Bursaws texted me about the pot thing. Tipped me off that something
was up—even some idiot pothead wouldn't do something *that*
moronic. This was a pretty terrible plan from the start, if you want
my opinion. Melting us one at a time without giving us a chance to
warn one another? I mean, it's *fine*, I *guess*, but only if every one of
us suddenly forgot how to use our phones. What'd you do, Tackety
Wax the OUT door to trap the Hollows in the tank?" she said, laughing as she saw the tube of wax at Poppy's feet. "Pathetic."

"Shut up, Anita—"

Before Poppy could make a move to escape, Jill pinned her arms to her sides with an impossible amount of strength for her size. She picked Poppy up with no effort at all and walked to the edge of the tank's roof, dangling her over a hundred feet of nothing.

She was squeezing Poppy too tight for her to scream. Why wasn't Dud jumping in to help? Poppy closed her eyes and wriggled, panic flooding her brain so fast, she almost didn't hear the voice.

"Oh, put her down, my doll."

She felt Jill's hands get tighter, but not intentionally — more in a surprised, flinching way. Jill backed up from the edge and set Poppy down on the roof, still restraining her as she glared at the source of the voice. "What's going on?"

Dud took a few steps toward Jill and gave her a pitying look. "Dear me, Anita. And here I thought you were the smart one," he said.

Or rather, *she* said. Though the voice was Dud's, the inflection was unmistakably Madame Grosholtz's — that musical, lilting pitch that anyone who'd heard her speak would recognize in a flash.

The stern look remained on Jill's face, but her eyes were questioning. "Tussaud? That you?"

"Indeed it is."

Poppy's body went ice-cold. Instantly she flashed back to Jill/Anita accusing Dud of being one of them, speaking those words that Poppy had refused to hear.

Snake.

Dud coyly shook his head. "I know, I know, you tried to get rid of me," he said. "And it was a good plan, yes, it was! It worked for a little while. But you should know by now that I am not so easily discarded."

Jill released Poppy. Poppy rubbed her arms but remained silent, and she didn't make a move to run away. Jill was captivated; Poppy didn't want to break the spell.

Plus, Poppy hadn't the first inkling of what was going on. Madame Grosholtz had said in her message candle that she had set the fire on her own. Was it all a lie? Had the Chandlers tried to get rid of her themselves?

Jill studied Dud, trying to look calm. But Poppy could tell it was an act. Jill was scared. "I didn't try to kill you," Jill said. "I didn't set that fire."

"Of course you didn't," said Dud. "Preston did."

Jill's face went slack. *"What?"*

"He said . . . Oh, what did he say . . . ?" Dud said, remembering. "He said that our interests did not align, and he decided that if you two were to continue to live on, to go ahead with your plan, the only thing standing in your way was me. And so I had to go."

"Preston said all of that?"

"Oh, and he said it wasn't personal." Dud gave his hand a flighty little wave — it looked funny on him, but it was dead-on, just as Madame Grosholtz would have done. "I beg to differ, of course," he said with a chuckle. "In fact, I wish . . ."

He looked out over the town. Jill waited for an answer but grew impatient. "Wish what?"

"I only wish," said Dud, "that you had consulted with me first.

Before burning me up. Did it not occur to you that perhaps our interests were aligned after all?"

Jill stared at Dud. "What do you mean?"

"Your continued existence has been impressive," Dud said, pacing slowly. "I admit that. But as you know, there were two of you, and there was only one of me. As you can see, I am still here, and I have done well for myself. So why, then, would I not want to keep living? Do you think you are the first ones to desire to overtake a town in order to secure a full population as backups? Why do you think I went along with your plan all these years?"

Jill frowned. "Wait. *You* were going to —"

"Yes!" Dud laughed — or, rather, Madame Grosholtz laughed, that beautifully weird tinkling of glass. "Of course I was. I only wish you'd consulted me first. We could have avoided this entire mess."

Poppy practically heard herself hit rock bottom. She'd been duped. The stone candle was nothing but fiction. Probably planted by the Chandlers. And Dud —

He shook his head, amused. "Ah, well. We are here now, and it is not too late. As long as we do things my way, of course."

Jill got suspicious all over again. "Your way?"

"Well," Dud said, teasing, "you must admit that your way is quite foolish. Killing the girl and continuing on as you have, slowly taking over, two at a time? Poppycock."

"You got a better idea?"

"Of course I have a better idea. *Blitzkrieg.* I am German, remember?"

"What?"

341

"We overrun them all at once. In one fell swoop. *Schwoop!*"
Dud clapped twice, with the utmost efficiency. "One and done."

Jill scratched her head. "But how? We —"

"Tell me," Dud interrupted. "Below us, in this tank, is a duplicate of every person in town, no?"

"Yeah. Multiple duplicates for most."

"So why not inhabit all of them, right now — and *invade?*"

Jill looked flabbergasted. "We can't," she sputtered. "We need to replace them slowly enough to hide the bodies, we need —"

"You need *me*," said Dud, "and nothing else."

Jill stared at her, hungry. "How?"

"Oh, no, no, no," Dud said, wagging his finger. "I will not be making that mistake again. You agree to partner with me first — *then* I will show you how. No more stabbing in the back. No more betrayals."

Jill thought about this, working her jaw. "An invasion . . ." The fire in her eyes grew brighter. "They wouldn't be able to stop us . . ."

Dud blew a raspberry. "Those gutbags? Of course they could not. Any resistance they could scrounge together would be useless; we could overpower them in no time."

Jill was nodding, but she still looked hesitant. "Yeah. Yeah, maybe . . ."

"Oh, no 'maybe' about it," Dud said with a dismissive wave of his hand. "It will work. Don't you remember who I am? I *made* you." His voice became choked with emotion. "You — we — have survived all these years, in bodies that were pure works of art. That is something to be proud of. Why would I want to destroy my most glorious creations?"

Jill took a deep breath and gave a final, decisive nod.

"Okay. Let's do it."

Dud grinned. "Excellent!" Again, the double clap of efficiency. "Into the tank, my doll, into the tank. We have work to do."

The look Jill gave Poppy was infuriating — smug, taunting, and vindictive all at once. "Told you not to trust him," she whispered.

Tears welled up in Poppy's eyes.

Dud gestured at the hole in the roof. "Beauty before age."

Jill sat down and dangled her feet through the hole. "What about her?" she asked, nodding at Poppy.

Dud let out the loudest, coldest Madame Grosholtz laugh yet, kicking the Tackety Wax tube in her direction.

"Leave her."

With that, Jill disappeared into the hole, her feet clanging as she landed on the catwalk. Dud hopped in behind her, never glancing back.

* * *

Poppy stood alone on the roof, stunned. A wind whipped across the roof, chilling her right down to her devastated bones.

How had it all gone so wrong?

No — she knew exactly how it had all gone wrong.

Jill wasn't Jill.

Dud wasn't Dud.

And Poppy had failed.

Again.

* * *

She was back on the stage of Radio City Music Hall. The shiny, slick floor felt cold on her cheek. Her ankle throbbed where she had twisted it. Her head rang.

Time had stopped; every person in the theater held their breath, the air itself billowing with anticipation, peppered with the staccato shouts of worried audience members and production assistants.

She felt a drop of blood trickle down her face.

She closed her eyes.

Her career, her future, her life —

It was all over.

* * *

But . . .

But they'd done everything right. The Plan had gone off without a hitch. Every member of the Giddy Committee had played their part. All the animate Hollows had been destroyed. With the exception of Jill, *everything had gone exactly right.*

Poppy let out a small gasp.

Wait.

Everything *had* gone right.

All the animate Hollows had been destroyed.

No one was left to relight the Chandlers' flames.

Dud had led Jill into the tank. But why take the dangerous

catwalk route instead of going down the staircase, the same way they'd come up?

Dud had kicked the Tackety Wax toward her. But why? Madame Grosholtz wouldn't have noticed it lying there, wouldn't have had any reason to kick it.

The voice coming out of Dud hadn't been Madame Grosholtz's at all.

* * *

Get up.

Still lying on the stage, she didn't know where the voice had come from. The shouts were growing louder now. Someone had called for a medic. No one had cut the music, which kept playing, mocking her.

Yet there it was, a voice cutting clear through the static, booming through her head.

GET. UP.

Maybe her career had ended before it began. Maybe her future had been cut adrift like a balloon, floating wildly up and away into unknown territory. And her life — well, it would take a lot of work to put it back together, but she could do it. She'd have to.

With a burst of unstoppable energy, she got to her feet.

The show must go on.

* * *

Poppy did not give herself time to think. She couldn't. She had a job to do: cross off the last item of The Plan. Wrenching herself

345

from the spot she'd been rooted to, she grabbed the Tackety Wax, tiptoed back to the hole, laid out the plastic tarp, and carefully glued it down along the edges, creating an airtight seal.

She pounded down the metal stairs of the tank to the large red button that stuck out of its wall. Her hand wavered over it, her brain screaming at her to push it, but her heart screaming louder not to.

Because she knew what was on the other side of that wall.

Dud. Not Madame Grosholtz. The real Dud. Her Dud.

Who had heard enough Madame Grosholtz in his memories to know how she spoke.

Who had picked up a lot more acting skills from the Giddy Committee than they ever could have realized.

Dud, among his waxy brethren.

Urging her to push the button.

Telling her it would be okay.

And probably waving.

~~8:20 a.m.: Melt all Hollows in the reinsulated tank~~

346

25

~~Pay a visit to the Grosholtz Candle Factory~~

THE FIRST THING POPPY HEARD WAS SCREECHES OF TERROR.

Not from Tank #2 — the second she pushed the button, she fled down the hill, past the ruins of Madame Grosholtz's studio, all the way to the front of the candle factory store.

She must have looked a fright, all wild-eyed and blotchy from crying, but hardly any of the tourists threw a glance her way; they were streaming out of the main entrance in droves, fleeing to the parking lot. Old people held fluttering hands to their chests. Mothers pushed their screaming children's faces to their thighs to shield them from the horrors inside.

Poppy, fighting against the traffic, pushed her way in.

Chaos now ruled the Grosholtz Candle Factory. The floor was littered with broken glass and abandoned fudge. The massive surge required to turn on the storage tank's heat must have knocked the store's power out, because the lights were off. Store maps had been tossed hither and yon with a lack of ceremony that must have made

Barbara furious. Vermonty lay on the ground, helpless, flailing, unable to get up because of the bulky suit.

Poppy took pity on the poor state and helped him to his feet. He muttered a thank-you and tottered directly into a wall, then fell back into the streaming masses and was carried via collective momentum out the exit.

Poppy kept on pushing through the hordes until finally she could see what it was they were running from.

The diorama.

The air-conditioned display, now robbed of its climate control, had quickly grown too warm for its citizenry to survive. The farmers' waxy flesh melted away from the metal armature that served as their bones, glass eyes drooping in their sockets, plinking to the ground and rolling around like marbles.

But the melting wax figures, as scary as they looked, weren't what the tourists were screaming at.

They were screaming at the corpses.

Some of the figures' waxy outer shells did not reveal metal frames beneath. Some of the figures' shells — eight, to be exact — melted away to reveal:

Rotting flesh.

Human bones.

And plenty of blood.

Poppy gaped in horror, identifying features that were recognizable even in death — a strong chin, a ski-slope nose, a garden gnome paunch —

Poppy kept frantically scanning the kidnapped victims until

an eerie, creaking noise sounded from above. She looked up. For a split second she saw it happen — the plastic repair patch of Tank #1 ripping down the middle, then finally detaching altogether.

She ran from the glass-domed roof just seconds before it imploded.

A deafening, splintering noise shook the store as the glass shattered and thousands of gallons of Potion poured through the now-open dome. Poppy grabbed the leg of a café table and held tight as it surged through the store, shattering the diorama's glass. When it stopped a minute or so later and she staggered to her feet, the liquid came up to her knees.

The drenched storegoers thrashed about like panicked fish, groping for help, while the diorama figures floated in the fetid liquid, corpses mixing with sculptures mixing with tourists, all taking on the same pale, waxy look in the milky Potion. The shoppers rose up in a chorus of agony, moaning, one of them grabbing Poppy's ankle and crawling up her leg.

"Fudge," the thing rasped. "Fuuudge . . ."

Poppy scooped a glob of wax off the groper's face — and gasped. *"Jill?"*

26

Take a week off

"IF THERE IS ONE THING THAT TREADING POTION FOR TWENTY-four hours with nothing to sustain me but my own will to survive has taught me to appreciate, it's the humble appetizer," said Jill. "So beautiful in its simplicity. A fry . . . a ring . . . a stick . . . a finger . . ."

Poppy gazed out upon the Friendly's appetizer landscape that had overtaken their table. "Nothing simple about this."

"Oh, shut up, traitor."

"Would you stop calling me that?"

"Sorry, but I still can't believe you thought it was me," Jill said, inserting a waffle fry into her mouth. "I'd like to think that my best friend — my *best friend* in the *entire world* — would have at least gotten tipped off that something was amiss. That her best friend had been replaced by a *wad of inanimate material*."

"I think we've firmly established that there was nothing inani-mate about any of this," Poppy said, reaching over to Jill's Munchie Mania basket to steal a mozzarella stick.

"No!" Jill stabbed a fork at her, defending her mountain of fried food. "The doctor said I need to fatten up!"

"And she prescribed a deep-fried diet, did she?"

"Not exclusively. Frozen dairy treats are encouraged as well."

Greg danced over to the table to deliver the extra bottle of ketchup Jill had requested. "Anything else I can get for you two?" he asked in an almost awestruck voice. The level of local celebrity to which all members of the Giddy Committee had risen over the past week was rivaling Poppy's in her *Triple Threat* days. Connor had been offered his own public-access television show. Banks was doing cabaret shows on Friday nights at the bowling alley lounge. "Another round of chicken fingers?"

"Greg," Jill said seriously, looking him dead in the eye, "another *three* rounds."

"Right-io!"

"I can't believe you suspected him," Jill said, dumping half the ketchup bottle onto her platter. "The man is one of a kind. Inimitable. Kind of like *me*, or so I thought."

"*I know.* Geez. Are you going to lord this over me forever?"

"Nah." Jill smirked and pointed at the NO LONGER TRAUMATIZED T-shirt Poppy had given her. "I'm over it. Mr. Crawford, on the other hand . . . I don't think he'll *ever* forgive you."

"Drat. I was so close to sealing the deal."

"I'm telling you, Poppy — over the course of a full day of panicking and screaming for help and making peace with our God, he still made time to curse your name. On an hourly basis. Like clockwork. Even *I* thought it was excessive."

Poppy let out a small puff of laughter — but it lasted only a second, dissolving into the morose funk that had infused the town over the past week. "Someone's got to pick up where Blake left off," she said darkly.

Mr. Crawford and Jill had escaped relatively unscathed, since they had been the most recent kidnapped victims — but no one else had been as lucky. Mrs. Goodwin, Smitty, Colt Lamberty, Principal Lincoln, Big Bob, Miss Bea, and Blake Bursaw — all dead and gone, with nothing for anyone to remember them by but the limited-edition candles that bore their scents.

It was a tragedy of epic proportions.

Which made it all the more infuriating that it was being swept under the rug.

Of course the town council wanted to keep it secret. If the Grosholtz Candle Factory went under, half the people in town would lose their jobs — and the other half would lose so many profitable tourist dollars that Paraffin's economy would all but collapse. So the interim mayor had gathered everyone together for a meeting — everyone who had been touched by the recent events at the Grosholtz Scandal Factory, as he called it, and not a soul more — to swear a vow of secrecy and to discuss strategies for how they should spin this story. After all, they were in a very lucky position — other than the Giddy Committee and those who had been kidnapped, there were no other witnesses. Townspeople may have noticed odd goings-on here and there and wondered why their loved ones were acting so strangely, but no one had *seen* evidence of the immortal wax demons. Nobody had proof. And as long as the legend of the Hollow Ones remained just that — a legend — Paraffin could continue selling the wholesome small-town Vermont image to visitors far and wide.

And so the strategy was fairly straightforward: Tell no one. Leak nothing to the media. Hush everything up; keep it all local. "It'll be our little secret," the interim mayor said with a wink.

As for the dead folk? They'd fallen ill and died after an outbreak of salmonella traced back to the yeast in improperly cooked bagels, just as Dr. Steve had warned. Smitty certainly wouldn't be able to defend himself. In making the café the scapegoat, the town council successfully diverted blame from the Grosholtz Candle Factory as best they could . . . but there was still the problem of what the tourists had seen that day in the store.

It was Poppy who had come up with the horror-movie alibi. That ghastly scene with the diorama, with all the decomposing corpses? The Chandlers were filming a movie; signs were posted on the doors as you walked into the store — you probably just don't remember seeing them. That contaminated-candle exposé that Banks and Louisa released? Part of the movie. Where were the Chandlers now? Certainly not trapped in liquid form in the storage tank up on the hill. They'd moved on to bigger and better things . . . in Hollywood!

And so once again Poppy had done what she did best: direct.

"To your masterpiece," Jill said, toasting with her milk shake. "Tell me: How does it end? I love spoilers."

"I don't know," Poppy said with a bitter edge to her voice, swirling her soup around the bowl. "Something super cheesy. *And they all lived waxily ever after.*"

"That blows. I'd demand a refund."

Poppy snickered. Who knew what sort of future she would direct for herself? She couldn't fathom it. The craziest fantasy she could think up held just as much possibility as anything else.

Jill crammed in an onion ring. "Have you figured out what to do with your tankful of melted enemies?"

"No. I convinced the foreman to keep it heated and in a liquid state, but all that wax — it would have to be dispersed way, way out. If flames of the Chandlers' souls are still lit somewhere, in a safe place, all it would take is for someone to make a Hollow for them again . . ."

"Oh, like that's gonna happen."

"I know. But we can't take that chance."

They chewed in silence for a moment.

"You okay?" Jill asked.

Poppy sighed. "I miss him."

* * *

She got home around ten. Her mother and father were curled up on the couch, watching a *Dr. Steve* rerun.

"Hey, Pops," her father said as she walked into the living room. "How's the family hero?"

"Full of ice cream."

"Friendly's again?"

"I am nothing if not loyal."

Her mother laughed. "I guess when you find your true love, you love it forever."

Poppy nodded and gave her a sad smile. They sad-smiled back.

And all three knew they weren't really talking about ice cream.

* * *

Poppy stared at her Broadway posters in the dark, at the whirly autographs that now looked to her like a hundred little arrows, all pointed at the thing in the backyard shed, as if to say, *If you miss him, go look at him! There's a startlingly good replica in there!*

But she couldn't, not yet. The thought was too distressing.

She tossed and turned some more. She didn't want to fall asleep. No, that wasn't right — she *did* want to fall asleep. It was the waking up that she dreaded, the fading away of all that transpired in her dreams.

She glanced at the closet. It was silent and mostly dark — except for a muted, flickering light.

This was getting ridiculous. A whole week had passed since . . . since. She hadn't opened her closet once in all that time, had gone so far as to borrow a bunch of Jill's clothes so she wouldn't have to.

But she couldn't avoid it forever.

Her breath caught as she opened the closet door. Everything was just as he'd left it: sleeping bag crumpled up into a ball, radio shoved to the side. The long-burning wax of the stone candle was still lit, but Poppy didn't bother to look inside — its message had ended more than a week ago. She fleetingly thought about blowing it out but banished the thought once again, as she had every night, unable to extinguish the one thing he'd left/sneezed behind.

At the memory, a giggle formed in her throat, followed by a lump. She hastily started to close the door—but stopped as she threw one last glance at the candle.

She carefully lifted it from the floor, brought the heavy stone up to her eyes, and gasped.

After seven inches of blank space and more than a week of burning, Madame Grosholtz had spoken one last time—way down at the bottom of the candle, in the shaky writing of one who knows the end is near:

AND YET, THOUGH MY REGRETS ARE MANY, MY GREATEST IS THIS: THAT I WAS NEVER ABLE TO CREATE A LIFE FROM SCRATCH. WITH ALL THE WAR AND SUFFERING AND EVIL I'VE SEEN OVER MY YEARS, I WANTED TO CREATE A PERSON WHO WOULD TRULY APPRECIATE LIFE, NEVER TREAT IT CALLOUSLY OR TAKE IT FOR GRANTED LIKE THE CHANDLERS HAVE. ONE WHO'D NEVER BEEN ALIVE IN THE FIRST PLACE—FOR ONLY THOSE WHO TRULY UNDERSTAND THE GIFT OF LIFE SHOULD BE THE ONES ALLOWED TO LIVE IT.

SO I PROPOSE ONE LAST EXPERIMENT. I WILL PLACE AN EMBER IN ONE OF MY EXPERIMENTAL HOLLOWS. NOT A FULL COPY OF MY FLAME-SOUL—IT IS FAR TOO RISKY TO ALLOW MY LIFE TO CONTINUE, TO LET THE CHANDLERS FIND IT AND EXPLOIT IT ONCE MORE—BUT MERELY AN

EMBER, A SHADOW OF MYSELF, AS PARENTS PASS ON THE GHOSTS OF THEIR SELVES TO THEIR CHILDREN. IT IS MY HOPE THAT THIS EMBER WILL CATCH FIRE AND CREATE A NEW SOUL ALTOGETHER.

I HOPE THE FLAME WILL GROW.

I HOPE THE FLAME WILL ENDURE.

Hardly breathing, Poppy stared at the flame.

Then turned her head toward the window.

Looked at the shed.

And bolted out of her room.

The Future

THE TOWN OF PARAFFIN SMELLED OF NOTHING.

Gone were the cloying, clashing scents of fruit mixed with sea-water, flowers mixed with cookies, licorice mixed with grass, old New England charm mixed with magazine-worthy modern living.

On the eve of its sestercentennial celebration, the town of Paraffin smelled *pure.*

Many things hadn't changed. Just as it had been at its bicentennial fifty years before, the gazebo was adorned with a large banner. Smitty's was packed with hungry donut eaters, though all that remained of Smitty was a Polaroid photo taped to the cash register. The lake still lured strolling citizens to its shore, where evil geese pecked at their ankles, their ferocity not tempered by time.

The Grosholtz Candle Factory was still in operation. It had been taken under new management forty years before and had catapulted into previously unheard-of levels of success. The CEO knew everything there was to know about candles and had replaced the retail shop with a world-class wax museum, attracting tourists from far and wide with his exquisite sculptures. Visitors often remarked that he almost seemed to be a wax sculpture himself — but of course, that couldn't be, as he aged the same way everyone else did. "He'd have to resculpt himself anew every few days," his partner would say when confronted with such rumors, "adding wrinkles and gray hairs one at a time! How ridiculous!"

Now the president of the factory herself, she was notorious for being a confident, tenacious leader, with a systematic way of doing things that couldn't be beat. She'd even written a bestseller outlining her process, titled *The List*.

But her business acumen wasn't her biggest source of fame. Not long after she and her partner had acquired ownership of the factory, she called a press conference that was to take place, oddly, *inside* Mount Cerumen.

The media were shocked to find themselves in a beautiful, soaring cavern, Gothic in its natural design and lit solely by candlelight. The audience took their seats — refurbished and reupholstered, taken from the local high school auditorium right before it had been demolished — sat back, and reveled in the inaugural performance, a fully staged production of *The Phantom of the Opera*. The acoustics were astounding, as was the lead actor, a Broadway star who had returned to his hometown for a special one-time performance. In the forty years since that night, the Candlelight Theater had been home to several productions staged every year, featuring just about every musical in existence — except for *The Sound of Music*. Never *The Sound of Music*.

But for Paraffin, the candles were still the main attraction. All agreed that the products now shipping to countless happy homes all over the world were the finest the factory had ever produced. No more pungent smells. No more cheesy names. Just pure, durable candles blazing longer and brighter than any that had come before, as if the wax itself were imbued with immortality.

And they all burned waxily ever after.